"I need

"And the company is prepared to offer you money, stock, a seat on the board—whatever you want."

"Oh, Casey," he said, his voice strangely sad. "What I want, you can't give me. No one can."

"How do you know? You haven't even told me what it is."

"And I don't intend to. I'm out of the corporate game now, and I'm going to stay out. You're wasting your time. And mine. You'll have to get someone else to help you."

"There *is* no one else," she insisted. "You're the only one who can help me. Don't you remember? We used to be married. I know what you can do."

A look of bitter anger crossed his face. "That's where you're wrong, Casey. You don't know me at all."

Dear Reader:

The year is almost over, but the good things go on in Silhouette Intimate Moments. For instance, this month we begin a special two-book series by one of your very favorite authors, Nora Roberts. *Time Was* is an exciting—and romantic—story of a love so special that even time itself can't stop it. Liberty Stone is a twentieth-century woman, while pilot Caleb Hornblower is a twenty-*third*-century man. Fate literally seems to be against them ever even meeting, much less finding a way to spend their lives together, but, as the saying goes, love conquers all. Next month look for *Times Change* and find out that adventure—and romance—seem to run in the family!

Think of the rest of this month's books as a bit of a Christmas present, because we have new novels from favorites Paula Detmer Riggs, whose *Tender Offer* will make you shed a tear or two through your smiles, and Linda Turner, who will introduce you to a very different—and very special—couple in *Flirting with Danger*. New author Joanna Marks rounds out the month with *Love is a Long Shot*, a book that once again demonstrates Silhouette Intimate Moments' knack for picking the winners.

Enjoy them all—and come back next year for more great reading.

Leslie J. Wainger
Senior Editor
Silhouette Books

Tender Offer

PAULA DETMER RIGGS

Silhouette Intimate Moments

Published by Silhouette Books New York

America's Publisher of Contemporary Romance

SILHOUETTE BOOKS
300 East 42nd St., New York, N.Y. 10017

ISBN: 0-373-07314-3

First Silhouette Books printing December 1989

Printed in the U.S.A.

PAULA DETMER RIGGS

discovers material for her writing in her varied life experiences. During her first five years of marriage to a naval officer, she lived in nineteen different locations on the West Coast, gaining familiarity with places as diverse as San Diego and Seattle. While working at a historical site in San Diego, she wrote, directed and narrated fashion shows and became fascinated with the early history of California.

She writes romances because "I think we all need an escape from the high-tech pressures that face us every day, and I believe in happy endings. Isn't that why we keep trying, in spite of all the roadblocks and disappointments along the way?"

For Leslie Wainger—
Brilliant editor and treasured friend.
With admiration and gratitude.

Chapter 1

I don't love him."

Perfect, Casey O'Neill told herself firmly. Her voice was firm and strong. Nicely confident, but not overly aggressive. Businesslike.

And she could find no flaw in the carefully drafted contract resting in her briefcase, which lay on the passenger seat of the car she'd rented at the airport in Albuquerque that morning. Nor in her attire.

The beige linen suit was the latest in the "power look" for women executives, tasteful and understated, but clearly expensive. Her calfskin pumps had been chosen with the same image in mind, and her dark blond hair had been newly styled and highlighted. She'd left nothing to chance.

Therefore, she reminded herself one more time, there was no reason to be nervous.

Slowly she flexed her tired shoulders, then climbed purposefully from the car and closed the door softly behind her. Standing close to the front fender, she watched a tumbleweed blow past the red subcompact and brush the back tire of the dusty black Jeep parked by a crumbling dirt wall. The Jeep and her rental were the only two cars she'd seen since she had turned onto the unpaved road leading to the Santa Ysabel pueblo.

This was a lonely place, she thought, glancing uneasily toward the distant horizon. And unforgiving of the unwary trespasser. But fortunately, if everything went as planned, she wouldn't be here long.

She glanced at her watch again. Surely more than five minutes had passed since she'd arrived, she thought, tapping her foot impatiently. It was nearly three, time for school to be out for the day. Or so the Indian woman at the gas station in the nearby town of Chamisa had told her when she'd stopped for directions.

She'd never been good at waiting. Her time was too valuable. Too tightly scheduled. But at the moment she had no choice.

She began to pace the rutted dirt road, glancing every few seconds toward the ramshackle adobe schoolhouse below the windswept mesa.

"This is business," she reminded herself firmly, side-stepping a clump of prickly brown weeds threatening her sheer designer stockings.

Casey knew all about business. She'd earned a Phi Beta Kappa key at Barnard and been first in her class at Wharton, where she'd received her M.B.A. Recruited by the most prestigious firm of management consultants in New York City, she'd chosen manufacturing as her specialty because, of all possible fields, it was the one that had the fewest women in the upper echelons. Her goal had been to become the first woman CEO of a major corporation by the time she was forty.

Much to her surprise, she'd discovered that she loved the hustle and bustle of the assembly line, and she reveled in the smells and the heat and the noise of a factory under full production.

In every plant where she'd spent any length of time, the workers had become almost family to her, and because she cared about them, they had worked harder and longer for her than for her more traditional colleagues. By the time she'd celebrated her twenty-sixth birthday, she'd acquired a reputation for being a miracle worker.

But now, at thirty-six, she'd run out of miracles.

Casey drew a deep, slow breath, forcing herself to relax. The air was so arid that it seemed to scour her skin, and she could feel each breath as it filled her lungs. Dust was beginning to swirl around her, and the swollen gray clouds over her head were casting misshapen shadows on the desolate landscape.

At the car agency she'd been warned about the sudden ferocious storms that lashed New Mexico in the summer. Apparently she was about to witness one.

Squinting against the rapidly rising wind, she pushed her bangs away from her brow. So much for the chic hairdo, she thought, sighing. Just then, a movement below caught her gaze. Someone had opened the schoolhouse door.

As she watched, students of all sizes spilled out into the barren yard. The sound of their high-pitched voices floated toward her across the heavy stillness, and her pulse began hammering in her throat.

This was not at all what she'd expected to find when she'd come looking for the man who'd once been the most respected and feared corporate raider on the Eastern seaboard.

Alejandro de las Torres. Alex. Her ex-husband.

The last time she'd seen him, she'd been blinded by tears, her throat clogged with the pleading words she'd been too proud to utter. She had loved him totally, adoringly, in every way a woman could love her man.

For a time her marriage had been idyllic. A man who'd waited until his thirties to marry, Alex was affectionate and exciting, a friend, a wonderful lover. And then suddenly, without warning, he'd simply lost interest in her.

It had been the cruelest kind of irony that the woman known for her skills at solving the insoluble had been helpless to save the one thing that meant everything to her—her marriage.

She should have known that a man as virile and competitive as Alex would soon tire of the same woman in his bed and in his life night after night, day after day.

After all, her father, a famous heart surgeon with a string of letters after his name, had left her mother for a younger and prettier woman when Casey had been ten.

She and Alex had been divorced for more than five years, two years longer than they'd been married. It had taken months to pull the remnants of her self-esteem together again, years before she'd stopped missing him. But gradually she'd made herself stop loving him, made herself face each day without him, until the hurt had faded and the wounds had healed. Now he was simply someone she used to know. Whatever they'd once meant to each other was history. Ancient history.

Moving closer to the edge of the scraped track, she waited and watched. All the students appeared to be Indian, with broad faces and sturdy bodies. They were speaking a combination of English and their native dialect, which sounded like an unintelligible jumble to her. But they seemed to be happy, the way children should be.

Alex must have looked like one of those stocky little boys as a child, she realized, with those same big black eyes and black straight hair. Their child would have looked like his father. If they'd had one.

Casey shoved the thought aside, just as she'd shoved it aside countless times when they'd been married. Alex hadn't wanted a child. Not right away, he'd told her whenever she'd brought it up. Not until he'd had her to himself for a good long time.

She shaded her gray eyes against the grit kicked up by the wind. Beneath the lightweight jacket, she was uncomfortably warm, but her hands and feet were unnaturally cold, and her lips felt numb. Her straining gaze was riveted on the doorway.

In her mind she saw Alex Torres on that first day when he'd come striding into the executive suite of the small foundry in Pittsburgh where she'd been completing a reorganization of the quality-control division. He'd just pulled off a surprise takeover of the undervalued company and had come to claim his victory.

She had heard of Alex Torres, chairman of Towers Industries. Who hadn't? He'd started with a small electronics parts company in California when he was in his early twenties, and by the time he'd turned thirty, he had been a multimillionaire.

His intense, unsmiling face had been on the cover of half a dozen business publications that year alone, and she could scarcely scan the society page of the *New York Times* without seeing his picture snapped at some charity function or other, always with a sophisticated and openly smitten woman by his side.

Still, Casey had been stunned by the man himself. Of Hispanic and Native American ancestry, he'd been incredibly handsome, tall and lean and dark, every inch the Spanish conquistador with his autocratic Latin features and mesmerizing black gaze.

Every line of his long, hard body had radiated strength and determination, and his corporate armor—the perfectly tailored, obviously expensive suit and the hand-sewn, highly polished loafers—had projected the image of a man who took what he wanted without apology or explanation.

Suddenly the schoolhouse door yawned all the way open, forming a dark rectangle in the drab mud wall. A spontaneous burst of deep male laughter floated across the emptiness toward her, and Casey froze, her hand over her lips. That can't be Alex, she thought numbly, staring at the man who stood in the doorway.

Alex wore a Savile Row suit with a vest and a custom-tailored shirt, not a soft-looking sweatshirt with a ragged neck and cutoff sleeves. And Alex's hair was razor cut and always neat, not curling in shaggy tendrils below his ears and tied back with a folded red bandanna across his forehead.

Evan Michaels, Alex's friend and attorney, had warned her to expect changes when she had finally bullied him into telling her where to find her ex-husband. But nothing could have prepared her for the man standing only yards away.

This man was a stranger with Alex's face.

This man exuded the raw masculinity and primitive force that she'd glimpsed only during the most passionate moments of their lovemaking. Sometimes he'd frightened her then with the power of his masculinity. He frightened her now.

And yet Alex had never been violent. In fact, he'd never raised his voice. He'd never had to.

But beneath the civilized facade had worked a dangerous man, a man driven to succeed, a man who used power the way his conquering ancestors had used their razor-sharp swords.

Casey edged closer to the crumbling adobe wall separating the road from the schoolyard. Nervously she pressed her fingers to the rough surface, feeling the heat that was still trapped in the mud.

She would wait until the children left before she went to him. What she had to say was better said without any distractions.

"Hurry up," she muttered, but the wind tore the words from her mouth before they reached her ears. The air tasted like dirt, and the sky was darkening more with each second that passed.

As though sensing her impatience, some of the children began running toward the cluster of two-story adobe buildings that made up the pueblo proper.

She shifted her gaze back to the school. Only one child remained, a small boy in an outsize orange shirt who was chattering happily and smiling up into the tall man's face. And then the child was gone, running behind the others, his short sturdy legs pumping furiously, and his shirttail flapping.

Casey inhaled slowly and threw her shoulders back. It was time.

Before she could move forward, however, Alex saw her. His shoulders jerked, and his hand went to his belly, as though he'd just taken a blow to the midsection.

Across the emptiness she could almost hear his resonant baritone uttering her name. In the beginning of their marriage his voice had sounded like a caress; at the end, he'd rarely said her name at all.

Casey cleared her throat, trying to ignore the sound of the sand driven into the side of her car by the wind. Her stomach was doing frantic flip-flops, and under the silky cinnamon blouse that had always brought her luck, her skin seemed unbearably sensitive.

"Stay calm," she told herself, lifting her chin in a gesture that the man below had once called her give-'em-hell pose.

Her ex-husband closed the distance quickly, his stride long and purposeful. He stopped a few feet from the half-ruined wall, as though deliberately keeping it between them.

He seemed bigger, especially his chest and arms, and his thigh muscles strained the seams of the frayed jeans. She'd never seen him in jeans before. Not once. When he'd been dressed casually, which had been seldom, he'd worn tailored slacks and custom-made shirts.

She managed a cool smile, which wasn't returned. Across the dry ground she could feel the hard-driving power of the man, but she ignored the prickles of unease that were raising the tiny hairs on the back of her neck. Something very volatile was bottled up behind that stoic Latin control, something primitive and uncivilized. Something she didn't want to see released.

For a moment she couldn't speak. And then, suddenly, she found her voice. "Hello, Alex," she said with forced lightness. "How are you?"

The first few minutes of any negotiating session were always the worst. And that was exactly what this was, she told herself. A negotiating session, nothing more.

Alex ignored the pleasantry. "So it *is* you. At first I thought you were a tourist, come to see a little local color. We get them sometimes, even way out here."

The stern lines of his dark face had weathered into a toughness that only enhanced the smoldering virility that had always excited her.

But not anymore. She was immune to his charm. He'd seen to that.

"No, I'm not sight-seeing, although I admit I'm...surprised to find you in...this place."

"I could say the same." One side of his mouth jerked upward in a brief half smile as he looked her up and down with the masculine arrogance that was such a part of him. "You look good, Case. Maybe a little thin, but you always claimed you wanted to be a size six. Looks like you made it."

Casey managed a polite smile. "Thank you," she said, because that was the first thing that came into her head.

"You're welcome."

Silence settled between them like an uneasy truce. She ran her palm over the pebbled brick. With the cowboy clothes and unkempt hair, Alex reminded her of the rangy tough-as-rawhide men who'd once fought the natives for this land. Only now he looked as though he would have been fighting on the other side.

"So you're a teacher now?" She made her voice matter-of-fact, as though she were conducting a job interview. Which, in a way, she was.

Casey watched his eyes grow impatient, and a spark of anger flared inside her. After six years of silence, he owed her five minutes at least.

"For two years now." He turned his head and glanced at the run-down building. "I have students in six different grades. It's a...challenge."

"But...but why here?" Her rose-tipped nails seemed garishly bright as she gestured toward the drab landscape.

He shifted his gaze to hers, and a bare suggestion of a shrug lifted his wide shoulders. "These are my people. My mother went to school in...this place."

Now that he was closer she could see the strands of gray salted into the thick black hair over his ears. And yet somehow he seemed younger than the forty-two that she knew him to be.

Except for his eyes. They weren't young. Just the opposite, she realized with shock. His eyes were shadowed and brooding, like those of a man who'd suffered terrible pain and survived.

She stared at him, fighting a smothering sense of unreality. Alex belonged in the rough-and-tumble arena of high-stakes power games, where the players stood to win or lose millions. He'd been the best. A winner. What could he possibly stand to win in this place?

"I've been away from New York since, well, since a few months after the divorce. I didn't realize that you'd, uh, retired," she said with slow deliberation, weighing her words.

When he didn't comment, she asked quietly, "Why, Alex? Why did you give up the life you loved for . . . this?"

He looked around slowly, his hands on his hips, as though trying to see the place through her eyes. His stance was relaxed, even indolent, but Casey sensed an alertness behind the casual pose.

"I've been working since I was ten. I was tired, burned out. I had plenty of money. My brothers and sisters were older." He hesitated, then added with a suggestion of a smile, "Maybe I'm having a second childhood, who knows?"

Silence fell again. This was harder than she'd expected. Much harder.

"How did you find me?" he asked finally, his voice strangely hoarse, as though he'd swallowed some of the dust that was blowing around them.

"Evan told me."

"You must have been very persuasive. That information is confidential."

Casey inhaled swiftly. "Even for your ex-wife?"

He hesitated only slightly. "Yes." He shifted his booted feet and glanced up at the sky. Every line of his tall body showed resistance. He didn't want her here.

Casey swallowed, determined to keep her voice steady and businesslike. "Could I buy you a drink, or a cup of coffee? I have something important I need to discuss with you."

A strong gust of wind shoved at her back. The storm was coming closer.

"Must be damn important to bring you all this way." Suddenly he smiled with wry amusement, crinkling the weathered skin of his temples. "Why don't you tell me about it before we both blow away?"

At the gentle tone of his voice, her well-rehearsed speech suddenly flew from her mind. She'd forgotten how quickly Alex had been able to disarm her when he'd wanted to.

"I need your help," she blurted out.

His face changed, and he took a step forward. For an instant she thought he was going to take her in his arms, but he stopped abruptly, frowning. "What's wrong?" he asked, his voice low and steely.

"Conrad Deshler is after my company."

His expression hardened again. "So this is . . . business?"

"Yes, of course," she told him impatiently. "Why else would I come?"

"Right. Why else would you come?"

Some powerful emotion came and went quickly in his dark eyes. One thick black brow arched sardonically as he shoved his hands into his back pockets and waited. He wasn't coming any closer, and he wasn't making this easier for her.

Okay, she thought, fighting down an irrational but powerful urge to close the distance between them until only inches separated them. She'd always loved being close to Alex, close enough to feel the heat from his restless body, close enough to inhale the clean male scent of him, close enough to run her hands over the thrilling width of his shoulders.

She cleared her throat. Imagine him across the desk in your office in Summerville, she told herself. You're in charge here. It's your play.

"For five years now, I've been CEO of Summerville Foundry. It's in the town of the same name located about sixty-five miles northwest of Cincinnati." She let a rueful smile cross her face. "When I was offered the job, the board of directors was desperate. The company was about ninety days from bankruptcy; the work force was down to a skeleton crew and the company stock was virtually worthless." She stopped to clear her throat. The air was making her mouth painfully dry.

"Worse still, none of the bread-and-butter contracts had been renewed. There had been too many missed delivery dates and quality-control problems."

His mouth quirked. "In other words, the buzzards were circling."

Casey gave in to the smile that wanted to form. "Were they ever! The foundry has been around since the Civil War, when it began making rifle parts for the Union army. Some days I was sure that the ghosts of all the men killed by those rifles were hovering, waiting for the foundry to collapse around me."

Alex stripped the bandanna from his forehead and ran a hand through his unruly hair, leaving finger tracks in the raven thickness.

A heavy gold ring gleamed dully against his skin, drawing her gaze. It looked just like the one she'd once slipped on his finger with such love and trust. The wedding band he'd given her now rested in a drawer of the Queen Anne highboy in her bedroom.

Casey managed to keep her features expressionless. This isn't personal, she reminded herself. This was for all those people who had been there when she needed them, people who would almost certainly lose their jobs, maybe even their homes and their savings, if she failed to defeat Deshler's bid. She couldn't give up now. If she did, she would never be able to face herself again.

She forced herself to concentrate on her carefully prepared presentation. Alex had always dealt in facts, not feelings. "A man named Bennett Jameson is my head of research and development. He's invented a lightweight alloy that has brought us more orders than we can handle. He's working on another alloy for the computer industry. Deshler wants the patents for his own foundry in Gardena."

Alex whistled. "That's a tough one. He's never lost a fight."

"Neither have you."

"No, I've never lost." His voice roughened. "Not in the way you mean, anyway."

The wind caught the edge of her jacket and threw it open. Alex's dark gaze instantly traced the curves under the silk blouse, and Casey stopped breathing. But his expression didn't change.

A fleeting feeling of pain caught her unawares, but she ignored it. There were bound to be some leftover feelings of bitterness that she hadn't managed to erase, but she could handle them.

"He's been buying up stock steadily for the past six months," she rushed on. "The annual shareholders' meeting is in one month, on July first, and according to the papers he's filed with the SEC, he's going to make a play to take over a majority of the seats on the board. As of midnight last night I didn't have the votes to stop him."

Alex propped a booted foot against a low section of the wall and rested his hand on his thigh. Casey ignored the dull glitter of gold that taunted her. Their divorce was old news.

"And you want me to tell you what to do, is that why you've come all this way?" His voice was as flat as the land on which they stood.

"No, I want to hire you to stop him, and we don't have much time to do it."

He stared at her, his gaze narrowed against the wind. "You want to hire me to stop him," he repeated slowly, as though the very idea was unthinkable.

"Yes. Of course, the foundry will pay for . . . for a substitute teacher for the time you'd be away. And I'm prepared to offer you carte blanche—money, stock, a seat on the board, whatever you want."

"Whatever I want." His hand slowly tightened into a large fist against his thigh.

"Yes, within reason, of course."

Casey knew that her voice sounded wooden, but she didn't dare let Alex read the panic that was lurking behind her controlled facade. He was her last hope; he *had* to help her.

"No, Casey," he said firmly, his voice sounding strangely sad. "What I want, you can't give me. No one can. Not in this life, anyway."

"How do you know? You haven't even told me what it is."

"And I don't intend to." His foot dropped to the ground. "I'm out of the game now, and I'm going to stay out of it."

"But, Alex—"

"You're wasting your time," he said impatiently, glancing toward the sky again. "And mine. You'll have to get someone else to help you."

He was turning her down, sending her away, just like that. As though she were a . . . a stranger he scarcely knew. As though he'd never touched every part of her with passion. As though he'd never smiled at her with love.

Casey realized that she was trembling, and she folded her arms over her midriff so that he wouldn't see how much his dismissal had hurt.

"There *is* no one else. I know what you can do, Alex. I've seen you defeat better men than Con Deshler without raising a sweat. You're the only one who can help me."

His mouth twisted, and a look of bitter anger crossed his face. "That's where you're wrong, Casey. You don't know me at all."

She blinked. "I . . . what are you talking about? Of course, I know you. We were married—"

"You knew the image," he interrupted, his voice savage. "The guy behind the reputation. You didn't know the man inside."

Something in his tone frightened her. He sounded bitter, as though there was something twisting painfully inside him, something that never relaxed its clawing grip.

"I could only know what you let me know," she told him stiffly. "Which was damn little. I didn't even know you planned to divorce me until Evan showed up with the papers."

He flinched, but the stony look on his face didn't change. "Best be on your way, before the storm hits," he said. "These roads can get slippery."

Her face stung with sudden heat, and she lifted her chin to the wind in an effort to cool her hot skin. Losing her temper wouldn't win her anything but a quick turnaround to Ohio.

"I'm not giving up—"

A crackling bolt of lightning sliced the clouds close above their heads, filling the air with the smell of sulfur. Beneath their feet the ground shook as thunder reverberated in a booming shock wave across the emptiness. The storm was directly over them.

Before she could move, Alex vaulted the wall and grabbed her arm. "C'mon," he shouted as the first fat drops pelted them. "You shouldn't be standing here. It's too dangerous."

He hustled her to the Jeep and jerked open the door. Before she could move, he lifted her into the seat.

"Wait, I need my things!" she protested, snagging her nylons on something rough. Her ribs felt bruised where his hard fingers had gripped.

"I'll get 'em. You stay here," he yelled over the roar of the wind. "I'll just make sure all the kids have gone home."

Before Casey could answer he left her, running back toward the schoolhouse with long, loping strides that covered the ground quickly.

She shifted in the seat and listened to the metallic pinging of the rain hitting the roof a few inches above her head. Puffs of dust rose around the car as the rain beat down on the parched road.

None of this made sense. All these years apart, she'd thought that Alex had moved his base of operations to Los Angeles, to the Chandler Aerospace plant that he'd acquired shortly before everything fell apart between them. That had been his plan, and she'd had no reason to doubt that he'd carried it out.

All right, so she hadn't seen his name in the business periodicals she read faithfully, but he'd never courted publicity, and she'd just assumed that, living out of the Eastern limelight, he'd managed to maintain a low profile.

The rain was coming down in slanted sheets when Alex returned. He pulled her things from the red car, then ran to the Jeep. With a quick motion he tossed her purse and briefcase into the back seat, then slid behind the wheel and slammed the door, shutting out the storm.

His sweatshirt was soaked and clung to his chest like a cotton breastplate, emphasizing the breadth of muscle above his lean waist. Dark blue patches of moisture outlined his thigh muscles, and water dripped from his thick hair.

Without a word he started the Jeep and swung it around toward the main road. He maneuvered the four-wheel drive with the same casual skill and at the same breakneck speed as he'd driven his classic Porsche. That much, at least, Casey realized, hadn't changed.

"Where are we going?" She had to raise her voice to be heard over the roar of the engine and the pounding of the rain.

Alex gave her an impatient glance. "To my house. I'll bring you back to your car when the storm lets up."

To his house? Where he lived with the woman who had put that ring on his finger?

Her pulse raced furiously, then settled into an erratic pace. "Are you sure you shouldn't call your wife and tell her we're coming?"

Alex turned to frown at her, the Jeep swerving wildly before he controlled it. "What the hell are you talking about? I don't have a wife."

Casey blinked in confusion. "Then why are you wearing a wedding band?"

His frown deepened at the note of accusation clouding her voice. "This is your ring, Casey. I've . . . gained some weight. I can't get it off."

She stared at the smooth wide band. It looked snug, but not unusually tight. Still, why else would Alex continue to wear a symbol of a love that no longer existed for either of them?

"You could have it cut off," she suggested tersely.

Alex's jaw flooded with dusky color. "Does it bother you that I still wear it?"

His gaze went to her hands, which were folded in her lap. The third finger of her left hand was conspicuously bare.

"Yes, it bothers me." The bitter taste of truth was strong in her mouth. "We both know that the reason you wore it no longer exists."

Of course it bothered her, she echoed silently. She could still hear his husky promise at the moment when she'd slipped it onto his finger. "As long as I wear this, *mi amor*, you'll know that I love you."

"And I love you," she'd answered, lifting her face for his kiss.

At the time she'd believed that his love would last forever, just as she'd known that hers would never die. But a man in love with his wife wouldn't have filed for divorce without even giving her a reason why.

A charged silence filled the Jeep, broken only by the labored screech of the wipers on the glass and the steady drumming of the rain overhead. Casey stared at the gloomy landscape faintly visible through the sheeting rain. Inside she felt as bleak and barren as the storm-battered land outside.

Alex was silent, staring straight ahead, his hands steady on the wheel. The stop sign at the intersection with the state highway suddenly loomed out of the wet wall ahead of them. He braked, and the Jeep slid to a stop.

He let the engine idle as he turned to gaze at her. His eyes were dark, cryptic, filled with brooding amber lights, but as they searched her face, they seemed to grow even darker, more shadowed, more unreadable, as though he were turning inward to that place where she could never follow.

"You're right, Casey," he said in the clipped, even tones that his enemies had learned to fear. "I'll get rid of the ring. After all, as you say, the reason I wore it no longer exists."

Chapter 2

Twenty minutes later Alex turned off the highway onto a narrow access road, slowing almost immediately to a crawl, and the Jeep lurched from side to side in the deep ruts.

Casey peered through the steamy glass with growing uneasiness. There had been no mailbox by the track, no street sign, nothing but a muddy trail leading off into the emptiness.

She sat perfectly still, counting the strokes of the wipers one by one, her back straight, her hands folded neatly in her lap as she'd been taught at Miss Porter's School for Girls. But the blood was pounding through her veins with more force than the rain on the roof, and her nerves were stretched taut at the sensation of danger that Alex's presence was generating inside her.

"That's my place," he said suddenly, startling her.

"Where?" Peering through the streaming glass, she saw only rock and sand ahead.

"In those cottonwoods by the creek."

The Jeep jolted down a slight incline, and the movement threw her leg against Alex's. He jerked away as though she'd stabbed him, and Casey held on to the door handle, her gaze focused directly ahead. That hadn't changed, either, she thought with a pang of hurt. In those terrible last weeks of their marriage, Alex hadn't touched her at all.

Ignoring the empty feeling in her stomach, she searched the land ahead for a house. "I see the trees and the stream," she told him, her eyes straining. "Oh, there it is. I see it now."

Ahead and slightly to the left was a small stone building half hidden by the towering trees. It was low and sprawling, like the adobe haciendas she'd seen in magazines, with a flat roof and strong, clean lines. At first glance it seemed a part of the wild, untamed land around it, its spare facade softened only marginally by spikes of purple flowers growing in clumps next to the drab brown stone.

Beyond the house was the creek, swollen now by the downpour, surging with a spray of angry white water over dun-colored rocks lining both sides of the channel.

Casey saw no other houses nearby, no other man-made structures of any kind. She and Alex were alone.

"Watch the mud when you get out," he said, his obsidian gaze slanting down to her feet, then back to her stiff profile. "Those shoes aren't much suited for slogging through puddles." He took his time returning his gaze to the road.

"Thank you for the warning," she said in her best boardroom voice, "but I've had mud on my shoes before."

A small muscle at the corner of his mouth tightened, giving his expression a hard-bitten remoteness. "Suit yourself. You're the one who'll have to walk around in soggy shoes."

The silent impact of his intimate scrutiny left her shaken, but she refused to show it. Six years ago she'd vowed never to let her emotions rule her head again. She didn't intend to break that vow now.

Alex downshifted, his big hand dangerously close to her knee. The Jeep bounced over a large half-buried rock, and she braced her hand against the dash. Tension crackled between them like a third presence in the small vehicle.

As soon as the they reached the shelter of the largest tree, he angled the Jeep close to a small adobe shed to the rear of the house and killed the engine. Pocketing the keys, he reached into the back for her case.

Through the screen of her half-lowered lashes Casey watched his chest muscles flex under the wet shirt. He'd always been physically strong, but now, for some reason that she didn't fully understand, his strength made her feel terribly fragile. It's this place, she told herself, not Alex. But whatever the reason, she didn't like feeling vulnerable.

A woman made mistakes when she was vulnerable. Hadn't she made one when she'd fallen in love with a man who'd loved the chase more than he had loved the prize?

"Stay here," Alex ordered, glancing past her to the drops beating furiously against the window. "I have an umbrella inside. I'll come back for you."

"Don't bother. I won't melt."

She opened the door a crack, then stopped and gazed around curiously. "I don't see the Porsche. Is it parked behind the house?"

"No." His hand tightened around the wheel. "I gave the Porsche to Miguel when he graduated from Stanford a few years ago."

Casey swallowed the hurt that rose to her throat. Alex had kissed her for the first time in that car. No doubt he'd forgotten that. Just as he'd undoubtedly forgotten a lot of things about their time together. About her.

A memory could hurt for only a moment, she told herself resolutely. A few seconds, really. With careful dignity, she lifted her chin and smiled.

"How...generous of you," she said, phrasing her words with her usual precision. "But then, you were always very generous with your family. I'm sure Miguel was thrilled."

Her voice cracked, startling her and jerking Alex's gaze toward her. It's the storm, she told herself hastily. No wonder she was upset. She'd better get a grip on herself before she brought up the subject of the foundry again.

Alex stared at her, his brows drawn together over the straight blade of his nose. "I offered it to you, but you told Evan you didn't want anything from me. What the hell was I supposed to do with it?"

Casey's jaw dropped. All she had ever wanted from Alex was his love, not his money or his possessions. And at the divorce hearing she had requested the restoration of her maiden name, nothing else.

"It was yours to keep or give away. It ... it was never mine. I kept only what I brought to our marriage."

An emotion she'd never seen before flashed into his eyes. "Damn it, I couldn't keep it! I couldn't keep anything that reminded me—"

Suddenly the passenger door flew open, ripped by the wind from Casey's grasp. Rain blew in torrents into the Jeep, drenching them instantly.

"Hang on," Alex shouted before opening his own door and struggling out into the wind.

Casey grabbed her purse from the floor in the back and was turning around to the front when Alex reached in to help her. His hand brushed her breast, and they both froze. His face turned a dusky red, and the tendons stood out in his neck as though he were gritting his teeth.

"Give me your hand," he ordered brusquely, his shoulders hunched against the cold deluge.

She ignored the hot rush of blood through her veins as he folded his big hand around hers and helped her climb down. He kept her close to him, his hip rubbing hers with disturbing intimacy as he led her around the puddles to the carved pine door.

It wasn't locked.

Alex ushered her in and pushed the door closed behind them. Inside, she had an immediate impression of rough white walls and sparse furnishings that were oversize and almost primitive in design.

An entire wall of windows faced the tumbling creek, and the rain beat like stinging needles against the steamy panes.

"Wait here," Alex ordered, tossing his car keys onto a rough pine table by the door. "I'll get you something to put on."

"That's not necessary," Casey assured him stiffly. "I'm fine."

"Oh, yeah? Then how come you're shivering?" His shuttered gaze lingered briefly on the wet splotches on her shoulders and breasts. His lashes lowered, obscuring the expression in his eyes, but not before she'd seen a flare of potent male awareness in their depths. The tremors that shook her increased.

"I'll be fine," she repeated.

Without replying, Alex turned his back on her and walked away. His boots echoed sharply against the unglazed terra cotta tile, each rangy step leaving wet marks on the clay. He disappeared into an open doorway beyond which she could see the massive footboard of a large four-poster bed covered with a nubby burgundy spread.

Alex's bed.

Hastily she averted her gaze. She didn't want to think about him lying naked on that outsize mattress, his arms reaching for her the way they once had. She refused to think about the nights she'd spent alone, staring at the empty space where Alex should have been. Those nights, those times together, were over.

Crossing her arms over her chest, she clenched her teeth to keep them from chattering. The room wasn't abnormally cold, but she was, inside.

Alex reappeared, a black velour bathrobe tossed over his shoulder. "This should keep you warm." He inclined his head toward a short hall. "Bathroom's to the right."

He held out the robe, and after a momentary hesitation, she took it and walked quickly away.

Alex watched her go, his stomach hitched into a painful knot. He realized that he was holding his breath and let it out slowly. When he began breathing again, he noticed that her perfume still lingered, taunting him with a fragile scent of spring flowers that had always excited his hunger.

Had she worn that scent intentionally for him? he wondered, staring at the empty hallway. Or had she simply forgotten how much he had liked that particular perfume?

His money was on the latter, he decided, turning away abruptly. He returned to his bedroom and closed the door, shutting out the tantalizing scent.

Casey had never played sexual games to gain an objective. She was too classy and too honest. She had to love a man before she would invite him to her bed. He should know; he'd nearly gone out of his mind until he'd won her heart.

He'd never had to work harder at anything in his life. Nor, he admitted, had he ever been more patient.

He'd been aware of her from the first instant he'd walked into her office. He'd noticed her eyes first. They were a rich shade of gray, the exact color of the Pacific just before dawn on a cloudy winter day, and when she'd smiled up at him, they'd warmed to the color of a young gull's wing.

And he'd been fascinated by her shiny sun-washed hair. He'd grown up surrounded by women with lush black hair worn long or in fat gleaming braids, women whose eyes were as dark and seductive as the lilting language they spoke. But Casey's hair had been golden and worn in cascading waves, like the shining tresses of a sleeping princess he had once seen in a storybook when he'd been a little boy.

Casey was more than pretty, though, he'd discovered. In fact, she was incredibly bright—he'd figured that out right away.

And wonderfully loving—though he hadn't found that out until later.

He remembered the way she'd looked at him with cool indifference that first day.

"Mr. Macho," she had called him, but she'd said it with such an adorable smile he hadn't been angry, merely intrigued, because his famous Latin charm hadn't made a dent in her ladylike demeanor. So he had decided to seduce her.

But Casey had had no intention of being seduced.

"No thanks," she'd told him briskly every time he'd asked her out. "I'm not your type." Which had surprised the hell out of him.

No woman had ever said that before.

Until he'd met Casey, his affairs had been strictly on his terms. No long-term entanglements, no promises, no illusions of love—take it or leave it. He'd rarely had to ask a woman twice.

So he'd pushed, and Casey had pushed back. The stronger her resistance had become, the more he'd wanted her. At first it had been a game, another takeover bid, a pleasant diversion. And then he'd seen her with another man, and for the first time in his life he'd been jealous. Violently, obsessively jealous.

A murderous urge to wipe the possessive Ivy League grin from her date's bland Anglo-Saxon face had consumed him for days. And then he'd gone looking for Casey. Staking out a chair in her outer office, he had refused to leave until she'd agreed to have lunch with him.

In the intimate French restaurant he'd selected with meticulous care, she had teased him mercilessly, making him laugh in a way he'd never laughed before, not even as a kid. She'd made him feel like a kid, too.

When he'd been with her, he'd wanted to ride on a carousel and run barefoot in the waves and have popcorn at the zoo, things he'd never been able to do when he was young and growing up in a rat-infested barrio in East Los Angeles.

And for the first time in his life, he had wanted to take care of someone, not because it was his obligation, but because it was his pleasure. For the first time in his life, he had hated the thought of being alone.

By the time he'd returned her to her office that afternoon, he'd been half in love with her. He'd also been scared as hell that he was going to lose her.

Alex felt a sharp pain in his wrist and realized that he was gripping the tall post at the corner of his bed so tightly that the tendons in his hand were bulging.

Carefully he relaxed his grip and flexed his fingers. The wide gold band on the third finger caught his gaze. Casey was right; he should have gotten rid of the damn thing a long time ago. Six years ago, in fact.

He muttered a vicious curse and pulled the sodden sweatshirt over his head, hurling it toward the hamper in the corner. He didn't want to think about the reason why he no longer had the right to wear Casey's ring. He didn't want to think about the past at all. He'd made himself stop caring a long time ago.

His hands shook as they reached for the waistband of his jeans. He'd been so sure he would never see Casey again. He'd lived with that belief so long that it had become a part of him, like a chronic agony from which there would be no relief.

But now that she was here, in his house, wearing his bathrobe, he was suddenly feeling things that he had no right to feel. No damn right at all. He would do well to remember that.

When Casey returned to the living room, she found a fire crackling in the massive stone fireplace that took up most of the east wall.

She glanced around, looking for Alex, but she was alone. Giving the sash of the oversize robe a tug, she padded across the cold tile to the sofa facing the fire, but she was too nervous to sit down.

"Casey?"

Alex's voice came from behind, and she whirled around, her hand going to her throat.

"God, Alex, you nearly gave me cardiac arrest," she blurted out, gathering the floppy lapels of the robe closer to her neck. A heady masculine scent of cigar smoke and soap rose from the soft fabric. Alex's robe smelled like her memory of him.

"Sorry. I thought you could hear me rattling around in here. I'm making coffee. You want some, or something stronger?" He was standing in the doorway of a small white kitchen, a coffee can in his hand. He'd changed into a red plaid shirt, open at the throat to reveal a V of curling black hair, with the sleeves rolled to his elbows. His tight Levi's were worn almost white, and his bare feet were encased in moccasins.

"Something stronger," she said, beginning to shiver again in spite of the warmth from the blazing fire.

He nodded, then disappeared into the kitchen, his moccasins silent on the tile.

Inside the thick walls the sound of the rain and the wind was muted, but outside, the storm still tore at the trees overhead, and drops of rain blown into the chimney by the force of the wind made the fire sizzle. Beyond the windows the creek ran in a torrent, small twigs and bits of weeds spinning wildly in the strong current.

Casey moved closer to the fire. She'd found a pair of white socks in the pocket of the robe. They were far too big and mismatched, but they were warmer than her wet high heels. She lifted the trailing hem of the robe and wiggled her toes, feeling distinctly self-conscious. If Summerville's stockholders could see her now, they would definitely vote for Deshler's deal, she thought, smiling to herself.

But the smile quickly faded. Her mission here was deadly serious, and so far, nothing had gone as she had planned. Worse still, she had only a few more hours before she had to leave in order to catch the red-eye back home.

She forced her thoughts back to her task. Maybe Alex *had* burned out—she knew what years of high-pressure negotiations and unrelieved stress could do to a person. And maybe he was enjoying his life as a teacher—she could understand that, too. Alex had always been good with kids, probably because he'd helped raise most of his nine brothers and sisters. But once he realized what a plum Summerville was, he wouldn't be able to pass up the kind of deal she was prepared to offer him.

After all, Alex was first and foremost a businessman. No matter how he felt about his ex-wife, he would be a fool to let this opportunity go by. And he was anything but a fool.

Her nerves under control again, she began to prowl the room, touching his things gingerly, as though trying to find the man she once knew. But his house was as different from her expectations as the man who owned it.

With growing curiosity Casey shifted her gaze to the wall of books opposite the fireplace. As she swiftly read the titles, she struggled with a wild sense of disbelief. Many of the books she'd read, others she recognized, some she didn't, but the subjects astounded her. When had Alex started reading books on philosophy and religion and history? For that matter, when had he begun to read for pleasure?

Her gaze searched the shelves. Nowhere did she find the periodicals on finance and marketing and industrial trends that he'd once devoured with his customary methodical thoroughness.

Curiouser and curiouser, she thought, drawn by the cluster of framed photographs that hung opposite the windows. As she got closer she saw that one of the pictures was actually a diploma from the University of New Mexico, granting Alejandro Mateo de las Torres y de Sanchez a bachelor's degree in education. So Alex had finally gotten the college education he'd always wanted.

What else had he gotten in this hard place that she hadn't been able to give him? she wondered, pushing her hands into the pockets of his robe.

Her gaze drifted to the next photo. It was an old-fashioned sepia print of a tall, broad-shouldered man with dark straight hair bound back by a beaded band and a hard, stern mouth, a warrior by the look of his attire. One large hand rested on the barrel of a rifle, while his other held a wicked-looking lance.

Casey felt a chill as she stared into the man's piercing eyes. They were like Alex's eyes, ablaze with victory, the way she'd seen them only once before.

That had been the morning he'd left for Los Angeles to finalize the takeover of Chandler Aerospace. It had been his greatest coup, one that had been long in coming because, for years, the stock had been privately held by the founder, Preston Chandler, and his family. But as soon as Chandler had taken his company public, Alex had started buying up stock until he'd finally attained controlling interest.

Uncharacteristically, he had asked her to ride with him to La Guardia, where he kept the company plane, and on the way he'd told her why that particular takeover had been so important to him.

He'd rarely spoken of his early years, and so she'd been shocked to find out that he'd once worked for the same company he now controlled.

He had been sixteen when he'd quit school to work full-time, and he'd taken a job at the same place where his father swept floors and cleaned toilets. Three years after he'd started, he'd been promoted to lead man on the first shift.

Thrilled and proud and grateful for the extra money, he'd been stunned when, one day six months later, he'd been abruptly demoted so that the owner's son, fresh out of college and without any experience, could take his place.

Alex had exploded, accusing Preston Chandler of breaking his word. When Bart, Preston's son, had muttered a racial epithet, Alex had hit him, so Bart had called in some men from the loading dock. Alex had ended up unconscious and out of a job. Emilio Torres had been fired, as well.

Uneducated and without skills, his father couldn't find work and sank deeper and deeper into depression, until Alex hadn't been able to stand it. Swallowing his pride, he had gone to Bart Chandler and begged for his father's job back. But the cocky young man had laughed at him, refusing outright.

Emilio, a proud man who'd been forced to apply for welfare to support his family, had died broken-spirited less than a year later.

Alex had found other work, but he'd never forgotten. Even as he'd pored over business textbooks at night and slowly amassed the capital to buy his first small company, he'd vowed to someday have enough money so that no one would ever have that kind of power over him again.

Casey reached out to straighten the old-fashioned photo, her fingers lingering on the heavy oak frame. She still remembered the celebration that she'd planned for Alex's return.

She'd chilled champagne, bought flowers, had the house-keeper make his favorite foods. The ivory negligee she'd chosen for that night had come from France and had made her skin glow and her eyes sparkle.

But the celebration had fallen flat. Alex had returned later than expected, looking wan and haggard, as though he'd been suffering from a terminal illness.

He'd drunk most of the champagne himself, and when he'd made love to her, he'd seemed strangely preoccupied, as though he were making love to a stranger. It had been over almost as soon as it had begun, leaving her aching and unsatisfied for the first time.

Nothing had gone right after that. Alex had stopped smiling, becoming more and more taciturn. He'd begun traveling even more frequently than usual, and on the rare evenings when he had been home, he'd shut himself in the den; alone.

At first Casey thought that something had gone wrong with the Chandler deal, but a few discreet phone calls had revealed that the deal had gone through with Alex's usual expediency.

She had grown more and more worried, and the more distraught she'd become, the more Alex had withdrawn from her. Her marriage had been in trouble, and she hadn't known what to do. She'd thought about it constantly, until she couldn't eat or sleep or concentrate, and her work had begun to suffer.

Finally she hadn't been able to stand it anymore. No matter what, she'd decided, she had to make Alex tell her what was driving him away from her and the nearly perfect life they had together.

So one dreary day a few weeks before Christmas, when he'd arrived home from yet another trip to Los Angeles, she'd been waiting, sitting stiffly on the sofa by the window overlooking Central Park.

The sound of the crackling flames faded as she allowed herself to drift into the past. She could still see the exhaustion in his eyes.

"It's cold as sin out there," Alex muttered, closing the door of the penthouse behind him. "I need a drink."

He dropped his heavy briefcase by the bar, shrugged out of his topcoat and tossed it aside. Without looking at Casey, he poured three fingers of Scotch into a glass, tossed it down in two swallows, then poured the same again.

Every time he came home from one of his trips, he seemed more tormented. But she didn't know what to do to bring him back to her.

Feeling more and more nervous, Casey pulled out a cigarette and lit it. At the scrape of the lighter, Alex turned to frown at her. "When did you start smoking?"

She took a quick drag. "About the same time you started drinking," she retorted, waiting for the nicotine to calm her frayed nerves. "Only you haven't been home long enough these past weeks to notice."

Alex jerked his gaze to the window, where sleet lashed the naked branches of the trees in the park. "Case, I'm dead tired. I don't want to fight with you tonight."

There was an edge to his voice that sounded like pleading, but Casey dismissed that possibility instantly. Since that one desperate time when he'd been nineteen, Alex had never begged for anything. He never would.

But she would. She was fighting for the one thing that mattered more to her than her skyrocketing career—her marriage.

Casey stubbed out her cigarette and stood. She wanted to touch him, but she didn't dare. Lately he seemed to hate her touch. Instead, she took a bracing breath, then said urgently, "Alex, we can't go on like this. Surely you can see that."

He studied the scene beyond the window, his distinctive profile as sharp and cold as the ice crystals pelting the city. "I don't know what you're talking about."

She ignored his distant tone. Alex wasn't a man to share his feelings or his insecurities. But he had to have them. Why else did he look as though he were being ripped apart inside?

Casey ran her hands down the tailored crispness of her skirt. Normally she changed into slacks when she came home from the office, but tonight she'd needed the extra power she'd always gleaned from her tough, competent image.

She moved closer, until the faint odor of cigar smoke and Scotch stung her nostrils. "Have I done something to hurt you? Is that why you're never here? Why you're . . . you're drinking too much? I know I've been working a lot of hours on this latest project, but maybe—"

"You haven't done anything," Alex interrupted, his gaze flickering to her face for an instant, before returning to the bleak vista beyond the thick pane. "I told you when we were married that I liked a woman who wanted to win as much as I do. That hasn't changed."

The light from the chandelier cast his face in harsh relief. He looked as though he'd lost weight, and his copper skin had a sickly gray cast.

"Then what *has* changed, Alex? Why are you withdrawing from me, from our marriage? Is it your business? Your family? *What?*"

He stared into his glass. "A man doesn't share his troubles with his woman, Casey. If he does, he's not a man."

"That's not true," she cried, wanting to kiss the bitter slant from his mouth. "You're the strongest man I've ever known.

There's nothing you could do that would make me change my mind about that.''

She touched his face with her fingertips, and he inhaled sharply, as though her touch hurt him. He took a deep, shuddering breath, and for an instant his control broke.

"I'm not so strong. If I were, I'd walk out of here right now, before you find out what kind of a man I really am."

"Then tell me," she pleaded. "I'm your wife, remember? For better or worse?" She managed a small laugh. "And lately, my darling, it's been worse."

His face twisted. Turning away from her, he bolted his drink, then returned to the bar for another. Soon he would be too drunk to reach for her, too drunk to make love....

Suddenly a horrible thought occurred to her. Maybe Alex was deliberately drinking himself into oblivion night after night so he would have an excuse for not touching her.

And if the most virile man she'd ever known no longer wanted *her*, who did he want?

Waves of nausea began churning in her stomach, and she clutched the back of the suede sofa for support. "Tell me the truth, Alex. Is there another woman?"

His head snapped up, and his gaze jerked to her face, then slid away, but not before she saw a flash of guilt in his eyes. He didn't answer.

"At least I lasted longer than any of your other women," she said in bitter self-derision, her voice unsteady and thin.

She waited, praying desperately that he would take her in his arms and kiss away the galling certainty that was beginning to eat into her soul like deadly acid.

But he turned away. "There's never been anyone but you since I met you. And I've been in L.A. on business." He threw down another swallow of Scotch. "Only business." With strong fingers he loosened the knot of his tie and unbuttoned his starched white collar.

Silence twisted between them, alive and electric with tension. Casey felt as though she were being slowly strangled, and she was powerless to release the knot. Alex didn't look at her.

Reading body language was part of her job, and his was screaming at her. He was hiding something.

"You're lying," she whispered, her voice breaking.

The glass fell from Alex's hand, and with a savage kick, he sent it spinning into the wall, where it shattered.

A sob escaped her lips, and she clutched the back of the sofa for support. Hot tears filled her eyes and cascaded down her cheeks.

Alex turned away abruptly, his face drawn. "I've never seen you cry." He sounded almost accusing.

"I don't cry." She straightened stiffly, letting her hand fall to her side. "Alex, I have to know the truth. Please. I can't stand this . . . this coldness between us. It's tearing me to bits. I can't sleep. I can't eat. I can't even work."

His shoulders sagged for a moment; then he pushed them back, as though he were accepting a heavy burden. "I love you, Casey," he said in a dead-sounding voice. "No matter what happens, always remember that."

His gaze burned into hers for a heartbeat, and she thought she saw raw torment written in the black depths. And then his face stilled until his arrogant features seemed to be cast in bronze, and his eyes were like chips of black slate.

With two long, quick strides he was past her. Silently he retrieved his coat and briefcase and turned to go.

"Is that your answer?" she cried, her heart breaking.

Alex didn't respond. At the door he turned and looked at her. His brow furrowed, as though he were suffering. And then he was gone, the door closing quietly behind him.

Casey stared at the door, the salt from her tears stinging her cheeks. She began to shake. Alex had really left, and this time she wasn't sure he was coming back.

Because at the moment when he'd walked through the doorway, he had looked exactly like the man he'd been when he'd walked into her life. He looked like a man who always walked alone.

The next day she had received the divorce papers. Her marriage was over.

The fire popped loudly, and Casey jumped, her heart skipping a beat. She hadn't thought of that bleak winter evening in years. She shouldn't have thought of it now.

The image in the faded photograph in front of her grew sharper and sharper until she saw the shadowed lines around the somber mouth and stark loneliness in the warrior's proud carriage.

"That's my great-grandfather. His name was Cadiz."

Casey turned slowly to find Alex standing a few feet away, two mugs of steaming coffee in one hand, a bottle of brandy in the other.

"Cadiz . . . suits him. Is that his last name?"

"First and last. He didn't need more than that. Everyone knew him. And most feared him, even the U.S. cavalry."

"He fought?" she asked in fascination, looking again into the man's fierce eyes.

"Fought and won. That's why his people, my people, still have this land."

"He sounds like a remarkable man." Gently, she touched the dark head of the man in the portrait with her finger. "He looks like you." Turning, she surprised a stark look of pain on Alex's face.

"Does he? I hadn't noticed." Alex set the mugs on the weathered trunk in front of the sofa and poured a hefty slug of brandy into one of them. He drank from the other as he waited for her to sit down.

"Whatever happened to him?" she asked, her gaze going irresistibly to the portrait.

"He died in federal prison."

"Oh, no! That's *terrible*."

"That was the government's price for granting him the victory. His life for the lives of his people."

A chill shook her, and she huddled into the robe for warmth. "But . . . but that's a horribly unfair price to have to pay for . . . for winning."

"Who says life is fair?" His gaze rested for an instant on the man in the picture.

"But to put a man in a cage because he won. That's monstrous!"

Alex acknowledged her impassioned words with a raised brow. "Legend says that he paid the price because his people were more important to him than his freedom."

But no matter what the legend said, his freedom was the one thing he valued above all else, Casey guessed silently, knowing that a man with Cadiz's proud eyes would suffer the worst kind of agony locked away from the thing that was most precious to him, the land he'd fought so hard to keep.

"Sounds like he was a very brave man," she said with a sad smile.

Alex dropped his gaze to the steaming liquid in his mug. "Maybe he wouldn't have been able to live with himself if he'd done anything else."

His voice sounded raw, and Casey felt tiny bumps shiver along her skin. Rubbing her arms, she padded silently across the room and settled into the corner of the sofa, pulling her legs up under her. Curling her arms around her knees, she made herself breathe slowly and evenly until the ragged edges of her nerves smoothed.

Had Alex known this story before? she wondered. Or was that one of the things he'd learned in this self-imposed exile of his? There were beginning to be more questions than answers in this place, and that made her extremely uncomfortable.

Without looking at her, Alex stretched out in a chair by the fire, his long legs extended, his ankles crossed. He rested the mug of coffee on his turquoise-and-silver belt buckle.

It was a familiar pose. They'd sat this way in his den countless times. Then the silence had been a warm, intimate cocoon. But now it was cold and lonely, like the land outside.

Casey hated it.

"This is an interesting house," she said, filling the thick silence with conversation. "Is it old?"

She was stalling, but she couldn't seem to help herself. Now that she had Alex's attention, she was afraid to reopen negotiations. That wasn't like her, but then, she'd never felt quite herself when she was around him.

Alex glanced around the room. "It's about two years old. Most of it, anyway. I finished the bedroom this year."

Casey gaped at him. "*You* finished it? You mean, you built this place?"

He nodded. "Stone by stone."

She took another look. It was small, only three rooms and a bath. But the house had a stark, even impressive grandeur about it, as though its solid strength came from its simplicity.

It would stand for generations, she thought, impervious to the assault of the elements. She decided that she liked Alex's house, and the thought added to the growing sense of unreality that was threatening her control.

"I admit I'm surprised, especially considering the promise you told me that you'd made to yourself."

"What promise?"

"That once you had made your first million, you would never do any work that couldn't be done in a three-piece suit."

A stain of red ran along his jaw. "People change."

"Not that drastically, Alex. Not without a very good reason."

"I had a reason." He shifted his gaze to the fire.

For an instant Casey wanted to ask him why he was here alone. But that was personal, and this was business. Besides, she insisted to herself, she no longer cared.

Without looking at him, she reached for the mug in front of her and took a cautious sip. The coffee was strong, but the brandy was stronger, like a fiery lash against her tongue.

"Too strong?" Alex raised a brow toward the mug in her hand.

Casey shook her head and forced herself to swallow. "Just right." She took another sip. The alcohol hit her empty stomach in a hot rush, spreading quickly to her veins.

"Take it slow. You need to be alert for the drive back to Albuquerque."

Casey bristled at the edge of command in his voice. "Don't worry about me, Alex. We're divorced, remember?"

He turned away from her, his gaze focused once more on the fire in the grate. "I remember too many things I need to forget." His voice sounded strained, as though his memories were hard to bear.

If they were, Casey thought with a flare of pain, they couldn't hurt any worse than hers had during those first few months after the divorce.

She concentrated on her drink. Somehow she had survived, and now she no longer wanted to think about that time.

Alex watched the play of emotions across Casey's face. She'd gotten better at hiding her feelings, but he knew her too well to be fooled. He'd hurt her again.

The familiar feeling of self-loathing settled inside him, as strong as it had been in the last days of the marriage that had become an intolerable prison for both of them.

Stifling a sigh, he tried not to look at her. It had been years since he'd felt this sick anger at himself, years since he'd spoken without thinking, years since he'd made his decision to leave the only woman he'd ever been truly happy with.

He dropped his gaze and stared at the tile he'd laid one hot day last summer. He'd thought of Casey that day, just as he'd thought of her every day. Just as he would think of her every day after she left.

Slowly he flexed his knees, trying to work out the sudden tightness in his muscles. Why did she have to look so pretty, with her butterscotch hair framing her face in a soft halo? he thought angrily. And why did her big gray eyes still search for his soul when she looked at him?

"Alex, I didn't come here to fight with you," she said with a sigh. "I need your help, and it's not easy for me to ask. But I simply have no choice."

"I understand, Casey. Believe me, I do." He drained his mug, then stood. "There's more coffee in the kitchen, if you want some."

Suddenly, before she had time to do more than blink in surprise, he walked across the room, grabbed a brown Stetson from the wall rack and reached for the doorknob.

"Where are you going?" she asked, astonishment thinning her voice.

"For a walk. I need some air."

He watched the soft corners of her mouth tighten at his abrupt tone, and something twisted inside him. But he refused to give the sharp visceral pain a name.

"But...but you'll catch your death out there in the storm," she protested, her gaze flying to the windows, where the rain still pounded the glass.

Alex settled his hat low over his forehead and opened the door a crack. The wind plastered his shirt to his wide back, and the rain spattered the cotton like buckshot. The sound of the blowing rain filled the room, forcing him to raise his voice.

"Believe me, Casey, there are worse things than death."

Without looking at her, he turned and walked out into the storm.

Chapter 3

Alex stood next to a twisted, half-dead piñon, his palm flattened against the wet bark. The wind shook the branches above his head, and rain stung his cheeks.

Closing his eyes, he bowed his head and let the needle-sharp drops pound his shoulders. Why now? he thought. Why did she have to show up just when he was beginning to find a little peace?

He'd tried so hard for so long to live his life by new rules. He'd tried even harder to change the man he'd come to hate. The man she'd once loved. The man he never wanted to be again.

But now that she was here, all he could think about was his reason for leaving her. The reason he'd made himself stop feeling, stop wanting, stop loving her.

He spat out a curse, then jammed his hands into his back pockets and began walking, because he couldn't stand still any longer.

"Damn you, Evan," he muttered into the wind. The man was supposed to be his friend. At the very least he should have called to say that Casey was on her way. If he'd had any warning at all, he would have been gone when she arrived.

But his old buddy had always been on Casey's side. Maybe he was even a little in love with her himself. Alex cursed again, this time in fluent Spanish, but it didn't help.

Suddenly lightning flashed overhead, and the thunder boomed around him, shaking the ground beneath his feet. The wind blew the rain sideways and bent the uppermost branches of a young cotton wood against the roof of his house.

He stopped short, staring at the familiar square lines he knew as intimately as he'd once known Casey's soft body. He'd carried each one of those stones to this site himself. And he'd single-handedly fitted each one in place.

Some days his hands had blistered and bled, and his eyes had blurred and stung with hot sweat, before he'd let himself stop. And some days he'd been so tired by nightfall that he'd fallen asleep leaning against the stones he'd just wrestled into place.

He had needed the hard manual labor and the mind-numbing monotony to keep him sane. And even more urgently, he'd needed the day-to-day challenge of this unforgiving place to keep him from thinking of Casey.

Only it hadn't worked. And it sure wasn't working now.

Rain dripped from the brim of his hat as he bent to gather a handful of smooth round rocks. One by one he hurled them across the stream toward the stunted oak that stood on the far side.

He wanted her to leave. And, damn it, he wanted her to stay. But even if she would consider it—which she wouldn't—having Casey here, *anywhere*, in his life would be hell for him, a worse hell than he was living now.

The last stone pinged against the twisted trunk, the sound echoing over the flat terrain like a sharp cry of pain.

Alex lifted his face to the sky and closed his eyes. The need for her was still inside him like an open wound that would never heal. And there wasn't one blasted thing he could do about it.

Inside his house she was waiting for him. He owed her the courtesy of hearing her out, at least. And if he could help by giving her suggestions, he would do that, too. But that was all he would do. All he could do. He couldn't go back to the life that had taken everything from him but his will to survive. Not even for Casey.

He cleared the thickness from his throat. In a few hours she would be gone. He could stand anything for a few hours.

Casey heard the click of the door latch and looked up quickly, relief flooding over her. She was pressed back against the cushions, her coffee mug held in front of her like a shield.

"Help," she whispered as Alex entered the room and stopped short, a look of astonishment lighting up his face.

He burst out laughing, and Casey bristled.

"This isn't funny, Alex," she exclaimed, her voice squeaking as she shifted her gaze to the wild-looking animal growling at her from atop the trunk in front of the sofa. "I closed my eyes for a minute to...to rest, and when I opened them, this...this creature was about to pounce."

The creature looked like a tomcat, she decided, except that it was missing one yellow eye and half an ear. And its fur, sticking straight out from its arched body, was an ugly mix of orange and black. It was also bigger and more ferocious looking than any ordinary house cat she'd ever seen.

"Looks like you've got it handled, Case."

"Are you kidding? If I move, I'm dead."

The manic gleam in the animal's one eye intensified, and its strident shrieks grew more frantic.

Alex grinned, his teeth flashing against his dark skin, and for a moment Casey could almost feel the blazing warmth of his mouth on hers. His kisses had been like a drug to her. Even now, she could feel the pull of that addiction. But she'd learned to control her dangerous urges. The hard way.

Alex closed the door and shook the water from his Stetson. He'd never seen Casey in such a state, but he had to admit she looked cute as all get out, with her cheeks flushed and her soft mouth quivering with indignation. Her very kissable mouth.

Abruptly he dropped his gaze to his hat and ran his hand around the band, but in his mind he saw himself leaning over her, his mouth taking hers. He forced the fantasy away.

"That's Butch," he told her. "You're sitting in his favorite spot."

Casey gaped at him. "You...you know this animal?"

Alex nodded. "He showed up one night after a tangle with a coyote. I managed to keep him alive. Now I feed him, and he lets me live here. Works out fairly well most of the time."

He tossed his hat onto the table and ambled closer.

The cat began growling again, low in his throat, his tail twitching like a warning flag. "Stop that," Casey ordered, fixing the creature with her best icy glare.

The growling increased, and he lowered his head, ready to spring. "Whoa, Butch," Alex called out, ambling closer. "We know you're tough. You don't have to prove it."

He scooped the bristling animal into his arms, and Casey stiffened. "Watch out, I think he's insane," she warned.

Alex chuckled. "Naw, he's just used to being on his own. He doesn't trust too many people." His big hand kneaded a spot behind the cat's scruffy head, and a loud rumbling purr filled the room.

Casey stared in speechless shock as the creature turned his face into Alex's neck and nuzzled his chin. She'd done that very same thing herself once. She still remembered how warm his skin was. And how comforting it felt just to be close to him.

"He obviously doesn't like women," she muttered, then took a bracing sip of the brandy-laced coffee.

Alex watched her mouth droop, and a feeling of deep tenderness stirred inside him. Casey was always very conscious of her dignity. He thought it was because she was so soft-hearted and caring under the patrician courtesy. He knew a little about self-protection, and he was touched by her struggle to appear undaunted by a seedy house cat.

"Here," he said suddenly, plopping Butch into her lap. "You two make friends while I dry off."

The cat scrambled for solid footing, and his heavy haunch pressed Alex's hand against Casey's thigh. His knuckles scraped the inner curve, and she recoiled. He pulled back his hand quickly and rubbed it against his wet hip.

"Behave yourself, Butch," Alex ordered, his face tight. "The lady is a guest."

The cat stopped purring, but he curled into her lap, his front paws resting against her hip. Alex inhaled slowly. Damn, but he envied that cat, he thought grimly. He turned away and began unbuttoning his dripping shirt.

He tugged the tails from his jeans, then grabbed the back of his collar and pulled the shirt over his head. He wiped his face and chest, then wadded the shirt into a ball and tossed it next to a pair of scuffed running shoes lying to one side of the hearth.

Without seeming to, Casey watched. Was this really the man who'd been almost fanatically neat in his personal habits? The man whose life had been organized into five-minute blocks of time?

He looked the same, and yet, not the same. In the flickering light from the fire, his skin was as dark as an old penny, and his muscles moved like fluid steel. A ragged triangle of curling black hair spanned his chest, tapering to a narrow line that trailed toward his navel. Below the heavy belt, his jeans were water spotted and sticking to his skin, outlining the rugged masculine contours that she knew far too well.

Heat blossomed in the hollow between her breasts, and her breathing changed. Hastily she dropped her gaze to the cat.

Butch stared back, his single yellow eye intimidating. You're not wanted here, it seemed to say.

Believe me, cat, I know that, she told him silently. The animal blinked, then moved restlessly, as though he was as uncomfortable as she was.

Casey touched him gingerly, her fingertips feather light on his furry back. He didn't flinch.

Slowly, watching his unblinking yellow-green eye, she began to pet the beast. His fur was surprisingly soft, his body well muscled beneath that thick pelt. Like Alex's, she thought suddenly, and her hand stilled.

He'd purred, too, in his own way when she'd touched him and petted him. And he'd moaned in relief when she had massaged the tension from his temples when he'd been suffering from one of his frequent headaches. Even after he'd become a multimillionaire, he'd driven himself almost beyond the bounds of human endurance, and only she had had the power to make him let up on himself. Sometimes, at least.

She looked up to find Alex watching her with a strange, almost haunted look in his eye. "Looks like you two made friends, after all." One side of his mouth rose in a reluctant smile.

"More like an armed truce, I'd say." She rubbed the cat's ear, and the end of its tail began twitching back and forth like a metronome, while its back claws dug into her leg.

"Don't worry about Butch. He's really a softy deep down."

Alex kicked off his muddy moccasins and turned to the fire. In silence, he moved the screen to one side, then stirred the coals to flame again and added a log from the basket by the hearth. The wood sputtered and cracked as the fire blazed high.

"In an hour or two it's going to be too hot in here," he told her as he replaced the screen and returned to the same chair he'd left less than an hour before. "That's the way it is in this country. Hot one minute, cold the next. Nothing here is predictable.''

As soon as Alex sat down, Butch opened his eye and arched his back. Shaking off Casey's hand with a imperious blink, he jumped from her lap and, with two fast strides, leaped onto Alex's thigh.

Alex leaned back and extended his legs, giving Butch room to curl up. The cat threw Casey a hooded look, then stretched and closed his eye. One paw was extended along Alex's thigh, the other rested on his belly button.

A kernel of primitive warning exploded deep inside her. There were two male creatures in this room. Both were battle scarred and wary. And both were dangerous.

Nervously she rubbed her thumb against the pattern etched into the heavy mug. She glanced at the window. "Looks like it's stopped raining.''

"Yeah, the driveway should be drained pretty well in an hour or so.'' Alex rubbed the cat's flank absently.

Casey shifted her gaze to the fire. He was wrong. It was as cold as ice inside his stone house. "Okay, I get the point,'' she said stiffly. "You don't want me here. But before I go, you're going to listen to what I have to say.''

One arched brow lifted. "I am?''

Casey ignored the sardonic tone. "I need a strategist, someone who can predict what Con's going to do and head him off before he does it. Like chess, you said once. The best players think three and four moves ahead at all times.'' She inhaled slowly. "You beat me every time we played, remember?''

"Casey, listen—''

"No, you listen. As you so graciously reminded me, I don't have a lot of time, so I'll give you the bottom line. When I took over at Summerville, there were whole families that had lost their jobs—grandfathers, fathers, sons and daughters.''

She waved toward the sheltering walls. "There were one hundred and sixty-three homes for sale and no buyers. Churches in the area were taking up collections of food and clothing to give to the people of the town. Children were wearing shoes with holes and school clothes that didn't fit. In other words, good people had been reduced to poverty because a few greedy and inept men had ruined the company that had supported entire families for over a hundred years.''

Casey paused, giving Alex a chance to comment, but he remained silent. He was too still, his eyes matte black and cold, his mouth tight. She wasn't getting through to him.

"I lived with one of those families when I first moved there," she said in a voice gentled by memory. "The Johnsons. Grandma Johnson made me chamomile tea every night when I came in late and insisted that I take her own hot-water bottle in winter to keep me warm. Because I was too skinny, she used to say."

Casey felt the tears well, and she blinked hard. "She died two weeks ago and left me her few shares of stock. To help out, the will said, because she believed in me."

Alex stared at the ceiling he'd plastered with his own hands. He didn't want to hear these things. He didn't want to care about these people. He *couldn't* care. When a guy cared, it hurt too much if he made a mistake.

"How many shares?"

"Two hundred and sixty-four. When her grandson was killed in Vietnam, she used his insurance to buy them, as...as a kind of memorial, she told me. Because she knew that the foundry would have had a job for him if he'd come back from the war, the way she wanted it to have a job for his little boy someday, the one he never saw." Her voice sharpened. "People who know him tell me Deshler is sure to close the foundry and move everything to his facility in California."

Alex stared at Butch's scarred face. "Makes sense. Minimize administrative costs and the profits go up. His bottom line will look impressive as hell to his shareholders."

"I don't care about Con Deshler's bottom line! Robbie Johnson graduates high school next month. I want him to have a place to work."

Alex's hand tightened on the cat's flank, and Butch yowled in protest. "Find another company to relocate to your town. Generate new jobs in a new industry. That's what I would do."

Casey leaned forward, the heat of the fire reflected in the color in her cheeks. "You don't understand, Alex. The foundry is the heart of the town. The people love those ugly old buildings, and the smell of iron and dirt, and the noise and heat." Her voice softened. "And I love the people who've worked overtime without pay and opened up their homes to me and believed in me. They're my family, now."

Alex felt the barb twist in his gut. He'd been her family once, just as she'd been his. Never once had he doubted her love for him, nor her need for his love in return.

Alex slid Butch off his thigh and stood. The cat didn't stir as Alex deposited him gently on the cushion that still bore the imprint of his own body.

"Con Deshler is dangerous, Casey," he said flatly, without raising his voice. "If you take him on, you may lose more than your company. He could ruin you. He's done it before, to more experienced CEOs than you."

"I know that, but—"

"Do you? Do you really?" He began to pace, his long legs hobbled by the small room. "He's a shark, a damn feeding machine. He doesn't care what kind of destruction he leaves behind as long as he wins."

Casey sat perfectly still. Something in Alex's voice warned her that he was talking about himself. But he was wrong. He had never been like that. *Never.* In fact, in almost every case, he'd increased benefits for the companies he'd absorbed, and in many instances he'd also raised wages and added to the work force.

"I *need* you, Alex," she said softly, playing her last trump. "Desperately."

He stopped pacing and whirled to look at her. "Don't make this personal, Casey. That won't help either of us." His eyes glittered with anger—or was it frustration? She wasn't sure.

Alex had been a master at hiding his emotions. Half the time she hadn't known what he was thinking unless he chose to tell her. And as for feelings, he kept them well shielded from her, from the world, maybe even from himself.

"You...that is, Evan said you offered me a substantial settlement. I didn't want your money. I still don't, but I do want your help." She swallowed the sour taste of fear. If he turned her down, she was lost. "Bottom line, if you feel you...you owe me, this will clear the books."

Alex stared at her, his hands bunched into fists on his hips. "You've learned to fight dirty, I see," he said in a silky voice.

Casey felt sick inside, but she'd come too far to back down now. "You're the one who insulted me by offering money. One million dollars in exchange for three years of my life. Did you really think that would take away the humiliation, Alex? Did you?'' She choked and swallowed the harsh words that welled against the dam of her pride.

He stared at a spot over her head, as though seeing another time, another place. "No, Casey," he said with a heavy sigh. "I just didn't have anything else to give you. I still don't."

Casey ignored the strain that roughened his voice. If she started talking about the past, she would be lost. "But you *do*. You can give me a month of your time. And your expertise. That's all I want, Alex. Nothing more."

Alex turned his back on her and rested his forearm against the mantel. Silently, he stared into the dying flames. She had him pinned to the mat. Neatly, cleanly, with no escape.

He'd failed her once and learned to live with it. Could he stand to live with himself if he let her down again?

Alex closed his eyes and let the embers warm his face. He'd never been afraid of anything in his life, but he was afraid now. Hell, he was scared to death. He didn't know if he could hack the business world anymore. No, it was more than that. He didn't know if he could fight no holds barred against a man like Con Deshler and still hang on to the self-respect he'd fought so hard to regain.

"Please, Alex," Casey said softly, her voice a whisper away from pleading. "These people were there for me when I needed them. I can't let them down. I just can't."

Alex took a deep, steadying breath. He could hear tears in her voice. But Casey didn't cry. She'd told him that once—on that rotten night when he had walked out of their flat for the last time. He'd never forgotten the helpless rage that had filled him at that moment, rage at himself for putting those tears in her eyes. And rage that there wasn't one damn thing he could do to take them away.

Slowly his fist clenched against the hand-hewn mantel. "I'll give you my answer tomorrow." He turned to face her. "That's the best I can do."

Casey glanced toward the door. "But I have to leave *tonight*. I have a reservation on the midnight flight."

One brow rose. "Then I'll call you."

She sank back against the cushions. Intuition told her not to leave until she had his firm commitment. "No, there are papers you need to see, lists of shareholders, P and L statements, R and D projections. I can't leave them."

"If you want my answer now, it's no."

Casey opened her mouth to protest, then closed it. When Alex used that tone, he meant what he said.

Slowly she nodded. At the moment he held all the cards. But then, he'd always held a pat hand where she was concerned.

His image blurred until she could no longer see him clearly. It was safer that way. "I need to use your phone," she said, glancing around. "I, um, should change my reservation, call my secretary."

He hesitated, then glanced toward the bedroom. "In there."

Casey slid her legs to the floor and stood. Her toe caught in the hem of the robe, and she pitched forward, her hands outstretched to break her fall. Alex lunged toward her, catching her against his chest. Automatically, his arms closed around her, lifting her to her toes.

His body was lean and firm, the way she remembered, and incredibly strong. Too strong. His chest crushed her breasts, and she could feel his heart pounding like a war drum. Or was that her own heart racing out of control?

She felt his muscles flex, then relax, as though he were holding himself under a tight rein. He set her carefully on her feet, his hands sliding down her arms. Lingering. Nearly caressing.

"You would have hit your head on the corner of the trunk," he told her, visibly trying to control his breathing. His hands fell away, then somehow ended up on her shoulders again. His fingers pressed. Massaged.

"Yes."

His mouth was close. She tilted her head slightly. His mouth was closer.

He didn't move. Neither did she.

The fire snapped in the grate, the only other sound in the room besides their mingled breathing.

She wanted him to kiss her. The thought hit her with the force of a blow. She wanted to feel his mouth on hers. To feel his hands on her body. To feel *him*.

Casey wrenched herself away and reached for her cup. She must be out of her mind. What was she thinking? What was *wrong* with her?

She didn't look at him as she drained her mug, then set it carefully on the trunk. "I'll just, uh, make my calls now."

Alex nodded and walked over to the fire. His face was lined with tension, and his arrogant brows were drawn, as though he were hurting someplace inside.

Casey turned and hurried into his room. Her hand shook as she shut the door behind her.

Damn, Alex cursed silently. For a minute he'd forgotten why he'd left her. He'd forgotten the bitter feelings that had lain between them at the end.

But Casey hadn't. She didn't want him. And it hurt.

What the hell was wrong with him? he thought. He didn't love her. He couldn't allow himself to want her. He didn't *want* her to want him.

He grabbed his mug and headed for the kitchen. He needed more coffee.

Casey was shaking all over by the time she sat down on the edge of the bed. The bed was so tall that her feet dangled above the floor, making her feel even more vulnerable.

His bedroom was just large enough to accommodate the oversize bed and a couple of dressers. There was a small wooden trunk at the foot of the bed and another on the left side, where the phone sat next to a lamp and a book on Native American folklore.

"Great move, Case," she whispered, pressing her hands to her mouth. She'd planned for every possibility but this rash burst of leftover lust.

It's a red flag, that's all, she told herself. A danger signal. There was still an attraction between them. Purely physical, to be sure, but still . . .

She would be on guard while she was here. For a few heady seconds she had forgotten why she'd come. But she wouldn't forget again. This was business.

Feeling more confident, she picked up the phone.

Chapter 4

The storm had spent its fury, and the setting sun was threading through the clouds when Casey returned to the living room an hour later.

Alex was standing by the window, his hands pressed against his spine, his fingers shoved under the waistband of his jeans. He turned as she approached, a quick frown creasing his brow.

"I was beginning to get worried about you." His hair was rumpled, as though he'd combed it with his fingers, and tension radiated from the stiff line of his shoulders.

"I wish I hadn't called," she muttered truthfully, crossing the room to stand a few careful feet from him.

"Trouble?"

"I'll say! Becky, my secretary, was frantic. Deshler's arrived in Summerville with his accountants and his attorneys and his bodyguards. He's rented a house and arranged a party for the local shareholders. Two weeks from Saturday, Becky thinks. My staff's in a panic."

Her people were dedicated and well trained. She trusted them implicitly. Still, conflicting needs tore at her. The foundry needed her there, but she couldn't leave. Not while there was still a chance that Alex would agree to help her.

So she'd spent most of her time on the phone issuing detailed orders for each member of her management team. Summerville Foundry was in the game now, for better or worse.

"I should have known he'd pull a stunt like this," she said with a sigh she couldn't quite suppress.

Alex walked over to the bookshelf and picked up a heavy stone that had been carved into the head of a tomahawk. Absently, his expression absorbed, he ran his fingers over the blunt surface.

Casey felt a shiver of hope run down her spine. Alex thought best with something in his hands, maybe because most of his life he'd been so used to working with them.

"How many shares do your employees control?" His voice gave no hint of his feelings.

Casey quoted the exact figure, then added tersely, "A woman named Rachel Eiler is the majority shareholder. My broker tells me that she could tip the scale."

"Do you have her proxy?"

Casey shook her head. "Not yet, but she likes me. I'm pretty sure I can count on her."

Alex turned to face her. "You'd better be absolutely certain when you walk into that meeting on the first of July."

"I will be."

"Good." Alex tossed the heavy stone in the air and caught it. "Deshler must be getting soft. I would have expected something more intimidating, like a big spread in the local papers with rumors, innuendos, even outright lies planted by unnamed sources, all having to do with 'problems' at the foundry. That way management is forced onto the defensive from the start."

Casey went pale, and her mouth went dry. "I never thought..." She stared at Alex helplessly. "My secretary also had a message for me from the town marshal. Someone... someone broke into my house after I left to go to the airport." The words left a nasty taste on her tongue. "Mrs. Morrow, my neighbor, heard glass breaking, and she called the marshal."

Alex swore succinctly. "Did he catch the guy?"

She shook her head. "Becky said the... the person made a mess of my bedroom before he left. Sam, Marshal Rickert, told Becky to tell me that it was probably a transient who was looking for money or jewelry and got mad because he couldn't find anything worth stealing.'' She took a careful breath. ''I keep a lot of highly sensitive papers in a safe in my bedroom, but fortunately I have most of them with me. Do you . . . do you think Con sent someone to steal those papers?''

''If he did, he's made a bad mistake.'' Alex's voice was low and tightly controlled.

''But you think he might be responsible?'' she pressed, watching his eyes go completely still, like the deadly stare of a range-tough hero in a Western movie. Only Alex wasn't acting.

''It's possible.'' He dropped his gaze to the primitive weapon in his hand.

''So what do we do to counteract this . . . this first move?''

''*We* don't do anything. I haven't said I'll help you.''

''I realize that, Alex,'' she said carefully. ''I was speaking rhetorically.''

Casey tucked her hands into the sleeves of the robe, kimono fashion, and turned to stare at the lengthening shadows beyond the windows. The desert was a place of secrets where a man could lose himself forever. But why?

Alex had never explained his actions to anyone. She didn't expect him to explain now. She only knew that his coming here had nothing to do with her. He'd shut her out of his heart long before he'd walked out.

She repressed a shudder. She hated the feeling of insecurity that had held her captive since she'd driven off the familiar wide lanes of the freeway and headed for this out-of-the-way pueblo. She didn't want to stay in this place a second longer than she had to.

''I'll just go change,'' she said, carefully lifting the hem of the robe to keep from stumbling again. ''I imagine my things are dry by now.''

''You're going back to Ohio, then?'' She heard nothing in his voice, not even the pretense of interest.

A bit of scar tissue tore deep inside her. It would be so much easier to leave now. To walk out of this incomprehensible new life he'd made for himself and never look back. Easier, and by far the smartest thing she could do.

But she couldn't. Too many people were counting on her.

''To a motel,'' she corrected calmly. ''The nearest one will do nicely, I'm sure.''

His cheeks creased into a half smile. ''Chamisa is the closest town, and the only motel closed a few years back when the new

road went through. Now there's not even a rooming house.
You'll have to stay here." His tone was a little weary, a little
harsh.

"*No!*"

"Believe me, Casey, I'm not any happier about it than you
are, but there's no alternative."

He left her standing by the sleeping cat, disappearing into his
bedroom to return a few minutes later dressed in dry jeans, a
short-sleeved gray sweatshirt and white socks. A pale blue dress
shirt with long sleeves dangled from one finger.

"Here, you can sleep in this. It's clean."

Casey caught the shirt he tossed her way, crushing the crisp
Oxford cloth between her hands. Her heart lurched. It was one
she'd bought for him at Brooks Brothers, with his initials embroidered in tiny stitches on the French cuffs.

"Alex, this is silly. There must be a place—"

"There isn't." He retrieved his running shoes from the hearth
and sat down on the sofa to put them on.

She couldn't stay here, she realized instantly, wearing his
shirt, with only a few feet of empty space between his big bed
and this sofa. It was impossible.

"You must have stayed somewhere when you were building
this house," she persisted, her voice rising in desperation.

"Yeah, I lived in a tent under the trees. It leaked when it
rained, and in the winter it was as cold as a . . . it was damn
cold."

Alex's head was bent toward his shoes as he knotted the
frayed laces. The nape of his neck was covered by shaggy tendrils of thick hair, and for an instant Casey had an urge to run
her fingers through the soft-looking thatch. She had always
loved Alex's hair, even when it had been cut into the severe
quasi-military style that he'd favored in the past. But now she
found she liked the way the disheveled look softened the arrogance that had sometimes set him apart from her.

Curling her fingers into her palms, she looked around
frantically. Her stomach began to flutter wildly. "It's only a
couple of hours to Albuquerque," she said. "I don't mind
driving."

Alex stood. "It's settled, Casey. I realize that you don't want
to spend any more time with me than you have to, so I'll get out
of your way. There's plenty of stuff in the refrigerator. Make
yourself at home."

"But—"

"No buts. It's a long drive back to the nearest town of any size, and the weather's unpredictable this time of year. I don't want to worry about you running off the road in another storm. I have enough on my conscience as it is."

Two strides took him to the door before she could react. He opened the door, then looked back over his shoulder. "Take the bedroom. At least it's better than a tent."

She forced a smile. She was trapped, and they both knew it. "Thank you, but I'll take the couch."

"Suit yourself. When I come home, I'll just pick you up and toss you onto the bed."

She opened her mouth, then shut it. The thought of his big hands touching her when she was most defenseless made her go warm and then cold inside. She would be safer in the bedroom, but from whom? Alex or herself? Her decision must have been clear on her face.

"Good move, Casey." His eyes crinkled at the corners, as though he wanted to smile. But he didn't. Instead he gave her a quick nod. "Don't wait up for me."

Without waiting for an answer, he disappeared into the twilight. Casey was left alone.

Alex pulled his Jeep into the crowded parking lot in front of the Prickly Pear Bar and Grill and killed the engine. He intended to get drunk. Blind, stinking drunk. So drunk that he wouldn't remember that Casey was at his house, sleeping in his bed. So drunk that he wouldn't have to remember why he wasn't sleeping in that bed with her.

Alex stared at the blinking beer sign in the window. He hadn't been to this place in months, and he hadn't been drunk in years. But there had been a time, right after he'd left New York, when he'd rarely been sober.

For days and nights on end, he'd sat alone in one Albuquerque bar or another, drinking steadily until Casey's face had blurred into an alcoholic haze and the pain inside had dulled enough for him to sleep. And then in the morning, when he'd had to face the frustration and self-hatred that never left him, he'd started all over again.

Alex dropped his forehead to the steering wheel and closed his eyes. When would he be allowed to forget? When would he be free again? Dear God, when?

He rubbed his brow over the hard plastic. He'd nearly blown it a few minutes ago. Nearly said things he had no business saying. But he'd been away from the slash-and-parry arena of corporate negotiations for a long time, and he was too rusty to deal with Casey when she wanted something from him.

He uttered a vicious curse and yanked the key from the ignition. He'd made his world here so damn safe. No one, not even the kids who listened to him day after day with such trust, expected more from him than he chose to give. No one in this place knew who he'd been. No one knew the secret he carried inside himself day after day, night after night.

He had worked hard to become a different man. But what kind of a man? Did he have the courage to risk everything he'd worked so hard to achieve because Casey asked it of him? God help him, he simply didn't have the answer.

Slowly, feeling sick inside, Alex climbed from the Jeep and pocketed the keys. He glanced across the pitted blacktop road that had once been a section of Route 66. Wild Horse Mesa stretched for ten or more miles along this road, its jagged red sides rubbed raw from countless years of wind and rain.

He returned his gaze to the blinking red, white and blue sign. Some of the kids at school had learned to read by matching signs like this one with the commercials they saw on T.V.

He'd talked to them about drinking. About how bad it was and how stupid. Only a coward or a fool tried to drown his problems in a bottle, he had told them. And they'd believed him, because he was their teacher. A role model, the only one some of them had.

"No, damn it," he muttered aloud, aiming a vicious kick at a flattened beer can at his feet. This time he wasn't going to numb the pain with Scotch. This time he would face it cold sober and alone.

He would run until his legs burned and his wind gave out. And then he would go home and hope he was tired enough to ignore the fact that Casey was sleeping only a few feet away, behind a door that didn't lock.

Alex raised his face to the wind and listened to the familiar sounds of twilight. He could hear her voice in the soothing wind song, calling his name in that special lilting way that had always made him smile inside.

He remembered the way she had welcomed him with a drowsy smile and a kiss on those long-ago nights when he had come home tired, with the pressure of his high-stress life still heavy inside him.

No matter how late it had been, she'd never been too tired to love away the loneliness that was always with him when he was away from her. The loneliness that was with him now.

Madre de Dios, he felt empty. A thousand times over the past six years he'd wished that he'd been different, or circumstances had been different, or it had all been a bad dream. But wishing never changed a thing. He was what he was, a man who'd made a terrible mistake and was paying for it.

Muttering a plea for strength in the language of his mother's people, he began to run, letting his stride lengthen naturally until he found his rhythm.

Casey was in his head, in his blood, just as she'd been from the moment he'd met her. And he couldn't have her. He'd forfeited that right by making one stupid error in judgment on a malignant sunny day in Los Angeles, and nothing he could ever do would be enough to earn him the right to have her again.

For a moment, as he looked into the setting sun, his eyes blurred. He blinked hard and looked away from the bright orange ball. Damn, he wanted a drink.

Casey pulled the long tail of the shirt over her bent knees and huddled under the thin cotton blanket. It wasn't quite ten, but her inner clock was still on eastern time, and her eyes burned with fatigue.

Now that the rain had stopped, the night air was surprisingly warm, and the wind had ebbed into a gentle breeze that sighed like a lonely child outside the bedroom window.

Burrowing her cheek into the feather pillow, she tried to get comfortable. But her body was stretched as tight as the string of the ceremonial bow hanging on the wall over the headboard. And her mind refused to shut down.

She couldn't stop thinking of Alex. Nothing made sense anymore. Nothing.

Once they'd been so close, so much in love. From the first moment she'd seen him, she'd felt a nearly irresistible urge to touch him. No, she corrected. To love him.

Intuitively she'd sensed a fiercely guarded gentleness beneath the tough masculine exterior, a gentleness that had drawn her to him, even as she'd experienced a premonition of danger. He had the power to make her feel more like a woman than an executive. To demand more than she'd ever had to give before.

And he'd cosseted her with a rough, almost awkward tenderness that had gradually healed the pain of a lonely childhood spent in a succession of boarding schools where her emotionally frail mother had parked her after her father's desertion.

He'd seen through her tough career-lady facade. He'd understood her loneliness and her pain.

But *his* toughness hadn't been a facade. From the time he'd been a little boy, he'd had to fight to survive, and the battle had seasoned him to a hard, cutting edge.

He'd been the eldest, the responsible one, the one who'd frequently gone hungry so that the newest baby could have milk, the one who had to be strong. He'd driven himself mercilessly until he had gotten it all—success, money, prestige.

So why was he here in this rustic place, teaching school? And why was he still alone?

Or was he? Even though he wasn't married, he could still have a lover. Evan had told her once that Alex attracted women like a powerful magnetic field, and she herself had felt the irresistible pull of his sexy grin and brooding eyes.

She curled into a tight ball and tried not to think about him making love to another woman in the bed where she now lay. But she had no right to be jealous. He was a free man. A bored-looking judge in a cold and dreary courtroom in New York City had said so.

Just as she was a free woman.

All of a sudden she didn't feel free. Not lying in the middle of Alex's bed, with the familiar clean scent of his shampoo still clinging to his pillow, and the masculine clutter of his everyday life around her.

She sighed and turned onto her side. The slide of the sheet against her bare legs was nearly unbearable, and the weight of his shirt against her breasts made the nipples swell into painful buds.

"I'm just tired," she whispered into the darkness. But the ache that was growing inside her refused to go away. Instead, it swelled and pulsed and crackled through her nerve endings, tightening her muscles into stinging knots.

She rocked back and forth on the mattress, trying to push the memories out of her mind. But they refused to go.

The first time they'd made love had been in her bed, not his.

She'd made dinner for him in her loft in SoHo. After dinner she'd taught him to dance. He'd never had the time to learn, he'd warned her as she'd fitted into his arms. The slide of his heavy thighs against hers had made her knees shake with the need to get closer to him.

But Alex had been tense, his strong body radiating some powerful force, like a volcano ready to blow.

She'd been determined to get him to relax.

Shivering suddenly, she pulled the blanket closer against her neck and rubbed her chin over the wide satin binding. She closed her eyes, and the small sounds of Alex's house faded as she let herself sink into memory.

"You're very graceful for such a big man," Casey whispered into the pleated front of his crisp white tuxedo shirt.

"I'm a big ox," he said, turning red. "None of my sisters could manage to teach me, and the one time I went to a dance, I nearly crippled my poor date for life."

He'd discarded his tux jacket almost as soon as he'd arrived at her door. The black bow tie had come off during the main course, and he'd rolled his shirtsleeves to the elbow during dessert, showing corded forearms thickly covered with downy black hair.

"Poor Alex," she teased, laughing. He stopped moving, holding her motionless against him. He smelled of musk, the kind that came from a man's pores instead of a bottle.

"No one laughs at Alejandro de las Torres and gets away with it, *querida*," he said in a silken purr.

"I just did."

"So you did." His thumb brushed her bottom lip gently. "Now you must pay the price, sweet Casey." His bold gaze fell to her lips, and a slow, determined smile pushed into the hollows under his arrogant cheekbones. For such a hard, uncompromising man, he had a surprisingly sensuous mouth. A beautiful, masculine mouth. Her pulse rate soared, but she managed to keep her lips from parting in anticipation.

"What price is that, Mr. Torres, sir?" she asked, lowering her lashes to keep him from seeing her thoughts in her eyes.

"I want you, *mi amor*, naked and ready, under me."

He pushed the thin rhinestone strap of her evening gown off her shoulder and kissed the soft white skin. His other hand pressed against the small of her back, forcing her closer.

Both of his workman's hands slid possessively down the bare length of her spine, leaving her skin tingling. Slowly, his raspy fingers pushed under the ivory silk where it rested against the curves of her hips.

A honey-warm sensation spread inside her, moving outward to the inner surfaces of her thighs. Her sleek dress was suddenly too tight, her silk stockings too constricting. She ached to feel her skin against his.

"You ... sound serious." Her voice was low and sultry, not from artifice, but from the passion shaking her.

"I *am* serious, Casey. I don't know how to be anything else."

One hand left her spine to cup her chin, forcing her head up so that she had to look at him. There was a fierce look in his eyes, a look that curled her toes in her satin slippers. He was right. He was a man who didn't know how to play games for fun. Whatever he did, he did to win. Including making love.

Run! an inner voice said, but it was too late.

Somehow, sometime when she hadn't been looking, Alex Torres had slipped beneath her guard and taken her prisoner.

She loved him.

"Alejandro," she whispered, loving the sound of his name. Loving him.

His brows drew together quizzically. "Yes, *querida*?" Light from the overhead fixture caught in his short hair, turning the well-brushed strands to gleaming ebony.

She raised a steady hand and threaded her fingers through the dark thatch, loving the feel of the springy thickness. Released from its careful grooming, it was unruly and very manly. Like Alex himself.

"Claim your prize," she whispered, her voice soft and welcoming.

His mocking smile grew gentle. "Are you sure?" he asked gruffly. "I won't force you."

"I know. That's why I'm sure."

The fierce glow in his eyes warmed to a vivid golden gleam that inflamed her.

"Casey," he whispered in rough caress.

His fingers were hard and possessive as they slid the other strap from her shoulder. "I'm glad your skin is too fair to tan. You look like a woman of light." His breath was warm and deliciously moist against her lips. Alex drew back, his eyes smoldering. "I warn you, *querida*, once I have you, I'll never let you go." His large scarred hand slid along her cheek, holding her captive. "You'll always be my woman."

"I know." Slowly, her lashes fell, and she turned into his palm. She kissed the rough calluses. "I love you."

Alex shuddered, his body shaking hers, as well. He whispered urgent words in Spanish, words she didn't know, his deep voice caressing the vowels in a way that made her go soft inside.

"Love me, Alejandro," she murmured against his crisp white collar.

"I want you, Casey. More than I thought I could ever want a woman." His warm, moist breath whispered into her ear, and she shivered with pleasure. His hands were busy with her zipper, sliding it down over her rounded bottom with one easy movement.

"I've thought about doing this from the first moment I watched you walk away from me, twitching your arrogant little bottom in dismissal." His voice was a low growl of triumph.

"I didn't." Her breathing was becoming erratic, and it was hard to make her voice properly indignant.

"You had me roped and hog-tied that first morning, and you knew it. I let you have your victory then, but this is mine."

He slid his hands around to her hips, then down her thighs. His fingers snagged on her silky panty hose, the only undergarment she wore under the sleek dress, and a charge of purely feminine exaltation shook her. This was a man, a raw and intensely masculine protector, a man with rough hands and a flinty core that would never accept defeat. With him, she would always be safe.

She smiled and touched the slight cleft in his chin with her fingertip. As soon as she raised her arm, the shimmering silk fell away from her breasts, brushing her thighs as it fell.

Alex's heated gaze followed the wisp of ivory down her body, then returned to the small rosy-tipped breasts that were only inches from his chest.

"Beautiful," he murmured, cupping them possessively. She closed her eyes and let bliss pour over her. Her breasts were swollen and tingling with a wonderful ache that only his touch could ease.

There was a rustle of sound, and then his soft hair brushed her skin as he kissed first one hard nipple, then the other. His tongue inscribed a figure eight, encircling one rosy peak, then the other and connecting them in the hollow between.

Casey pressed a kiss into his hair, her lips as sensitive as her breasts. His hair felt cool and smelled of pine trees in the winter.

"I've been patient a long time," he whispered, his voice a groan. His hands were urgent and uncompromising as they pushed the filmy nylon down her thighs. She was as eager as he was, kicking off her shoes and holding on to his shoulder as he lifted each small foot in turn and slipped the panty hose off her toes.

Casey smiled up at him, her mouth soft and willing at the corners. Her hands were still on his shoulders, and she used them to push herself to her toes until she could reach his mouth.

"Kiss me," she whispered.

His face was tortured, his eyes fiery. "*Gatita*. Little wildcat," he muttered in a thick voice. "I thought I knew..."

Her kiss swallowed his words.

She clung to him, her hands laced behind his neck. His body moved fluidly, and then she was in his arms, held high above the floor.

He stopped kissing her long enough to ask in a furious growl, "Which way?"

Casey's blood sizzled through her veins. "To the left and down the hall," she managed between kisses.

Alex muttered something indistinct as he crossed the room and headed down the narrow passageway, cradling her against his chest like a knight striding to his horse with his prize.

Her bed was covered by a satin coverlet that gleamed silver in the faint light from the street outside. Shadows softened the furniture, and the scent of two dozen red roses in a vase on the nightstand perfumed the air.

He kissed her, long and hard, and then set her gently onto her feet. His eyes glittered like black stars as he started to strip.

"Hurry," Casey whispered, helping him with his studs.

He shrugged the suspenders over his shoulders and ripped away the cummerbund. She tugged at the tails of the starched shirt, pulling them from trousers that were suddenly tighter as his arousal pushed against the fabric. He angled his broad shoulders from the shirt and tossed it away, his hand already going to his zipper.

Casey stared at him, her pulse pounding in her throat. He was magnificent, a perfect male animal.

His chest was broad and covered with curly black hair in an inverted triangle. His muscles were clearly defined and shaped with perfect symmetry. There were no ugly bulges from pumping iron, no misshapen lines or angles.

In the shadowed room, he seemed to glow, inviting her kiss. His skin was hot and tasted salty.

Even as he bent to shed his shoes and socks and trousers, she was touching him, trailing her fingers over his spreading shoulders.

He straightened, wearing only dark red briefs that barely covered his potent manhood.

"I need you," he said, his voice low and urgent. His breath was a harsh whisper in the quiet room, and hers was coming in short, quick bursts.

"I love you."

He groaned. "You're mine now. Only mine. No one but me will ever have you again."

She moved, and he moved, shedding his briefs, and then they were on the bed. His hands caressed her with a feverish need. Sweat glowed on his forehead and cheeks as he kissed her until she was breathless.

He touched her possessively, intimately, his warm fingers exploring every secret, sensitive place on her eager body before cupping the soft, throbbing spot between her legs.

Casey moaned and arched against his thick wrist. She was being conquered inch by inch, his hands and mouth delightful weapons that she was powerless to resist.

He was in control, taking her to a place where she'd never been before.

Casey felt the satin coverlet slide beneath her thighs as she moved, out of control, ready, eager.

Alex seemed to know the instant when she could take no more, the second when he was to make her his irrevocably. With a low growl of triumph, he parted her legs and sank into her.

Casey gasped and then began to move. She was alive, glowing inside and out, on fire. She met his hard thrusts eagerly, violently, clashing with him, moving with him.

Alex slid his hands under her and lifted her higher, until he filled her with unrestrained male power, thrusting faster and faster, releasing the greatest pleasure she'd ever known.

It was primitive. Elemental. Tempestuous.

With a guttural cry of triumph, Alex exploded into her. She was his.

Casey opened her eyes. Her heart was thudding in the dark silence, and her mouth was dry. Beneath her skin, her veins carried a rush of blood to her cold, shaking hands.

She could still hear Alex's voice, hoarse with satisfaction and spiked with arrogance. "We'll be married in Los Angeles, *querida*, in church, so that even God will know how much I treasure you."

Tears blurred the darkness, and she shut her eyes. Want you. Need you. Treasure you.

When he'd left her, he'd said he loved her.

But those had been empty words.

God, she thought. What a fool she'd been in those days. She'd been so much in love that she hadn't seen the signs of his cooling ardor until it had been too late. In the end one woman hadn't been enough for him.

Remember the guilt in his eyes, Casey told herself firmly, bunching her pillow into shape. Remember the endless days and nights without him. Remember that you don't love him.

Chapter 5

Alex stood in the doorway of his bedroom, a mug of hot coffee in his hand. In his bed Casey was sleeping deeply, her knees drawn up and her hands tucked under the pillow, as though she'd fallen asleep saying her prayers.

In the dawn light her hair looked pale gold, waving like a lacy mantilla around her face, and her cheeks were a delicate pink, the way they'd been sometimes when his whiskers had rubbed her skin during the night.

Her face was tranquil; a night of sleep had smoothed the tiny lines from her forehead. While he had prowled the living room like a prisoner in a cell, she'd rested. But that was only right, he realized. He was the one wrestling with ghosts, not her.

"Casey, wake up," he said, wincing at the harsh tone of his voice.

"Mmm," she mumbled, her lips curving slowly into a relaxed smile as she rubbed her cheek against the pillow.

Alex swallowed. His throat was suddenly tight, as tight as the muscles of his thighs after his punishing run. It took all of his control to keep from peeling out of his clothes and climbing in beside her.

He walked to the side of the bed, his boots echoing hollowly on the tile. "Casey, it's Alex. Wake up."

Her lashes fluttered, then settled once more against her cheeks like tiny little brushes. "Mmm," she murmured again, her hand lazily searching the empty place beside her.

His gaze fell to the curve of her hips outlined under the sheet. He hadn't asked her much about her personal life, but she was behaving like a woman who wasn't used to sleeping alone.

But why should she? Casey was too desirable, too vibrant a woman, to cloister herself from men. He'd told himself over and over that she would love again. He'd *wanted* her to love again. That was part of the reason he'd left her—so that she could find a man who would love her the way she deserved to be loved.

So why the hell did it hurt so much to think about it?

His hand jerked, sending scalding coffee sloshing over his bare wrist, burning the skin. He muttered a harsh expletive, then froze as Casey's eyes jerked open.

She sat up, blinking in confusion. The sheet fell away, revealing a considerable length of graceful white thigh beneath the pale blue shirt.

"What it is? What's wrong?" She pushed her hair away from her face, her eyes sleep glazed and unfocused in the dimness.

"Relax," Alex said in a voice that was too thick. He cleared his throat. "Nothing's wrong."

He managed a stiff smile as he transferred the cup to his other hand and wiped his stinging wrist on his jeans. "It's after five."

Casey gaped at him, her eyes fully open now, and wide with some emotion he couldn't decipher. Shock, probably.

"Five?" she asked, her voice husky. "Five in the morning?"

Alex heard the indignation threaded into the sensual tones, and he fought down a smile. "Yes, in the morning," he echoed gravely.

Holding the mug carefully, he crossed to the head of the bed and took one of her hands. It lay small and white against his darker palm, the fingers curled gracefully into a half fist as she blinked at him. He could still see the faint traces of sleep in the centers of her smoky irises.

"Here," he said, wrapping her fingers securely around the mug. "Drink."

Casey looked down at the strong fingers holding hers. His wrist was corded with tension, his palm pressed firmly against the back of her hand.

Warmth crept up her wrist, and her fingers gripped the cup so tightly that he frowned. "Is it too hot?"

She shook her head, and he removed his hand. For some strange reason she was disappointed. She had liked the sensation of his hand against hers. It made her feel . . . safe.

She bent her head over the mug, gratefully inhaling the steam. It was scalding hot and smelled strong, the way Alex preferred his coffee.

She took a cautious sip. "Mmm, cinnamon and sugar," she murmured. "My favorite."

She heard the sound of surprised pleasure in her own voice and glanced up to find him studying her with fathomless eyes as unflinching as the warrior's in the photograph. He stood completely still, his hands on his hips, one shoulder cocked higher than the other. His mouth was a firm thin line in the dark frame of his face, and his jaw looked as hard as the wall of his house.

"Is it? I thought it was mine." He watched the tiny drop of coffee shimmering on the fullness of her lower lip. His tongue pushed against the back of his teeth. She would taste better than any coffee, with or without cinnamon. And she would feel even better in his arms. He reached for the post at the foot of the bed and wrapped his hand around the smooth wood.

"I . . . this is just what I need," she said, faltering. She hadn't expected to wake up with Alex standing over her, and his presence made her feel as though her privacy had been rudely invaded. Except that it was his house, and *she* was the intruder.

Alex watched her tongue capture the tiny drop and sweep it away, and the emptiness inside him yawned wider. "You never did wake up easily."

"No, I . . . never did." She relaxed against the massive headboard, trying to escape the cobwebs trapping her brain. The room seemed smaller with Alex in it, but that was understandable. At six-two, Alex was taller than most men and bigger across the chest and shoulders, but even if he weren't, his air of assurance would make him seem so.

He looked down on her, waiting, one hand braced nonchalantly against the heavy post at the foot of the bed. He was dressed in jeans and a blue chambray shirt, with the sleeves rolled above the elbows. His hair was damp from the shower and slicked back from his wide brow, and his jaw had the shiny look of a recent close shave.

But six years had done more than change his outward appearance, she realized now. In some very basic way Alex himself had changed.

The arrogance was still there, but it had been tempered, as though he'd been tested in some desperate way and survived. And the cold and often impatient glitter in his eyes had disappeared, replaced by a strangely haunted look that aroused a feeling of compassion in her, even as she wondered what had put it there.

"Awake now?" The faint trace of a Latin accent was still there in the cadence of his deep voice.

"Yes, I'm awake." She met his autocratic gaze directly.

"Good. We need to talk." He cleared his throat, then continued in a matter-of-fact way. "I did a lot of thinking last night. And you're right. I was a bastard about the divorce, trying to force a settlement on you, but I was so used to... to providing for the people I... care about that I just reacted automatically. I didn't give a thought to how you might interpret the offer."

"I was hurt," she said quietly. And deep down, a part of her wondered even now what she had done to drive him away, wondered why he'd found her so lacking that he'd undoubtedly turned to another woman.

Her voice grew brittle. "Actually, I felt like a failure. But that's a word you don't understand, isn't it?"

"I understand it. I just don't... like it." He hesitated, then perched on the edge of the mattress, his lean hip against the footboard, one long leg braced against the floor. On his feet were a pair of black boots that looked new.

He must have come to this room while she'd slept to collect his things, she realized suddenly. Involuntarily she glanced down at the oversize shirt that covered her breasts. It was buttoned modestly to the second button from the top, but her nipples, uncomfortably full at the moment, were clearly visible through the blue cotton. And a shadow of cleavage peaked through the open triangle below the collar.

Suddenly she felt naked and exposed. No, defenseless was a better word. But Alex probably hadn't even noticed. And if he had, so what? Not only had he seen every inch of her before, he'd also covered every one of those inches with his kisses.

Slowly she drew her feet closer to her body, putting more distance between them. "Maybe it would be better if we just put all that behind us," she said in what she hoped was a reasonable tone.

"Can you? I saw how uncomfortable you were with me yesterday. And how wary you look right now. If I do this...thing, we would be together for a month, sometimes day and night. Could you handle that?"

His words were uttered quietly, but his voice was oddly raspy, the way it had been that cold night in December.

The coffee churned sickeningly in her empty stomach, and she swallowed the scalding bitterness that rose to her throat. "Could you?"

"I've handled worse and survived." His voice turned crisp and cold again, his eyes grew remote, just the way they had that night, when she'd asked him if he were seeing another woman.

Suddenly it came crashing down around her, the hurt, the uncertainty, the humiliation. "I've handled worse things, too," she said recklessly, her voice betraying none of the turmoil in her mind. "Like the time my husband left me for another woman."

His face flooded with color. "There was no other woman. I told you that." His voice grew colder.

Her heart began to pound. "I think I deserve the truth, Alex. After all, it no longer matters, does it?"

The corner of his mouth jerked upward. "You're right. It no longer matters. But just for the record, I left because we were destroying each other. You said so yourself. You couldn't go on, you said. I ended the misery—for both of us."

"But there was a woman, wasn't there? In L.A.," she persisted, her pride refusing to let him cavalierly dismiss her. Not this time.

His body didn't move, but the air in the room changed, reminding her of the static-charged moments before yesterday's storm hit.

"Is that the kind of man you think I am, Casey? A man who would betray vows made in front of God?"

He sounded angry and...and what? Hurt?

A bitter chill came over her. Why should he be hurt? He was the one who stopped coming home, stopped wanting her, the one who had wanted the divorce.

"What else should I think?" she asked in a cutting tone that hid the pain that was beginning to spiral inside her. "Whatever you wanted, you took. That's the kind of man you were."

Alex smiled, a cold, painful smile that nearly made her gasp. "You're right, Case. I was that kind of man." He stood and walked out of the room.

Casey took one last look in the bathroom mirror and fluffed her hair around her face. She'd applied extra blush, but she was still far too pale.

Sighing in defeat, she picked up her small makeup kit and returned to the bedroom. Quickly, ignoring the sick feeling churning under the band of her rumpled linen skirt, she made Alex's bed, then glanced again at the clock radio. Almost thirty minutes had passed since he had walked out on her. He was still in the house; she'd heard him in the kitchen. But she had a feeling that he was avoiding her.

A faint sound from the doorway startled her, and she turned. Butch was standing on the threshold, his tail waving lazily above his mottled back, his chartreuse eye glaring at her.

"Yeah, I'm still here," she muttered. But not for long, she added silently. Alex was sure to turn her down now, and much as she hated to admit it, she didn't blame him.

She'd told him that she was here on business, but all of a sudden it hadn't been business anymore. She'd been a fool to dredge up the past like that.

Thank goodness only the senior people, her two executive vice presidents and Ben Jameson, knew that she'd gone to see Alejandro Torres. And none of them knew that Alex was her ex-husband.

Great going, Casey, she told herself sarcastically. Now you can go back and tell them the trip was a dismal failure.

She took a step forward, then stopped. Butch growled and arched his back, his teeth bared. "I'm not afraid of you, cat. I'm just as tough as you are."

"I'm not so sure." Alex appeared in the door frame, his Stetson in his hand, a battered canvas backpack slung over one shoulder.

Butch yowled, then shut his mouth with a snap. Turning tail, he sauntered away with a feline arrogance that made her want to laugh, but the look in Alex's eyes stopped her. He looked as though *he* hadn't laughed, really laughed, in a long time.

"Things got out of hand a while ago," he said coolly. "I told you I was . . . out of practice. I should have headed that off."

"I should never have brought it up. All of a sudden things got . . . personal, and I know how you hate that."

One side of his mouth stiffened. "I couldn't hate anything about you, Casey."

An instant of shared awareness flashed between them. Her breathing shortened, faltered, then began again. Why couldn't she get this man out of her heart? Why did she still long to walk into his arms? To rest her head on his broad shoulder for the comfort that she needed so desperately now? To draw on some of his magnificent strength to shore up her faltering confidence?

"If you want to hitch a ride to pick up your car, I'm leaving for school now." He took a step backward, giving her room to pass.

"Yes, thank you." She heard the brittle tension in her voice and felt it in the air. "I'll get my things."

She started to walk past him, but he reached out and caught her arm. She flinched, and he dropped his hand.

"You're right, Case," he told her, his stance stiff. "I owe you. And I pay my debts. But I need time to figure out how to pay this one. Maybe I can help you without going to Ohio."

"How?"

Alex inhaled slowly. "Let me make some calls, see what I can come up with. Stay one more day. Give me the time I need."

"But Deshler's already started his final push," she blurted out. "I can't stay here any longer."

Alex smiled without humor. "You can do anything if you have no other choice."

Casey chewed on the inside of her cheek. She hated this feeling of helplessness, but what else could she do? Intuitively she sensed that if she pushed Alex, he would refuse.

"Okay, Alex. You win. I just hope I'm not making a terrible mistake."

His mouth twisted. "Everyone make mistakes, Casey," he said in a flat voice. "Learning to live with them, that's what's hard."

Without another word he turned, walked across the living room and out the door, leaving it open behind him.

The ruffled flounce of her new white denim skirt lightly brushed her bare legs as Casey carried her purchases to the cashier in the front of the narrow old-fashioned store.

The selection in Echevarria's Dry Goods Emporium had been severely limited and far more suited to the casual Southwestern life-style than the fast track she was used to. But there was a definite charm to the cluttered place, and an old-world kind of peace in the high ceilings and rutted floor.

As she'd tried on the simple clothes, she'd felt herself slowing down, even relaxing, and she felt wonderfully lighthearted in the white fringed skirt and matching T-shirt.

Her new sandals, soft white leather studded with turquoise and silver, made her feel as though she could walk for miles along the dusty, poorly maintained road that formed Chamisa's main thoroughfare.

"Everything fit all right?" the sloe-eyed Indian woman at the counter asked solicitously when Casey approached, arms laden, the mud-spattered pumps she'd replaced dangling from her fingers.

"Yes, thank you," Casey said with a smile. "I managed to find everything I needed."

"I'm glad. Most of our customers are local. They buy mostly larger sizes."

The clerk had a motherly smile, and a quiet, almost shy way about her that was reinforced by a gentle melodious voice. Casey liked her instantly.

"I don't suppose you have any more earrings like the ones you're wearing," she asked impulsively, eyeing the twisted silver hoops dangling from the woman's ears.

Some of the formality left the woman's stance as she leaned forward to allow Casey to finger the silver. "Not exactly like these," she said with a lilting accent. "Garcia Crowe never makes any two pieces alike, but I have something similar." She bent down to retrieve a scrap of black velvet cloth from the case. Her slim brown fingers unwrapped it almost reverently to reveal delicate silver hoops studded with turquoise.

"I love them," Casey said at once, touching the delicately feminine design with growing delight. "How much?"

The woman quoted a price that seemed supremely reasonable, although her voice sounded hesitant.

"I'll wear them," Casey said instantly, removing the plain gold ovals from her earlobes and replacing them with the silver.

She tossed her head, loving the feeling of freedom the dangling earrings gave her. She dropped her old earrings into her purse and pulled out her wallet.

"They look lovely on you," the clerk said in softly accented English. "Garcia will be pleased."

"Please tell him that his work is exquisite. As good as any I've seen. Better, in fact."

"He'll like that."

Meticulously checking each handwritten price tag, the woman rang up the purchases one by one on an ancient cash register.

There were three tops, a pair of jeans, underwear and a hopelessly skimpy nightshirt, the only thing the store had in the way of feminine sleeping attire—all for the price of one business suit in her favorite boutique in Cincinnati. Or a very plain cocktail dress in that little store in SoHo where her mother's sister was part owner.

"Will that be all?" The clerk waited, her hand poised over the register.

Casey frowned, glancing around for one last look. The midday sun streaming through the dusty windows made her squint. Sunlight seemed brighter in New Mexico, maybe because the air was so clear, or maybe because, growing up in Manhattan the way she had, she was used to the shadowy world beneath the tall buildings.

Spying a rack of sunglasses, she selected a pair framed in red and added it to her purchases. "I'd like these, too, please." She opened her wallet and pulled out a credit card.

The middle-aged clerk's face clouded, and her dark, soft eyes flickered to the considerable sum displayed in the register's cracked window.

"I'm sorry, but I must ask you for cash. Most of us don't even have a credit card, and this pueblo is so far off the interstate, we don't get a lot of tourists." She sounded apologetic and decidedly disappointed.

"No problem," Casey told her with an understanding smile. "I'll just write you a check."

She returned the card to her wallet and pulled out a leather-bound checkbook and a gold pen. She rarely carried more than a few dollars in cash, preferring the record-keeping convenience of charge slips.

The woman looked uncomfortable. "Is your bank local? Albuquerque? Santa Fe?"

Casey shook her head. "Ohio, I'm afraid."

The woman sighed. "I wish I could..." She shrugged regretfully. "It's not that I don't trust you, but I can't risk losing that amount. I hope you understand."

Casey thought of the water-stained silk blouse and wrinkled linen skirt buried under the pile of new things on the counter. She wasn't going to fly home in rumpled clothes.

"I'm staying with...a friend not too far from here. He could vouch for me." She hesitated, then added winningly, "Alex Torres is his name. He's the teacher at the Santa Ysabel School."

Shock warred with relief on the woman's smooth face before a wide smile of obvious delight replaced them both.

"Then of course you may write a check. Alejandro is a friend to all of us. Under those black frowns of his, he's a very sweet man."

Casey's pen dug into the crisp paper. A sweet man? Alex?

"How, um, long have you know him?" Casey asked, her brows pulling into a frown. Alex Torres had been called many things, but never sweet. Not by her, and certainly not by his rivals.

The woman thought a second. "Nearly two years now. I was on the tribal committee that selected him as teacher. He had no teaching experience and talked little about his past years, but his professors at UNM spoke very highly of him. And most important of all, we could see that he loved children very much."

This time Casey's pen jerked to a complete halt. Surely this woman wasn't talking about the man who'd refused point-blank to father a child. Not once, but repeatedly.

She gripped the pen tightly to stop the sudden shaking. With carefully precise strokes, she signed her name and handed over the check. The woman scanned it silently, then placed it in the register drawer and clanged it shut.

"You are the first friend of Alejandro's to visit him here," she said, breaking into another smile. "You have known him many years?"

"Yes," Casey said hollowly. "Many years."

Too many years to pretend that they were mere acquaintances, and yet she didn't want to say something indiscreet. She had no idea what Alex had told these people about himself—or his background.

The clerk's efficient brown hands took the embroidered white blouse from the top of the stack and began to carefully fold it.

"It's good that you are here," she said in a somber tone. "He is alone too much. Everyone has tried to make him feel welcome, but he is a man few of us can understand."

Casey swallowed. "I know what you mean. He's not like most men."

Feeling more and more uneasy, she glanced over her shoulder at the empty street. A miniature dust devil danced drunkenly along the faded white line in the middle of the gray tarmac, sucking up bits of paper and small jagged pebbles as it went.

The woman's gaze flicked from Casey's face to the street outside and back again. "I have seen that he carries a heavy silence inside. Like a grief that is too terrible to speak of. My husband says that Alejandro is like many of the men he knew in the army during the Vietnam War. Many men lost friends in those bad times, but Alejandro has told us that he has never been a soldier, so I believe that his grief is for another reason."

The woman pulled a large brown-paper bag from under the counter and began to put the folded clothes inside.

Casey drew a careful breath. "Why do you think that?"

The clerk's voice grew pensive. "When he first came to the pueblo, he was called the man who never smiled by some of us. Only the children could lighten the deadness in his eyes."

Taking the sunglasses from the pile, Casey slipped them over her nose. "Does he . . . I mean, is there a special woman in his life? That you know of?" Her hands felt clammy, even though the air was warm.

The woman shoved the last of the purchases into the bag and pushed it across the counter toward Casey. "Many would like to be, that I know, but Alejandro is a man who keeps his passions private." She threw Casey a half-shy, half-shrewd look. "Me, I think he still loves the woman whose ring he wears."

Casey felt her face freeze. You're wrong, she thought. He never really loved her. He only wanted her physically.

The matronly clerk folded her hands over her stomach. "My eldest son is . . . in prison in Santa Fe," she said in a small sad voice. "For a robbery committed while he was drunk. His wife was shamed unbearably and returned to the home of her mother. Even though my son knows it is for the best, he still grieves."

"I'm very sorry."

Kindness filled the woman's eyes as she acknowledged the sympathy with a nod. "I tell you this because I feel in my son the same silence that fills Alejandro."

She hesitated, then reached across the counter to lightly touch Casey's bunched fist. "Perhaps I say too much, but something tells me that you must be very special to him to be invited to visit. Maybe you are the woman to take the shadows from his heart."

Casey's own heart began thudding erratically. Somehow she managed to keep her voice matter-of-fact. "Unfortunately not. We . . . that is, I came here on business. Just . . . business."

The woman sighed and withdrew her hand. "Then forgive me for saying these things to you. I was so hoping . . . Alejandro has given much of himself to us. He deserves to be happy."

Casey forced a smile. For the first time in years, she found herself at a loss for words.

Stiffly, her face still frozen into a smile, Casey dropped her checkbook into her purse, then slung the strap over her shoulder and reached for the bulky paper sack.

"Thank you for your help."

The woman nodded, her expression blank. "Please tell Alejandro that Janetta said hello."

"I will. Goodbye." Casey turned and fled.

The same creek that ran past Alex's house wound through the center of Chamisa, and the town's main street followed its meandering path.

Frowning, she glanced down at the directions Alex had written for her on a scrap of line notebook paper. His handwriting was large and square, and she had no trouble reading the terse instructions.

"Left at the plaza," she read aloud. "Four miles down the road to the crossroads." She was meeting Alex for an early dinner. At the Prickly Pear Café, whatever that was.

Slowing the car to a crawl to avoid the large holes dotting the cracked pavement, she peered through the windshield. On the surface everything appeared drab and lifeless, but she was beginning to see subtle shades of red and yellow mixed with the dull browns. The colors tantalized her, daring her to look more deeply. To understand.

But it still seemed like a limitless wild place that had no beginning and no end. And the imposing shapes of the square mesas and the jagged shadows that darkened the desert floor made her feel insignificant and vulnerable.

But honesty made her admit that she'd felt even more vulnerable in Alex's house, surrounded by the walls he'd built and the private and personal things that were his. That was why she'd taken her time at Echevarria's and why she'd spent the afternoon exploring the pueblo.

It was a fascinating place, where time seemed to stand still. Most of the houses were two or sometimes three-story adobes, with crude ladders leading to the upper floors. In many places Casey had trouble telling where the dirt yards left off and the houses began.

There were few lawns and almost no trees. Occasionally she'd found a pot of bright flowers tucked here and there into a sunny corner, but much of the area was unrelieved brown.

And every building had a structure that resembled a hornet's nest near the front door.

At first, she'd been puzzled, until she'd seen an old woman in a long skirt and shawl removing a steaming loaf of bread from the mouth of one of them and realized that the beehives were actually primitive ovens.

Her mouth watered as she remembered the delicious aroma of that warm bread. She'd skipped lunch, and she was ravenously hungry.

She nearly laughed aloud as an elaborate, grossly misshapen cactus loomed in front of her, painted on a billboard stuck to the side of a rusting Quonset hut colored a sickly institutional beige.

"That just *has* to be the Prickly Pear Café." The large dirt lot near the road was filled with cars and trucks parked every which way, but there were only three vehicles in the smaller space to the back, two pickups and Alex's Jeep.

She parked next to the Jeep and tilted the rearview mirror so that she could see her face. Her wide gray eyes looked a little harried, a little tense and definitely apprehensive. And around the pupils the irises were a light gray that would, she knew, be silver in artificial light.

The sound of the wind sharpened until she heard Alex's voice. *I can always tell what you're thinking by the color of your eyes,* querida. *And when they're silver, I know that you want me. You do want me, don't you?*

She inhaled slowly, letting the pure desert air soothe the little muscles that were leaping like crazy in her throat. She was mistaken, she told herself, staring in the small mirror. Her eyes weren't silver. They were a nice clear gray. And that was the way they were going to stay.

She slipped from the car, locked it and pocketed the keys. The gravel beneath her sandals was still hot from the sun. The air smelled of dust and some pungent scent that she didn't recognize.

She opened the screen door, wincing at the shrill screeching of the rusty hinges. And even though a faded sign on the open inner door promised that the interior was air-conditioned, she felt a wave of heat rushing toward her as she entered.

Inside, it was dim and smoky, with the three small windows cut into the curved wall providing almost all the illumination.

A pool table stood in one corner, while an elaborate chrome-encrusted jukebox occupied most of another. A twanging country-music tune played mournfully to a half dozen or so men seated at the bar.

Casey searched the dark faces, looking for Alex. But he wasn't there.

"Who ya lookin' for, honey?" called the man closest to the door. He was the only one of those present who had light skin and eyes. He was also dead drunk.

"Shut up, Slade," ordered the bartender, a rotund man wearing a beaded headband and a spotless white apron. He moved to the end of the bar.

"May I help you, lady?" he asked, draping the bar towel over his sloping shoulder. His eyes were wary but not unkind.

Casey cleared her throat and walked over to him. "I'm looking for Alex Torres, but it doesn't look like he's here."

The bartender's eyes crinkled into a friendly smile. "You just come in the wrong door is all. Alejandro's in the restaurant, through there."

His head jerked to the opposite end of the bar, where a swinging door hung partly open. "I seen him when I went in to get ice. Looked mighty impatient, too, which ain't like him. Now I know why."

Casey was glad that the dim interior hid the color rushing to her cheeks. "Thank you."

She crossed the bar and pushed open the door, wincing at the sudden glare. The restaurant was as light as the bar was dark, brightened by a bank of fluorescent tubes suspended by wires from the ceiling.

The wooden tables were scrubbed clean, and the speckled white linoleum gleamed with fresh wax. A display case containing colorful artifacts stood next to the door to the front parking lot, and a counter with built-in stools lined one wall. All of the stools were occupied, along with a half dozen or so of the tables.

She saw Alex immediately. He was seated with another dark-haired man at a corner table, his hands cupped around a heavy brown mug. He looked up as soon as she walked in, and even from twenty feet away, she could see his face close up.

If he didn't want her here, he shouldn't have invited her to have dinner with him, she thought sourly, her hunger making her short-tempered. She was perfectly capable of feeding herself.

She walked toward the two men, conscious of the looks directed her way. No one smiled, no one acknowledged her in any way, and she had a sudden feeling that she'd entered a different land, or even another time.

She took a deep breath. For the first time in her sheltered, comfortable life, she knew what it was like to be in the minority, fair where everyone else was dark, speaking a language that was different than other's, an outsider. It was a scary feeling.

As she approached the table, Alex pushed back his chair and straightened slowly to his full height, as though bracing for a fight. She was a few feet from the table when the man next to Alex stood also and smiled politely. "Hello," he said in unaccented English.

A warm smile touched her lips. She liked his face. "Hello, I'm—"

"Ten more minutes and I was going looking for you," Alex interrupted in a biting tone.

"Why would you do that?" Casey asked, tightening her grip on her purse. "I'm only twenty minutes late." Annoyed at his rudeness and angry because he'd embarrassed her in front of a stranger, she tossed her head defiantly, and the dangling earrings swayed against her neck, drawing Alex's gaze. Something hot and primitive flashed in his eyes.

"Twenty minutes in the wrong place here and you could be dead. Do us both a favor and remember that."

"Yes, *sir*!" she told him haughtily, then shifted her gaze to the man who stood in polite silence across the table. "I'm Casey O'Neill," she said pleasantly. "I think it's only fair to warn you that I'm Alex's ex-wife. And I'm here on sufferance."

From the corner of her eye, she saw Alex stiffen. But what had he expected her to do? Lie?

The stranger's eyes crinkled into a smile, and she saw that they were a warm shade of brown instead of the black she'd expected. "I've already been warned, Ms. O'Neill. By hoss, here." He extended his hand, which was warm and large and exerted just the right amount of pressure. "I'm John Olvera."

He was several inches shorter than Alex, with smooth copper skin stretched over patrician cheekbones and jutting black brows. He was dressed in jeans and a tight Western shirt, much like the one that hugged Alex's broad chest, and his thick black hair was confined by a headband made from the skin of a rattlesnake.

"Are you joining us for dinner, Mr. Olvera?" she asked politely, feeling slightly confused. Alex had told her to meet him for dinner at five. And that was all he'd said.

"John, please. And yes, I've been invited to join you. Alex and I usually have dinner every Tuesday night."

"Oh, if I'm intruding . . ."

"Sit down, Casey," Alex said abruptly, pulling out the chair next to her. "If I'd thought you'd be intruding, I wouldn't have suggested that you meet me here."

Mindful of the other man at the table, Casey kept her smile stiffly in place. "Ordered, Alex. You ordered me to meet you here," she said sweetly. The ride to the school had been silent and tense. He'd escorted her to the rental car, made sure that it started, then told her they would have dinner out.

"You could have refused." His eyes narrowed.

"Is that what you wanted me to do?"

His fingers dug into the padded vinyl back of the chair. "What do you think?"

"I think you were hoping that I'd give up and leave so that you could stop trying to find a way to turn me down."

One stiff corner of his hard mouth jerked upward. "If that's what I wanted, then I must be disappointed, because you're still here."

She had to raise her chin in order to look him squarely in the eyes. A tiny fleck of blood near his ear suggested that he'd recently shaved, perhaps in a hurry. And a faint scent of musky after-shave mingled with the pungent smell of spicy cooking wafting toward her from the plates of her fellow diners.

A flutter of excitement moved through her, but she ignored it. In every way that mattered this was simply another business dinner, one of hundreds she'd had over the years.

Gracefully she slid into her chair and dropped her purse to the floor. His fingers brushed her shoulder as he returned to his chair and sat down. She looked up quickly, but his expression revealed nothing but stony anger.

"Looks like you've been shopping," John commented in a low, pleasant tone, his gaze resting for a heartbeat on the dangling earrings, a gleam of male interest shining in his kind eyes.

"I have, in a place called Echevarria's. I met a wonderful lady named Janetta." She shifted her gaze to Alex's shuttered face. "She said to say hello."

She waited for him to say something about her new clothes, but he simply nodded. Under his stiff brows his eyes glinted like ebony chips in the sun, and his lips were pressed into a straight, hard line. As she watched, he picked up the menu and began to look at it.

Disappointment caught her unawares, and she frowned. Why should she care if he liked how she looked? she lectured herself sternly. She'd bought the clothes for herself, not him.

But it still hurt.

"I admit that I couldn't resist," she told John with a quick grin that dimpled her cheek. "Who knows, maybe I was an Indian in a former life."

John laughed, and Casey noticed that he was a very sexy man. Almost as sexy as Alex when he was in one of his softer moods.

"I heard that you'd single-handedly raised the Echevarrias' net worth by a considerable amount."

"You did?"

"John is the head of the tribal council," Alex interjected, looking up from the menu abruptly. "I work for him."

"Technically," John said, one expressive brow arching wryly. "Except I know and the council knows that Alex doesn't take orders. From anyone." His eyes crinkled at the sun-weathered corners. "But I have a hunch you're not much for taking orders yourself."

"You got that right," Alex muttered sarcastically.

Casey's smile died halfformed. "Mr. Macho," she said, then nearly gasped at the wash of dusky red that colored his face.

"Sounds like she's got you pegged, hoss," John said with a chuckle. He gazed from one to the other with a curiously sympathetic look.

"I thought you wanted to talk about expanding the curriculum for the primary grades," Alex said with a bite to his voice.

"Hey, I'm easy," John shot back. "Whatever you want."

"Right now I want something to eat. I'm hungry." Alex bent his head over his menu, shutting them out. A muscle in his jaw pulled tight, as though he were clenching his teeth.

Casey was conscious of John's curious gaze roaming her face, but she felt rooted to her seat, the memory of those long-ago weeks when Alex had pursued her relentlessly, pressing down on her. He'd been single-minded and dauntless and so breathlessly irresistible that she'd had to fight with everything she had to keep from giving in to him on that first unforgettable date.

She'd known that she was lost the first time he laughed, really laughed. At that moment she'd seen the real person behind the predatory eyes, the person who had never learned how to play games for fun, the person who needed her.

Casey's gaze was drawn to Alex's bent head. There was a stark aura of loneliness hovering over the wide strong shoulders. Who makes him laugh now? she wondered.

And then she remembered the way he'd laughed at her battle with the blasted cat. His eyes hadn't laughed, though.

A deadness in his eyes. That was what Janetta had called it.

Suddenly, as though he sensed her thoughts, Alex looked up, and his gaze collided with hers. The banked fires in his pupils flickered as though fanned by some powerful emotion, and then suddenly they went out, leaving his eyes lifeless and cold again.

"Here," he said gruffly, handing her a menu. "Stay away from the chilies. You'd hate them."

Chapter 6

Does either of you want that last piece of fry bread?" Casey's hand was poised expectantly over the basket in the middle of the table. She'd discovered that the strange flat bread was delicious when drizzled with honey, the way John had showed her.

John held up a hand in surrender. "I'll let the two of you fight it out."

"It's all yours," Alex muttered. He'd relaxed somewhat during the meal, especially when he and John had been discussing the children and the improvement in their test scores, but whenever Casey had tried to join the conversation, he had fallen silent.

Now he sat with his arms crossed over his chest, the sinews in his wide forearms straining like ropes beneath the copper skin.

A tingling awareness skated across her shoulders and down her arms, urging her to touch him. To caress those strong, powerful arms. To warm her palms against his burnished skin.

Old habits, she told herself. That's all it is.

"I'll share it if you like," Casey persisted.

"No thanks. I've seen that determined look of yours before, and I'm not up for a fight right now."

Suddenly she wasn't hungry anymore. She moved her hand to the stem of her wineglass and took a tentative sip. She'd been so busy listening to John talk about the history of his people that she'd forgotten to drink the burgundy she'd ordered to go with her *carne asada*.

"That's too bad," she told Alex with a faint edge to her voice. "Because it looks to me as though you were born to fight. Remember your ancestor? That gorgeous man, Cadiz?"

To her surprise, Alex scowled. "He fought because he had to."

"And so did you," she countered, feeling her breath quicken. "To support your family. To make something of yourself. To win. I don't see how you could just walk away from something that was a part of you."

His matte-black eyes flickered over her, as sharp as the tip of a whip. "I was burned out. My brother Carlos runs Towers now. The shareholders are happy, and so am I."

"Tell me another one, Alex. You can't mean that you don't make *any* of the decisions?"

"I told you, I'm retired." The pulse at the base of his neck was beating slowly and evenly, but Casey saw the tautness around his mouth that always appeared when he was annoyed.

"This isn't retirement, Alex. It's . . . it's exile."

For some reason she had to prove to herself that, deep down, he was the same man who'd left her. Perhaps because that would help her to stay emotionally distant from him.

But she was finding it difficult not to admire the man she was slowly coming to know. According to the woman in the store, Alejandro de las Torres, teacher, loved the children he taught and they loved him. And according to John, Alex Torres returned his salary for teaching, as well as every cent of his quarterly dividends from Towers Industries to the tribal council to use as they saw fit. This year they planned to build a clinic in the pueblo.

Casey took another quick sip of wine and waited for the burgundy to blunt the sharp edges of her mind. Alex had been clearly embarrassed when John had been singing his praises— as though he didn't want her to see that side of him. But the Alex she'd known had never seemed embarrassed about anything. So who was this man sitting next to her?

She sighed inwardly, trying not to wonder about this man she didn't know. She didn't want to like him. She didn't want to care.

Alex watched Casey sip her wine, and his insides warmed as though the rich burgundy were flowing through his veins instead of blood. She had an aura about her, his woman of light, that made him go soft inside in a way that nothing in his life had ever done before.

He couldn't put a name to it, or maybe he was afraid to. He only knew that it made him feel like singing. And that was something that he'd done only as a very small child, before his mother got too busy with the other babies to spend time with him.

Slowly he ran his hand along the burn-scarred edge of the table, letting the conversation pass him by. Casey was good and decent and clean, all the things he wanted to be.

When she'd walked through the door an hour or so ago, her eyes sparkling with that inner glow that was such a part of her, he'd felt as though he'd just been kicked in the gut. He'd wanted to go to her, to swing her into his arms and kiss her breathless, the way he used to after a long, lonely trip.

Only she didn't want that from him now. She wanted the part of him that he'd been trying to escape, the scrawny street-fighting raider from the barrio who'd never been beaten. Except by his own damn arrogance.

He didn't want to be that man anymore. And if Casey knew why, she wouldn't ask it of him. But he would rather walk into the desert until he dropped than tell her about the woman in Los Angeles, the woman he'd hurt even more than he'd hurt Casey, the woman who had indirectly caused the end of his marriage.

Alex glanced at his watch. Wouldn't those two ever stop gabbing? he thought impatiently. He'd never seen Olvera so damn chatty.

"When are you going back to Ohio?" John asked when Casey had finished telling him about her impressions of the pueblo.

She risked a glance at Alex, but he wasn't looking at her. "I...soon. Probably tomorrow, first thing. I'm playing hooky as it is."

John chuckled. "Sometimes it's more fun that way. School's out here tomorrow. Stay on for a while and let hoss show you around."

With careful concentration Casey drained her glass and set it on the table before she shifted her gaze to Alex. She found him watching her impassively.

"So in one more day you'll be...available?" She tried to read the look in his eyes but failed. He was a blank slate, hard and impenetrable.

"In one more day I'll be on vacation. I have...plans."

"To do what?"

One arrogant black brow arched slowly. "As you reminded me just yesterday, Casey, we're divorced. What I do is my business."

The blunt rebuff hurt, but she refused to show it. Instead she gazed around the restaurant, which was now almost empty. Most of the family groups had gone home, leaving only a young Indian couple huddled together at a corner table. Her gaze moved to the display case. The bright colors made a cheerful slash against the dingy white wall.

"Those are pretty—what do you call them? *kachinas?*—in the case there," she said, giving John a friendly smile. She felt Alex's gaze on her face, but she ignored him.

"They're really dolls made for the children, so that they'll be familiar with the spirits," John told her quietly. "Our ancestors believed that was the way to teach the little ones to respect the gods without making them afraid."

"That makes sense, I suppose, although I have to say that most of them would scare me to death if I were a child."

A shallow crease appeared briefly at the side of Alex's mouth, and she realized that that was as close to a smile as he'd come all evening.

"Me too," he said, a wry note lacing his deep voice. "My mother had one when I was a child, and when I was bad, she told me that the evil spirits would get me if I didn't go to confession and do penance."

John chuckled. "Somehow the God of our Spanish conquerors and the sacred spirits of our people got all mixed up over the years."

Casey frowned. "Isn't that confusing?"

Alex merely shrugged.

"Sometimes," John answered, pushing his empty plate away. "Did Alex tell you that Cadiz was one of the Chosen Ones?" His big hand played with his coffee mug.

Casey shook her head. "What are the Chosen Ones?"

John glanced across the table. Suddenly the teasing light was gone from his eyes, replaced by an intense expression she didn't understand. "Explain it to her, Alex," he said. "Cadiz was your great-grandfather."

The slight movement of Alex's wide shoulders could have been a shrug. Or it could have been an involuntary flexing to ease the tightness of the muscles that strained the thin cotton of his shirt. Either way, the slow stretching made her acutely conscious of the power that lay beneath the blue material.

Alex's lips barely moved as he said slowly, "You brought it up, Olvera. You tell her."

John's white grin flashed briefly before his face resumed its somber expression. "Okay, I will. Unlike you, my cynical *amigo*, I happen to like this particular legend."

Alex merely grunted and tipped the chair back onto two legs, resting his head against the wall and his hands against the heavy thighs that tortured the seams of the faded denim. He stared straight ahead, his eyes half closed as though in contemplation, and the spiky lashes that used to tickle Casey's breast when he blinked cast arrogant shadows on his high cheekbones.

John leaned back, too, and hooked an arm over the chair. "See that *kachina* on the second shelf, the one with the man's body and the face of a mountain cat?" he asked Casey.

There were six large dolls behind the glass, all beautifully carved of wood and colorfully painted. She scanned the shelves until she found the one John meant.

It was larger than the others, and decorated with feathers and beads, and bright yellow and green paint. The body was undeniably male and fashioned to suggest great strength. The face was a good likeness of the nearly extinct cougar she'd seen in the guidebook she'd bought at the gas station in Chamisa.

But the *kachina*'s eyes were large and black, instead of the glittering amber of the animal's and the artist had painted tiny gold flecks in the places where the pupils should be. The figure itself had a fierce power that brought a shiver to her skin.

"Those eyes," she murmured. "They look as though they can see into your soul."

John looked pleased, but when she shifted her gaze to Alex, he merely lifted one brow mockingly.

She rubbed her hands up and down her bare arms and took another look at the figure. "What's it called?"

John pronounced a name that seemed to have more consonants than vowels. She tried to copy him, but her tongue got hopelessly tangled.

His solemn brown eyes applauded her attempt. "Roughly translated, it means 'one-who-is-great-among-men.'"

"And that's why Cadiz was chosen? Because he won a great victory?"

John hesitated, then shook his head. "There's more to it. Legend has it that during the first cycle of the sun after the earth was formed, one maiden, the bravest and the purest of heart, was chosen.

"On the night of her wedding, the father of us all came to her, giving her a son who was destined to grow bigger and stronger and more powerful than others. He in turn fathered many strong sons, ensuring the continuation of our people. And each first-born son of that first one-who-is-great-among-men carries the same seed of greatness."

Casey studied the intricate carving curiously. It was strangely compelling. "The doll has the same necklace Cadiz is wearing in the picture."

John nodded. "It's a sacred totem, made from the fangs of the mountain lions that used to roam freely on this land."

Casey felt a thrill shiver through her. What a wonderful story, she thought, turning to Alex. "Do you have the necklace? May I see it?"

He rubbed his lean belly with his hand, and the flash of gold on his finger taunted her. "I don't have it. It doesn't belong to me."

"But . . . but why not? If you're his descendant?"

Alex's chair hit the linoleum with a thud. "It just doesn't." His tone carried a heavy impatience. "I've heard this before. I'm going outside for some air."

He stood and pulled some bills from his pocket. Throwing them on the table, he gave John a look that could only be described as a warning. "Dinner's on me."

Casey's gaze followed him to the door. His long legs ate up the distance swiftly, and his buttocks bunched with power beneath the tight jeans. He looked even bigger than the man in the photo, wider across the shoulders and longer in the legs.

John's eyes were focused intently on her face, but when her gaze met his questioningly, he blinked away whatever expression had been written there.

"Interesting," he drawled with a half smile. "Man acts like he's got a thistle in his britches."

Casey felt the heat climbing past the fringed V of her T-shirt to warm her neck. John's tone suggested that she was the reason. But that was nonsense. Alex didn't care what she did. He just wanted to be left alone.

"I...he's never acted that way before," she said with a sigh. "I knew that he had a temper, but..." She stared at John helplessly. "I didn't mean to spoil your evening."

His smile grew broader. "Don't worry about me. I'm having a terrific time."

She managed a smile. "Me too, and I'd love to hear the rest of the legend."

She wasn't quite telling the truth, but she wasn't lying, either. She liked John very much, and from their conversation, she knew that he wasn't married. He was intensely virile and extremely attractive, but she wasn't drawn to him in the same combustible way that she was drawn to Alex. A part of her wished that she was.

John nodded and settled back in his chair. He extended his thick muscular legs to their full length and slid the tips of his fingers under the wide belt cinching his jeans.

"According to the stories that have been handed down by the storytellers for going on six centuries, the original seed that gave these special men their power also cursed each one with a flaw. With some it was pride. With others, greed. Still others, lust."

He lifted a brow, and she nodded. "Go on, please."

"The test for each of these men was to overcome that one fatal flaw," John continued slowly, as though he were taking care to choose just the right words. Or, she thought, translating the legend into English. Whatever the reason, she found herself hanging on to every word.

"It required awesome courage and much suffering before the demon, the flaw, was exorcised. Many died in the effort. Others gave up. Only a few rare men ever won the right to wear the sign of one-who-is-great-among-men."

Casey cast her mind back to the man in the faded photograph. She could still feel the power and intelligence of those hypnotic dark eyes. "Cadiz earned the right because he banished the demon of pride and allowed himself to be caged by his enemy so that others might live," she guessed.

John's eyes shone. "Exactly right." He studied the back of one large hand. "If Alex had been raised here, he would be head of the council, not me. I told him that once."

"What did he say?"

He raised his gaze to her face, and for the first time she noticed a hint of disapproval in those friendly eyes. "He said that he didn't want to be responsible for anyone but himself. Not ever again."

In the silence that fell between them she could hear the sibilant buzz of voices from the couple in the corner and the faint twang of the jukebox coming from the bar. She blinked in confusion.

"Is that the flaw?" she wondered aloud. "Is that why he doesn't want to believe in the legend? Because he's tired of taking care of others?"

John shook his head. "I don't know, Casey." He hesitated, then added tersely, "I just know that Alex is not a happy man. Not in the way that a man should be happy." He picked up his cup and drained it before returning it to the saucer with a loud clink.

She ran her finger around the rim of her empty wineglass. It felt cold against her fingertips. "What way is that?"

His eyes went blank. "Every man longs to belong to one special person. To love and be loved. To have a family. To leave a piece of himself behind." His mouth twisted in a brief smile laced with mockery. "That's one man's opinion, anyway."

Her nails raked her napkin until it was in shreds. Disgusted, she wadded it into a ball and dropped it onto the table. "You heard him. Alex has what he wants—solitude. Apparently he doesn't want anything or anyone else."

"If that's true, why are you still here?" His voice was both rough and gentle, but Casey ignored the hint of compassion in the deep tones.

"What do you mean?"

"If Alex didn't want you here, you would have been on the next plane home, even if he had to put you in a seat himself."

John pushed back his chair and stood. From the rack behind his head he took a black Stetson and pulled it low over his black brows.

"Ready?" he asked politely. "I imagine hoss has worn a rut in the parking lot by now."

Casey retrieved her bag and stood. Side by side they walked outside. The sun was low in the west, and grotesque purple shadows stretched across the desert floor.

She glanced around the lot, but there was no sign of Alex. And then she remembered that his Jeep, like her car, was parked in the other lot.

"Thank you for telling me about the legend, John," she said softly, extending her hand. "I enjoyed it very much."

He took her hand and pressed it between both of his. "My pleasure, Casey. I've learned a lot from you."

She blinked at him. "You have? What have you learned?"

"That my friend Alex, for all his street smarts, is a damn fool. If you'd been mine, I never would have let you go."

"Maybe the divorce was my fault."

"Was it?"

A breath of hot wind touched her cheek. "No," she said with desperate honesty. "I loved Alex, and I tried to make it work. He didn't love me. End of story. End of marriage."

A rueful smile touched his lips as he took her arm. "Where's your car?"

"In the front."

"C'mon, I'll walk you."

Before she could take a step, Alex materialized from the side of the Quonset hut, a slim cigar stuck between his strong white teeth. Seeing them, he threw the half-smoked cigar to the gravel and ground it out with the heel of his boot.

"That won't be necessary, Olvera," he said in a cold, unfriendly voice. "I'll take care of her."

John squeezed her arm before dropping his hand. "See what I mean," he said in a barely audible voice. "A thistle in his britches."

Casey burst out laughing, and John joined her before leaning down to brush a kiss across her cheek. The touch of his lips was pleasing, but not exciting. Not like Alex's had been the first time he'd kissed her. And every time since then.

"You're a very nice man, John Olvera," she whispered, meaning it.

"Yeah, I know," he drawled. "That's what all the pretty ladies say. For some reason, they think of me as their big brother."

He touched two fingers to the brim of his hat. "Take care, Casey O'Neill."

"You too."

"See you, hoss," John tossed at Alex, saluting him with a sideways sweeping motion of the same two fingers. There was an odd glint in his eyes that made Casey wonder if he'd been deliberately baiting his friend.

Alex grunted in reply and wrapped his hand around Casey's arm in the same place where John had been loosely holding her. But unlike John's, his touch wasn't gentle. His hard fingers were punishing, his grip inescapable, as he half led, half dragged her toward her car.

Her car and his Jeep were the only vehicles remaining in the lot. The dusty country road was empty for as far as she could see in either direction.

"Alex, stop pulling on my arm," she snapped, her sandals sliding on the slick stones beneath her soles. "What's the matter with you?"

"What's the matter with me?" he all but growled back. "I'm not the one kissing a stranger in a public parking lot."

"I don't believe you. I'm your ex-wife, remember? Why should you care what I do?"

His lips twisted. "I remember how you can twist a man in knots with one of those damn looks of yours." He backed her up against the fender of the car, his muscular thighs pressing her abdomen against the smooth metal.

"Give me your key," he ordered.

"I will not," she told him indignantly, her breath coming in short bursts and her heart slamming in her chest. "I don't take orders from anyone, and certainly not you."

"This time you do." One hand grasped her wrist while the other searched through her bag for the car key. Ignoring her gasp of protest, he opened the car door and stood to one side, his features unyielding against the blood-red sky.

"Get in the car, Cassandra."

"This is silly, Alex. You're acting like I did something wrong."

"You have two choices," he told her coolly. "One, you can get in the car and follow me home like the independent lady you say you are. Or, two, you can stand there and glare at me, in which case I'll throw you over my shoulder and carry you to my Jeep. What'll it be?''

An anger unlike any she'd felt before surged through her. ''There's a third choice,'' she told him haughtily, fighting to keep her voice steady. ''I can get in the car and drive to Albuquerque and never see you again.''

''You could do that, yes.'' His voice was silky and scarcely louder than a whisper. It was the tone he used when he was about to close in for the kill.

The truth hit her suddenly. She'd nearly been manipulated into making a tactical mistake. ''So *that's* what this is all about. I understand, now,'' she said, relaxing her militant stance. ''I'm supposed to get huffy and indignant and run back to Ohio on the next plane, leaving you with a nice clear conscience. Very ingenious, Alex.''

A white light as cold and deadly as lightning flashed in his eyes. She took a step backward.

''And are you going to do that?'' he asked in that same smooth, quiet voice.

Casey forced herself to stand her ground. In his boots he stood close to six feet four inches, and below the rolled sleeves of his shirt, his upper arms were hard with muscle. But she was determined not to be intimidated. She'd faced down angry, powerful men before and won, in the boardroom and out of it.

''No, damn you. I'm staying. I'm not making this easy for you. If my friends lose their jobs and homes because you didn't help them, it will be on your conscience, not mine.''

He absorbed her angry words without flinching, but a vein at the base of his neck throbbed visibly. ''What makes you think I have a conscience?''

Casey was thrown off guard. His tone was different, softer, more human, almost vulnerable. But that was ridiculous. Alex Torres was a lot of things, but vulnerable wasn't one of them.

''You and I both know that you don't care a hoot about what I think,'' she said, not bothering to disguise the bitterness in her voice.

Alex muttered an obscenity, then took her hand and pressed the key into the palm. ''Follow close, and don't make any detours.'' He scowled.

Her hand was trapped between his, and the jagged teeth of the key dug into the soft pad of her thumb. It hurt, but she had too much pride to pull away. Instead she raised her chin, challenging him. "I want to know your decision. Right now. You've had enough time to make your calls. More than enough."

His gaze locked with hers, and a ribbon of some wild and primitive emotion surged between them. She fought to hang on to her anger. That, at least, was safe.

But three years of loving this man were hard to forget. Snatches of sweetly intimate and loving moments crowded against her defenses. Long-buried memories rose to torment her.

"Silver," he muttered, his breath catching. "Your eyes are silver, like stars in winter."

Alex felt a wild exhilaration flare inside him. Her lips were only inches from his. He remembered how soft they were, especially against his skin.

But more than that, he remembered how giving she was, how sweet and trusting. She'd made him feel cherished for the man he was inside, not for what he could give her. He'd never felt that way before.

Just once more, he thought, as her image blurred. Dear God, just one more time.

His hand touched her cheek, and her lashes fluttered. She should break away. Get in the car. Run. Anything but this. She tried, but she couldn't make her legs move.

His fingers, warm and sandpapery rough, shook as they brushed wisps of golden hair away from her face. Something tightly curled began to uncoil helplessly inside her, spreading a sweet warmth.

"You're driving me crazy...." His pupils flared with golden light, and his head dipped toward hers. His mouth eased upward at the corners, and his lips parted, then came down on hers.

Her mouth opened under his, and she tugged at his shoulders, trying to get closer to him. Inside her head a voice was screaming a warning, but the heady rush of pleasure she was feeling overrode her usual caution.

She knew this man, the heady pressure of his hard lips, the moist warmth of his breath, the musky male scent of him. Familiar. Intoxicating. Irresistible.

She forgot the frustration, the humiliation, the pain of their parting, and remembered only the bliss he'd given her.

At first his kiss was light, tantalizing, experimental, as though he expected her to push him away. Her hands balled into fists against his neck, but she didn't try to escape. Tomorrow, tonight, a few minutes from now, she might hate herself, might hate him, but right now all she wanted was his kiss.

She let her lips soften, and his arms crushed her to him. Breathless, she exulted in the terrible shudder that shook him. Beneath her hands the muscles of his back bunched, as though he were restraining himself. Her fingers pushed into the tough knots, stroking away the tension. Slowly the muscles shifted, then relaxed under her palms.

She smiled against his lips, and Alex groaned. His tongue tasted the corner of her mouth, teasing her lips to part. She sighed her acceptance, and his tongue rasped against her upper teeth. He tasted of strong coffee and even stronger tobacco, just as she must taste of wine.

Dimly, Alex knew that he was making a bad mistake, but at the moment he couldn't make himself care. It had nearly driven him crazy, watching that sexy little dimple dart into her cheek every time she smiled across the table at John. And when she'd laughed at one of John's corny jokes, his dinner had stuck in his throat.

He closed his eyes and made himself concentrate on pleasing her. She'd always liked to be petted.

Casey gasped as his hands slid along the curve of her waist, then moved lower. At the base of her spine his hand began a circular exploration, lingering with maddening slowness on the slight curve of her buttocks. Even through the thickness of her new denim skirt, she could feel the heat of his hand.

She was spinning in space, his kisses and the wine she'd drunk making her light-headed. She didn't care about tonight, tomorrow. Her blood was singing. She wanted him to make love to her.

Alex heard the tiny whimper in her throat, and it was like a splash of icy water across his face.

What the hell was he doing?

He cursed silently, one vicious curse after another, and every one directed at himself. Sometime in the early hours of last night he'd sworn an oath to stay away from her. And he'd been determined to keep it, until he'd seen another man, a so-called friend of his, kissing her. His woman.

He made himself stand perfectly still, forcing his breathing into a calmer rhythm. When he had his emotions under the same rigid control that had served him for so long, he trapped her face between his warm hands.

"Casey," he whispered in a thick voice. "We have to stop."

"No, no."

"You don't want this. You don't want me. You've had some wine. Things got . . . out of hand, but tomorrow, you'll hate yourself."

Casey wet her tingling lips and stared at him. His face was drawn, the lines bracketing his mouth more deeply carved than before.

His message was clear, one she'd heard before. *He* didn't want *her*.

Moving slowly, she stepped out of his arms, careful not to brush against him. Fool, she told herself over and over.

"You're right," she said with an attempt at lightness. "It was the wine. I never did have a head for liquor."

She straightened the twisted neckline of her blouse and smoothed her skirt. What had happened was inevitable, she told herself firmly. A testing of old feelings for both of them. At least now she knew exactly how Alex felt.

She should be grateful to him. She *was* grateful.

What they'd just shared was an ending, not a beginning. An end to her memories. An end to her longing for a man who no longer existed, at least not in the way that she remembered. Or loved.

Smiling stiffly, she combed her hair with her fingers, trying to smooth the thick waves into place. But it was hopeless. Alex's big hands had tossed the expensive haircut into a tangled mess.

"Leave it," he said in a husky tone. He reached out to touch the tumbled curls, but before his fingers could reach her skin, they curled into a wide fist, and his arm fell to his side.

"See you at home," he muttered, then turned and swung into the Jeep.

Casey knew she should be congratulating herself on her narrow escape. The last thing she wanted to do was make herself vulnerable to the same man who'd nearly destroyed her.

But, strangely, as she slipped into the seat and reached for her seat belt, all she wanted to do was cry.

The satin negligee slid down her body and onto the floor. Casey felt the cool air of the penthouse swirl around her, but her skin was so hot, as hot as the fire blazing in Alex's eyes.

Her parched soul opened like a flower raising its petals to the spring rain, and she felt her spirit reach out to him.

He did love her. He did!

She was delirious with happiness. Months. It had been months since he'd held her. Since he'd touched her. Since he'd kissed her.

Her kiss-swollen lips curved against his shoulder. This was where she'd longed to be, in his arms, her body pulsing from his drugging kisses.

She'd nearly died of longing. But now he was coming back to her bed, to her heart.

Her man. Her husband.

Casey whimpered and pulled him closer, closer. She needed to feel his power inside her. She needed to be filled with him. Conquered. Loved.

The whimpering grew louder. The need built. His hands were caressing, possessing, stroking, and his breath was hot and urgent on her neck. But still he made her wait.

Casey was alive, burning, needing. She pressed closer and closer, feeling his throbbing body against hers. It was the primeval call of a virile man for his mate. Instinctive. Mystical.

His muscles tightened; his hands stilled, then clenched painfully against her spine. And then he was pushing her away, his face an empty mask of rejection.

The room grew cold, but the humiliation was scalding. He didn't want her. Didn't want her. Didn't want her...

Casey opened her eyes, her heart pounding, her hands clutching her pillow. The sheet was tangled around her hips, pinning her to the hard mattress.

Tears streamed down her cheeks, but her body was still alive, still yearning for his. And she could feel the hot blush of arousal on her cheeks.

A dream. It had been a dream. The same dream she'd had for months after he left.

Her heart lurched painfully, skipping one beat, then another, before settling into a steady rhythm.

She closed her eyes and tried to summon a picture of the green hills and white frame houses dotting the land around the foundry. That was her reality now, not a tempting male body and a pair of enigmatic dark eyes that no longer warmed when she walked into a room.

Turning onto her side, she pulled her knees close to her chest. The sheet rubbed her bare legs, the way his hair-roughened calf had once slid against hers.

Why hadn't he fought for their marriage the way he'd fought to get out of the barrio? Why hadn't he fought for their love the way he'd fought to amass his fortune?

Angrily Casey buried her face in the pillow, but his scent was still strong, taunting her. Impulsively, she threw the pillow to the floor, where it landed with a muted thud.

He hadn't loved her because he hadn't loved her. That was the only answer that made sense.

And Ms. Casey O'Neill was a sensible person. Everyone said so.

Except that a few hours ago she'd been ready to make love with him. No, she'd been desperate for him.

Annoyed with herself, she lifted her hips and tugged the sheet free. The room was surprisingly warm, although it wasn't yet dawn, and the curtains billowed lazily in the shimmering light. She stared through the opening between them at the morning star. It winked at her like a cold, stern eye.

Okay, she thought. So you're still attracted to the man physically. So you're still susceptible. A woman would have to be half dead *not* to be susceptible to Alex Torres. But that was sex, not love. If she loved him . . .

But she didn't.

Thank God, she didn't.

Otherwise she might be tempted to try to make him fall in love with her again. She might hope.

Chapter 7

When Casey awakened again, the gray silence had been invaded by the full light of dawn. She blinked slowly, fighting her way to full awareness. Her eyelids were swollen and tender, and her throat ached.

She rubbed her cheek against the sheet, her hand groping toward the headboard for the pillow. Suddenly she remembered. Alex's pillow was still on the floor where she'd thrown it.

Memory came back to her in a rush: the dream, the tears, everything. She must have dozed off again. Thank goodness the dream hadn't returned.

Sighing, she turned on her back and stared at the new day. Thick, angry clouds blocked out the sun, and the slender branches of the trees outside the window were bending with the force of the wind. Another storm was on the way.

"Great," she muttered. If it rained as hard as it had that first day, Alex's driveway would soon be impassable. She would be trapped in this house for hours.

Maybe if she left early . . .

She started to sit up, only to freeze at the sound of a man's voice. She held her breath and stared at the closed door, her ears straining.

It was definitely Alex's voice, although the words were indistinct.

Frowning, she slid from the cocoon of covers and fumbled into the black robe. Her feet were silent on the tile as she padded to the door and opened it a crack.

Alex was seated at the large pine table that he used as a desk, talking on the phone. He was fully dressed in tan jeans and a black shirt, the sleeves rolled above his thick wrists. Papers were scattered over the desktop, and her briefcase lay open on the floor by his dusty suede boots.

"Facts, Evan," he said, looking toward the ceiling in barely leashed frustration. "Not supposition. I can draw my own conclusions."

Casey suppressed a yawn. She hadn't heard the phone by the bed ring, so Alex must have called his friend while she slept.

Hastily she glanced behind her. The place where the phone had sat was empty.

Her hand crept toward the floppy lapels of his robe. Surely he hadn't been in the room when she'd been dreaming. Surely not.

The tip of her tongue touched the fullness of her lower lip. It felt slightly swollen. And his kiss had been so real....

Casey pushed the thought from her mind. She was never her best in the morning. Her mind must have played tricks on her.

"Okay, I understand," Alex continued in a steely tone. "Anything else I need to know?"

As he listened, he glanced her way. He was wearing glasses with thin dark frames, and lines of weariness bracketed his mouth. His expression didn't change, but Casey knew that he'd seen her.

Opening the door wider, she clutched the robe around her and walked toward the desk. The room was colder than the bedroom and smelled of wood smoke.

Outside the bank of windows the trees lining the creek looked like menacing black shapes against the dawn sky. She shivered and shoved her hands into the robe's large patch pockets.

Alex acknowledged her approach with a slight nod. In the glaring light from the desk lamp she saw the telltale throbbing of the little vein in his temple. He had another of his punishing migraine headaches.

Six years ago she would have offered to bathe his head in ice, the only thing that ever gave him any relief. Now she didn't dare. He would only reject her offer, and she'd had enough of that.

She started to perch on the corner of the table, only to jump back as a low hiss warned her away. Butch was curled into a tight ball near Alex's hand, his head resting on a yellow legal tablet that was half filled with Alex's large writing.

"Sorry," she muttered to the cat, who regarded her warily.

Without looking up, Alex began scratching the cat's ears, and the tension in the animal's scruffy body slowly released. As Casey watched idly, a flash of gold caught her eye. When was he going to have that damn ring removed? she wondered, stifling a yawn.

He sighed, his gaze shifting to the slashing notes in front of him. "No, don't do anything yet, Evan. I'll get back to you on that. Yeah, I know you're busy. Just tell Carlos that I need you. He won't give you any trouble." He hung up without saying goodbye.

"Have you been up all night?" Casey asked, her voice still thickened by sleep.

"Yes."

His face was a hardened mask, cast in copper-tinged bronze, his onyx eyes cold and emotionless behind the clear lenses.

Casey's breath snagged in her throat. "What's wrong?"

He ignored her question. "I just had an...enlightening conversation with Evan. He was doing some checking for me."

"Checking? You mean on...on Con?"

Cynicism tightened the corners of his mouth. "Yes, on *Con.*"

"What—"

He didn't let her finish. "You were wrong, Casey. Con isn't after your company. He's after you."

"Me, but...but that's ridiculous."

His expression didn't change, but his eyes impaled her like the war lance in the photo. "You're in bad trouble. Worse than you can imagine."

"Me?" She swallowed hard. "What...what do you mean?"

"Just this. Con Deshler isn't going to rest until your company is ruined and you, my dear ex-wife, are in prison."

Casey stared at him in shock. "P-prison?" Her voice was a frozen thread of sound.

The large hand that had soothed the cat was now pressed flat against the papers. As she watched, the veins crisscrossing the wide back stood out starkly. She was suddenly glad that hand wasn't around her neck.

"Yes, prison," he told her slowly, making every word count. "I can't prove it, but the word I got is that he's found a former employee of yours, some accountant named Plunkett, who'll swear that you had advance word of this takeover bid." Savage anger etched his dark face.

"But . . . but that's a lie." Casey stared at him in shock. "I didn't know until the SEC called and told me that Con had notified them of his intent to acquire more than five percent of Summerville stock."

Alex flexed his shoulders, but his face remained drawn with pain. "Did you buy a large block of shares less than two months before Deshler filed with the SEC?"

"Well, yes, I reinvested my annual bonus, just like I always do, but—"

"And did your mother buy Summerville stock that same week?"

Casey felt a chill shudder through her. "I don't know." Her eyes asked the question she was afraid to voice.

"According to Evan, she purchased five thousand shares the day after you bought yours. And that same former employee is prepared to swear under oath that he heard you tell your mother to buy as many shares as she could afford. That she was certain to double her money when Deshler Enterprises took over."

"But . . . but that's illegal."

"Exactly, and the SEC is extremely sensitive about insider trading. At the very least, you'll be ruined professionally." His voice hardened. "At the worst, you'll be fined and sent to prison. The bastard's got you cold."

The floor seemed to shift under her bare feet, and she reached for the edge of the desk to steady herself. The lapels of the robe fell open, revealing an expanse of white skin about the V neck of her nightshirt, but she didn't notice.

"It's not true," she said in a shaky voice. "I didn't know about his intentions. I swear it."

"Prove it. It's your word against the accountant's. And Deshler's." The lamplight outlined his profile, playing over the high cheekbones to shadow his cheeks and sharply define the cruel slope of his jaw.

Casey felt the blood drain from her face. "Your informant must be wrong. Con . . . Con wouldn't do that to me."

"You mean because he was once your lover?" Alex's voice was soft, but Butch must have heard the same violent undercurrent as Casey, because he opened his eye, leaped up and jumped from the table in one abrupt movement. He hit the floor running, and a second later Casey heard the swinging of the cat door in the kitchen.

For an instant she, too, longed to run—as far away from Alex's accusing stare as she could.

"What, no quick answer, Casey? That's got to be a first." She didn't know which she hated more, the sarcasm in his voice or the savagery in his eyes.

Casey swallowed the sudden sickness that filled her throat. Now she knew why a trapped animal preferred to bite off a foot rather than die a slow death. But this was a trap she had baited herself.

"We were engaged," she said truthfully. "For three months." Somehow she kept her voice steady and strong, but inside, her stomach was coiling into a frigid knot of fear.

"You were lovers, you mean." He picked up a pencil and rolled it between his palms. He didn't look at her, but the sudden flaring of his nostrils reminded her of a predator catching her scent.

"If you want me to say the words, I will. Yes, Con and I were lovers for almost a year."

A hot flame of jealously licked at Alex, but he sat still, accepting the scalding pain. Casey had a perfect right to give herself to another man, even a man like Deshler. She was no longer his wife, so why the hell did it feel as though she had cheated on him?

He leaned back on his chair and tried to ignore the pounding in his head. He needed sleep, but there was no time. There were things he had to find out, things he had to know, before he could figure out how to advise her.

"Do you love him?" he asked, studying her pale face. She looked as fragile as one of the tiny flowers that grew between the rocks after the first spring rain.

Casey's gaze faltered, then held steady on his. "I thought I loved him. He was there for me after you . . . after the divorce."

A muscle in his throat jerked, but his eyes went mirror smooth, reflecting nothing behind the glasses. "Did you make him wait as long as you made me?"

The blood returned to her face in a hot flood. Something snapped inside her, and all the old humiliation and pain came bubbling up from the place where she'd stuffed it all. "You want to know the details? You want me to acknowledge that I was a fool? Okay, Alex. I was."

She inhaled swiftly, letting the words rush out with the air. "I was a basket case when you left. Me, the unflappable Ms. O'Neill. I couldn't sleep. I couldn't eat. I felt empty. Cast-off."

Her raised voice made him wince, but she was too upset to care about the pain crashing in his head. He had no right to judge her. No right at all. Glaring at him, she began pacing, the robe billowing behind her, her hands slicing the air in anger and frustration.

"He was loving and admiring and, yes, sexy. He made me feel like a woman again. For a while, I confused gratitude with love."

Just as she had confused Con with Alex. In many ways they'd been alike, strong, powerful, intensely masculine. But the resemblance had been, at best, surface deep. When she'd realized the truth, she'd ended the engagement.

Casey repressed a shudder at the memory of that last ugly meeting. Con had changed right before her eyes, as though he'd suddenly ripped away a mask. His easy smile had become a sneer, and the charming demeanor she'd found so irresistible after months of Alex's brooding silence had disappeared, replaced by a crude vulgarity that had left her shaken.

"Maybe he hates me now," she admitted reluctantly, "but I really thought I loved him once. And I…thought that he loved me."

Alex uttered a vicious obscenity. "Don't kid yourself, lady. Con Deshler never loved anyone."

The derision in his voice hurt her more than she would have thought possible. Just because Alex hadn't loved her, that didn't mean no man could.

She stood straighter. "Don't be such a hypocrite, Alex. We both know you married me because you wanted me in your bed. I was just another conquest to you. Love had no place in your plan."

The pencil in his hand snapped, sounding like a pistol shot in the silent room. "That's enough."

Casey ignored the low throb of warning in his voice. He had no right to look at her as though she'd done something wrong. They'd been divorced for a long time before she allowed herself to want another man.

"You might not like it, Alex," she said recklessly, hurt driving her, "but when it comes to women, you and Con are just alike."

Alex tossed his glasses onto the desk and stood, his face going stark white from the pain. He walked toward her, his eyes brilliant with fury. His hand shot out to grab her by the nape of the neck, his fingers bruisingly hard as he pulled her toward him. Only inches separated his mouth from hers as he said slowly and deliberately, "Don't *ever* compare me to Con Deshler again. Just . . . don't . . . do . . . it."

Casey saw the barely restrained violence in his dark pupils. He was breathing hard, and his hand on her neck was hot, as though there were a furnace inside him, heating his blood.

"Then make me believe you're different." Her voice rose. "Tell me that you wanted me and not a trophy in your bed. Tell me that . . . that you loved me."

His face changed, and some of the fury left his eyes. His fingers eased their grip, becoming almost caressing. "And if I did, would that change how you feel about me?"

She stared at him. What did he want her to say? That she still loved him? That she forgave him? What?

"I . . . I . . ." The words wouldn't come. She didn't know how she felt. Not deep down.

Alex's face hardened. "Forget it. I have my answer."

Moving quickly, barely able to see where he was going, he turned and stormed out of the room, slamming the door so hard behind him that the pictures vibrated against the thick walls.

Casey stared at the heavy panel in stunned silence. Slowly she brought her fingers to her aching neck. Alex had been furiously angry, and his eyes had flared with the raw hunger she remembered. But she'd seen more than that in his face.

Right before he'd walked out, Alex had looked exactly like a man who'd just received a mortal wound.

Casey stood in front of the window and stared out at the storm-battered landscape. The rain was coming straight down, beating on the roof above her head in a monotonous, numbing rhythm. It had been raining for hours, and the ground outside was slick with puddles.

Inside the stone house, the walls that had seemed so sheltering when Alex was with her seemed to draw in around her, imprisoning her in this place that didn't want her.

Alex hadn't returned. Since today was the last day of school, she assumed that he was at the schoolhouse. He'd taken the Jeep and, in spite of her anger at the way he'd left, she was worried about him. He'd never driven before when he'd had a migraine.

When she'd tried to call him, however, the operator had told her that the Santa Ysabel Pueblo School wasn't listed.

But maybe that was just as well. He needed time to cool off, and she needed time to think about the things he'd told her about Con Deshler.

After the initial shock had worn off, she'd gotten coldly angry. The man was exactly what Alex had called him, a bastard. He was without conscience, without scruples, the kind of man who gave entrepreneurs with integrity, entrepreneurs like Alex, a bad rap.

The wind rattled the pane in front of her, and she touched a finger to the sweating glass. Had that been why Alex chucked it all? Because he'd been tired of being called a despoiler by the media and many of his peers?

"What do you feel when you look out these windows?" she whispered to his image in her mind, her voice scarcely louder than a sigh.

In a confused sort of way, she was beginning to understand why he'd been drawn to this place. There was a majesty to the land that called to a primitive longing lying dormant and protected inside her. Maybe it was the austere beauty that drew her, beauty that was hidden in the starkness, revealed only to one who chose to seek it out. Or maybe it was the sense of timelessness that she felt from a community that had been part of this land for centuries by the time Alex's Spanish ancestors arrived.

Slowly she turned to stare into the blazing eyes of one-who-is-great-among-men. One of the Chosen. How he must have suffered, she thought, with that magnificent body locked into a tiny cell year after year, unable to walk the land that he loved.

Her eyes misted with tears, and the stern face blurred. Did Alex share the special feeling Cadiz must have had for this place? Would he make the same sacrifice for something or someone he called precious?

Her lips curved into a bemused smile. John had said nothing about Cadiz's wife, the mother of Alex's grandmother.

A sharp needle of jealousy stabbed her, and she nearly gasped aloud. She was half in love with a man who'd been dead for over a century.

She managed a shaky laugh and started to turn back to the window when a wavering shriek pierced the silence. It was coming from outside the window.

"Oh my God," she cried, her stomach heaving. Butch was crouched on a large jagged rock at the edge of the stream, his back arched, his matted black-and-orange fur standing on end. Blood dripped from the scruff of his neck onto the granite, where the rain quickly washed it down the side to form a pink puddle.

A few feet away two coyotes circled restlessly. One was slightly larger than the other, with yellow-specked eyes that never blinked. Both stood with their heads down, their large dull-white teeth bared, and their heavy haunches braced for attack.

"Oh, no!"

Casey whirled in panic, her frantic gaze searching for a weapon. But she found none. No guns, no knives, not even a log in the basket by the fireplace.

"Hang on, Butch," she shouted, racing for the kitchen, her sandals slapping against the tile. The backdoor banged shut behind her, and she paused to catch her breath.

Rain lashed her face, blurring her vision. She blinked furiously, swallowing the water that streamed down her face and into her mouth.

She spied a broom resting against the side of the house and nearly cried with relief. Holding it in both hands, she rounded the house and advanced on the coyotes, the broom held in front of her like a staff.

"Get out of here," she shouted, waving the bristles toward the closer of the two. The animal skittered sideways, its teeth bared, its eyes gleaming malevolently as it watched her.

The other one took a step toward Butch, who growled, his tail twitching, his one yellow eye wild and alert.

"Go away. No one wants you here," Casey shouted again. The rain stung her eyes, making it hard to see clearly. She slipped on a half-buried rock, stumbling sideways. Suddenly one of the coyotes charged toward her, its mouth open, its powerful back legs churning.

Butch shrieked and leaped from the rock. He landed heavily, his back leg folding under him, distracting the charging coyote long enough for Casey to hit its slavering muzzle hard with the bristle end of the broom.

Stunned, the coyote turned on Butch, who lay within inches of his bloody jaws.

Casey knew that she had only seconds before Alex's pet would be dead. She took hasty aim, then swung the broom with all her strength. The heavy end hit the coyote's head with a sickening thud, and a sharp pain shot up her wrist. Somehow she managed to lift the broom again, whacking the other animal in the rump.

In a flurry of tawny fur and furious barking, the angry animals took off running. They spanned the creek with two long strides and headed for the mesa in the distance, their shrill yaps echoing across the empty expanse.

Casey stumbled to the rock and sat down, the broom falling unnoticed to the ground. Her heart was racing so fast she could scarcely draw breath, and her head was swimming.

The wet seams of her new jeans scratched her inner thighs, and her shirt was plastered to her skin. Muddy water had turned the white leather of her sandals to a sickly brown.

"I don't believe I did that." Her voice was coming in raspy jerks. "This place is making me crazy."

Something brushed her leg. She screamed and looked down in panic. It was Butch.

"Poor baby," she whispered, leaning down to pick him up. His mottled fur was soaking wet and slicked in pathetic tufts against his shaking body. Blood seeped from a deep gash under his chin, and his leg stuck out at a sickeningly crooked angle, but his tail jerked feebly, as though he were trying to show his gratitude.

"You're the ugliest cat I've ever seen," she told him with a shaky smile.

His yellow eye blinked, then closed, and he began to purr.

Casey promptly burst into hysterical laughter. Butch was even crazier than she was.

Casey was seated at the kitchen table, paging through Alex's only cookbook, when she heard the front door open. The storm had moved on, and a peaceful silence had settled over the house.

"Casey?"

His boots beat an urgent tattoo on the floor as he came toward the kitchen. He stopped in the doorway, one hand braced against the jamb. He was breathing hard, as though he'd been running.

Her lips were suddenly dry, but she managed to keep from sliding her tongue between the parched surfaces to moisten them.

"Hello, Alex," she said quietly, folding her hands in her lap. For some reason they'd begun to shake the moment she'd seen him.

"What the hell's going on here? Your car's covered with mud."

"I know. The rental people are going to be very annoyed." She wanted to keep the mood light for as long as she could. They needed to talk, but without the explosive tension that always seemed to crackle between them these days.

His eyes narrowed even further until they were dark slits. *"Casey?"*

She saw the telltale throbbing in his temple. No wonder he was in no mood for banter. "I, um, had to take Butch to the vet in Gallup. John said she was the closest."

"John said . . . what do you mean, the vet? What happened to Butch?"

"He was attacked by coyotes."

"He was *what*?" He pushed himself away from the door and came toward her. Deep grooves of pain scored his broad forehead, and his hair was wind tossed and damp.

Quietly she explained. When she got to the part where she'd hit the first coyote with the broom, he stopped her. His face was even whiter than it had been when he'd walked in.

"A broom? You fought off two hungry coyotes with a *broom*?"

"It was all I could find."

He stared at her, his eyes burning coals in his ashen face. "Did . . . are you okay?"

"Yes, of course. But my new sandals are ruined."

Alex glared at her as though he couldn't believe his ears. "Forget the sandals. I'll buy you a dozen pairs if that's what you want."

He pulled out a chair and slowly, bracing his arms on the table, lowered his body into the seat. Beads of sweat dotted his forehead, and his mouth was rimmed with white.

"Alex, are you all right? Can I get you some aspirin? Ice?"

She reached out to touch his clenched fist, and he recoiled, pushing her away with a swipe of his strong forearm. She stumbled, hitting her elbow on the table, but he didn't appear to notice.

"No, I'm not all right, damn it." His anger exploded into the kitchen, goading her into an answering fury. "This has been a bitch of a day."

"Personally, mine was wonderful," she threw back sarcastically, her frayed nerves finally giving way. "Just peachy, the best time I've had in years."

Alex stared at her, then groaned and dropped his head into his hands. His shoulders bunched beneath the black cotton, and a heavy sigh escaped from his lips. Slowly, as though the effort cost him dearly, he raised his head and looked at her.

"Promise me you'll never do anything that foolish again." His words were granite hard. "Otherwise, I swear, I won't let you out of my sight until you leave."

Casey heard the ragged note in his voice, and the determination. Alex never made idle threats. He would do exactly as he said.

Her spirit rebelled, but the businesswoman in her reminded her that she hadn't gotten what she'd come for: his promise to help. Grudgingly, hating herself, she gave in. "I promise."

A muscle worked in his tight jaw. "Good," he said, his voice strangely thick. He cleared his throat. "Good."

He pulled a red kerchief from his back pocket and wiped his brow. "Is Butch still at the vet's?"

Casey noticed that he held his head stiffly straight, as though the slightest movement hurt.

"No, he's in the bedroom. I made him a bed in a sunny spot in the corner. The vet had to knock him out before he would let her treat him. Poor baby, he's sleeping it off."

"But the vet told you that he'll be okay?" The anxious note in his voice touched her deeply. He had never had a pet, he'd told her once. His family hadn't been able to afford the extra food.

She smiled tightly, the anger seething inside her slowly receding. "He'll be fine. One leg was broken, and he had four sutures along the edge of his jaw, but Dr. Jimenez said he'll be almost as good as new in a few weeks."

One side of his mouth lifted wearily. "*Es un gato macho.* He's used up a lot of lives. I hope he knows that."

She laughed. "I don't think that'll stop Butch."

Alex tried to smile, but even that small movement made him scowl with pain. He muttered a curse under his breath.

Casey could feel the tension radiating from him. She hesitated, then stood and rested her hand on his shoulder. His muscles tightened under her fingers, and she could feel the dampness of his body through his shirt. Her fingers lingered at the nape of his neck, where the tension seemed the worst.

"Alex, there's plenty of time till dinner is ready. Why don't you take a nap?"

He frowned. "I'd thought we would eat out again." His pupils were dilated with pain, and his voice was taut with exhaustion.

She made her voice light. "I'm making my special chicken dish tonight. To repay your hospitality."

His pain-dulled gaze slowly shifted to her face. "What special chicken dish?"

Her lips curved into a reluctant smile. "The one I found in this cookbook. I had to read every one before I came to something that sounded easy enough."

"At least it's not an expensive standing-rib roast you're working on."

Casey shook her head. She couldn't speak. She was too busy fighting the memories that the softened note of affectionate teasing in his low voice had released.

Once, when their housekeeper had had the night off, Casey had tried to make a roast, but she'd gotten engrossed in a thorny time-management problem she'd brought home with her. By the time Alex had arrived home, hungry and tired, the roast had been little more than a charred black lump in the middle of the huge pan.

She'd nearly cried in frustration, and he'd ended up taking her to bed. Later they'd called out for Chinese food.

"It wasn't so awful, was it?" she asked in a shaky voice.

He tried to smile. "No. It wasn't awful." He sounded incredibly weary.

She swallowed a sigh and removed her hand. The feel of his rigid muscles remained on her palm, and she slowly curled her fingers into a ball.

"I'll call you when it's ready," she said, turning away.

Alex heard the slight catch in her voice, and the sad little sound tore into him like a knife. He wanted to tell her that the three years they'd been together had been the happiest time in his life. That sometimes at night he missed her small warm body curled into his arms so much that he couldn't sleep. But what good would that do? Nothing he did or said would make any difference. She'd told him as much this morning.

Hungrily, wanting to lay his head on her soft breast and close out everything but her sweet warmth, he let his tired eyes rest on the slender curve of her hip, drinking in the perfection of her dainty body. She looked like a golden Indian maiden in the frilly skirt and plain white blouse she'd bought at Janetta's store.

But Casey would never fit into this place. She was too ambitious, too driven to achieve. She needed challenge and competition to make her feel alive. And in the beginning of their marriage, when he'd been that way himself, it had been a real turn on to watch her eyes burn with the same passion for success that had flamed in him.

If she'd been different, less driven perhaps, or less ambitious, he might have taken a chance. He might have asked her to come with him into exile, but . . .

No, damn it. He'd done the right thing.

Alex nearly groaned aloud as the pain in his head shot down his neck. Nausea churned in his stomach, and phosphorescent zigzags of light shimmered in front of his eyes.

Bracing his hands on the table, he levered himself to his feet. "Call me if you need help," he managed to get out. Or at least he thought he did. His head hurt so much he wasn't sure.

Casey turned at the sound of his voice. He was in obvious torment. Without waiting for an answer, he turned and walked slowly out of the kitchen.

She stared at the empty doorway, listening to the sound of his heavy boots. Guilt stabbed at her. She was the reason he'd stayed up all night. Maybe even the reason he was suffering through another migraine.

Her gaze went to the door of the freezer. The least she could do was try to ease his suffering. If he pushed her away, at least she would have tried.

She grabbed a bowl from the cupboard and began filling it with ice cubes.

When she entered the bedroom a few minutes later, Alex was stretched full-length across the bed, his knees slightly flexed, his dark head resting on the same pillow that she'd thrown to the floor in anger. His worn boots were by the bed, and his large feet were encased in heavy white socks with yellow toes and heels.

One clenched fist rested heavily on his forehead, and his eyes were closed, his thick lashes looking like black shadows against his sallow skin. His lips were slightly parted, and he was breathing heavily.

As she deposited the bowl and a clean washcloth on the night table, his eyes slowly opened to pain-filled slits. "What's wrong? Is Butch worse?" His voice sounded lifeless.

Casey glanced toward the makeshift bed of towels in the corner. Butch was curled into a tight ball, sleeping peacefully, one front paw covering his nose. The fresh plaster of his cast was already scored where his tongue had worried it.

"He's fine. Just relax," she said in a soft voice.

"Casey..." She heard the protest in his voice and pressed her fingers lightly against his mouth to stop him. His breath was hot against her skin.

"Alex, I just want to help you. Don't fight me, please. It'll just make your headache worse than it is."

A grim smile creased his cheek briefly. "That's not possible." He closed his eyes and sighed in resignation. Or was it surrender?

Casey smiled sadly. All his life Alex had done for others. He didn't have much practice at accepting help.

She dipped the cloth into the ice water and wrung it almost dry. Gently she moved his hand to the pillow and began bathing his damp brow.

He groaned, and his fist tightened. His hair was curling at the ends, and the damp thickness brushed her fingers as she withdrew her hand to rewet the cloth.

"Feels good," he muttered.

"Relax," she crooned, knowing that the icy water would ease the pain enough for him to fall into a healing oblivion. For some sufferers, vasodilators or painkillers helped, but for Alex, the only thing that gave him any relief was sleep.

He muttered something unintelligible and licked his lips. The rigid lines of his face were beginning to relax into the natural arrogance that marked him as a descendant of the man named Cadiz. She could see the resemblance in the distinctive shape of his nose, in the proud curve of his lips, in the unforgiving line of his square jaw.

Alex sighed heavily, and his lashes fluttered, then opened. The lines in his temples deepened as he gazed up at her.

Casey filled the cloth with slivers of melting cubes, then folded it into a thick oblong, which she placed above his drawn brows.

Trying not to jostle him, she sat on the edge of the mattress and gently began massaging his temples. Her hip pressed against his side, and she felt the heat of his body warming her skin.

He sighed heavily and lifted his hand to cover hers. He let it rest there for a long moment, then dropped it to the pillow, where it curled into a half fist next to his ear.

"Nice," he said, weariness and pain slurring the single word into a caress. His lashes drifted lower again.

Casey inhaled slowly, fighting the urge to return that involuntary verbal caress with her fingertips. She longed to trace his lips from haughty corner to haughty corner, feeling them soften just for her.

The skin beneath her fingertips was smooth and hot, unblemished except for a short jagged scar between his brows, and she was tempted to explore that tiny flaw with the tip of her tongue.

Her lips parted with the need to trail kisses along the line of his brow, to taste the salty moisture dampening his skin. Beneath the thin cotton covering her breasts, her heart began racing. She wanted to take his pain into her own body, to give him the peace that he craved. She wanted to erase the tortured lines that the last six years had chiseled into his proud features. She wanted to love him.

Casey's hands froze against his throbbing temples.

Dear God, she *did* love him. Now. This minute. She loved the man he was now.

"Casey?" he said in a rusty voice, his skin furrowing under her stiff hands.

"Wha—?" Shock clogged her throat. "What?" She had to force her lungs to breathe.

His eyes opened slowly. They were dull with pain, but she still felt the impact of his intent gaze.

"Thank you," he said slowly, his rough hand coming up slowly to rest against her cheek. "For saving my cat. He's not much—" his lashes drooped, then rose again to reveal a sad, mocking gleam in his pain-filled pupils "—but he's all I've got." He turned his head and kissed her wrist. Then his eyes closed, and his hand fell away. His breathing slowed, becoming regular and shallow. He was asleep.

Chapter 8

The room was hot and stuffy. Alex wiped the sweat from his face with his hands and turned his head toward the window. He'd built his house with the front facing east in order to be in harmony with the land, and the breeze blowing into the bedroom was from the south.

It was after five. He could tell from the length of the shadows made by the trees sheltering the house. The door to the bedroom was ajar, and he could smell something cooking.

Had Casey said something about chicken? Something about making dinner for him? He felt a smile come to his face at the thought. She tried so hard to be domestic, but her mind had a way of zooming off on to other things whenever she walked into the kitchen. Not that he cared.

He would gladly eat charred roast every night of his life if that meant he would have Casey in his arms afterward.

He lay perfectly still, his body heavy with the sick lethargy that always came after one of his headaches. He could still feel the gentleness in Casey's hands as she'd bathed his forehead. She'd talked to him, said words that he didn't remember now, but he'd heard the caring in her voice. He sucked in a ragged breath against the clawing need that rose in him whenever he thought of her.

During their years together, she'd been a woman of many moods: sophisticated, sultry, playful, kittenish, all wrapped up in an exciting package of femininity that he'd never found in another woman.

When they had made love, she'd unexpectedly made herself completely vulnerable to him, and he'd felt as though she'd given him a rare and precious gift—her trust.

Had she done the same with Deshler?

His belly tightened at the thought, and his mind drifted, dipping into a caldron of jealousy for a long bitter moment, then sharpening to stab him with Casey's own words: *I thought I loved him.*

How could she have given herself to that bastard? he thought, feeling a gnawing rage buffet him. Anyone but Con Deshler.

Alex pushed his fist under the pillow and stared at the ceiling, trying to push the image of Casey, naked and glowing with love in Deshler's arms, out of his mind. She had gone to Con on the rebound; he understood that all too well, even if she hadn't come right out and said it. And that made him responsible for the mess she was in now.

"Alex, are you all right?" Casey was standing in the doorway, a dish towel wrapped around her waist, a smudge of flour on her chin. Her cheeks were flushed from the heat of the kitchen, and the bare skin above the edge of her white shirt was covered with a faint sheen of pink.

A few drops of sweat had been trapped in the hollow of her neck, and in his mind he saw himself licking the moisture slowly, greedily, from her skin.

Alex's breath quickened, and a violent possessiveness shuddered through him. She was beautiful, with the sun shining across the living room to streak her hair with light. So damn beautiful.

His teeth ground together. She was his. Even if they could never live together again, in his dreams she would always be his.

"Alex? Did you hear me?"

He managed a careful nod. "I'm okay. Just a little groggy."

"Are you sure? I can bring your dinner in here."

Promise her you'll go with her, a part of him urged. Promise her you'll save her foundry. But the words refused to come. He no longer made promises he wasn't sure he could keep.

"Give me a minute." His voice was hoarse, and he cleared his throat. "I'll . . . be right there."

Casey nodded, then disappeared.

Alex raised himself slowly to his elbows and waited for the dizziness to pass. Even if he proved Deshler was a blackmailer and a liar, there was no guarantee he could save the foundry.

Because he didn't have much time, Casey would have to trust him blindly. That was the only way he could make it work. And even if she could force herself to blindly accept his lead, the odds were against their winning.

But, damn it, he wanted to make her the promise she wanted to hear. He just wasn't sure he had the guts to keep it.

Casey sat on a thick patch of coarse grass at the edge of the rippling creek and lifted her face to the sky. In the distance she heard a coyote howl, then another. A bleak smile curved her lips as she stared at the streaks of deep orange and fuchsia stretching over her head.

It was twilight, the time between day and night when the land changes shape and texture. The time between the worlds, someone had once called it, and that was the way it seemed—especially here. Here, the day seemed to linger, as though time moved more slowly in the vast emptiness.

Lowering her gaze, she leaned back against the rock behind her. The limestone slab was knobby against her spine, and she shifted position until she found a smooth, cool place.

The air swirling lazily around her was thick, almost oppressive, and hot. She could feel a thin trickle of sweat flowing between her breasts toward her belly. If she'd been alone, she would have erased the moisture with her fingers, but Alex sat next to her, one long leg raised to support his muscular forearm, the other extended casually in front of him. He was watching the sun die, his face in stark profile, alone with his thoughts.

"I never thought I could stand to live more than a few hours away from the ocean, but I've come to love the desert," he told her suddenly in a low, oddly meditative voice. "Except for the heat and the dust. I'm not sure I'll ever get used to them."

Casey managed a smile, anxious to maintain the uneasy truce between them. "I thought I'd suffocate in the kitchen with the oven on. I should have made a salad. At least I'm good at that."

His slow smile flashed in the twilight shadows. "I'm not complaining. I like charred chicken."

"I can't believe you ate it all."

His gaze flickered over her, and an expression that might have been a smile lingered for an instant in his eyes. "I was hungry. I missed lunch."

"Me too."

The smile warmed until she had trouble with her breathing. "Yeah," he said in the lilting cadence she loved, "you were too busy fighting off coyotes with my broom."

His words were chiding, but his tone was almost tender. Or had she only imagined the gentleness?

Casey pulled her knees to her chest and hugged them. This new Alex was as hard to understand as the strange, guttural language he'd spoken in his sleep as she'd stood watching over him.

"You've changed," she told him, drawing circles on her skirt with her fingernail.

His eyes bored into her as though searching for something. "How?"

Casey was suddenly flustered. For some reason her answer seemed important to him. She rubbed her hand along the stringy grass and tried to organize her thoughts.

"In some ways you're...more human now. More, I don't know, approachable, I guess. But in others..." Her voice trailed off.

"In others?" he prompted.

"It's like you're trying to...to deny your power. Like you're trying to be...ordinary."

He bowed his head. "I am ordinary."

Casey shook her head. She wanted to touch him, but she was afraid to break the mood. "You could never be ordinary. You were born special, like...like the man in the picture, like Cadiz."

His lips twisted. "He was a savior, Casey. I was a destroyer. That's what I did best."

"No!" she cried. "You were always fair."

"Was I?" He shook his head. "I don't think so."

"Alex, why did you come here?" she asked suddenly, staring down at the land around them. The storm had left little impression on the sunbaked earth, just as she'd left little impression on this hard man next to her.

"Would you believe for a little peace?" Alex picked up a stone and rubbed his thumb over the rounded edge. It was smooth and warm, like Casey's skin.

"Are you happier now? Happier than you were in New York?" Happier than you were with me? she added silently.

He heard the sad note in her voice, and in his mind he reached for her. But only in his mind. "I haven't had a lot of experience with happiness, Casey," he said truthfully. "I'm not sure I know what it is. I only know that I sleep better now."

He stared fixedly at the scuffed toes of his boots, fighting the need to watch the reflection of the setting sun in her eyes. It had been a mistake suggesting a walk after dinner. In the glow of the fading light she was more desirable than ever.

More than anything, he wanted to warm himself in the glow of her loving nature, if only for a heartbeat. But he didn't dare. It would make it too hard when he had to go out into the darkness again—alone.

With a silent cry of pain, the only kind he allowed himself, Alex hurled the stone toward the setting sun.

Casey watched the arching trajectory of the rock until it hit the desert floor, spattering dust into the stillness.

"I called my office while you were sleeping," she told him with a calm she didn't feel. "Becky said that Con's spreading a rumor that I've already abandoned the employees I'm supposed to be championing. That . . . that I'm out of town interviewing for another job. She's managed to cover for me, but my staff is beginning to ask questions she can't answer. He's serious, Alex. I think for the first time I really believe he might win."

His mouth slanted into a cynical line. "Con doesn't bluff, Casey. And he always plays with a stacked deck."

She bit her lip, then blurted out softly, "I've made reservations on the 9:00 a.m. flight tomorrow." She hesitated. "For two."

He stood and turned away from her, a lonely figure silhouetted against the blood-red glow on the horizon. Suddenly the blazing sunset seemed garish and ugly, and the air smelled of dust.

"As far as I've been able to discover, he's got every angle covered," he said tonelessly. "My gut tells me it's a done deal.

You'd be better off walking away from this fight, Case. If he gets the company without an expensive proxy fight, odds are he won't go after you personally. If you fight, it could get bloody."

He was turning her down. She could feel it. Slowly she got to her feet, feeling the stress of the past few days rip away her control. "I'd rather go down fighting than...than run away," she said heatedly. "I'm not much for doing penance in a cold stone house in the middle of nowhere."

He spun around, his eyes alive with emotion. "You little idiot. This isn't about me. It's about you. I don't want you to go to prison."

"Then *help* me!"

He lifted his face to the sky for an instant, then looked at her. "And what if I can't? What if I make it worse? Then what?"

Casey managed a shaky laugh. "Then you can visit me in prison."

Alex muttered a vicious curse. "Damn you," he said in a furious tone. "Damn you for making me feel again."

Before she could respond, he spun away from her and walked with pounding, furious strides upstream.

A dozen different emotions swamped her, and she swallowed hard, her eyes filling with the tears that she hated.

"Damn *you*," she whispered at his retreating back. "Damn you for making me love you again."

Casey stared out the window at the crescent edge of the moon slicing through a dark bank of clouds. The landscape below looked cold and barren, and the gnarled branches of the trees bordering the creek reminded her of bony fingers reaching out to trap her in this stark and lonely place.

Her mouth moved, forming the words she'd said on that first day in Santa Ysabel. "I don't love him." I can't, she added silently. It hurts too much.

But she did.

He'd been the first man to awaken the dormant fires that had slept within her for so long. And he'd been the only man she'd ever met who'd encouraged her to be herself. To fight for her place at the top. To win.

Six years. Long, painful years of forgetting. And still she'd let herself hope.

Never again, she vowed.

The mournful sound of a night bird filled the silence. The air was still unbearably hot, lying heavily against her skin.

She moved her head on the pillow, trying to find a cool spot, and kicked at the sheet. The thin covering slithered to one side, exposing her bare legs.

She closed her eyes, willing her mind to shut down. The room was so silent that she could hear the cat's raspy breathing and the faint hum of the clock by the bed.

Absently she reached out to rub the empty space next to her. Nowhere in this house had she found a sign of a woman. Any woman.

There was no silky robe on the back of the door, no cosmetics or female notions in the bathroom, nothing in the closet.

And Janetta didn't know of a special woman in Alex's life. Nor, she had a feeling, did John.

From all that she'd heard of Alex, all that she herself knew of him, it wasn't like him to go without a woman for very long. So where was she, that other woman?

She'd thought about her so often that she'd even taken on a face, an image. She would be attractive and bright and sophisticated. That was Alex's preference. His style. His way of armoring himself against the humiliation of his poverty-stricken past.

Casey rubbed the cool cotton sheet with her fingertips and thought about the ring that still gleamed on his finger. The pueblo was filled with skilled silversmiths. Hadn't she just bought earrings made by one of them? If Alex had really wanted to have her ring cut from his finger, he could have done so easily. He could have done it yesterday or today.

But he was still wearing it.

The hope that had shriveled inside her revived. Maybe she'd been wrong about his reason for ending their marriage. And if she'd been wrong, maybe there was a chance she could make him fall in love with her again. After all, she'd fallen in love with him all over again.

The edges of her mind began to blur, and she sighed. She felt like Butch, chasing his own tail and getting nowhere. All her thoughts kept returning to the same question. If he hadn't been unfaithful, why hadn't he fought to make her believe him?

And the same answer came back to haunt her. Because he had wanted to get out of a marriage that had begun to bore him, and she'd given him the perfect out.

Casey rubbed her tired eyes and gave in to the weariness gripping her. Tomorrow, she would leave this place. Tomorrow...

Suddenly she heard a sound. Someone was outside.

She sat up, her heart pounding, her wide eyes searching the silvered landscape outside the window. Alex was standing by the jutting rock where they'd sat side by side on the wild grass, his head bent, his shoulders forming a rigid silhouette against the moonlit horizon.

The end of the cigar he was smoking glowed orange for an instant, and the acrid scent of smoke filled her nostrils. He stood alone, looking out over the land that was part of a brave man's legacy. He carried the stamp of Cadiz on his chiseled features, but what about inside?

Casey sighed. Once he'd promised to love her and cherish her and keep her above all others. Had he kept any of those vows, even for a little while?

As she watched, Alex suddenly flung the cigar into the water and headed for the house, his steps oddly reluctant. The door opened, then shut. The living room was in semidarkness; she'd left a light burning in the kitchen for him.

The door to the bedroom was ajar, open far enough for the cat to hobble through. She held her breath as Alex prowled his house, his tread slow and weary. The door to the bathroom opened, then closed, and an instant later she heard the sound of the shower.

She squeezed her lids hard against her lower lashes, but the image of his rugged, masculine body wet and slippery with soapsuds refused to disappear.

Once she'd lathered every inch of that lean, burnished body, relishing the steely resistance of his muscles against her hand.

The places where he'd once touched her, too, throbbed to life again, just as he'd throbbed against her palm. She moaned and twisted against the hot sheet, trying to ignore the fire inside her. In spite of everything, the humiliation, the loneliness that was worse when she was with him, the aching love that wasn't returned, she still wanted him. Her body called to his, begging for the fullness of his possession.

She pressed her clenched fist against her teeth and closed her eyes. Tomorrow, she repeated silently over and over. Tomorrow.

"Casey, are you awake?"

Her startled cry died in her throat. He was standing in the doorway, his hair-roughened chest still damp from the shower, a white towel riding low around his lean hips. In the dim light from the kitchen, his body was a study in brown and black, a bold conquistador chiseled in seasoned mahogany.

"Yes, I'm awake," she said quietly, her heart a loud and angry pounding in her head.

"What time did you say your plane left in the morning?" His hair was slicked back from his forehead, revealing the harsh lines of a frown on his brow.

Her stomach churned with a sick feeling of defeat. *Your* plane, he'd said. Not *ours*. She'd guessed right. He wasn't coming with her. She'd failed.

"Nine," she answered, suddenly conscious of the glistening brilliance of his devil-dark eyes.

Something that might have been a smile curled one corner of his hard mouth. "Set that clock for five. That should give us plenty of time."

"Us?"

"Yes, us." Casey heard the thread of humor in his voice, but his face was an impenetrable mask. "I'm going with you."

Alex stood at the bathroom sink, methodically scraping his straightedge razor through the lather covering his jaw.

A cold shower had taken the edge off the exhaustion that had blurred his vision and hampered his concentration, but his eyes still stung from a night spent poring over the printouts in Casey's briefcase.

He'd read until he knew the foundry's financial position as well as Deshler and his people could, maybe even better, because Casey had given him access to corporate secrets. The new alloy for computer components developed by her man Jameson should double the profits in five years or less, if the tests of the prototypes proved out.

Alex tilted his head to one side, wincing at the twinge of pain in his temple. Most of the work he'd done these past two years had taxed his muscles, not his brain. He was out of practice, and his mind was tired. The only competing he'd done had been against the clock. Some nights he'd finished his work in the dark, but at least he'd finished it.

Scowling, he stopped to rinse the razor under the tap before taking a sip from the big mug of scalding coffee at his elbow.

It was not yet dawn, and the house was quiet. Casey was still asleep, curled up in the middle of his bed, her honey-tipped hair framing the relaxed face on his pillow with seductive softness.

He knew that she would wake up slowly, stretching and muttering in a husky little voice that used to make him smile whenever he'd heard it.

Absently, the way he did whenever he thought of her, he rubbed his thumb over the smooth warmth of his wedding band, relishing once more the memory of her skin against his.

Holding her the other night, he'd felt at peace for the first time since he could remember, and his starving soul had been nourished in a way that made him hunger for all the things he'd given up when he'd left her.

His thigh muscles bunched against the towel riding low over his hips, and he remembered the eager way she'd responded to him. But he couldn't take what she'd been offering. He still felt dirty inside; maybe he always would. And he couldn't take the chance that his past would someday soil her as well. He'd been the one who'd made the mistake. He had to be the one to pay.

The familiar bitterness of wanting what could never be again settled over him, and the warmth he'd felt faded into the harsh light flooding the small room. He muttered a particularly crude Spanish insult at his reflection in the mirror, then began stroking the dark skin under the soap.

His eyes were half closed, and his mind had begun to drift aimlessly when he heard a sound behind him. The latch clicked, and the door was pushed open. Casey stood on the threshold, blinking in the glare.

"Sorry, I didn't see the light," she murmured in a voice that was still thick with sleep. Her feathery lashes rose and fell rapidly as she tried to blink herself awake.

Her hands were clutching the makeup bag containing her things. Her borrowed robe hung open, revealing the skimpy white nightshirt.

He turned back to the mirror, but the glass seemed to intensify the flush on her cheeks and the vibrant colors of sunshine and fire in the waves framing her face.

"I must have forgotten to lock the door." His voice sounded hoarse in the cool morning air, and he cleared his throat. "I'll be done in a minute."

Embarrassment prodded Casey awake, and she realized how she must look to him, walking half asleep into his bathroom, his robe hanging off one shoulder.

"Take your time," she said, managing an apologetic smile. "I, um, could use some coffee, anyway." She turned to go, but the rug skidded under her foot, and she grabbed the edge of the sink to keep from falling.

Her bag fell from her hand, and the cuff of her sleeve caught the cup on the sink, dragging it off the edge. Steaming coffee splashed over her thigh and soaked through the thin cotton nightshirt, burning her skin.

Casey cried out in pain, but before she could move, Alex stripped the robe and the sodden shirt from her, then scooped her into the shower stall. She gasped as her bare feet hit the cold tile, and she stumbled. He caught her, then climbed in behind her and closed the glass door. Reaching past her, he turned on the tap and directed the spray toward her naked thigh.

Stinging cold water cascaded over her, and an icy chill penetrated to the bone. She began to shiver.

"Relax, *querida*," Alex whispered against her shoulder. "The cold water will take away the pain."

His body braced hers while his hands held her steady. The water pounded over them, easing the pain in her thigh, but exciting another more urgent one deep inside.

Even knowing that she shouldn't, she wanted him. Just the feel of his thighs against the backs of hers made her go weak, and the warmth of his solid chest made the cold bearable.

She'd been the strong one for so long, the one who others habitually turned to in moments of crisis or pain. She'd been there for all of them, her mother when her father had left them, her employees, even the people of the town, but no one had been there for her when she felt scared or tentative, or when she felt alone and lost. Not for a long, long time.

Tentatively, Casey let her body relax against him. His muscles hardened, reminding her of the power of his lean body, and his arms came around her waist to crush the breath from her lungs.

As though he couldn't help himself, Alex buried his face in the curve of her neck, and lime-scented lather slid over her breast. In spite of the cold water his skin felt hot, and his breathing was loud in her ear, becoming more labored with every breath he took.

"Just a few more minutes and the sting will be gone," he said in a low growl, his arms wrapped around her waist.

Water played over his thick forearms, running in erratic rivulets over his taut muscles.

He was wearing only a towel, the same white towel he'd worn last night, and her bottom was cradled against the heaviness of his sex. Her heart skipped a beat before accelerating into a gallop.

Without thinking of the consequences, she turned in his arms and boldly lifted her face toward his. "Don't push me away," she pleaded. "Not this time."

Pain contorted his face for an instant, and then his mouth came down on hers.

Casey responded eagerly, knowing that this was all she would ever have of the man she loved. Her mouth opened under his, and he took what she offered, his tongue seeking hers. She met each bold thrust with equal boldness, loving the taste and the feel of him.

Water pounded her back and drained down her body to pool under their feet. She pressed closer, stumbling slightly under the heavy spray. Alex lifted her and swung around, shielding her from the icy water with his broad back.

His face was a tortured mask as he gazed down at her. "I thought I could forget you," he whispered in a strangled voice. "I tried. Every damn day for six years, I tried. But I can't get you out of my head."

Her hand shook as she reached up to brush the thick wet strands of glossy black hair away from his furrowed brow. His hand trapped hers against his cheek, and he turned to kiss the pulse that was throbbing in her wrist. His other hand slid up to cup her breast, and the nipple, already puckered by the cold, hardened even more.

She reached for him, her hands sliding over his sculpted chest, her palms slowly massaging the hair-roughened plane.

"Mi Casey," he whispered, giving her name a Latin pronunciation that brought a lump to her throat. How she'd missed that special lilt in his deep voice.

He moved his hand to her cheek, and it shook as he caressed her with just the tips of his fingers, as though he was afraid of his own need. Casey closed her eyes, savoring the touch that she had longed for without being able to admit it, even to herself.

"*Mi mujer.* My woman." This time his voice was demanding, and she smiled inside. The Alex she loved took. He never asked.

His hands slid down her body until they reached the flare of her hips. His fingers spread, but instead of pulling her against him as she expected, his hand stilled.

She held her breath, waiting. His breathing was erratic, out of control, and beads of sweat shone like teardrops on his copper skin. The need was alive in his eyes, she could see it. Why was he hesitating?

Suddenly he removed his hand and turned off the water. He kissed her hard, then opened the shower door and pulled a towel from the rack.

Slowly he wiped the water from her body, warming her face, her neck, her shoulders, with his breath, his kiss. By the time his mouth reached her breasts she was tingling all over.

Eagerly she smiled at him, all the love she felt shining in her eyes. "I've never forgotten, either," she murmured, her voice tremulous. "Not ever. Not even with..." She faltered, then stopped, and she bit her lip.

An expression of leashed violence tightened his face as his gaze raked her dripping body. "With whom, Casey? Who are you comparing me to?" He didn't move, but she could feel the fierce tension running through his body.

"Alex, I didn't love him," she cried softly, her hands curling into fists against his chest. Not like I loved you, she added silently.

His hands removed hers from his body and pushed her away. She stumbled over the rug but managed to keep from falling.

"What you do or don't feel about Con or anyone else has nothing to do with me. I gave up the right to care a long time ago." His brows were drawn as he tried to regain control.

Not this time, she pleaded silently, holding the towel in front of her, her hands shaking. I won't let you shut me out.

"But I want you to care. Because I care. About you. I fell in love with you all over again. Can that be so wrong?"

Alex gripped the edge of the sink and struggled against the need to pull her into his arms again. Because he wanted her love so damn much, he'd come so close to losing control.

"Don't love me, Casey," he ordered harshly. "I'll only hurt you, the...the way I hurt you before. There are things about me, things I've...done, that you don't know."

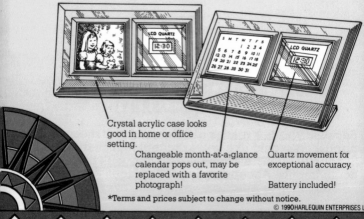

WE EVEN PROVIDE FREE POSTAGE!

It costs you *nothing* to send for your free books — we've paid the postage on the attached reply card. And we'll pick up the postage on your shipment of free books and gifts!

Business Reply Mail

No Postage Stamp
Necessary if Mailed
in Canada

Postage will be paid by

Silhouette Reader Service ™

P.O. Box 609
Fort Erie, Ontario
L2A 9Z9

Canada Post
Postes Canada
125

She clutched the towel more closely around her. "What things, Alex? Why can't you tell me?"

He clenched his teeth against the thought. "Because I can't. It's enough that I know."

"Alex, what *happened*? Why are you doing penance in this place?"

Penance, he thought bitterly. If only it were possible. But there wasn't a priest alive who could absolve him.

He raised his gaze and found her staring at him, her face pale, her eyes filled with confusion. A black heaviness filled him. She deserved the truth, as much of it as he could bear to tell her.

He cleared the thickness from his throat. "One morning I woke up and discovered that I'd become the kind of man I'd always hated. A man like . . . like your buddy, Deshler. Ruthless, consumed with winning at all costs. A shark. I couldn't face myself."

Casey went very still. "Or me?"

She watched the lines around his eyes deepen as he winced. For an instant his guard dropped, and naked pain shone in his eyes. "Or you."

"And that's why you left?"

He hesitated, then nodded. "Yes."

"There never was another woman, was there?" Casey asked softly.

Slowly he shook his head. "Not in the way you think." His voice was rough.

"But something happened in L.A., something that made you . . . hate yourself?" She was feeling her way, putting the pieces together as she spoke.

He raised his gaze and looked at her, his face lined, as though with grief. "Yes, something happened."

"Will you tell me what it was?"

Slowly he raised his hand and touched her cheek, his fingers lingering, as though he couldn't bear to let her go. "No," he said, his voice nearly inaudible. "I'll never tell you." His hand dropped away.

Her eyes filled with tears. He sounded so tortured. So bereft. She had to try one more time to reach him. They'd had so much. . . .

"I love you. Please let me help—"

He stopped her with a finger against her mouth, and her lips began to tremble. He removed his hand and closed it into a fist.

"Don't, Casey." His voice sounded as though a part of him were being rubbed raw. "You'll only hate yourself for saying these things. Because I can't...I won't love you in return. Whatever we had is over."

"But I won't accept that!" she cried. "I know you want me."

"Accept it. I have," he said with a cold finality that finally penetrated the lingering haze of desire surrounding her. "I'll help you fight Deshler, and then I'll come back here where I belong. And no matter what, I'll never see you again."

His deep voice slashed at her heart. All her life she'd taken risks. It was part of her nature to fight for what she wanted. And she'd been so sure that if she stripped away the pretense and the hurt, if she bared her soul, Alex would do the same.

And, obviously, he had. It wasn't his fault that he couldn't love her.

"Thank you for being so honest with me," she said with as much dignity as she could manage. Bending, she retrieved his robe from the floor and slipped into it. Moving very carefully, she stepped backward toward the door.

The light from above threw his face into shadow, and for an instant she thought she saw tears glistening on his thick black lashes, but that was just another illusion.

"I'll be ready to go when you are." She turned and walked out.

Alex turned slowly, feeling as old and barren as the land outside. He stared at the dark face of the man in the mirror. All these years he'd worked hard to change. He'd thought he *had* changed. That he'd become a better man. A man he could respect.

Yeah, you're one hell of a man, he thought bitterly. With a vicious guttural cry, Alex lifted his hand and smashed his palm against the mirror.

Chapter 9

"And the weather in Cincinnati at four-thirty, eastern daylight time, is eighty-nine degrees..."

The amplified voice of the flight attendant droned on, but Alex shut it out. In forty minutes they would land, and the fight for Summerville Foundry would begin. The fight that he had to win, no matter what.

But God help him, what happened if he failed? he thought. How could he live with himself if Casey were locked away in a cell for something that she hadn't done? Wouldn't even think of doing? While he, who'd done far worse things, went unpunished—by man's law, anyway.

Alex shifted restlessly in his seat, trying to ease the tenseness in his tired body.

Casey was seated next to him, her shoulder resting against the plane's bulkhead, her hands wrapped around her third glass of wine. She hated flying. In the past, when they'd flown together, it had been in the company Jetstar, fitted out with all the comforts of a private home, and because she'd trusted him, she'd been able to relax. He'd taken that trust for granted—along with her belief in him.

Alex rested his head against the seat back and watched her through half-closed eyes. The New Mexico sun had touched her skin with color, and there was a smattering of freckles over the bridge of her nose, making her look deceptively fragile.

His jaw clenched, and his eyes closed. He was so damn tired.

At the Albuquerque airport, because he was too big to fit comfortably in the smaller seats in the rear compartment, he'd exchanged their economy tickets for seats in first class. He and Casey were alone in the forward compartment except for one other couple.

Seated directly across the aisle, they were young and obviously in love. From the moment the plane had left the ground he'd been touching her, whispering to her, touching her again. And she kept holding up her hand and gazing at the shiny gold band on the third finger.

Honeymooners, Alex thought, hearing the man whisper something that elicited a throaty giggle from his bride.

Something hard and cold turned over inside him, and he opened his eyes and tried to concentrate on the papers in front of him, but the figures blurred. He took off his glasses and rubbed his eyes.

"Tell me more about this guy Bennett Jameson," he said evenly, watching Casey's hand tighten around her glass of wine.

Casey's gaze flickered to Alex's face, then dropped to the clumsy white bandage on his left hand. She'd heard the sound of shattering glass and seen the bloody remnants of the mirror in the sink. Before they'd left, she'd offered to redo the awkward gauze wrapping, but he'd curtly refused her help.

After that, they'd spoken very little. Since they'd dropped Butch off at John's place early this morning, their conversation had revolved around business.

On the ride to Albuquerque, Alex had begun to withdraw from her, shutting her out more and more with every mile they traveled. It was as though he'd gone inside himself, making himself ready to face the battle. Now he was like a remote stranger—or, she realized, like the man in the photograph. Compelling, frightening and totally beyond reach.

Rousing herself, she forced herself to focus on his question. "I hate to use the term, but boy genius comes closest to describing Ben," she said slowly, picturing the young scientist's thin face and pale features. "He's a brilliant metallurgist and a whiz at computers. There isn't anything he can't do if he puts his mind to it." Her voice faded as a movement across the aisle caught her eye.

A blond young man was kissing the neck of the tiny brown-haired woman next to him, and she was responding enthusiastically, so enthusiastically her skirt was halfway up her thigh. Casey averted her gaze and took another sip of wine. Her hand inched down her own skirt to the hem, and she gave it a surreptitious tug.

"Sounds like it was quite a coup for the foundry when you hired him."

"It was," Casey said, with a humorless smile. "NASA went crazy over his lightweight alloy, and once the word got out, we had more orders than we could handle."

Across the aisle the woman rubbed the man's hand with her cheek, her big dark eyes shining with love. Casey took another sip of wine.

"You did a hell of a job," Alex told her, and he meant it. He'd seen the figures and understood all too well how high the odds had been stacked against her. If she won this proxy fight, she'd be able to write her own ticket.

A pleased smile drifted across her face. For the first time since she had walked out on him in the bathroom, she looked comfortable in his presence. "We did, didn't we."

Across the aisle the man nuzzled the woman's white neck, and she giggled, then sighed as his mouth moved up to her jaw. Small feminine sighs of pleasure rose over the drone of the engines, filling the small space.

Casey licked her dry lips, then took another quick sip. She really hated flying. "If...if Ben's latest experiment works out, we could double our business in five years. The plant manager and I have even talked about adding a third shift. And next year there will be money for a day-care center and an expanded benefits program. If Con wins, none of that will happen."

Alex stared down at his bandaged hand. Slowly, wincing inwardly at the pain, he closed his hand into a fist. Con was going to pay, one way or another, for putting Casey through this hell. But that had to come later. Right now he had to use his wits instead of his fists.

He closed the folder in front of him and picked up his pen. "Once we blunt Con's blackmail threat, Bennett Jameson becomes the pivotal player in this game," he told Casey matter-of-factly, drawing her startled gaze.

It was obvious that she'd been thinking of something else. Or someone. Con, maybe? How long had it been since they were together? he wondered, then immediately blocked out the thought.

"I would have thought Mrs. Eiler would be." Casey's gaze darted past his shoulder, then returned immediately to his face. "Because . . . because she's the majority stockholder."

Across the aisle the man was running his hand up the woman's leg, and she was kissing his jaw. Alex felt his own jaw clench, and he forced himself to relax. The next time he flew, he was going to commandeer the Jetstar. Hell, he'd bought it to use.

"She's pretty much committed, you said. And if Jameson stands firm with you, he could swing a lot of votes your way. After all, without your boy genius's research, Con will be getting a one-product company."

Alex heard a muffled sigh, the faint sibilance of a kiss, the sounds of two people enjoying each other. He shifted his position. These damn seats weren't much better than the economy model.

"Bottom line here is money," he continued, propping one booted foot against the seat in front. "We have to convince the shareholders to opt for long-term gains versus a one-time windfall generated by the sale of their stock to Deshler Enterprises."

"How do we do that?" From the corner of her eye, Casey saw the man across the aisle bend his head to kiss the bare skin exposed by the woman's frilly low-cut blouse.

"First of all, I want you to sell me one share of stock. And then I want you to agree to take out a loan, contingent on conditions that I'll dictate, encumbering the foundry with debt."

The woman giggled again and threaded her hands into the man's wavy blond hair. He groaned, and his hand moved dangerously close to her breast.

Casey cleared her throat. "A poison pill?" she asked tautly.

"Exactly. No company, no matter how profitable, is ripe for takeover if the debt to asset ratio is too high."

Alex heard the man whisper a very intimate suggestion to his new wife, and his palms began to sweat. "In . . . this case," he continued, "I doubt that Deshler will be deterred, but it couldn't hurt."

Another suggestion. Another sigh. A kiss.

Casey watched Alex's fingers tighten around his pen. "Where will we get the loan from?"

The sighs from across the aisle grew louder, more heated. Alex's knuckles grew whiter. "From me."

"But—"

The woman moaned softly, and Casey broke off to take a quick sip of wine. The rim of the glass was smooth against her tongue.

Alex scowled. "Evan's already drawing up the papers." He ran his hand down the side of his thigh.

Casey risked a quick glance toward the young couple. They were completely absorbed, her small body pressed against the seat by his larger one. They were so young. So much in love.

Nervously she averted her gaze, watching the clouds streak past the window. The plane was descending. In a matter of minutes she would once more be the cool and efficient Ms. Casey O'Neill. But for some reason the thought of returning to the world she loved wasn't as appealing as it should have been.

The plane was nearly two hours late, and the passengers milling around the luggage carousel were vocal in their complaints. By the time Alex had retrieved his luggage, Casey had a pounding headache, and the wine she'd had instead of lunch was churning in her empty stomach.

"Ready?" Alex slung his garment bag over his shoulder and picked up his other bag, along with a large canvas tote containing the things Casey had bought during her stay.

"I was ready hours ago," she retorted, her hastily erected defenses strained to the limit after four hours in the air.

"Let's go, then. You know this place. Get us out of here."

He pulled his Stetson low over his brows and scanned the crowded causeway. His face, tanned even darker by the hot Southwestern sun, carried that same look of stony remoteness that had greeted her over the breakfast table.

In his worn jeans and faded Western shirt he looked more like a Spanish vaquero than a corporate executive. Until a person looked into his eyes. They were cold and piercing, like a tempered blade that she'd aimed at Conrad Deshler.

This was the hard-charging man she'd married, the fighter she'd gone to find. She'd seen this man quiet a room of a thousand angry stockholders with just a look. And she'd seen him bend them to his will just as easily.

You should be pleased, she told herself impatiently, as she sidestepped a mother and two chattering toddlers. This was the man she needed. But a part of her missed the brooding schoolteacher whose best friend was a mangy old cat with one eye and a tattered ear.

Casey switched her heavy briefcase to her right hand so that she could see her watch. It was five-fifteen, right in the middle of rush hour. The traffic on the bridge taking them from the airport in Covington across the Ohio River into Cincinnati would be a nightmare.

"This way. I know a shortcut." She set a fast pace that Alex's long legs matched easily.

The door to the outside concourse slid open, and the hot, humid air rose from the pavement to hit her like a wet towel. On the access strip, arriving and departing passengers bustled around double-parked cars, competing for harried-looking redcaps.

In the right lane of the ramp, a long line of yellow cabs snaked slowly forward to the taxi stand, where impatient travelers stood in a ragged line, waiting. Near the crosswalk a black stretch limousine waited, a burly uniformed chauffeur standing at attention next to the rear fender.

The air smelled of exhaust fumes and dust. Wrinkling her nose in disgust, Casey thought of the clean, crispy sky over the desert. She was going to miss that bright, cloudless blue.

Glancing up at Alex's face, she said, "My car's in the east lot. If we hurry, maybe we can beat most of the traffic."

Alex squinted into the setting sun, then dropped his bag and the canvas satchel. "I'm not going with you."

"*What?*" Casey stared at him, her eyes widening with surprise. "You promised—"

"I'll keep my promise," he said, cutting her off. "But first I have things to do."

The shock constricting her throat eased enough that she could speak. "What things?"

Alex's grim mouth softened slightly. "For one thing, I have to get a haircut." He removed his hat and combed the flatness out of his long hair. "And then I have to get some new clothes. I'm not up on the latest 'power' ties, but Evan is."

"Evan?"

"I asked him to meet me here. We have a lot of work to do before we're ready for Con and his boys."

Casey glanced over Alex's wide shoulder, searching the area for his friend. The rear door of the limo was now standing open. Evan Michaels leaned against the fender where the chauffeur had stood, his copper hair gleaming in the sun, his craggy Irish face uncharacteristically somber.

As her gaze met his, the attorney raised a hand in greeting and grinned. She smiled and waved back, but her stomach was lurching as though she'd just stepped on a fast down elevator.

"You've been busy," she said.

"Not as busy as I'm going to be." Alex replaced his hat, giving it an extra tug, then rolled his sleeves one more turn, exposing two more inches of tanned forearm. The grimness that seemed permanently implanted on his rugged features seemed more pronounced than ever.

Here was the chairman of the board of Towers Industries. Coldly efficient, focused unerringly on his goal, the man who'd never lost a takeover bid.

Casey fought down a sudden pang of loneliness. "When . . . when will you arrive in Summerville?"

For an instant his face changed, and the man who'd held the cat so gently in his lap this morning on the way to John's smiled at her. "As soon as I can. I promise."

"I . . . good." She cleared the thickness from her throat. "We don't have much time."

A stiff smile hardened the corners of his mouth. "We never did."

He picked up his suitcase and walked away from her. In spite of the turmoil inside her, Casey couldn't help noticing the purposeful set of his wide shoulders and the long lines of solid muscle beneath the tight jeans.

Brown dirt from the desert floor clung to his tan suede boots, and the heels were worn down at the back and scuffed. She had a feeling that he'd walked weary, punishing miles in those boots. But what were the demons that had been driving him?

After three days, she still didn't know. And now she couldn't afford to care. Once she was home, sleeping in her own bed and surrounded by her own things, she would be able to put the past few days out of her mind.

She started to turn away, then stopped herself and swung back in time to see Alex and Evan shake hands. Alex said something in an abrupt voice, and the shorter man nodded, then stepped back to let Alex enter the back seat. Alex pulled off his Stetson and tossed it onto the seat, then started to follow.

"Alex!" At her shout, he straightened and looked over his shoulder. "Don't let them cut your hair too short. Butch won't let you in the house if you do."

He looked startled, and then his face relaxed into a slashing grin that made her go warm inside. She grinned back, and for an instant the magic that had first bound them together sparked between them.

Then his face changed. Once more he was the deadly weapon that she'd wanted. He climbed into the car, and Evan followed, closing the door behind him.

Casey shaded her eyes and watched the limo pull smoothly into the line of traffic. A feeling of déjà vu assaulted her, and she remembered that long-ago morning when he'd gone off to Los Angeles in triumph to wrap up the Chandler deal.

That had been the last time she'd heard him laugh. Really laugh.

"Be careful," she'd told him that foggy winter morning, thinking of the flight. "I couldn't stand it if something happened to you."

He'd kissed her then. "As long as you love me, nothing bad can ever happen. You're my beautiful talisman."

Tears flooded her eyes, blurring the crowded street in front of her. She had loved him then. She loved him now.

Suddenly she was very frightened.

Alex settled into the plush interior of the Cadillac and tried to relax. His lower back ached with fatigue, and his gut was hard with tension. He'd had too little sleep and too much caffeine, and his nerves were raw.

"I see Casey hasn't changed," Evan said with wry amusement, watching her through the rear window.

"No." Alex stared fixedly at the glass partition behind the chauffeur's head. He hated the thought of leaving her to face Deshler alone, but at the moment, he didn't have a choice. Right now his priority was Evan and the things his friend had dug up.

"Looks great, too," Evan muttered, eyeing the slim ankles under the denim ruffle. "Terrific legs."

A muscle along Alex's left forearm jerked wildly as the bandaged hand resting on his thigh balled into a fist. "Touch her and I'll break your neck." His voice was deadly quiet, like the hiss of blade before it severed the neck of an enemy.

Evan stiffened. "Back off, Alex. This is me, Evan. I was your best man, remember? The guy who saw how anxious you were to have her."

"Things change. I got tired of being married."

"If you say so."

Alex pushed his boots against the plush carpeting and tried not to remember the way Casey had felt in his arms just a few hours ago.

He stared down at his hand. Slowly he flexed his fingers, causing the cut on the heel to throb. Fresh blood seeped through the gauze. The cut wasn't long, but it had gone to the bone.

Evan noticed the blood, too. "Did you win or lose?" he asked with a chuckle.

"I lost."

But maybe when this was all over...

No, he warned himself viciously. There was no way back for him.

"We might as well get started," Alex muttered, leaning back against the soft cushions. For some reason he preferred the hard seat of his Jeep. "Give me what you've got so far."

Evan leaned forward, released the lock on the briefcase resting on the jump seat and opened it. Inside was a stack of file folders in neat piles.

"I talked to the town marshal like you wanted. Casey's place is a mess." He hesitated, then added in a rough tone, "Someone scrawled obscenities all over her bedroom, along with the words, 'Vengeance is mine.'"

Alex swore under his breath. "Deshler?"

"Maybe, but we'll never prove it."

"Go on."

Evan regarded Alex warily. "You're not going to like it."

"Okay, give it to me. All of it."

Evan reached into the case and extracted a red folder. Quickly he riffled through the pages inside until he found the one he wanted. "This is the preliminary report on Jeffrey Plunkett, the accountant who's accusing Casey of having insider information."

"Anything we can use?"

"Not much. In a nutshell, the man's a wimp, but paradoxically, the weakness that makes our investigator certain he wouldn't break into a woman's house will make him a superb witness."

Alex sighed. "Cut to the chase."

Evan handed Alex a grainy picture of a serious-looking young man standing with his arm around a frail-looking woman in a plain blue dress. He was holding an adorable blond toddler in his arms.

"Nice-looking all-American guy."

Casey should have a little girl like that, Alex thought sadly, with silky gold curls and big gray eyes. She would have been a terrific mother.

That was another mistake he'd made. He should have given her the child she wanted. His child. A hard knot formed in his gut, reminding him of all he'd lost. Silently he handed the photograph to his friend, and Evan returned it to the folder.

"See the problem?" Evan said in a gritty tone. "On the surface Plunkett is a straight arrow. There isn't a jury anywhere in Ohio who wouldn't love him."

A jagged star of light exploded in front of Alex's eyes, and a sharp pain stabbed into his right temple. Leaning his head back against the slick leather, he tried to will away the headache he knew was coming. He couldn't afford to lose his concentration.

"So what's the key to this guy?"

"That's just it, Alex. Plunkett once worked for Deshler in his components company in South Carolina, but he resigned to take the job in Summerville, his hometown. His references were satisfactory. Not great, but not bad."

"His bank account?"

"Modest. As well as his savings. He's working for a local bank now, in the new-accounts department. There've been no complaints. None that we know of, anyway."

Alex inhaled sharply, fighting the nausea. The sunlight filtering through the tinted windows were nearly unbearable. He reached for the edge of the seat and held on.

"Any unexplained trips out of town? Any strangers visiting?"

Evan frowned, then flipped open the folder again. "Let me see..." He scanned the unemotional lines neatly typed under the letterhead of the best detective agency in Manhattan.

"Three months ago he took his family to visit his wife's parents in Cleveland for a week. Apparently he goes every year." He closed the folder. "Nothing else."

Alex nodded, then winced at the slicing pain even that small movement caused. The drone of the tires on the pavement was like a needle piercing his brain, making it hard to think.

"Tell the agency to put more people on it. By this time next week I want to know everything about this man, right down to his shoe size and his daughter's blood type. Something in that homogenized life is phony. Before I go to the wall with Deshler, I have to know what it is."

Evan pulled out a small leather-bound notebook and a gold pen and began making notes.

Alex rested his head against the seat and closed his eyes. Casey's hands had been so cool. And her soft voice had been so sweet, easing some of the soul-deep pain that was with him day and night. He stifled a sigh and tried not to think about the look on Casey's face when he'd told her that he couldn't love her.

Por Dios! he thought. She would never know how much he needed her.

The sky was purple and the streetlight in front of her house was glowing when Casey pulled into the short gravel driveway and parked in her usual spot near the side porch.

Because she was wrung out from the plane trip and exhausted from the drive home, it took her a minute to realize that a man in an unfamiliar khaki uniform was standing to one side of her favorite lilac bush, his hand on the butt of his holstered gun.

"What now?" she muttered, reaching for her things. Before she could open the car door, he was doing it for her.

"Ms. O'Neill?" he asked in a polite Kentucky drawl.

"Yes, I'm Casey O'Neill. Who are you?" She had to crane her neck to meet his cool blue gaze. In earlier times this man, with his stringy body and hawklike features, might have been a companion of Daniel Boone.

"Francis Newton, ma'am. I'm with TriCounty Security." He didn't actually tip his hat, but Casey had the feeling he wanted to.

She waited, but apparently the man thought he had explained sufficiently. "Mr. Newton, what exactly are you doing in front of my house?"

He straightened, as though preparing for inspection. "Guarding it, ma'am."

Casey blinked. In the semidarkness her Victorian three-story, with its twin spires and lacework trim, looked like a storybook gingerbread cottage. How could anything hurt her there? She fought down a smile.

"I'm afraid I don't understand. Marshal Rickert told my secretary that there was no danger."

"Yes, ma'am, and I aim to keep it that way."

Casey blinked in impatience. "On whose orders?"

It was the guard's turn to blink. "Mr. Michaels of Towers Industries, ma'am. My orders are to, uh, stick with you like glue."

"You'll do nothing of the kind," she said sharply. "I don't need a bodyguard."

This was Alex's doing, she realized. In spite of his self-imposed exile, he was still the major stockholder of the company he used to rule. And in every way that counted, Evan was still his executive assistant.

"Sorry, ma'am. I have my orders." The guard was eyeing her warily, his eyes a shade cooler. No matter what she said to him, she had a feeling the man wasn't going to leave.

"Wait here. I'll have Mr. Michaels rescind those orders."

The man watched silently as she retrieved her tote from the trunk of her vintage Mercedes. Before she could sling it over her shoulder, however, he took it from her, his large bony hand hefting it easily.

Her frustration mounted, but the look on his homely face told her that further argument would be useless. He had been hired to do a job, and he intended to do it, no matter what she wanted.

"This way, please," she muttered, following the narrow sidewalk around the house to the front steps. He walked one precise pace behind her, his eyes alertly sweeping the wrap-around porch.

I feel like an intruder in my own house, she grumbled silently, fishing her keys from her purse. Always before, the scarlet paint on the entry door had seemed welcoming and gay, but tonight it looked like blood.

Lord, she thought, I've got to get a grip here, before I lose it completely.

Casey opened the door and slipped inside, the guard still only one step behind. Inside, the air was hot and smelled musty. She snapped on a light, her eyes narrowing against the sudden glare.

The small foyer was exactly as she'd left it, with one exception. The giant marigolds in a crystal vase on the small rosewood table were drooping and dead.

Ignoring the brown blossoms and withered leaves, she hurried down the narrow hall to her den. Newton followed, his heels clicking on the polished parquet floor.

In the den Casey snapped on the light and went directly to the phone. The red light on the answering machine blinked monotonously, but she ignored its signal. She would listen to her messages later.

She had punched out half the numbers of the Towers corporate office when she remembered that Evan wouldn't be there.

No matter, she decided. If Alex's organization was functioning in its usual highly efficient manner, Evan could be reached in seconds if necessary. And this was certainly necessary.

"Towers Industries, security."

The crusty voice was achingly familiar, and for an instant, Casey couldn't speak. "Mr. MacGregor? Is that you?"

"Yes, ma'am. May I help you?"

"Angus, this is Casey... Torres."

There was a brief pause. "Mrs. Torres! It's mighty nice to hear your voice again. How're you doing these days?"

"Fine, and you?" Her heart was pounding painfully as the commonplace words rolled over the line. She'd adored the middle-aged night guard whose bull-like exterior concealed a sentimental soul. And now she realized just how much she'd missed hearing his gruff voice.

"Mighty fine," he said with a chuckle. "I... uh, well, I was real sorry to hear about your divorce."

"Thank you." She cleared her throat. "I need your help, Angus. I need to speak with my . . . with Mr. Torres. He's with Mr. Michaels. Would you give me his local number, please?"

There was another pause. "I can't do that, Mrs. Torres. None of us guards is allowed to give out information like that over the phone. You know, because of security and all."

Casey sighed. She knew, all right. Corporate espionage was almost as much of a problem as international spying, especially in a company like Alex's, where the subsidiaries held numerous contracts with the Department of Defense.

"Will you have him call me, then? It's urgent." She recited her number slowly.

"Will do, Mrs. Torres."

"Thank you. I . . . it was nice talking with you, Angus."

"You too, ma'am. This place sure ain't the same without you and Mr. Torres around." He hesitated. "But maybe all that's changing?"

Casey heard the question in his voice and smiled sadly. "I'm afraid not. Nothing has changed. Nothing at all."

They said goodbye, and Casey hung up. She glanced up to find the guard watching her from the doorway, the canvas tote still dangling from his hand.

"Just put the bag on that chair there." She pointed toward the small recliner that was the only modern piece in the pastel-and-white room.

"Yes, ma'am." The guard did as he was told, then returned to the doorway, where he stood silently, his arms crossed over his chest, his long, thin face impassive.

As she waited, Casey surveyed the familiar room, her eyes lingering reflectively on each carefully selected piece. She'd spent hours finding period pieces to go with the ornate 1880s interior, and when the room had been finished, she'd pronounced it perfect.

But now, strangely, the expensive antiques and chintz upholstery seemed fussy and overdone. Worse still, the heavy velvet curtains seemed garish and suffocating.

An image of the clean lines of Alex's stone house popped into her mind. Sadness filled her as she realized that she would never again feel the security of those clean Spartan walls. Nor would she be able to stand at the window and gaze out at the wild country that she was beginning to love. And as for that crazy old cat . . .

She felt a melancholy smile tug at her lips. Butch had actually purred this morning when she'd given him his pill. And he'd licked her nose when she'd bent down to say goodbye at John's place.

Goodbye, you rotten creature, she told him silently. Take care of yourself and . . . your friend, Alejandro. He needs you.

Blinking hard, she took a deep breath, then spun around to face the wary guard. "Would you like some coffee, Mr. Newton? I'm going to make a pot."

His expression brightened. "I'd purely love some, ma'am, if it ain't . . . isn't too much trouble."

"No trouble at—"

The ringing of the phone interrupted her, and she smiled an apology as she lifted the receiver.

"Casey O'Neill."

"What's wrong?" It was Alex. Over the phone the slight Latin flavor accenting his deep voice seemed more pronounced. Depression filled her as she realized how much she loved the fluid sound of those slurred Latin vowels.

"You know what's wrong." She swallowed the lump that was thinning her voice. "I don't need a guard, Alex, so I'd appreciate it very much if you or Evan would ask him to leave. Nicely, of course, and with full pay."

She heard him sigh. "Your place was ransacked, remember? The guy could come back."

"Marshal Rickert believes the person was a transient."

"And if he wasn't? Then what?" Alex sounded harried, as though he were barely hanging on to his patience.

"I'll manage. I'm not helpless, you know."

"Casey, I'm dead tired, and I don't have a lot of patience left. Let the guard do his job, and we'll talk about it when I get there."

Casey thought about the look in his eyes that morning in the bathroom. For an instant, before she'd turned and walked away, he'd looked like a man at the end of his endurance.

She closed her eyes, fighting an urgent need to tell him how much his coming here meant to her; he didn't want her gratitude. She'd asked him to pay whatever debt he felt he owed her, and that was what he was doing. Nothing more.

Nervously she wound the phone cord around her finger. "I realize that your intentions are good," she said carefully, "but if I showed up at the office with a . . . a bodyguard, my employees would think I didn't trust them. That I thought some-one here might be trying to hurt me. They would feel betrayed, Alex. I can't do that to people who are my friends."

"It's possible one of your 'friends' has been leaking infor-mation to Con." He went on to explain.

"I don't believe it."

"Casey—"

"Alex, even if that's true, a bodyguard just might alienate some of those people who plan to vote for me. You said every vote counts."

There was a lengthy silence. For some strange reason she had a feeling he was rubbing his closed eyes, just as she'd seen him do countless times in the past when he was trying to make a difficult decision.

"Okay, point taken. But before I give you what you want, I want something from you."

"What's your price?" she asked sharply, too tired to care how she sounded. She craved a cup of coffee, a hot bath and twelve hours of uninterrupted sleep in her own bed.

"Your promise that if you even suspect there might be something wrong at your place or at the office, you'll call the marshal." His voice had the ring of iron on steel, and Casey knew that he wouldn't give up until he got what he wanted.

"I promise."

There was a slight pause. "Casey, I did this for your own good. I . . . don't want anything to happen to you."

She stared helplessly at the darkness outside the window, tears pressing her throat. He sounded raw, as though he was hurting as much as she was.

But that was an illusion.

This morning she'd come close to begging for his love. If he'd loved her, he would have told her so then. And if he'd wanted her, he would have taken her that moment in the shower when the passion between them had flared out of control. He'd done it many times before when they'd been married.

But she'd felt the desire leave his body, just as she'd seen the fire fade from his eyes. He didn't love her, and he didn't want her. It was well and truly over between them. She had to get used to that. Again.

"Here's Mr. Newton," she muttered, her voice shaking. Si-lently she held out the receiver, and after a moment's pause the lanky guard took it.

Casey picked up her bag and hurried up the stairs. At the end of the short hall she came to an abrupt halt, her breath shuddering through her open mouth.

Her room was a shambles. Red paint spattered the walls, the furniture, even her bedspread. All the drawers had been emptied, her things trampled. Silently she read the words gouged into the wallpaper and painted on the mirror.

Vengeance?

Would Con really do such a thing? she asked herself in growing shock. She remembered the cold, brutal look on his face the night she'd given him back his ring.

"Yes," she whispered aloud. "He could do this."

Slowly she turned, listening to the guard's footsteps below in the hall. Should she ask him to stay? She shook her head.

No. The people of this town were kind and decent. She trusted them. Didn't she?

Chapter 10

Three days later Casey was at her desk, working at top speed, when a spry old lady in a rust-colored gabardine suit swept into the office unannounced.

"Cassandra, I am greatly disturbed," she chirped in a reedy voice, her sparrow-brown eyes snapping at Casey over the thin gold rims of her spectacles.

Casey stood quickly and, in her haste, caught her heel on the leg of her chair. She stumbled against the desk, ripping her stocking on the ornate drawer pull. Rats, she swore silently. Nothing had gone right since she'd come home.

Rebecca Williams, Casey's secretary, followed the old woman into the office, her expression harried. "Sorry, Ms. O'Neill," the young woman muttered, her shoulders lifting in a helpless shrug.

"Mrs. Eiler is welcome anytime, Becky." Casey circled her desk to meet Rachel Eiler near the door. The little woman offered her cheek, and Casey stooped to kiss her. The woman's skin was parchment dry and smelled of lemon verbena.

"Tea, Mrs. Eiler?" she asked politely, hoping that Becky hadn't run out of tea bags.

"Tea is for old ladies," the elderly woman muttered testily, her voice as trembly as her hands. "I'll have bourbon, neat."

She tottered on small delicate feet to the chair in front of Casey's desk and sat down, her back arrow-straight, the feather in her old-fashioned pillbox hat quivering. Primly she removed her spotless white gloves and placed them in her handbag.

The woman was reputed to have been a Ziegfeld girl before she married the staid and proper heir to the Eiler fortune, but her manner suggested a woman of the old school, a lady who had very strong ideas about what was proper—and improper.

Casey shot a pleading glance at her secretary, whose features relaxed into a smile.

"Yes, ma'am, bourbon neat." Becky mentioned the two most expensive brands then asked, "Which would you prefer?"

A gleam of admiration sharpened the old woman's eyes even more as she voiced her choice. Casey made a mental note to give Becky a hefty bonus as soon as this mess was over. Young as she might seem to others, at twenty-three Becky was still the best assistant Casey had ever had.

Sneaking a glance at her watch, Casey returned to her desk and sat down. What a shrewd old darling, she thought, watching the measuring glint come into the faded eyes. Thank goodness she's on my side.

Rachel owned thirty-three percent of Summerville's stock, inherited at his death from her husband. Judge Harrison Eiler's family had built and operated the foundry until the first World War, when they'd brought in younger men to modernize the facility for war production. They'd lost controlling interest in the stock-market crash of 1929. Mrs. Eiler was the only remaining member of the family.

"Stop looking at your watch, young lady. Listening to me is the most important thing you have to do today, I promise you that." The feather atop the old lady's head shook even more violently.

Casey felt her cheeks grow warm. "I love listening to you, Mrs. Eiler," she chided in a gentle voice. "You know that."

The older woman acknowledged Casey's warm words with an impatient nod. "I've come for the truth, Cassandra. Did you know about that man Deshler's plans before they happened?"

Casey stared at her. "Of course not! How could I know?"

"Jeffrey said that you two were once...involved, as you young people call it." All of a sudden her tone was surprisingly vigorous.

Casey took an urgent breath. "We were engaged, yes, but that was years ago. I didn't know about his run on the stock until he filed the papers."

The old woman's eyes took on a look of calculation, but before she could speak, Becky walked in.

"Your 'tea,' Mrs. E. I...made it myself, just the way you like it." With a polite smile, she placed a small linen napkin on the desk in front of the birdlike woman, then set a cut-glass tumbler in the middle of the cloth square.

Mrs. Eiler grunted her thanks, reached for the glass and daintily sipped until half the contents were gone.

Becky's lips twitched, but her face remained impassive. "Ms. O'Neill, I've informed Mr. Jameson that you'll be delayed for your two o'clock appointment. He said that he'll be in the lab when you need him."

Casey stifled a sigh of relief. "Thanks, Becky. Please close the door when you leave."

"Of course."

A second later Becky was gone. Casey was alone with the one person on the lengthy list of shareholders whose goodwill she had to keep in order to win.

"Mrs. Eiler, I assure you—" she began, but the old woman cut her off.

"I'm afraid I'm going to need proof, Cassandra. As my Harrison always said, take a man's word, but only after you've seen proof that he keeps it."

Casey picked up her pen and ran it over her palm. "What about Jeff Plunkett? It seems to me that you're taking his word without any proof." There, she thought. The ball's in your court.

The woman blinked but didn't flinch. "I'm Jeffrey's godmother, in case you don't know. I took him to Sunday school when he was a boy and often listened to his prayers at night." Mrs. Eiler brushed impatiently at a wisp of thin white hair feathering across her cheek. "What reason would he have to lie?"

Casey fought down a surge of fear. A week ago she would have staked all she owned on this woman's loyalty. Damn Con, she thought, her heart pounding.

"Maybe, for some reason I can't imagine, Jeff thinks that it's true, but he is mistaken." Her voice shook, and she took a moment to compose herself.

Mrs. Eiler took another swallow of her drink, then pinned Casey with her bright gaze. "You're a brave woman, Cassandra. I admire that in you. Harrison always said that a coward turns away from the battle that can't be won, but a brave man chooses to fight. You're fighting, and that's good."

She raised the tumbler to her lips and drained it, then put it on the desk with a loud thump. Her tiny hands seemed terribly frail as she wiped her lips with the napkin, then clutched it in her lap.

"Prove your innocence and you will have my proxy." Casey started to smile, but Mrs. Eiler waved a warning hand. "But I won't have Jeffrey hurt. If you attempted to discredit him in order to make yourself look good, I would take that as a personal insult. And much as I would hate it, I would side with that dreadful Deshler person. Whatever you do, you must have proof. Do I make myself clear?"

Casey forced a smile. "Perfectly."

"Good." Removing her gloves from her purse, Mrs. Eiler pulled them on, then rose slowly, using the arms of the chair to steady herself.

Casey hurried to help her, but the older woman waved her off. "You're busy, dear. That youngest Williams girl will help me down to the automobile."

Once again she presented her cheek, and Casey bent to kiss her. Mrs. Eiler turned to go, then seemed to think better of it. Turning back slowly, she raised her gloved hand and gently patted Casey's cheek. "You're so pretty, my dear, and bright as a new dime. But your eyes are so sad."

The quavering voice was filled with sympathy, and Casey felt her defenses sway. Sad? she wondered. Is that how I feel? For three days she'd tried to feel nothing at all, so she wasn't sure.

"I'm just . . . tired," Casey told her. "But thank you for caring."

Rachel waved aside her thanks. "Nonsense. I know what sadness looks like. I see it in my own eyes even now, after fifteen years alone." Her eyes took on a soft sheen, as though she were thinking of her late husband. After a moment's silence she roused herself to ask softly, "Is he dead, your man?"

Casey shook her head. There was no use pretending to this woman. Behind the doddering facade was a lively intelligence and eighty-some years of experience. "No. We're...divorced."

"Your idea?"

Casey hesitated, then answered uneasily, "No. His."

The watery eyes glinted suddenly. "Neglected him for your career, I suppose, like those modern women I read about in my magazines." She sighed. "I made my Harrison feel like a king from the moment I met him until he was taken from me." Her smile was sadly sweet as she dropped her hand.

For an instant Casey couldn't speak. Could Mrs. Eiler be right? Had she neglected Alex?

He'd said no, but what man would admit to wanting more than his wife was willing to give? Certainly not a man like Alex, who'd had to fight for every scrap of affection he'd gotten from his overburdened parents.

"Don't look so upset, Cassandra. It's not too late. It's never too late, not if you really love him. Go after him. Tell him."

I did, Casey thought, feeling the hurt all over again. It just didn't matter to him.

Casey opened the door for the old lady and followed her into the outer office. Becky was talking on the phone when they entered. She glanced up, a look of concern on her face.

"She's available now, Coop. I'll tell her. Yes, right away. Goodbye." The secretary hung up, then rose from her seat and hurried around the desk, her brows raised as she met Casey's gaze.

"Becky, will you please walk Mrs. Eiler to her car?"

"Certainly. I'll be right with you, Mrs. E." Becky smiled warmly at the old woman before handing Casey a stack of messages.

"A man named Torres asked for you downstairs about fifteen minutes ago," she said in a low voice, "but since there was no one by that name on your appointment list, I told Marie to explain that you were in conference."

Casey's heart began to pound, and her palms started to sweat. So he had come. For the first time she acknowledged the kernel of doubt that had lodged in her subconscious at the airport. A part of her was still very wary of the man who'd abandoned her.

"I'll see him now."

Becky's gaze shifted to Mrs. Eiler's impatient expression, then back to Casey's face. "He must have talked his way past Marie, because Cooper just called from the plant. He says that two men in city suits are watching his crew pour a heat, and he wants to know if they're authorized."

"Don't worry about it. I'll handle it." Casey waited until Becky escorted Mrs. Eiler to the elevator, then returned to her office, grabbed her hard hat and the folder containing her notes for the meeting with Ben, and hurriedly left her office again.

"Casey, wait up!"

Halfway across the gravel yard between the main building and the newer one on the other side, Casey turned to find Ben Jameson running toward her.

Small of stature and painfully thin, with long legs and vulnerable amber eyes, Ben reminded her of the half-grown fawn that had wandered into her backyard last spring to eat every one of her newly planted flowers.

"Are you going to the reception next Friday night?" He sounded out of breath. "If you are, I thought we could go together, sort of like a mutual protection society. I hate parties."

Casey heard the shudder in his voice and reminded herself that Ben, already a college graduate at the age of fifteen, had spent most of his life in a laboratory in one place or another. Socially, he was as awkward as an adolescent. That was part of the reason no other foundry had taken a chance on him.

"I don't mind parties," Casey answered, pushing her yellow hard hat to the back of her head. "It's Deshler I'm not crazy about."

Ben flashed the puckish smile that always startled her. "I hear ya." His grin took on a hard edge. "I applied for an R and D job with Mr. 'C as in Crook' Deshler's foundry when I left MIT. Did you know that?"

Casey frowned. "No, I didn't. What happened?"

"Turned me down flat." He lifted a bony shoulder. "I knew someday, if I was patient, I'd get my revenge."

Casey returned his grin, but inside she felt a vague uneasiness. Ben was a man of many moods, but she'd never heard that hard, biting tone in his voice.

"Ben—"

"Too strong, huh? Okay, I'll tone it down. I get carried away sometimes." He pushed a shock of unruly blond hair away from his forehead. "Let me know. About Deshler's bash I mean."

"I will."

She started walking, and he fell into step beside her. "What were you doing in the main building?" she asked. "Becky said you were in the lab."

"I was, but I got restless and came looking for you."

Casey nodded. "I was just on my way to see you in the lab. But first I have to see to an important visitor."

An image of Alex as she'd last seen him, in scuffed boots and worn jeans, his Stetson pulled low over his brow, flashed into her mind and stayed there.

"So who is this punk who's beating my time?" Ben shoved his hands into the pockets of his baggy cotton slacks and looked at her curiously, his intense eyes reflecting avid curiosity.

"The man I went to see in New Mexico, Alex Torres. He's agreed to help us." Just the sound of his name made her stomach flutter.

Ben shook his head sadly. "What's this world coming to? We're attacked by a big shark, so we go out and get a bigger one to eat up the first one."

He was kidding, but Casey's patience was stretched too thin to answer in kind. "Would you rather work for Conrad Deshler Enterprises?"

Ben blinked, and his expression grew serious. "I know I was outvoted, but I still think it's a dumb idea to set one raider against another. They're all crooks."

"That's not true, Ben."

"Isn't it? After you mentioned his name, I did some research on this dude, Torres. Did you know that he was flying high, grabbing up everything he looked at, and then wham! he dropped out of sight? There were rumors that he'd used strong-arm tactics to steal this little company in California called Chandler Aerospace."

"What rumors? I didn't read anything like that."

"In the *L.A. Times*, for one. Down in a little box in the corner of the back page of the business section, but I know how to do research, remember? The guy who wrote the piece postulated that your *important visitor* went underground to avoid getting nailed with criminal charges."

Casey started to protest, but the words stuck in her throat. Was that it? Was that why Alex had suddenly gone into hiding?

She wanted to deny the very idea, but it made a certain terrible sense. He *was* living with guilt. He'd admitted that much. And he'd refused to tell her what had driven him to make such drastic changes in his life-style and in himself.

Was he a crook? Had the man she loved deliberately and willfully broken the law?

No, she thought. No matter what had been written about him, Alex was not dishonest.

"There's something you should know, Ben. Alex Torres is my ex-husband."

Ben stopped in midstride, forcing Casey to stop, too. "I don't believe it." He looked stunned.

"It's true. We've been divorced for more than five years."

"Good," he said with a smirk. "You're too classy to live with a crook like that."

Casey made herself smile. Dear Ben. He thought he was making her feel better. If only he knew.

"If the schmuck gives you trouble, you just say the word and I'll...I'll punch his lights out." Awkwardly he reached out and punched her shoulder gently with his fist.

Casey was touched by his obvious affection. The conversation on the plane flashed into her mind, and she realized that she had the answer to Alex's question. Ben *was* loyal to her, no matter how quirky he might seem at times.

"Thanks, Ben," she said, letting her gratitude show in her voice. "I'll remember that."

He flushed, but held her gaze, his strange gold eyes warm with admiration. "Anytime, Casey. I owe you, and I always pay my debts."

A memory from the past wavered, then grew stronger. Alex had said something like that just a few days ago. She cleared her throat and focused on Ben's open features.

"Here are the sales and production figures for the last five years, as well as the projections for the next five," she said, handing him the thick folder. "What I need from you is a detailed estimate of the cost to complete your present tests on this new alloy, as well as your best guess, in layman's terms, on its possible uses, especially in the aerospace and medical industries. I want to have this ready to send out to the shareholders by the end of next week.''

As though he'd passed a hand in front of his pale features, Ben's face changed. He no longer looked like a gawky boy but rather a highly dedicated scientist.

He opened the folder and squinted at the handwritten text, his face screwed taut against the sun's glare. "I'll get started on it right now," he said, his voice vibrating with eagerness. "Actually I've been doing some thinking..."

He ambled off toward the laboratory wing of the long flat building, muttering to himself, and Casey fought to contain a laugh.

Talk about a nutty professor, she thought, resuming her quick pace. What would I ever do without him?

The plant, as everyone called it, was the heart of the foundry. Two stories tall, the concrete block structure was as long as a football field and almost as wide. Here were the shops where Ben's designs were translated into patterns, then into working prototypes for testing and, finally, into high-precision parts.

Strategically placed around the perimeter were three state-of-the-art gas-fired cylindrical furnaces, or cupolas, that always reminded Casey of something out of a science fiction movie. Today the crew was using the largest, and noisiest, of the three.

She paused in the doorway, listening to the comforting roar underscore the shouts of the men as they carried large ladles of molten metal from the mouth of the furnace to the tightly packed sand molds arrayed in neat rows on the concrete floor.

Every time she walked onto this floor, she marveled at the difficult combination of brute strength and delicate skill that it took to convert the white-hot liquid into a perfect casting that might someday go to the moon or beyond.

The trick was to fill the cavity inside each mold slowly enough to prevent air bubbles, but not too slowly, or the metal would cool too quickly, becoming brittle.

It hadn't taken her long to figure out that every man on the crew had a purpose, and each was indispensable. It had taken her months to instill that same knowledge in her employees, but once she'd succeeded, absenteeism had dropped to almost nothing, and production had soared.

Pausing at the entrance to the restricted area, she searched the area quickly, but saw only the sweating men of the first shift, their faces black with soot, their eyes hidden behind safety goggles. Roy Cooper was nowhere to be found.

Taking a deep breath, she settled her hard hat over her bangs and waited for the butterflies in her stomach to subside. It's only natural to be nervous, she thought. Now that Alex was here, the fight would begin in earnest. Prebattle jitters, that was what she had. As soon as she faced her fear, the nerves would disappear. The flutters in her stomach increased, as though her body was ignoring her logical rationale.

"Keep it businesslike," she muttered. "One ally to another." That would work. Of course it would work. Wouldn't it?

In spite of the huge air vents blasting down from above, the air swirling around her was stifling and smelled of rust. Her skin quickly grew damp, causing her tailored blouse to stick to her body. Through the damp material her nipples looked like tiny buttons.

She rotated her shoulders, pulling the damp cotton away from her skin, but she was still conscious of the sensation of fullness in her breasts.

Ignore it, she told herself. No one will know but you.

Making a quick about-face, she headed toward the foreman's office tucked into a relatively quiet corner of the huge building. Before she reached the office, however, she spotted the burly Scotsman.

And Alex.

He was with Evan, standing ten yards or so in front of her and slightly to the right. Both men wore the white hard hats reserved for visitors. Alex's had been pulled low over his forehead, like the battered Stetson that had seemed such a part of him, and his thick hair curled over his starched collar. Casey felt her stomach clench. He'd left his hair long, just as she'd asked him to.

Alex shouted a question over the din, and Roy nodded. He pointed toward the furnace and began talking. Alex listened intently, his gaze focused on the ironworker controlling the flow of the metal.

He'd removed the jacket of his tan suit, carrying it carelessly over his arm, and the sleeves of his striped shirt were rolled to his elbows. His collar was open, his muted plaid tie loose. Below the perfect break of his trouser cuffs, his feet, shod in polished cordovan loafers, were spread wide, like a man claiming the land upon which he stood.

He wasn't as tall as the massive foreman, nor as burly, but Casey saw the deference in the larger man's stance and in his face.

A shiver made a quick trip down her spine. In the five years she'd known him, Roy Cooper had never let anyone stay on his floor without proper clearance.

But Alex was still here, and Roy was treating him like an honored guest. She took a deep, slow breath, feeling the hot air singe her lungs.

As she watched, Alex braced his right hand against the steel I-beam supporting the catwalk overhead and ducked his head in order to hear something that Evan was saying. His left hand rested on his hip, and she noticed that a small Band-Aid had replaced the gauze.

Casey felt a lump come to her throat. Somehow she had to forget that she'd ever felt that strong hand caress her body in all the special places that only he knew. Somehow she had to find a way to stop loving him.

But how?

She started forward, a fixed smile on her face. Evan saw her first. He broke off what he was saying to draw Alex's attention to her approach.

Alex's chin came up, and his hand dropped from the steel post. His face was controlled, impassive, as darkly compelling as she remembered. He didn't move. He was making her come to him.

Her hopes sank. It was the right move, the power move, showing her that he was taking charge. It was what she had wanted from him.

A faint noise from the catwalk above startled her, and she started to look up. Before she could find the source of the strange scraping sound, Alex lunged toward her.

His shoulder plowed into her stomach, and she flew backward. Her legs tangled with his, and his arms held her, bruising her ribs as they rolled.

A flash of red streaked by her, followed by a loud crash close enough for her to feel the flying pieces of concrete thrown up by something hitting the floor in a violent collision.

She landed on top of Alex, his arms holding her tightly against him. Her hat and his went spinning across the dirty floor, and her elbow jabbed him in the stomach.

She gasped for breath, sucking in a mouthful of hot, dusty air that hurt her throat. She began to cough.

"Easy," Alex muttered close to her, the concern in his voice nearly overshadowed by the savage anger she saw in his eyes.

Less than five feet away a workman's toolbox nearly four feet long lay in a jumble of tools on a cracked section of concrete. One sharp corner had stopped at the exact spot where she would have been standing if Alex hadn't reacted when he did.

She began to shake. Some of the fury left his face, as though his concern for her now took precedence.

"You're safe now," he whispered hoarsely against her ear. Slowly, still cradling her, he pushed himself to a sitting position. He was breathing hard, and his voice was raspy as he issued orders to the men clustered around the two of them.

Roy took off running. Shouts from someone in the distance blended with the thunderous noise of the furnace. Casey tried to move, but her arms and legs felt numb. Shock, she thought vaguely.

"Don't move, Casey," Evan said from somewhere above. "The foreman went to call the nurse."

"I'm fine," she mumbled. "Just need to rest." She buried her face against Alex's collar and gave in to the tremors shaking her. She would be dead now, if it hadn't been for him.

Vaguely aware of Alex's deep voice whispering to her in Spanish, she tried to quiet her galloping pulse, but she couldn't seem to stop shaking.

Beneath her legs she felt his stomach muscles tighten, and she realized how intimately they were entwined, with her thighs straddling his, and her breasts pressed tightly against his chest.

"That was close," she muttered, clutching his shirt with her fists. At the moment she didn't care who saw them like this. Right now the unflappable Ms. O'Neill was shaking in her designer pumps, and she needed him.

This might be the last time he would hold her, the last time she would feel his strength. Fighting an insistent urge to cry, she snuggled closer, trying to ignore the heat and the dirt and the noise—and the fact that he was only holding her because it was the kind and decent thing to do.

"Casey, sit up," he ordered against her temple, his voice threaded with tension. "The nurse is here."

She raised her head slowly to find Alex's unsmiling mouth an inch away from hers, the corners controlled by two small commas of tension. She lifted her gaze to his eyes, her lashes sweeping up and down, trying to clear her sight. Blacker than black, his eyes were narrowed menacingly, but the deep lines framing those dangerous eyes suggested an unbearable pain.

"Are you hurt?" she asked, her voice shaking uncontrollably. "Alex, are you all right?"

He closed his eyes tightly and pressed his face into her hair. "No, I'm not all right," he muttered, his breath raspy and labored. "You shouldn't be out here, damn it. This is no place for a woman."

She felt a shudder rip through him, and she pressed closer, wanting to hear the words of love and caring that she craved. Now, please, now, she pleaded silently. I almost died. Please tell me that you care.

Slowly she raised her hand and touched the unruly tendrils of damp hair lying against his neck. Her fingers trailed down to rest against the skin under his collar.

Alex muttered something in his mother's language, but this time the harsh, guttural words had a gentle sound.

"What?" she whispered. "Tell me so that I can understand."

Alex gritted his teeth against the violent need to take what she was offering. To tell her what she wanted to know. He'd carried it all alone for so long, the guilt, the self-hatred, the frustration of living his life like a monk, without warmth and comfort and love.

Alex ran his hand down her smooth back, feeling her tremble under his palm. If only she knew how much he wanted her, how much she was torturing him with each breath she took. He wanted to pick her up from this filthy floor, to take her to her bed or his, and to make love to her over and over again, until he was purged of the unbearable guilt that twisted inside him.

But more than that, he wanted some of the peace that she'd always given him. That she still gave him, whenever he dropped his guard enough to let her. But that would be taking what he could never give in return.

Let me go, Casey, he pleaded silently. Don't make me want you.

He made himself relax, made himself drive the thoughts of her from his mind. He had a hard, dirty fight ahead of him. Victory was the one gift he could give her. The only one.

"Case, we'd better get off this floor." He was forced to raise his voice over the din. Her eyes grew wide with hurt, making him wince. He hadn't meant to sound so uncaring, but maybe it was better.

The dazed look in her eyes lifted. Her tongue ran over her lips, leaving a film of moisture behind. Alex swallowed hard and pressed his teeth tightly together. She would taste salty, and her lips would be soft and welcoming. For all her brilliance and drive, Casey was the most feminine woman he knew, and the most giving. Her kiss would be healing. And God, he needed that.

His concentration blurred, and he lost track of the people around them. Of the stench and the heat and the place on his hip that had crashed against the concrete. He couldn't seem to take his eyes away from that soft, sweet mouth.

Casey drew back, her neck arching away stiffly. Her breasts brushed his chest and he held his breath. Deep inside a fire as hot as any blast furnace roared to life, taunting him.

"Of course. You're right," she said, brushing a lock of tawny hair away from her face. "We must look very silly. Thank goodness our more...proper shareholders aren't here to see this." She lifted her chin in that little gesture he remembered so well. Alex felt his gut twist. His lady hated to show when she was hurting.

She pushed against his chest with her small fists, and he let her go. Because he had nothing to give her but her freedom, he would always let her go.

But damn, it hurt like hell.

Alex stood at the window, looking out. The boardroom was air-conditioned, but he was sweating, and his hip ached.

Behind him, seated at the head of the large oval table, Casey was presiding at a hastily called meeting of her senior staff. News of the incident in the plant was already spreading like a virus throughout the foundry, and she'd decided to stop the rumors, at least among management personnel, before things got out of hand.

She was damn good, he thought, taking a sip of the cold coffee in his nearly empty Styrofoam cup. Better than good. She was concise and tactful and very much in charge. He would trust her with one of his companies anytime—if he were making those decisions these days.

He drained his coffee and crushed the cup slowly in his fist. Raider. Shark. Despoiler. He'd been called all of them. Because that was what he'd been.

What he *was*.

I still have it, he thought. The urge to fight. The blood lust, coiling inside him like a poisonous snake, ready to strike.

Alex ground his teeth on the thought. With every day that passed, the need to win was growing stronger. He knew now that it was an integral part of him, the worst part, and he was scared as hell he wouldn't be able to control it.

God, he thought, feeling tension pull tighter around his spine. He hated meetings.

"...and I'm pleased that the shift finished the heat, in spite of the, um, interruption," Casey told the gathering reassuringly.

Casey transferred her full attention to the middle-aged man at the end of the table. Dutch Shrader had been chief of security at Summerville Foundry for thirty years. He was short and stocky, without an ounce of fat on his thick frame, and had never once used the gun that was strapped low around his hip.

"Can you tell us anything about the toolbox, Dutch? Who it belongs to? Why it was there?"

He cleared his throat. "It was there because the cooling unit in that part of the plant is busted. Been busted for a week, in fact. Maintenance started working on it two days ago and..."

Casey appeared to be listening attentively, but from the corner of her eye she intently scanned as much of Alex's face as she could see. During the confusion in the plant he'd taken charge. He'd done it smoothly and diplomatically, and her people had carried out his orders without hesitation.

Alex Torres was now in charge.

But Casey couldn't stop thinking about Alejandro, the man who had built a stone house with his own hands, the man who taught reading and arithmetic and social studies to a bunch of black-haired kids and lived in self-imposed exile.

During their marriage she'd loved Alex, adored his style, admired his brilliance, but she realized now that she hadn't really known him well enough to say that she truly liked him.

But it was clear that most of her staff liked him enormously. Especially the two women, Becky and Marisa Bergman, Summerville's controller, who was sitting to Casey's left, sneaking glances over her glasses at Alex whenever she thought no one was watching.

Jealousy spiraled through her, startling her. Why was she still thinking of him as hers, when it was clear that he had no intention of ever being hers again?

Angry at herself and more tired than she wanted to admit, Casey tried to ease the tightness in her shoulders, but whenever she moved, a viselike pain pinched her lower back. Somehow she'd wrenched it during the tumble she'd taken.

Tonight, after the Chamber of Commerce dinner where she was to be the featured speaker, she was going to soak in the hottest water she could stand.

"...and no one saw the man climb onto the catwalk. Worse than that, no one saw him leave it. That's all I've found out so far."

She sighed and glanced across the table. Evan was watching her intently, his freckled face solemn. She'd had little time to talk with him, only a few minutes before the meeting had begun, but she was glad he was there. For some reason Alex seemed more approachable when the affable Evan was at his side.

"Any other thoughts or suggestions, Dutch?" she asked, glancing around the table.

"It's your call, Ms. O'Neill. Say the word and I'll be on the horn to Sam Rickert right now."

"That won't be necessary," she said as forcefully as the pain would allow. "For publication, it was an accident. The man repairing the air conditioner—"

"Was having coffee in the cafeteria when his toolbox nearly took you out," Alex interrupted in a cold, sharp tone. He turned and met her startled gaze squarely. The remote look that she hated was back in his eyes.

"Then who was up there on the catwalk?" she persisted. "I saw a man in blue overalls."

"So did I, twenty feet in the air. That's all any of us saw. But it wasn't the man who owned the toolbox. You heard Shrader here. Six witnesses swear the guy was telling dirty jokes and swigging down black coffee at the exact moment that box fell.''

Alex stepped toward the table, his black gaze challenging anyone to dispute him. ''Anyone could have taken a pair of coveralls from the supply locker, and everyone looks alike in them. Who knows? It might even have been a woman.''

A buzz of comment arose, but Alex ignored it. Tossing the crumpled cup onto the table, he perched on the arm of the vacant chair to Casey's right, one leg dangling, the other braced against the floor.

''But that means that someone deliberately pushed that toolbox over the edge,'' Casey protested. ''Someone... someone who works here.'' She repressed a shudder. She was still shaken, and no matter how hard she tried to tell herself to forget the sound of the metal box splintering the concrete, she couldn't. ''What possible good would it do to spread that kind of poison all over town?''

Alex's cool smile didn't ease his grim expression. ''It might make that person think twice before he tried to kill you again.''

A collective gasp rose from the seven people seated around the table. The air around Casey's head seemed to crackle with tension. She turned to look at Alex squarely, but a stabbing pain shot down her side and into her leg, and she cried out.

''What's wrong?'' he asked in a low voice.

''Nothing. Just a...twinge in my back.'' Her voice was equally low.

''Like hell.'' Alex leaned forward and took the pen from her hand. Casey started to protest, but he cut her short.

''That's all, ladies and gentlemen,'' he said, letting his gaze touch each face around the table, his crooked half smile giving each person the impression that he was speaking only to him or her. ''I think you'll agree that Ms. O'Neill has had one hell of a day. Even though she won't admit it, I think she needs some time to regroup, don't you?''

His smile broadened into a charming grin of conspiracy, and the others responded with a chorus of agreement. Whatever they'd thought of Alex initially, he was now firmly established as a thoughtful but decisive ally.

Casey felt the impact immediately. In a one-on-one contest with Alex in the arena of corporate power, she would lose every time. But that didn't mean she couldn't win—in her own way.

Hiding her irritation, she smilingly thanked her staff for their attention and issued orders to Dutch Shrader to continue his investigation.

She waited until they had all gone, then turned to Becky and said quietly, "I'll be back in my office in fifteen minutes. If the man from Warner Medical is early for our four o'clock appointment, please explain that I'm in an important meeting."

"Will do, Ms. O'Ne—"

"Forget it, Casey," Alex interrupted in a low voice. "You're going home—now."

The secretary's dark head swiveled from one to the other, her attentive attitude swiftly changing to avid curiosity.

"I'll keep my appointment, Becky," Casey said firmly. "And tell Mr. Jameson that I'll stop by the lab before I go home."

"Damn it, Casey," Alex said in a biting voice. "Don't be so stubborn."

The woman was impossible, he thought in mounting frustration. She was dead on her feet, and her face was paler than he'd ever seen it. No doubt about it, she needed someone to take care of her. To give her warmed brandy, to kiss the lines from her forehead, to put her to bed. To . . .

"Don't be so bossy," she grumbled irritably, tossing her head in the familiar gesture of defiance that never failed to fascinate him.

Her gold earrings flashed in the diffused sunlight streaming through the blinds, reminding him of the sexy silver ones she'd worn in Chamisa. His fingers flexed, then curled into loose fists at his side.

"It's not going to do Evan's public relations campaign a damn bit of good if you end up in traction."

"I'm fine." Three more weeks, she told herself. Surely she could manage to control her libido for twenty-one days. Then, for better or worse, this would be over.

"Right, fine," Alex muttered in disgust.

Casey and her secretary exchanged looks. "Might as well give up, Mr. Torres," Becky said with a sympathetic grin. "Sooner or later, Ms. O'Neill will get her way."

"This time." Alex moved to the window, deliberately turning his back on the others. Three dozen kids in one small room were a dead-bang cinch to control compared to one Casey O'Neill. Hell, a billion-dollar company was easier to handle than she was when she got that mulish look on her face.

He shoved his hands into his pockets to keep from tossing her over his shoulder and hauling her off. He'd vowed to keep this strictly business, and that was exactly what he intended to do.

Rubbing his thumb absently over his ring, he stared at the town spread out like a scene on a postcard, with its houses prettied up in white paint and a small redbrick church at the end of Main Street looking out over the town like an old-fashioned duenna.

Ohio was too green for his liking. And there wasn't enough room in the narrow valley between the hills around here for a man to breathe.

He followed the cluttered horizon absently, trying to decide what to do next. He'd been in town for five hours, and already things were damn near out of control. And at the moment he didn't know what to do about it.

"Anything else before I go?" Becky asked, gathering her notes.

Casey hesitated, then smoothed her skirt over her lap. "Actually, I'd love a cup of... of Mrs. Eiler's tea when I get back to the office." She gave her assistant a tiny smile.

"Yes, ma'am. I know just what she likes."

Becky was smiling as she left, her four-inch heels beating a sharp tattoo on the bare wood floor.

Evan meticulously stacked his notes into a pile, then slid them into his case. "Listen, kiddo," he told Casey with a slight frown, "maybe you shouldn't push it. You do look a mite tired." He snapped the latch on the case and rested his hand on the smooth leather. "Although on you, darlin', the pale look is very... stylish."

Casey managed a smile. "Now I know why I never forgot you."

He grinned. "Maybe I should cancel my appointment with that guy Plunkett, and we can run away together."

"What appointment?" she asked sharply, looking from one to the other.

Evan's expression grew serious. "Our investigator turned up the fact that Mr. Jeffrey Plunkett once worked for Charleston Tool and Die, which, you'll be interested to hear, is wholly owned by Deshler Industries."

"There must be more to it than that." She caught the questioning look that Evan shot to Alex, and she seethed inside. She wasn't used to filtering her questions through a third party.

Alex leaned against the wall and crossed his arms. "Word is, the guy was on the fast track to controller, so why did he suddenly resign and take a lower-level job with Summerville Foundry? Some people think he had sticky fingers."

Casey sighed. "Alex, you can't accuse the man of stealing unless you have some kind of tangible proof."

His eyes flashed, controlled fire on a dark night. "The hell I can't. That's exactly what he's doing to you."

Casey ran her nail along the stitching of her leather notebook. "Just before I came looking for you, I had a visitor. Mrs. Eiler. Remember I told you about her?"

He nodded curtly. "Majority player in this deal along with you and Deshler."

Casey's smile was tinged with irony. "She's Jeff Plunkett's godmother." Swiftly she recounted her conversation with the elderly woman, omitting the personal digression at the end. "Without hard proof that Jeff is lying about me, she's going to vote with Con."

Evan whistled softly. "We've got trouble."

Alex stared at the floor, thinking, his body radiating leashed control. "That's it, then," he said finally. "Ready or not, we go on the offensive. You're the lawyer, Evan. There's got to be a noose somewhere that we can jerk around Deshler's neck."

"Alex, I've looked—"

"Then look again. You're the paper person. Find me a loophole to hang the bastard with."

Evan dragged his briefcase from the table. "I'll get right on it." He hesitated; then, with what looked like a defiant shrug, he bent down to give Casey a quick kiss on the lips.

Evan hurried out. She and Alex were alone.

The hiss of the air vent ten feet above their heads and the rumble of a delivery truck backing into the loading dock across the yard were the only sounds in the cavernous room.

Seconds ticked by.

Casey stared at her reflection in the gleaming mahogany table, aware that Alex was watching her with stony, unreadable eyes. Something was locked away in those black depths, something that had hurt him so terribly that he'd given up everything because of it. Like Cadiz, Alex was a man who walked his own road proudly and alone.

"You really believe what happened is Con's doing, don't you?" she asked, breaking the silence.

"It's the savvy move, and you can bet your next bonus that he's got himself well insulated. Even if we catch the guy who was up on the catwalk, he'll never lead us to Con."

He crossed to the chair next to her and reached for the suit coat hanging over the back. An ugly abrasion ran the length of his forearm, and there were spatters of blood on his shirt. Her stomach twisted. He could have been killed as easily as she. Only his quick reflexes had saved them.

She felt her face grow cold.

"What's wrong?" Alex asked, watching her. "Should I get the nurse?"

A queasy nausea replaced the tightness in her stomach. "You could have died, and it would have been my fault," she said in a thin voice, a shudder running through her.

"No, Casey. Not your fault."

"Yes." She stared at her small white hand. The nails were carefully manicured, and her skin was soft and unblemished. "I would have killed him if you had died. Somehow—" she choked. "Somehow I would have made him pay."

Alex knew that nothing showed on his face, but in his gut, he felt as though he'd just taken a hard left, and for an instant he couldn't move.

She would do exactly what she said. If need be, she would take on Con Deshler, or this town, or anyone else if she had to. For him.

Casey was more worthy of Cadiz's legacy than he would ever be. She'd risked humiliation and worse to plead for the people that she loved. And she would fight for them at the risk of her own freedom.

More than anything, he wanted to fight alongside her. And he wanted to win. But not for himself, this time. This time he wanted to win for Casey.

A coldness settled inside him. A resolve. A promise.

He touched her cheek. "Don't worry about me, Casey," he said in a low voice. "I don't want to cause you any more pain." Grabbing his jacket, he turned and left the room, leaving her staring after him.

The rented farmhouse where Conrad Deshler was staying with his staff overlooked the town's only cemetery. The lane leading to the large white-frame home wound through the older section, where many of the gravestones had toppled onto the unkempt grass.

The chauffeur slowed for a sudden hairpin curve, and the heavy car swayed to the left. "Sorry, sir," Miklos said, glancing into his rearview mirror.

"No problem," Alex told him curtly. He hated graveyards. In fact, he'd avoided them from the day they'd put his father into the ground. It had been raining in Los Angeles that morning, and the mourners had left as soon as the priest had uttered the benediction.

But Alex had stayed.

Kneeling by the grave, the mud seeping into the fabric of his only decent pair of pants, he'd sworn an oath to avenge his father's humiliation.

And he had. Only he'd been the one who paid the price. He was still paying.

The chauffeur braked smoothly, and the car came to a stop in front of the crumbling limestone steps leading to the small front porch.

"You want I should come with you, Mr. Torres? Them two guys on the porch don't look too friendly." The chauffeur glanced into the rearview mirror.

"Thanks for the offer, Miklos. But those guys are just for show." Besides, he didn't want a witness.

Miklos scrambled from the driver's seat and opened the rear door. "You sure, sir? The one with the red hair is packing a gun."

The chauffeur's narrowed gaze dropped pointedly to Alex's bloody shirt. He hadn't taken time to change after he'd left Casey in the boardroom. Instead, they'd driven directly to this place.

"Actually," he told Miklos in a low voice, "Red Cagney is a former Secret Service agent. Con pays well for the image."

Alex climbed out, and the heat from the parched ground hit him with a damp rush. Within seconds sweat began trickling down his spine, sticking his shirt to his back. He began walking toward the house, adrenaline making his heart beat faster.

One of the men had disappeared inside as soon as the limo had braked to a stop. The other, younger and stronger looking, was standing at the foot of the steps, his face completely blank.

"Mr. Torres," Cagney said, his Boston accent stronger than Alex remembered. *"Como esta?"*

"Hello, Red. I see you're still pulling baby-sitting duty."

Alex didn't stop. The bodyguard, his face mottled with anger, was forced to fall in step with him.

Alex reached the steps and started up, but Cagney managed to get between him and the door.

"Get out of my way," Alex said in a low, cold voice.

Cagney's gaze flickered, but he didn't move. "Is Mr. Deshler expecting you?"

"No, but he'll see me." Alex's brief smile was icy.

Cagney started to refuse, but a carefully modulated tenor voice cut him short. "That's okay, Red. I'll handle this."

A tall man in tennis whites pushed open the screen door and sauntered out. With his perfect smile and dimpled cheeks, Conrad Deshler had always reminded Alex of an ad for mouthwash. An image of that mouth on Casey's made his blood run hot.

He thought of the time he'd broken a man's nose with one punch, just for making a suggestive comment to one of his sisters, but he ignored the violent urge to ruin that plastic smile with a quick uppercut. At the moment there was too much at stake.

"Hello, Alex," Deshler said pleasantly, offering his hand.

Alex ignored it. Instantly an expression of anger crossed the other man's face, but it was quickly masked.

"Let's talk, Deshler. Now."

"I heard you'd bought into this game." Deshler took a lazy sip of his drink.

"Bought in and upped the stakes."

The ice cubes tinkled in the sweaty glass in Deshler's large hand. "That sounds interesting. Why don't you come in and we'll talk about it?"

Alex shook his head. "Let's take a walk." He nodded toward the empty expanse of sunburned grass sloping toward the burying ground.

Deshler's blue eyes narrowed, and his mouth drew into a thin line of suspicion. Seconds passed while he scrutinized Alex's unrelenting expression.

Finally he shrugged. "Why not? I could use some exercise." He drained his glass, then handed it to his bodyguard. "Stay here," he ordered curtly.

"But, Mr. Deshler—"

"You heard me."

"Yes, sir."

Alex turned his back on the man with the gun and walked down the steps. After a slight hesitation, Deshler followed.

The two men walked in silence, their steps crunching loudly on the dried grass. Alex stopped at the rusted iron fence and ran his hand over the pointed tip of the gatepost. His face was carefully controlled, but inside a cold rage filled him.

"There's something you need to know, Deshler." He turned his head, letting the man see the cold fury in his eyes. "If Casey is hurt *in any way*, I'll kill the man responsible."

Deshler stared at him, his jaw slack, his face frozen. Alex almost believed the man was innocent. Almost.

"You got a . . . reason for this threat, Torres?"

"Yeah, I got a reason. Last week someone vandalized her bedroom. Today a toolbox fell and nearly split her skull. I don't need any more reason than that."

Deshler smoothed his styled blond hair with his palm. "I had nothing to do with that, Alex. I'm . . . very fond of Casey."

Alex heard the taunt in Deshler's cream-cheese voice, but he made himself ignore it. "Tell me another one."

"It's true. It's also true that she's got herself a good little company. It'll make me a lot of money when I take it apart and sell off the assets."

"Try to sell, and I call in my note."

Deshler's eyes narrowed in suspicion. "What note?"

"The loan I made Summerville Foundry two days ago. One million for research and development. Cash. Last time I checked, the foundry didn't have nearly that amount in ready assets."

"I don't believe you. Not even a company like Towers could grant that kind of a loan without board approval. You haven't had time to call a special meeting."

Alex grinned coldly. "Not Towers. Me personally. And I have the right to decide where that money will be used—no matter who sits in the executive suite. Have your attorney check with mine if you don't believe me."

A small yellow butterfly flew a fluttering circle around the two men, then settled onto a clover blossom at their feet. Deshler scowled, then deliberately crushed the tiny creature beneath his rubber sole.

"I'll live with it," he told Alex with a placid look. A smug grin spread across his face. "I've got the votes, Torres. Casey would be wise to concede now, before I turn Plunkett loose on her. Maybe we can . . . strike a deal."

Alex regarded the man impassively. "What have you got on the guy? Drugs? A charge of embezzlement?"

Deshler's gaze narrowed. "Hey, the guy came to me. Said he used to work for me and thought I ought to know something important. I didn't believe his story at first, of course. But that Boy Scout face is very convincing. Wait 'til you see him in action."

He started to leave, then turned back, a lascivious look crossing his face. "Casey looks great, doesn't she? Even though she's lost some weight. Still, I imagine in bed she's still as sexy as ever. We had some very good times, Casey and me." He glanced disdainfully at the dark spots on the front of Alex's wrinkled shirt. "Too bad you weren't man enough to keep her, muchacho. She's a hell of a lay."

Alex hit him squarely in the belly. Deshler doubled over, his breath coming in wheezing gasps.

"You'll . . . pay . . . for . . . that, Torres," he managed to grind out.

Alex flexed his fingers and stared at the abandoned graves. "You know where to find me. Muchacho." Without a backward glance, he walked away.

Chapter 11

Casey stared at the face of the clock radio by her bed, watching Friday tick second by second into Saturday. The dormer windows were open, but the lace curtains hung lifeless and still against the sills. The air in her bedroom was sultry and smelled of the talcum powder she'd applied after her bath.

Sighing restlessly, she turned onto her side, trying to find a comfortable position. The mattress felt too hard, and her eyes were grainy with weariness. She'd come home from the Chamber dinner around eleven, taken a hot bath and two aspirins, then gone directly to bed.

Now, an hour later, the pain in her back was gone, but she was still wide awake. And the more she tried to concentrate on sleep, the more wired she became.

"Hot chocolate," she muttered, flinging off the sheet and sitting up. "Never fails."

Yawning, she switched on the bedside lamp. The light hurt her eyes, and she squinted against the glare. Slowly she climbed out of bed, standing for a moment on the new rug she'd bought to replace the one ruined by the intruder. In her mind's eye she saw again the torn wallpaper and obscene letters smeared in lipstick over every flat surface.

She'd scrubbed everything with disinfectant twice and hired a painter and wallpaperer to come in next week to completely redo the room, but she knew that she would never forget the sense of violation that had raced through her when she'd seen the damage for the first time.

Maybe I should sleep in one of the guest rooms, she thought as she padded into the hall and down the stairs. Or the old nursery next to the master bedroom.

No, she thought hastily. Not the nursery.

She shivered. She'd never noticed before how many empty rooms there were in her house. When this was over, she should really think about leaving Summerville, finding another challenge. In the West, maybe.

Her hand tightened on the handrail. The highly polished walnut was smooth and cool under her palm, and the Persian runner felt scratchy and stiff against her bare soles. What was the matter with her? she thought. This was the house she'd always wanted. Why would she want to live anywhere else?

At the bottom of the stairs she snapped on the overhead light and made her way down the hall. On one side was the door to her den. On the other was the entrance to the kitchen. Yawning again, she turned right, snapping on the kitchen light by the door.

Eyes half closed, she made her way to the refrigerator and fumbled for the milk. She found a small pan and put it onto the burner, then poured in the milk.

"Now where in blazes did I put the cocoa?" she muttered, opening and shutting cupboards at random, trying to find the small brown container.

The old house creaked around her, the little sounds familiar and comforting. Outside, a hoot owl screeched in the distance, and nearby, a cricket began a mournful courting song.

"Aha! There you are." She dragged the hot chocolate mix from the middle shelf of the last cupboard and snapped off the lid.

She started to look for a spoon, thought better of it, and dumped a sizable amount into the pan. Squinting, she watched the brown granules sink into the milk. "What the hell . . ." she said, dumping in more.

After returning the can to the shelf, she reached into the next cupboard for a large ceramic mug.

Suddenly a fist pounded the kitchen door, rattling the frosted glass window. Casey whirled around, her heart racing. The mug fell from her hand and hit the floor, shattering on impact. Through the opaque pane, she saw a man's upper body and a long arm raised to knock again.

The door shook on its hinges from the force of the pounding, and she glanced around frantically, her gaze finally settling on the wall phone by the table. She held her breath and began picking her way through the broken glass. She had to pass the door....

"Casey, are you all right?"

Relief ran through her like a wave. It was Alex.

"No, I'm not all right," she muttered, her heart still pounding, but for a different reason.

She hadn't been able to stop thinking about him. In her office, in her car, even in her bedroom. Especially in her bedroom. Hastily she glanced down at her short nightgown. It was designed for comfort in the hot, muggy weather, not protection from hypnotic black eyes.

"Casey?"

She took a deep breath. By the time she ran upstairs for a robe, Alex would have the entire neighborhood awake. Besides, what did it matter, anyway? He'd made it very clear that he wasn't interested in her physically. He probably wouldn't even notice.

"Coming," she shouted. "I'm coming."

She managed to make it to the door without stepping on a piece of ironstone. She turned the bolt, then opened the door a crack and peeked out. The porch light cast his face in shadow, making him look gaunt, as though he'd lost weight in the few days they'd been apart.

"Are you all right?" he said as soon as their eyes met. "What the hell took you so long?"

"Alex, it's past midnight. People are sleeping."

His angry gaze fell to the ruffle at the neckline of her gown, then jerked back to her face. He scowled. "Right, and every light in your house is on."

He shifted his feet until they were braced wide apart, and his fists settled angrily on his hips.

Casey bristled. "So?"

"So I thought you might be in trouble."

Alex felt the sweat sticking his clothes to his body and knew that he must smell like a locker room. His irritation increased, and his brows drew together in a black frown. What the hell was she doing, answering the door in that skimpy little thing, anyway?

Anyone standing where he was could see the white triangle of her bikini panties through the thin material. And the silhouette of her lush hips and tiny waist above the lacy band.

"Thank you for your concern," Casey said with a fixed smile, "but as you can see, I'm perfectly fine. I couldn't sleep. I was just making some hot chocolate."

Alex was beginning to feel like a fool. His irritation increased.

"Hot chocolate? It's got to be eighty-five degrees outside. Isn't that a bit illogical?"

Casey prickled at his sarcastic tone. Pointedly she stared at the shorts and sweat-soaked tank top he was wearing. "I suppose it's logical to jog in this humidity."

His eyes crinkled into a brief smile, and some of the strain in his face eased. "Actually, I was running. Jogging is for women."

His damp hair gleamed in the overhead light. His bare shoulders had a sweat-burnished glow, like the gladiators of another time. Beneath the white shorts his legs looked long and powerful in the shadowed light, and the little hairs were damp and sticking to his skin.

Her pulse rocketed, her senses coming alive in a way that felt like arousal, but she reminded herself of that last morning in his house, when she'd all but begged for his love. She would never allow herself to want him again.

"Excuse me," she said on a little rush of breath. "I'd better check the milk." Without thinking she stepped backward, and her heel came down on a a fragment of the cup. A sharp stab of pain shot up her leg, and she gasped. Lifting her foot, she stared at the trickle of blood slowly running down her heel.

"Oh, dear," she said in a small voice.

"Don't move." Alex scooped her into his arms and cradled her against his chest. Her arms went around his neck, as though it were the most natural thing in the world. And it had been, once, he reminded himself stiffly. He'd held her this way the first time they'd made love, and countless times after that.

Still, it was always amazing to him how light she was. And how pliant her small body could be when she was clinging to him like this.

Holding her tightly, he carried her to the table in the corner of the kitchen and set her down gently, her legs dangling over the edge.

She blinked up at him. Her face was scrubbed and glowing, and her hair smelled fresh, like flowers after a rain. He rubbed his sweaty palms on his shorts.

"Where's your first-aid kit?" He sounded out of breath, as though he'd started to run again.

"There's some stuff in the bathroom at the top of the stairs, but—"

"Sit still and keep your hands off your foot. I'll be right back." He disappeared.

Before she had time to take more than a dozen deep breaths, he was back, a box of Band-Aids in one hand and a tube of antiseptic in the other.

"Scoot backward so I can see your foot," he ordered in a flat voice, putting the bandages and ointment next to her thigh. Casey did as she was told.

Her gown rode up on her hips, revealing the lace edge of her panties. Immediately Alex jerked the material over her thigh, his knuckles raking the sensitive inner curve.

Humiliation flooded her. Surely he didn't think she'd done that on purpose? That she was trying to seduce him? She took a slow breath.

Bracing herself, she watched as Alex lifted her foot and bent over it. A folded blue bandanna was tied around his forehead, and his jaw was dark with whisker stubble. He looked tired.

"Stop wiggling, Casey," he ordered tersely, sparing her face an impatient glance. "You're as fidgety as my students just before recess."

"Then stop squeezing so hard." He scowled, but the pressure of his hard fingers on her heel eased marginally.

"It doesn't look serious. Not much bleeding." His fingers wiped across her heel, then across the front of his white shirt, leaving a swatch of blood that looked rust colored in the light.

"There's a towel in the drawer. You're going to ruin your shirt."

His head shot up, and he scowled. "We're not in the executive suite now, madam president. Stop giving orders." He sounded harried.

"Suit yourself. It's your shirt that's ruined."

Alex's eyes narrowed, and he returned his gaze to her foot. With his right hand he held it securely, while he applied the cream to her heel with his left. His touch was gentle, his fingers rough, as he smoothed the bandage over the cut.

"All better?" she asked, her voice more breathless than it should be. She expected him to drop her foot, but it remained securely braced in his palm.

His breathing seemed suddenly very loud in the quiet room. Hers, too, sounded labored. As casually as she could manage, her hand crept to the top of her nightgown, covering the bare skin exposed by the ruffled straps.

"You'll be fine," he said tersely, rubbing his thumb over her arch. Little shivers of pleasure rode up her leg.

She should tug her foot from his grasp. She should thank him politely and send him on his way. But she didn't seem to be able to do those things.

"Next time wear slippers." His free hand slid up her ankle, and Casey started shaking inside.

"I will," she said with a rush of breath.

He couldn't stop looking at her. With her pale hair framing her face and her smile soft and sleepy, she looked like an adorable angel. Except this angel had a body that could drive even a saint over the edge.

A savage frustration ripped through him. Leave, Torres, he ordered silently. Now.

But he didn't seem to be able to move.

He was dead tired, and his leg muscles, worn out by his marathon run, had seized up while he'd been standing out there on her back stoop and were tight and aching.

And inside, his feelings were in the same tangle that had driven him from his bed to run for miles in the saunalike heat.

Night after night he dreamed about her, waking up in a cold sweat, his body hard and ready to love her.

Alex muttered a frustrated curse under his breath. He lowered her foot, then reached up to untie the bandanna from his forehead and wipe his brow. He shoved the kerchief carelessly into his back pocket, stepping away from the table, his feet crunching over the broken fragments.

Damn, he'd forgotten about the glass. Stifling an impatient sigh, he glanced around the large, old-fashioned room.

"Where's your broom?"

"In the pantry. There, by the fridge."

He heard the edge of exasperation in her voice, but he made himself ignore it. In silence, without looking at her, he found the broom and began sweeping up the pieces of yellow crockery.

Casey rubbed her palms together nervously. He would have to know sooner or later. Maybe it would be best to tell him here, away from the office.

"Actually I'm glad you're here. I . . . have something I need to discuss with you. Something happened tonight at the Chamber of Commerce dinner."

He glanced up, his expression emotionless. "It was my understanding, Casey, that you were to clear your calendar through Evan or me." He spoke with cold emphasis, the only sign that he was angry.

She ignored the queasy feeling in the pit of her stomach. She had planned to tell him about her speaking engagement after the staff meeting, but from the way he'd reacted to her not going home to rest after their "accident," she'd known he wouldn't okay it.

She took a deep breath. "It was a disaster."

He emptied the dustpan into the trash container at the end of the counter, then returned the broom to the pantry. He leaned against the counter, his ankles crossed, his arms folded over his chest. "Okay, start."

Casey glanced around the pale blue kitchen with the fussy accessories and beautifully restored pine plank floor. Suddenly the room seemed too big, too unfriendly. And the bright light from the brass fixture made her feel undressed and at a definite disadvantage.

"Not here," she said in a voice that sounded thin. "Let's go in the parlor."

A strange look crossed Alex's face, as though the idea wasn't very appealing, but she was feeling far too uncomfortable to care.

She slid off the table, putting her foot gingerly on the floor. There was only a small twinge of pain.

In silence she turned off the burner under the forgotten milk, then walked past him, her head high. She sensed him behind her as she led the way to the parlor, but she made herself look straight ahead.

She switched on a small Tiffany lamp, then curled into the large platform rocker facing the black marble fireplace. The room was large enough for a tea party or a small gathering, but small enough to feel cozy and welcoming. She had decorated it in colors of rose and fuchsia, with brighter accents of blue. The wallpaper was an authentic nineteenth-century print.

"Nice room," Alex commented, his shuttered gaze taking in the oriental rug and sprigged walls. "I like the high ceiling." He shoved his hands, palms out, into his back pockets and looked around for a place to sit.

"It's my favorite room," Casey told him, feeling oddly self-conscious. "I've put all my special things here, including the English antiques I inherited from my grandmother. They've been in the family for four generations."

Alex nodded, trying to decide which of Grandma's spindly chairs would take his weight. All of them looked as though they'd been designed for ladies, even the high-backed sofa that was covered in some kind of shiny pink-and-white material.

"The couch is your best bet," Casey said dryly.

"Damn thing looks as though it should be in a bordello." One black brow arched sardonically.

Casey struggled to hang on to the professional distance she needed. "It was, once," she admitted, fighting the smile that wanted to bloom. "In Hamilton. I bought it from the daughter of the last madam. I think it adds a certain cachet to the room, don't you?"

Alex lowered himself cautiously, careful to keep his back from touching the slinky material. "I don't know about cachet, but the thing is about as comfortable as a church pew. The only thing you're missing is a kneeling bench."

"I'll work on it for you," she told him tartly. She loved her couch, and she didn't appreciate his sarcasm.

"Not for me. I spent enough time on my knees when I was a kid. I swore I'd never do it again."

Something unusual in his tone caught her ear. "Don't you believe in prayer?"

Alex lifted one bare shoulder and stared down at the intricate swirls in the carpet. Did he believe in prayer? He had once. In his early years he'd prayed a lot to his mother's gentle, loving God. And sometimes, when he'd thought he couldn't stand the loneliness another minute, to his father's sterner deity, but neither could deliver him from the burden he carried now.

"Right now I believe in a strong offense," he said flatly. "And you've stalled long enough. Tell me exactly what happened tonight."

"I'm not stalling."

"Yes, you are. You always chew on your lip when you're trying to hide something."

Casey immediately released her lower lip from between her teeth. She hated this feeling of vulnerability that Alex always seemed to evoke in her.

Frowning, she curled her legs under her and cast her mind backward, trying to decide where to begin. Try the beginning, when you walked in and saw Con again, prodded a tiny voice. She felt her cheeks grow warm.

Con hadn't changed. He was still sophisticated and charming and, inside, completely self-involved.

Lord, how could she have thought she loved a man like that? A man who would do anything, tromp over anyone, to win. She'd been such an idiot.

She took a deep breath and plunged in. "It started innocuously enough, I guess. I was seated on the dais, while Con was sitting someplace in the back. I didn't even see him until right before I stood to speak."

Alex's belly tightened in a sharp spasm of pain. "Was that the first time you'd seen him since . . . you broke your engagement?" Since you slept with him? he added silently, feeling the knot in his gut twist tighter.

"Yes. He looks . . . good. Very trustworthy."

Alex grunted. "Yeah, everyone trusts a blue-eyed blonde with a perfect smile and a pedigree going back to the *Mayflower*."

"And they don't trust a black-eyed Mexican-Indian with roots going back to Cortes and beyond?"

His smile was fleeting. "Mestizo. People with mixed blood like mine are called mestizos—among other things. Your friend Con and his Wall Street cronies have a nice long list. I've heard most of them."

Casey watched his hands clench on his knees, and she hurt inside. For all his money and power, Alex still carried a lot of that angry nineteen-year-old inside him. But she couldn't let herself care. He didn't want her caring. Hadn't he told her that?

Casey drew a steadying breath. "Before the meeting was over, I felt like a clay pigeon in a shooting gallery. Everyone but the woman serving the meal took a shot at me."

"It was rough?"

"Rough is mild compared to what it was. By the time I left I was half convinced that I owed it to the town and my shareholders to take my dirty skirts as far away as possible."

Picking at the decorative cord framing the pad on her chair, she forced herself to tell him the rest. "I saw the faces of the people in the audience, Alex. They were with me all the way—until one of Con's stooges stood up and started asking questions. I did my best, but the more he pushed me, the madder I got."

"Did he ask you about insider information?"

"Not exactly. He alluded to unconfirmed rumors of . . . improprieties." Her lips curled in disgust. "People started whispering and looking at Jeff."

Alex muttered a succinct curse. "He was there, too?"

"Yes, along with Rachel Eiler. He looked like Mr. Clean, sitting there behind his CPA image." She chopped the air with her hand. "He might as well have stood up and accused me of fraud."

Alex frowned thoughtfully,. "What about Deshler? Did he say anything?"

Casey nodded slowly. "Oh yes. He came to my defense like some knight on a charger. 'I'm certain Ms. O'Neill would never do anything wrong,' he told the audience in his best let's-all-give-her-the-benefit-of-the-doubt voice. It was sickening."

"But shrewd. He knows better than to attack you directly."

Silence fell between them. Outside, a car drove slowly by, and a dog somewhere close began barking.

Alex rubbed his thumb over his ring. There had to be a way to cut the bastard off at the knees without compromising the promises he'd made to himself when he'd walked away from it all. But how?

It was nearly impossible to stick to the rules when a man like Deshler was sending in the plays for the other side.

"What do we do now?" Casey asked quietly.

"We fight." He would find a way. He always had.

He extended his legs, trying to ease some of the tiredness in his muscles. He flinched as a sudden cramp stabbed his left hamstring. He stood, rubbing the knot until it eased.

He paced the small room, working off the rest of the cramp, then stood in front of the bay window and stared out at the street. Everywhere he looked in this town he saw pretty little houses with swings in the backyard and bicycles in the front.

Slowly he ran his hand over the frame of the Victorian cradle holding a bushy fern. Like the couch, this was something he'd never seen before.

"This come from the madam, too?" His hand gave the tiny bed a shove, and it swung easily on its brackets. Ready for use.

There was a sudden tense silence. Finally Casey answered softly, "No, I . . . Con bought it for me. As an engagement present."

Alex fought down the feeling of revulsion shaking him. "You wanted his child?"

Casey uttered a soft little cry. "Please, Alex. I don't want to talk about him."

He had his answer. A quiet rage filled him. In front of his eyes the pretty street blurred. He felt as though he were strangling.

In his head he hated Deshler for taking his woman. In his gut he hated himself more for not being able to keep her.

"I could kill you for getting mixed up with that *cabron*," he told her in a barely controlled voice. "Anyone but him."

Casey stared at his stiff back. His hand tightened over the smooth rail of the cradle until the knuckles looked ready to explode through the skin.

She thought about the night he'd left. His voice had carried that same harsh note of frustration. But why? If he didn't care, why was he so angry?

A startling thought nearly made her gasp aloud. He sounded like a man who'd just caught his wife cheating on him.

"I thought he was like you," she confessed, wanting him to understand. "I wanted him to be like you, so I wouldn't miss you so much. But he's not like you. He hurts people. I hate that about him, Alex. I *hate* it."

"I've hurt people, too, Casey." His voice was flat, controlled.

"But not like Con," she said fervently. "He ruins people's lives."

Alex heard the words and the contempt behind them. If she only knew.

"Is that why you quit, Alex?" she whispered into the silence. "Because you hurt someone?"

He bowed his head and stared at the scuffed toes of his shoes. "I told myself it was business. That my stockholders deserved to make a bigger profit. I told myself a lot of things. Except the truth."

Casey heard the tortured note in his voice. "Tell me," she urged quietly, afraid to move.

He closed his eyes, trying to find the courage to do as she asked. Over the past few days he'd wanted to tell her so badly that he was like a man pacing a dark cell hour after hour, day after day, with no hope of escape. He hated the half-truths and evasions. He hated himself for telling them.

A feeling that might be hope grew within him. Maybe they *could* try again. Maybe they could pick up the pieces he'd tried so hard to stomp into the ground.

He took a long, deep breath, then let it out slowly. He braced his shoulders and slowly turned to face her. She looked puzzled and almost frightened, as though whatever he said was very important to her.

"You . . . remember what I told you about old man Chandler and Bart, his son?"

Casey nodded. "That they fired your father and you. And that you swore to get even—which you did, when Towers absorbed Chandler Aerospace."

Alex's face was stiff with pain. "Yeah, Alex Torres always keeps his word."

"Is that wrong, Alex?"

He forced himself to meet her gaze. It was hard to breathe, and a cold sweat was beginning to trickle down his spine. The words were going to hurt like hell. He'd rather do anything than say them. But no matter what happened, Casey deserved the truth.

"It's wrong if people die."

Casey felt as though all the air had suddenly been sucked from the room, and her hand went to her throat. "You can't mean . . . you're not trying to tell me that you . . . killed someone?"

Alex felt sick. He swallowed hard and tried to keep his voice steady. "Indirectly, yes."

"Oh my God."

Alex heard the horror in her voice, and it felt like the lash of a whip on his back. But he'd started this. He had to finish.

"Bart Chandler couldn't believe that he'd lost his company, but it was even worse for him knowing that he'd lost it to me, the 'stupid greaser' he had tossed out on the street so many years ago." His hand combed his hair in quick, nervous movements.

Casey put her hand to her lips, her eyes filling with sympathy. "How did you feel when you saw him again?"

Alex's mouth twisted into a cruel, self-mocking smile. "Like I had my foot on his throat and couldn't wait to trample him into the dirt where he'd once pushed my face. I was so damn proud of myself. I'd waited sixteen years, but I'd finally gotten my revenge."

He walked slowly to the couch and sat down again. Leaning forward, he clasped his hands between his knees and watched her. "I expected him to be furious and frustrated as hell, but I . . . I never expected him to beg."

"He begged?" Casey asked in a near whisper.

"Yes. Chandler Aerospace was his whole life, he said. And someday his son, Randy, would take over from him the way he'd taken over from his father."

"What did you say?"

Alex hesitated. "I told him that my father had lost everything because of him—including his dignity and his life." He dropped his head, his gaze focused on the floor. "He cried then, and pleaded with me to let him stay on as CEO. If he lost his job, he kept saying, he would never be able to hold up his head again. He had a . . . a position in the community to uphold, to pass on to his son." His mouth hardened. "Can you believe it, Case? When I was growing up, my father just worried about putting enough food on the table. He didn't even have a damned 'position.'"

"So you said no."

He sighed. "I said no, and then I . . . laughed at him, the way he'd once laughed at me."

Casey bit her lip. She'd never heard Alex sound so angry. But his anger seemed directed at himself.

He slowly raised his gaze to hers. "The next day he drove off the Coast Highway in his Mercedes. Randy was with him. The . . . the coroner said that—" his voice broke "—that the boy lived for an hour or so after the crash. His neck was broken."

He stood and began to pace. "Bart had a picture of his boy on his desk. Blue eyes. Blond hair. A big smile. I kept seeing that kid, Casey. When I was awake. When I was asleep. I . . . I couldn't get him out of my head."

He returned to the window and stood looking out, his back stiff, his head bent. "I'd become the kind of ruthless bastard I'd always hated. Every time I'd taken over a new company, I'd told myself I was better than the rest of the sharks because I cared about my people." He snorted in self-derision. "Some caring, huh? An innocent ten-year-old boy died because Alex Torres wanted revenge." His voice was slivered with pain.

Casey slid her legs to the floor and stood. One foot was asleep, and stinging needles pricked her nerves, but she ignored the pain. Limping, she went to him.

"Alex, it wasn't your fault," she said earnestly. "Bart Chandler was a coward. He couldn't face his own failure. He killed his son, not you."

She touched his shoulder. He flinched but she didn't remove her hand.

"I wanted to destroy him, Casey," he said in a tortured voice. "The way he'd destroyed my dad. I didn't think about his family. It didn't cross my mind that a happy little boy would never grow up because of me. Or that an innocent woman would spend the rest of her life in an institution because she couldn't deal with her loss." His voice grew strained. "I didn't think about anything but my damn pride."

He pounded the wall next to the window. Plaster fell from the hole he'd punched through the wallpaper, and a large photograph of her grandmother slid to the floor, the glass shattering.

Casey jumped at the noise but kept her gaze riveted on Alex's downcast head. He was suffering.

"Now you know," he muttered in a thick voice. "Aren't you proud of me?" He straightened his shoulders, then turned to face her, steeling himself to accept the revulsion in her eyes.

But instead of the contempt he expected to see, there was the soft sheen of tears in the gray depths and a look of terrible pain on her face—for him. His throat felt raw.

"Don't," he whispered hoarsely. "Don't cry for me." His hand shook as he wiped the tears from her cheeks.

"That's why you left me, wasn't it?" Casey said slowly, her voice shaking. "Because you didn't want me to know."

He looked away, then slowly turned back to face her, as though it was the hardest thing he'd ever had to do. "I was ashamed, Casey. Every day I looked in the mirror and hated the man I saw there. I didn't want you to hate yourself because you were married to a man who'd done what I had."

"I could never hate you. I tried, but I couldn't."

His faint smile was bitter. "Believe me, it would have happened. You would have hated what I did. And sooner or later it would have destroyed your love for me. I . . . couldn't handle that."

"And that's why you've been punishing yourself all these years."

He nodded. "Doing penance, I think you called it. It hasn't helped much."

Casey nearly cried out at the stark pain in his eyes. He'd been living with his guilt and shame for a long time—alone. Because he'd wanted to spare her.

A deep tenderness welled up inside her. How could she hate a man who shouldered such a terrible burden in silence because he couldn't bear to hurt her?

Gently she placed her hands on his shoulders and looked deeply into his eyes. Beneath her palms his muscles jumped, then stiffened with tension.

"Hold me, Alex," she pleaded. "Please. I need you to hold me." She began to shake. He looked so terribly lonely.

His face contorted, and his eyes squeezed shut. His arms came around her gently, and she rested her cheek against his heart. His breathing was harsh against her neck, and beads of sweat dampened his skin beneath her palms.

"I love you," she said in a gentle voice. "Even knowing what happened, I love you."

He squeezed her tighter, as though a sudden spasm of pain had gripped him. "You shouldn't," he whispered in a strangled voice. "I don't deserve it."

"But I do. I'm not sure I can ever stop." She caressed the back of his neck, trying to ease some of the tension punishing him.

"I want to love you, Casey," Alex said in a hoarse whisper. "*Dios*, I want that. But . . ."

"But what?" she pleaded, her face pressed into the damp space between his shoulder and his neck.

"I don't know if I can. When I left, I made myself stop feeling. It was the only way I could survive. I don't know what I feel right now."

"I'm willing to risk it."

Alex lifted his head and looked at her. His face was ravished with some powerful emotion. "I've missed you so much."

Casey traced the lines of strain around his mouth with her soft gaze. "And I've missed you."

He lowered his mouth to hers, and she clung to him, her small body pressed against his.

He made himself be gentle. He had months, years, of ugliness inside him. He didn't want them to touch her.

But holding her, kissing her, this was a reprieve, a moment of grace, a gift. He should be skinned for doing this, but he couldn't make himself stop. Not yet.

He teased her lips with his tongue until they parted. She tasted tart, like the lemon drops she used to keep in a jar by the bed. He'd been hungry for so long.

"Alex, Alex," she whispered against his mouth, and a wild, desperate longing erupted inside him.

Slowly, like a newly blind man unsure of his touch, he rediscovered the soft feminine lines he had once known intimately, his hands gentle and at the same time urgent. He wanted to touch all of her, to feel the helpless little shivers of her response beneath his hands. He couldn't get enough of her, not in a thousand years of trying.

His heart hammered in his chest, and his breathing grew labored, painful. He lifted his mouth from hers and took a deep breath. He had to stop.

"You do want me," Casey whispered, her voice unsteady. "I can feel you wanting me."

He buried his face in her hair and fought for control. She was right. He wanted her so much he ached with it. He had thought about little else since she'd come into his life again.

But he'd wanted her before, and it hadn't worked out. The more he'd tried to make things right between them, the more he'd hurt her.

That was then, an urgent voice prodded from someplace inside his head. You're a different man now.

He kissed her again, this time with a possessive fire that made her go soft inside. His mouth slid over hers, taking what she

offered freely, his hands folding over her shoulders
against him.

Desire spread through her, tingling her skin and heating h
muscles. A strange ringing sounded in her ears. Time seemed
to stop, and the night sounds around her faded.

"Make love to me, Alex," she whispered. "I'm tired of being
alone."

A jagged look of doubt came into his eyes. "I wanted to keep
you safe, *mi amor*. From what I did, from the shame—"

With an eager sigh, Casey stopped his words with her mouth,
her tongue probing until he opened his mouth for her. He tasted
like well-aged brandy, strong and smooth and incredibly potent.

His mouth moved over hers in the lazy, possessive way that
she remembered, exciting little ripples of desire inside her. His
hands slid down her waist to press against the swell of her hips.
The soft material of her nightgown was the only barrier between his warm fingers and her skin.

Her body came alive, bursting with the raw need that the
days with him had built inside her. Her breasts swelled and
hardened against his chest, and she pressed closer.

Alex groaned in what sounded like surrender and moved
against her, his hands roaming her back, her hips, the rounded
contour of her bottom.

His fingers burrowed under her nightgown to caress her bare
spine. His breathing grew more rapid, and so did hers. The
same need that she felt in him coursed through her. She met his
bold, hungry kisses eagerly, aggressively, shyly, feeling all over
again the exhilaration of that first time they'd made love.

His hands moved up her spine and then down, mapping her
body in the same aggressive way he always had. She gasped as
his fingers slid under the elastic of her panties. His hands
cupped her buttocks, then slid around to caress her hips.

His thumbs stroked the sensitive skin where the flare of her
inner thighs began. She pressed closer, trying to rub against
him, to feel him harden against her, but he made her wait.

"Easy," he whispered. "We have plenty of time."

Before Casey could answer, he lifted her into his arms. She
gasped, then buried her face in the hollow of his neck.

"Upstairs?" he asked, his voice a deep rumble.

"Yes. At the end of the hall."

... her heart thrumming loudly in her ears. He
... up the stairs, his labored breathing coming
... exertion.

... id her on the rumpled sheets, then braced his
... hands to kiss her, one kiss leading to another until
... ssible to tell when one ended and another began.

... impered against his mouth, and he released her.

"Are you sure, *querida*?" he asked in a tortured voice. "I
can't promise you anything but tonight."

"I'm sure." Her voice was nearly breathless because of the
need shaking her. She wanted to feel him against her, in her.

He stared into her eyes, his own eyes swirling dark pools of
some intense emotion. Abruptly he straightened and pulled off
his shirt.

The mattress dipped under his weight as he sat down and
pulled off his shoes and socks. "Your turn," he said in a low
voice.

He was asking her to come to him. To make herself as na-
kedly vulnerable as he would be without his shorts. Tenderness filled her as she realized that he wasn't quite as self-assured
as he seemed.

Slowly, her eyes never leaving his, she sat up and slipped out
of her nightie, then rocked back on her hips to slide the panties over her legs, each movement offering herself without
words to the man she loved.

For a few heart-pounding seconds Alex couldn't breathe.
He'd forgotten how fine boned and delicate she was under the
tailored clothes she wore as her working uniform.

He stood and rid himself of the rest of his sweat-soaked
clothes. Sliding in next to her, he pulled her toward him.

"Tell me what you want, *querida*," he whispered. "I want
to please you."

Casey slid her hands over his shoulders and looked up at
him. She loved the arrogant tilt of his head, his shaggy hair and
the musky man-scent of him. She loved his mouth, which could
be so hard and yet so tender. She loved him. Her smile spread
as she gave a sigh of pleasure.

"You," she whispered, her throat thick with happiness. "I
want you."

His blood raced through his veins, pushing him almost beyond the limit of his control.

Patience, he told himself. This time is for her. For all the times you've wanted to love her and couldn't.

Gently he pressed her to the mattress and began kissing her again. This time he was in charge, tempting her, teasing her, his hands working their magic on her.

Her fingers ruffled through his hair, teasing the damp strands into a curling midnight thatch.

He whispered words she didn't understand, words that were urgent and deeply felt. "In English," she whispered, but he shook his head. Instead he kissed her nose, her eyes, her cheekbones. His teeth nipped at her earlobe and then moved lower to trace the faint line of her collarbone inward to the tender hollow of her neck.

It had been so long since he'd touched her, so long since he'd felt her body pulse against his, so long since he'd been able to bury himself deep inside her.

His hands shook as they rediscovered her flat belly, her tiny waist, the moist crescents under her breasts. She was beautiful, soft and sweet smelling, just the way he remembered her.

Inside, the part of him that longed for the peace she'd once given him stirred to life, tempting him with unbearable urgency. He groaned and bent his head to her breasts, suckling each nipple until the tiny bud was hard and round against his tongue. He licked the moisture from between her breasts.

Casey moaned, and beneath his lips her chest rose and fell in tiny, eager gasps. He swept his hand down the curve of her hip to her belly and below, to the silken tangle of soft curls that disappeared between her thighs. His fingers stroked and kneaded gently, then explored the warmth and wetness that filled the air around them with exquisite perfume.

She began to tremble, her breath coming in short, gasping bursts between her parted lips. "Alex," she whispered, her voice thinning to a moaning plea.

"Soon, *mi amor*," he answered, his breath warm against her breast. He moved lower, planting eager, moist kisses along her body.

He loved the fresh powdery smell of her and the feel of the taut skin around her belly button. She tasted salty on his tongue, and he knew that he'd never tasted wine that was any more delicious. He'd never been so high, so drunk with feelings he wasn't sure he would be able to control.

Casey was half gasping, half sobbing in her need to feel him inside her. His fingers stroked her lightly, then more insistently, moving down her body in demanding circles, sending wave after wave of pleasure through her until she was clinging to his shoulders helplessly, her hips arching against the heel of his hand, the exquisite friction shaking her.

"Casey, *querida*," he crooned, his fingers gently rubbing the sweet, moist spot that had given him the greatest pleasure he'd ever known.

She twisted against his hand until it moved to her hip. His heavy thigh brushed hers as he repositioned himself, and she held her breath. And then his mouth was hot on her, his tongue teasing, stroking, devouring her.

She moaned and tossed her head from side to side. The pressure built and built, and just when she thought she couldn't stand it anymore, his tongue lifted her on a tidal wave of mind-shattering pleasure. She lay limp and exhausted, her hands threaded into his hair. He rested his head on her thighs, his breathing coming in harsh, rasping gasps.

Her eyes filled with tears of happiness as she whispered his name. She stroked his hair and his sweat-damp face, filled with a deep sense of peace. It was all out in the open now, his reason for leaving, the guilt, the shame. He would begin to heal, and she would help him.

"Sleepy?" he whispered, kissing her thigh.

"Mmm." She smiled. "Just drifting."

He chuckled, then sat up and piled the pillows against the wicker headboard. Silently he cradled her damp and tingling body against him, his hand lightly stroking her thigh, gentling her, soothing her. Her arms twined around his neck, and she rested her face against the heat of his chest.

"Stay with me tonight, Alex. Just for tonight." Lovingly she nuzzled the soft springy hair tickling her cheek.

"If that's what you want."

She smiled drowsily. "Oh, it is."

"Then that's what I want, too. Tonight I want to please you, *mi amor*."

Please her? He'd done more than that for her. But she'd done nothing for him.

"Alex?" she whispered, her voice slurred with the heaviness inside her. "Why didn't you—"

"Shh, *querida*." He stroked her cheek with gentle fingers. "It's all right. Tonight was for you."

A deep, glowing lethargy settled over her like a warm blanket, and she yawned. Blinking drowsily, she fought to keep her eyes open. She wanted to stay in Alex's protective arms, listening to the heavy beat of his heart forever.

"Tomorrow," she promised, her lids becoming more and more heavy.

Alex brushed her mouth with his and cradled her close. "Go to sleep, Casey. We'll take care of tomorrow when it comes."

Sunlight filtered through the gently blowing curtains to touch her cheek. Casey lay still, enjoying the warmth on her skin. Bird song filled the air, and the clean smell of morning dew tickled her nostrils. From the bathroom came the sound of her shower.

"Mmm," she muttered, rubbing her cheek against the soft pillow. Her body was heavy with bone-deep relaxation, and she felt like singing. A dreamy smile curved her lips.

It wasn't a dream. Alex had made love to her last night. And he'd stayed with her. In her bed, his body curved protectively around hers.

Casey stretched her arms and legs, yawning through her smug smile. She turned her head, remembering the sight of his dark head on the pillow next to hers. Now only the wrinkled case showed that he'd slept there.

No, that wasn't quite right, she corrected, wiggling her bottom against the smooth sheet. Her nightgown lay in a puddle of white cloth on the floor by the bed. And the lamp was no longer lit.

She smiled and stretched. Her nipples were still swollen from Alex's mouth, and her face was faintly sore where his whiskers had rubbed.

But his lovemaking had been more than physical. Much more. His caring had been in his hands and his mouth and his eyes when he'd carried her over the edge into glorious pleasure. He didn't have to say the words. Last night he'd told her all that she need to know.

Alex loved her.

She closed her eyes, loving Alex in her mind. For so long she'd felt like a woman in mourning, her life tinged with black, and now, suddenly, she wanted to sing and shout and dance with happiness.

The shower stopped. A few seconds later the door opened. Alex emerged wearing only his shorts and shoes without socks. His morning beard was a black shadow on his strong jaw, and his hair was damp and curled over his forehead. Drops of water glistened in the dark hair covering his chest. He smelled of soap.

He approached slowly, his face intense. He reached the bed but made no move to touch her.

A flutter of anticipation tickled her throat. He was magnificently male, and he was hers. She smiled.

"Good morning," she said, her husky voice carrying a hint of shyness.

"Morning. How...do you feel?" At his cool tone Casey's welcoming smile grew smaller.

"Wonderful."

He cleared his throat. "Good. We have things to talk about."

Alex reached down to retrieve her nightgown. Silently, he held it out to her. A feeling of uneasiness came over her as she took it from his hand. "You mean about last night? About the things you told me?"

"That's part of it." He turned his back on her and walked to the window. His back was stiff and visibly tense. He braced his arm against the wall by the window and dropped his head. "I'm glad you know, but it doesn't change things. I thought it might, but your knowing just...complicates things."

Casey scrambled out of bed and struggled into her nightgown. She made no noise as she crossed the room, but Alex heard her, anyway. His back tightened as though he were bracing himself for her touch.

"Why is it a complication?" She leaned against him and wrapped her arms around his waist. He inhaled sharply, but he didn't move away.

"Because...nothing has changed."

"Of course it has!" she exclaimed. "It all makes sense now. I love you for trying to protect me. But that's all in the past. I want to be with you, to show you how much I love you. We have so many years to make up for, you and I."

"I wish it were that easy." He turned suddenly, breaking her hold, and she stumbled. He caught her arms, but he looked at a spot over her head.

He didn't want to see her smile or hear her voice full of love and hope. He couldn't care. Damn it, he couldn't love her.

"But it *is* easy, Alex," Casey whispered, her smile breaking across her face like a sunburst. Rising to her toes, she pressed against him, her arms wound around his neck. "Why are you fighting this feeling we have between us?"

His skin was hot where it touched hers, and his shoulders were stiff with restraint. "It won't work, Casey. No matter how much I want to love you, I . . . I can't."

"It will come. I can be patient. Love is always patient."

She pressed closer, rubbing her breasts enticingly against him. She'd promised him tomorrow and tomorrow was now. Her hand caressed his muscular shoulders, his strong biceps, the sensitive skin inside his elbows, her touch lightly provocative. Instantly his body hardened against her, all man and ready to be loved. A heady excitement surged through her. How could he not love her when he wanted her so much?

Alex groaned and buried his face in her sleep-mussed hair. "Casey, you . . . we have to stop," he whispered hoarsely against her neck. A hard tremor shook him, and his arms tightened until she could scarcely breathe.

She hugged him, her heart pounding. "Come back to bed, darling," she whispered, her voice low and promising. "It's tomorrow. This time is for you."

She felt the corded muscles beneath her stiffen, and then he was pushing her away. "No, not for me. Not ever for me."

Casey started to reach for him again, but he grabbed her wrists and held her away from him. He looked as though he were in mortal pain. His breathing was labored, as though he were fighting for his life.

"Alex, what's wrong? Don't you want to make love to me?"

He swallowed hard, and his shoulders drooped. "I want to. God help me, I want that more than I've ever wanted anything in my life." His voice was ragged and low, as though each word caused him terrible pain. "But . . . I can't. I'm not capable. I can't make love to any woman."

Chapter 12

Casey blinked in disbelief. "But just now," she said slowly, "you wanted me. I could feel it."

Instinctively her gaze fell to his shorts. She tried not to stare, but she couldn't seem to help herself. Only minutes ago his body had surged against hers, hard and ready. But now his arousal was gone.

She felt as though she'd fallen through a trapdoor into a black pit. She didn't know which way to turn.

"See what I mean?" His voice was icy with sarcasm.

Casey's mouth went dry. "But surely, one time—"

"*Every* time, Casey. This is the way it is with me. No matter how much I want you, as soon as I start making love to you, I stop being able to. I can't do one damn thing about it."

Alex didn't bother to hide his bitterness. He'd carried his shame and frustration for so long that he'd really thought it would be a relief to tell her. But the longer she looked at him with such shock, the more naked he felt.

"Last night . . ." Her voice trailed off. Last night he'd made love to her, all right, but only with his hands and his mouth.

"Exactly. No matter how much I wanted to . . . to be inside you, I couldn't." His face flushed. The small muscle beside his mouth jerked uncontrollably. "Now you know it all. Why I left. Why I stayed away. Why I wish like hell I'd never come here!''

He turned away, his body blocking out the sun streaming through the lace curtains. Tension radiated from him like an electric force field.

Casey took a step forward, then stopped. She twisted her hands together in front of her. ''But why, Alex? Surely there's a reason.''

''Oh, there's a reason, all right.'' He turned to face her, his expression rigidly controlled. ''Remember the night I came home from L.A.? The night we celebrated my greatest triumph?''

She nodded. ''We . . . we made love that night.''

His mouth twisted. ''Did we? As I recall, it lasted about five minutes.''

''You'd had too much to drink.''

Alex filled his lungs with air, but he still felt as though he were slowly strangling to death. ''It wasn't the liquor, Casey. It was me. I kept seeing Randy Chandler, bleeding, dying. . . .''

Casey gasped. ''No!''

His face contorted with pain. ''After I . . . realized what was happening to me, I went to see a doctor I knew about in L.A. His diagnosis was blunt. I'd built myself my own private purgatory, and until I worked out my guilt, I was going to stay there.''

Casey took two steps backward until she felt the bed behind her. Slowly she sat down and folded her hands in her lap. ''It wasn't your fault, Alex. You're the only one who thinks so.''

''You're wrong.'' His gaze dropped, then rose slowly. ''A few hours after . . . after the accident happened, Bart's widow came to see me at the plant. I had no idea why she was there. To plead for her husband, I thought. She was very calm, very matter-of-fact. I'd killed her family, she told me, just as surely as if I'd pushed them over that cliff. And I would pay. Someday I would want something as badly as she wanted her child returned to her. And then I would suffer the way she was suffering. Divine punishment, she called it. God's way.''

Casey was very cold, and her stomach was shaking uncontrollably. ''Alex, she was distraught. Hysterical.''

''Rationally, I can almost believe that, but inside, I know that I have to pay. Maybe it isn't God's way, but . . . it's mine.''

Her throat stung with pain. For him, for herself, for that faceless little boy and his suffering mother. "But...but to give up your marriage?"

"What was I giving up?" he said in a low voice. "Our marriage would have ended anyway. You're a sensuous woman, Casey. After a while, you would have been as...frustrated as I was. And eventually you would have resented being tied to a man who couldn't make love to you."

She took a slow breath. "Alex, let me help you. There are ways—"

He heard the pleading in her voice and knew that the punishment he'd borne in silence all these years wasn't nearly enough to pay for the hurt he was causing her.

Inside he was bleeding to death, but Casey was the one who was suffering. He'd left her because he had wanted to spare her this anguish. Now it seemed he'd failed at that, too.

"No one can help me, Casey. Not even you. If I hadn't owed you, I wouldn't be here. And as soon as this is over, I'm leaving. It will be better for both of us if you remember that."

He could tell her of the endless nights he'd longed to come to her. To try one more time. To let her do for him what he'd done for her last night. But in his heart, he knew that he would only fail one more time, and that would be torture for both of them.

Without looking at her, he retrieved his shirt from the floor and slung it around his neck. "I'll see you later. At the office." He walked past her.

"Alex, wait."

He turned. His jaw seemed set in granite, and his eyes were shuttered. Once again he was shutting her out.

"I'm not giving up," she told him in a quiet voice. "You were more to me than just my lover. You were my friend and my confidant and a dozen other wonderful things. Sometime during those few days in New Mexico I fell in love with the man you are now, and this time I'm not giving you up without a fight."

"You don't have a choice." For an instant he looked unbearably sad, and then the hard mask dropped over his face again. "And neither do I."

He walked out.

* * *

"...and when I told him thanks but no thanks, our good buddy Deshler looked like he was about to split a gut."

Ben Jameson perched on the side of Casey's desk and grinned. He was clearly proud of himself, and Casey didn't blame him. Not too many men had told off a powerful man like Con and gotten away with it.

Casey sat back in her chair and summoned a warm smile. "I really appreciate that, Ben. I had a feeling Con would get around to offering you the brass ring."

He bunched his shoulders awkwardly, a shy look of pleasure replacing the triumphant grin. "Hey, I can't break up the team. Like I told Dierdre before... before she died, you and I understand each other. Don't we, Casey?" His voice was almost pleading with her.

She fought off an urge to put her arms around the gawky young man and hug him. Ben had always been mercurial and sometimes acted like a spoiled brat, but deep inside he was hungry for love and acceptance. Since his sister's death, he sometimes seemed like a lost soul. But he was almost thirty years old, too old to be mothered.

"Of course we understand each other, Ben. I don't want to break up the team, either. And I'm very pleased that you've signed your proxy over to me. With the others we have locked up, we're very close to having the shares we need to win."

Mentally she crossed her fingers. They *were* close, but they still needed Rachel Eiler's shares to win. Unfortunately, the fiery little woman still refused to commit herself.

Casey had worked nonstop for a week, giving interviews to the local press, speaking at community clubs, maintaining the high profile of a progressive businesswoman. With Alex at her side she'd hosted luncheons and dinners and given tours of the plant to anyone who asked for one. Slowly, public opinion and, more importantly, shareholder confidence were swinging her way.

But she was worn out.

Being with Alex, wanting to touch him and love him, was tearing her apart. But every time she tried to talk to him, he became silent and remote. It was driving her crazy with frustration.

"What time should I pick you up tonight?"

Casey blinked. "I'm sorry, Ben. What did you say?"

His sensitive fingers toyed with the fragile porcelain dancer atop a small music box on the corner of her desk. Alex had given her the valuable antique for their first anniversary, claiming that the tiny woman in ivory lace reminded him of her.

"What time should I come by? For the shareholders' reception. We're going together, remember?"

Embarrassment warmed her cheeks. "Oh, Ben, I'm so sorry!" she exclaimed with genuine regret. "After all that's happened, I just plain forgot. Alex is picking me up." She leaned forward to place her hand on Ben's forearm. "Why don't you come with us?"

Hurt traveled slowly across his freckled face, finally settling into the tense corners of his almost feminine mouth. "No, that's cool. I can hack it by myself. No problem."

Something in his tone told her that he was not only hurt, but angry. "Ben, listen. It's just because of... of what happened the other day that I'm going with Alex. He thinks I need protection."

Against her strong protest Alex had arranged with Tri-County Security for around-the-clock guards. But she'd adamantly refused to attend Deshler's party with an armed guard by her side.

"I can protect you as well as he can," Ben muttered, getting to his feet. Inadvertently his hand brushed the music box, sending it crashing to the floor, where it shattered on impact.

His face turned chalk white. "God, I'm sorry, Casey. Maybe... maybe it can be fixed."

He bent down, gathering up the fragments awkwardly, like a scared little boy afraid to face his mother's wrath.

Casey's distress quickly turned to sympathy. "That's okay, Ben. Really," she said soothingly, averting her gaze from the shattered pieces of porcelain and polished wood in his hands.

"I'll work on it," he said, his voice dull. And then he grinned. "Don't worry. I can fix it. When I was growing up Dierdre always claimed I could fix anything."

Casey smiled reassuringly. "I believe you can."

His eyes warmed, and his smile grew affectionate. "I'll see you tonight, okay? At the party. I have a new suit."

He left, talking to himself again. Casey sat back and closed her eyes. She would enjoy the quiet for a few minutes before she headed home.

But as soon as she closed her eyes, the scene in her bedroom flashed into her mind. Over and over she'd made herself hear the words. She'd conjured up Alex's face a dozen times, searching for a clue, a hint of softening, a look of doubt, anything she could use to change his mind.

She would do anything to help him. *Anything.* But first he had to let her try.

She was beginning to drift when the phone shrilled. It was after five. Both the receptionist and Becky had left for the day so, rousing herself, she reached for the receiver. "Summerville Foundry."

"Let me speak to the person in charge." The voice was arrogantly male and bordered on rudeness. Casey sat up and glared at the phone console.

"I can help you," she said in her haughtiest Barnard accent. "This is Casey O'Neill."

"Hey, the lady herself. Maybe this is my lucky day." His voice changed, becoming unctuous. "This is Peterson of the *Middletown Daily Mail.* What can you tell me about this backdoor deal you've cut with Alex Torres of Tower Industries to merge Summerville Foundry with Chandler Aerospace?"

Casey gasped. "I beg your pardon?"

"C'mon, doll. I got a deadline. Polk of the *Cincy Times-Leader* has already scooped me. It's all over the afternoon edition, and the wire services have already picked it up. I mean, Alex Torres coming out of retirement is big news. Give me an exclusive and I'll make you look like Snow White to the folks with the votes."

"No comment." Casey slammed down the phone, her heart pounding.

"The nerve of that man," she muttered, looking around for something to hit.

"Trouble, madam president?"

She glanced up to see Alex standing in the doorway, his collar open, his tie loosened, a folded newspaper in one large fist.

"That was a . . . a very nasty man who claimed to be a reporter."

His frown was weary. "Yeah, I imagine. Deshler's trying an end run."

"A planted story?"

Alex's smile was deadly cold. "You might say that." He closed the door and crossed the office in three long strides and spread the paper in front of her. His finger tapped a box in the lower left corner of the front page. The bold black type seemed to reach up and slap her in the face.

Keeping It in the Family? —See Article, Page C-1

"Oh no," she whispered. "This is terrible."

The reporter had dredged up an old picture of Alex and her, taken just a few days before he'd gone west to finalize the Chandler deal. He was grinning, his smile a sexy white curve in his dark face. His raincoat was thrown over one shoulder, and he carried his familiar bulging briefcase in his left hand. She was wearing her favorite wide-brimmed hat and had been caught looking up at him, an adoring smile on her face.

"Oh, Lord." Silently she scanned the article.

Corporate raider Alex Torres is back. Or so it would seem. According to an unnamed source, the legendary Torres, founder and chairman of the board of multibillion-dollar Towers Industries, has agreed to help his ex-wife, Casey O'Neill, win her proxy battle with rival raider Conrad T. Deshler.

Torres, reputed to have been living in the Southwest since turning Towers over to his brother, Carlos, six years ago, is staying at a local inn with Towers's corporate counsel, Evan Michaels.

"Alex Torres never does anything without getting paid for it," an unnamed source told this reporter. Could it be that his fee for this "service" is the eventual inclusion of Summerville Foundry under the Towers umbrella? It's something for the shareholders to think about when they vote on July first.

A wave of cold anger washed over her. "For unnamed source read 'Conrad T. Deshler.'"

"More like one of his aides. They get paid for taking the heat in case of a libel suit." Alex's face was unnaturally pale and lined with weariness, and the telltale pulse was throbbing at his temple.

"You have another migraine, don't you?"

He perched on the corner of her desk, massaging the back of his neck. "Actually," he said in a dry voice, "I think it was the four cups of Mrs. Eiler's tea that did me in."

Casey stared at him. "You saw Rachel?"

"I just told you I did. For 'tea.' For a little woman she sure pours with a heavy hand."

Dumbfounded, Casey slumped back in her chair. Her mind was numb. "You didn't tell me you were seeing her. I would have gone with you."

"This was my play, Casey. A crapshoot, but this time we got lucky." Alex watched her. "Mrs. Eiler has agreed to read the statements from Jeff's former co-workers intimating that he'd been fired for taking corporate funds. Even better, she's agreed to ask him to explain the rumors. Evan has an appointment to see her at seven tomorrow morning."

Casey jumped up and ran around the desk to fling herself at him. "Oh, Alex, that's wonderful. We'll win now. I know we will."

His face twisted as though the pain in his head had suddenly increased tenfold.

Immediately, Casey stepped out of his arms. "I'm sorry," she said softly, aching for him. And for herself.

For an instant the fire was back in his eyes. "Believe me, so am I."

"Then why are you giving up?" she burst out. "Why won't you fight this?"

"Fight? Fight what?" Alex grabbed her hand and pressed it flat against his fly. He was aroused. Her heart soared—until she saw the tortured look on his face. "Feel that, Casey? All you have to do is touch me, and I want you so much I could take you right here on your desk." He flung her hand away. "But I can't, damn it. As soon as I try, I . . . that part of me is dead."

Casey took a deep breath. Slowly she began unbuttoning her blouse. He stared at her, his expression frozen. Her fingers shook, but she made herself reach for the next button.

"Stop it." His voice was harsh.

"Alex, we can try...." Her heart stopped its frantic pace and began beating with a leaden slowness.

His hands weren't gentle. He jerked her against him. "I want to do more than try. I want to bury myself so deep I won't see that poor little boy smashed against the rocks. And I want to tell you all the things I feel for you that I can't get out of my head. Damn it, Casey, I want to *love* you, but I can't. Not physically. Not the way a man loves his woman. And every time I'm with you, I feel like I'm a half-crazed animal in a cage, wanting and wanting and never having."

Tears welled in her eyes and slid down her cheeks. "Oh, Alex," she whispered helplessly. He was suffering so much, and she didn't know how to help him.

He groaned out a curse, then thrust her away. "This is what it would be like for us, Casey. Day after day, month after month, until we ended up frustrated as hell, hating each other. I can handle the loneliness. I couldn't handle that."

His face was grim as he picked up his jacket and headed for the door. "Mr. Newton," he called, beckoning curtly.

A second later, Francis Newton suddenly appeared. "Yes, sir?"

"Ms. O'Neill is ready to go home now. I'll pick her up sometime after eight, so you can tell your relief that he doesn't have to be at her place until eleven."

"Yes, sir. I reckon Buddy'll be pleased to have more time with that little waitress he's been seeing down to the Corner Café."

Alex scowled. "Tell him if he's one minute late, he's out of a job. Got that?"

"Yes, sir. I got it." Newton touched his finger to his cap.

Without looking back, Alex abruptly left the office, his footsteps sounding lonely in the empty corridor. A second later she heard the elevator doors slide shut, and he was gone.

It was almost eight-thirty when Alex rang the bell. Casey fluffed her hair one more time, grabbed her beaded evening bag from the dresser and hurried down the stairs.

Francis Newton appeared in the doorway leading to the parlor, his hand on his gun, his chilly gaze fixed on the door.

"It's okay, Mr. Newton," she said, her reassuring smile on the shaky side. "I'll get it. It's Mr. Torres."

"Yes, ma'am," he said agreeably, but he stayed where he was, ready to protect her if necessary.

Adrenaline flooded her, warming her cheeks and accelerating her pulse. She took several deep breaths, then pulled open the door.

Alex was standing with one hand in his pocket, the other loosely clenched at his side, gazing up at the huge beech tree in her front yard. His profile was drawn with bold, slashing strokes against the purple sky, reminding Casey of a painting by Remington.

But instead of jeans and a Stetson, he was wearing a dark blue suit that had been skillfully cut to accommodate his wide shoulders, and a white shirt crisp with starch that made his copper skin look even darker.

At the click of the latch Alex turned to look at her. His mouth seemed hard, even cruel in the porch light, but she had the strangest feeling that he wanted to kiss her.

"You look...lovely," he said in a low voice, his gaze lingering on the wide tapestry belt cinching the waist of her tailored silk dress. "Off-white or whatever you call that color makes you look very sophisticated."

His gaze traced the flaring line of softly shimmering fabric to her legs, which were covered in the sheerest nylon, to her plain taupe pumps, then slowly returned to her face, where it rested for a heartbeat on her lips.

"That was the idea," she told him, wanting him to kiss her so badly that she was having trouble breathing properly. "Presidential, but...approachable."

A warm breeze rustled the leaves overhead and tossed his hair onto his forehead. Her breath fluttering in her throat, Casey watched his hand brush it back. Somehow the combination of stiff white cuff, onyx cuff link and muscular brown hand seemed intensely masculine.

She stepped out onto the porch, forcing Alex to take a step backward. "I'm leaving now, Mr. Newton," she called over her shoulder. "I have my key."

Newton appeared just inside the open door. "Yes, ma'am. I'll just get my lunch box before I lock up."

"Thank you."

"See you tomorrow at 6:00 a.m. sharp." Newton disappeared.

Alex's hand was politely supportive as he helped her down the steps and into the back seat of the limousine. Casey sat stiffly, conscious of his long thigh brushing hers every time the big car rode over a bump in the poorly maintained road.

Alex still had a headache. She could see the signs, but she knew that he wouldn't admit it. Not unless it became so unbearable he could no longer hide it.

In silence they rode through town to the Grange Hall, rented for the evening by Deshler and Associates.

Alex tried to ignore the throbbing heat in his temple, but the jagged lines in front of his eyes were getting worse, and even the sound of his own breathing was painful.

He took a slow, careful breath and tried to relax. Casey was wearing a new perfume, he realized, the pain intensifying. Different from the one that had been his favorite. More provocative.

Frustration knifed through him. If she was trying to turn him on, she didn't need perfume. All she had to do was smile at him and he wanted her. But along with the wanting came an instant reminder of his own inadequacy as a man.

"Leave it to Con to find the biggest place in town," Casey muttered, leaning closer to Alex for a better look.

Alex edged away, the need for her like a fire inside him. It would always be like this for him. He'd accepted that, finally.

He ran his hand along the seat by his thigh. He hadn't slept worth a damn since the morning he'd told her the truth about himself. He doubted that he'd sleep tonight.

"Half the town is here," Casey muttered, leaning back. "I just hope I don't forget any of their names."

The chauffeur stopped in front of the brightly lit entrance and hurried around to open the door. Alex got out first, then reached back to help her.

She stepped out and took a deep breath. *Why am I so scared?* She thought anxiously, her nerves mounting. *Because,* came a faint answer, *if you lose the foundry and Alex, you'll have nothing left.* Her mouth went dry, and she licked her lips nervously.

"I'll be glad when this is over," she muttered.

Alex bent his head to whisper, "Wish you had your broom?" For an instant their eyes locked, and they shared a memory. Of a mangy cat. Of a house and a place. Of a time together.

"Yes, actually, I do. There is a certain resemblance between Con and those two coyotes."

His grin flashed. "I couldn't have said it better myself."

Side by side they walked toward the old building, now blazing with lights from every window.

Built in the early part of the nineteenth century, it had been wired for electricity and equipped with plumbing, but other than those changes, the long, narrow brick building remained unchanged.

"Oh, look," Casey whispered. "There's Ben, by that sickly looking hydrangea bush."

Alex allowed her to lead him toward the skinny scientist in the powder-blue suit. "I have to hand it to you, Case," he said in a low voice that only she could hear. "No way would I have hired that guy to run an R and D department, no matter how desperate I was. He looks like he belongs in a sandbox instead of a lab."

Casey gave Alex a warning look, then called Ben's name. He looked around nervously, searching for her. She waved. "Over here, Ben."

He shambled toward them, the jacket of his light blue suit flapping open to reveal a dark plaid shirt and red suspenders. One hand was hidden behind his back.

"I was waiting for you," he said to Casey, his grin flashing eagerly. "I wanted to give you this."

The hand that had been hidden now held a small florist's box. Beneath the clear plastic was a single white rose.

"Oh, Ben," she said, deeply touched. "It's lovely."

He ducked his head, fumbling with the lid. "Here, let me help you put it on."

His hand hovered over her breast, his face growing redder and redder. "Uh, maybe you should do it," he finally suggested.

Silently Casey handed her bag to Alex, who raised one black brow, but said nothing. She took the rosebud from the box, removed the pin from the wrapped stem and carefully affixed the corsage to her dress.

"It looks great, just great," Ben muttered. In the glare from the floodlights his amber eyes appeared almost white. Straightening his shoulders, he shot Alex a strange, almost vicious look. "Doesn't it, Torres?" Then, his freckled face flaming, he turned away to hurry with that strange, loose-jointed walk toward the crowded entrance.

"Madre de Dios," Alex muttered, handing over her bag. "The kid is in love with you."

Casey touched the flower with her fingertip. "He's just . . . vulnerable. He'll get over it."

"Don't be so sure. He looked at me like he wanted to slit my throat just because I was standing next to you."

"He's just young. Remember what you were like in your twenties."

Alex took her elbow, guiding her carefully over the cracked sidewalk. "At Jameson's age I was supporting my mother, five of my brothers and sisters, and five thousand employees. I didn't have time to fall in love."

At the door they were greeted by a man with flaming-red hair and a charming smile who asked to see their invitations.

Casey dug into her bag and pulled hers out. "Thank you, Ms. O'Neill," the man said politely, handing it back.

He turned to Alex. "Mr. Deshler asked me especially to check for *your* invitation, *Mr.* Torres," he said, his charm evaporating before her eyes.

"This party is for shareholders. I'm a shareholder."

The man's eyes narrowed. "You aren't on the list."

"I am now." Moving deliberately, his eyes never leaving the other man's, Alex pulled a folded stock certificate from the inside pocket of his suit coat. It was the one share Casey had sold him.

Deshler's lieutenant inspected the elaborately engraved certificate thoroughly, then—reluctantly, it seemed to Casey—handed it back. His gaze returned to her. Like a light bulb suddenly being switched on, his incandescent smile flashed again. "Have a nice evening."

Alex refolded the stiff parchment carefully, then returned it to his pocket. "We intend to," he said with a hard grin, brushing the man with his elbow.

The redhead looked as though he wanted to explode.

Admiration for Alex's foresight shot through her. He seemed to know what Con would do before he did it—which was exactly why she needed him.

She risked a look at Alex's face. It was cold and impassive, a mask. Only she knew how sensitive he really was. And how deeply he cared. So deeply that he'd sacrificed a part of himself to spare her.

He glanced down, catching her gaze on him. A cynical smile slanted across his face. "Okay, let's get this behind us."

Without waiting for her to answer, he took her arm and guided her through the crowd to the end of a short line of guests waiting to shake the hand of the host.

Con was standing alone on a small stage, his carefully brushed blond hair gleaming in the light. His suit was one shade lighter than Alex's and tailored in the latest style. His shirt was white, his tie expensive, his tasseled loafers gleaming. Everything was perfect.

Like Alex's attire.

But there was no comparison between the two. Strength and pride, she thought that was what Alex had innately. And an animal magnetism that was more compelling than mere good looks. Those things he had inside, wherever he was, no matter what he was doing.

Con's power came from outside. From the things he owned and the image he projected. He would never be the man Alex was, no matter how many so-called victories he piled up.

"Valor, gatita," Alex whispered close to her ear. And she smiled. He was behind her, his body nearly touching hers. She longed to lean back until she could feel his strength, steady and implacable.

At that moment Con finished with the person ahead of them and turned to shake the hand of the next person. Casey.

"Casey, honey," he murmured, his voice deepening into a caress. "It's been a long time." Swiftly, without telegraphing what he meant to do, he leaned down to kiss her hard on the lips.

Casey jerked away, but not before she saw a satisfied smirk cross Con's pale lips. Behind her she sensed rather than felt Alex stiffen.

"Back off, Deshler." His quiet voice sounded like a steel blade sliding through silk.

"I'm ready for you this time, muchacho."

"Anytime."

The men locked gazes, hatred pitted against power. The air crackled between the two, and several people standing nearby turned to stare.

Mindful of the hundreds of curious eyes all around, Casey pasted a party smile on her face and stepped between them, offering her hand. "How are you, Con? I'm not going to say it's nice to see you, because it isn't."

His palm was smooth and moist, and she tried to pull away, but his fingers tightened. "But it's wonderful to see you, Casey. You're even more lovely, if that's possible. Maybe it was the New Mexico sun, hm?"

"Or the fresh air." She tugged her hand free. "Speaking of which, if you'll excuse me, I think I need some."

Behind her she heard Alex chuckle. His hand slid around her waist, supporting her without seeming to. Her knees were weaker than she'd thought.

"I thought he was going to hit you," she said, her voice thin.

Alex led her to the bar, his hand warm against her waist. "Not on his best day." His grin flashed, devilishly white and boyishly pleased. "What do you want to drink?"

Casey touched the tiny dimple at the corner of his mouth, and his grin faltered. "A double ginger ale," she managed to get out. "I need a clear head tonight."

Alex transferred his attention to the bartender. "A tall ginger ale for the lady. And I'll have a triple Scotch. No ice."

Casey glanced at the small watch on her wrist. It was nearly eleven, but the party showed no signs of ending. She hadn't seen Alex in over an hour, not since Mrs. Eiler had ordered him to keep her company.

Another hour and she would leave, she decided wearily, slumping against the chair in the corner where she'd taken refuge. In spite of the high ceiling, the smoke in the room was beginning to get to her. And her feet hurt.

Sipping her third ginger ale, she tried to tune out the noise that had grown louder and more raucous with each round of drinks.

She'd been talking nonstop since she arrived to people she knew and, more importantly, those she didn't. Over and over she had explained present management's plans for the future, emphasizing that a one-time gain from the sale of stock was hardly worth years of increasing dividends.

For the past hour Ben had frequently been at her side, disappearing now and then to refill her glass. Absently she glanced down at the corsage on her shoulder.

The white rose was beginning to wilt. I know how that feels, she thought, wiggling her toes in her new shoes.

"Miss O'Neill?" The young woman gazing at her warily was even shorter than she was. A mass of mousy-brown curls overpowered her small, pale face, and her blond brows and lashes gave her a naked look.

"Hello," Casey said, standing and smiling to put the obviously nervous young woman at ease. "Have we met?"

The woman shook her head. Pressing her hands together in front of her, she looked at Casey pleadingly. "I'm Emily Plunkett. Jeff's wife."

Casey froze. "I see."

"No, no, you don't. He's a good man, my Jeff. Loving."

"I'm sure he is," Casey said carefully, trying to figure out what this woman wanted. Whatever it was, she was clearly having a difficult time expressing herself.

"It's just that I...after Tessa, my little girl, was born, I...I couldn't seem to...function. I had these headaches, and sometimes when the baby cried and cried, I sat down and cried, too. I had trouble making myself take care of her. Finally I just packed up and went home to my mother."

Casey frowned. "Postpartum depression?" she suggested gently.

"Yes, that's what my...my therapist called it. At the hospital." The woman's voice was so quiet that Casey had to bend close to hear her. "That's where the money went. To the hospital."

Casey felt a pit open in her stomach. "What money, Mrs. Plunkett?"

The woman's face flushed a bright pink. "The money Jeff...borrowed from Mr. Deshler's company. He found out about it, but once Jeff explained...Mr. Deshler let him... resign. He didn't even make him pay back the money." Her voice broke on a half sob. "If Jeff is sent to jail..."

Her thin hand clutched Casey's tightly. "If you make Jeff admit he's lying about you, Mr. Deshler is going to file criminal charges." She was crying openly now. "Please, Miss O'Neill. Please don't hurt us."

Casey stood frozen, sick inside. The woman's nails dug into her wrist, but she barely felt the pain. So that's it, she thought sadly. Jeff had done a bad thing for a good reason.

Now, paradoxically, his fate was in her hands. Emily Plunkett was no match for Evan. All he had to do was ask the right questions, and the woman would spill everything. Of course, they wouldn't be able to use her words in court, but they *could* use them to convince Mrs. Eiler to demand an explanation from her godson. If he stuck to his story, he would be branding his wife a liar, and Casey had a feeling he wouldn't do that, Deshler or no Deshler.

Casey stared into the woman's pleading, tear-filled eyes. I can't do it, she thought, the heavy weight of sympathy making her shoulders droop. Sacrificing this woman and her child to win would be going against everything she believed in.

Taking a deep breath, Casey pressed Emily's hand between hers. "Don't cry anymore, Emily. I won't hurt you and your little girl."

The woman's smile was tremulous, but her eyes were bright. "God bless you," she whispered. Clamping her lower lip between her teeth, she withdrew her hand and disappeared into the crowd.

Feeling as if she'd just sustained a fatal blow, Casey looked around quickly, searching for Alex's dark head. He was at the bar.

Like a woman walking in her sleep, she made her way unerringly to his side. Her hand trembled as it touched his shoulder. He looked up quickly, his eyes glinting. As soon as he saw her face, he frowned. "What's wrong?"

"I have to talk with you."

"Cancel that coffee," he told the bartender, then took Casey's arm, leading her to a spot near the door. "Okay, let's have it."

As concisely as she could manage, she recounted her conversation with Emily Plunkett. When she was finished, Alex stared at her as though she'd suddenly punched him in the face. Tonelessly he began to swear. In Spanish. In English. In Spanish again.

"There goes Rachel Eiler's proxy," he said finally, running a hand around the back of his neck. "I didn't want to tell you this, but Evan ran some numbers today. With Rachel's proxy and without. With her, you win. Without . . ." He shrugged.

"Con wins."

"Yes."

Casey clutched his arm, needing his support. "I couldn't hurt an innocent woman. I know that's hard to understand—" Her words died in her throat. "I'm sorry," she whispered. "For a few moments I . . . forgot."

He stared at her, his gaze burning into hers fiercely. "Do you trust me enough to risk everything on one throw of the dice?" His expression frightened her, but she tried not to show it.

"Yes. I trust you, Alex. With my life, if it comes to that."

His control slipped for an instant, and she saw the vulnerable man beneath. And then a violent emotion came into his eyes. "It won't." He gripped her shoulder. "Put that confident smile back on your face and keep it there. No matter what."

With the rangy stride that she loved, Alex made his way to the front of the room. He was already taller than most of the people in the room. When he stepped onto the stage, he towered head and shoulders over nearly everyone.

"May I have your attention, please?" His voice rang out clearly, carrying a concise note of command that shocked the room into silence for a split second before a buzz of surprise began again.

Alex held up both hands and called for silence. All eyes turned his way, and the room gradually grew quiet.

"For those of you who don't know me, my name is Torres. Like all of you, I'm a shareholder in Summerville Foundry." There was a swell of comment, which Alex quickly quelled. "I'm sure few of you have ever read the articles under which Summerville Foundry was incorporated, but I have." His grin flashed, engaging and warmly persuasive, and Casey felt a shiver of desire. The man had charisma by the bucketful, when he chose to use it.

"Under special conditions for calling a meeting of the board, clause sixty-seven, paragraph A states that a vote of confidence for the sitting board may be called at any time by any shareholder. Paragraph B stipulates that said meeting will take place within forty-eight hours of public notice of same."

Alex's glance shifted to Con Deshler who was standing by the bar, a look of blank fury contorting his handsome face. "I hereby call such a meeting, which will be held at the foundry on this coming Sunday afternoon at one o'clock sharp. You are all invited to attend." His grin flashed again. "I intend to vote for Casey O'Neill and the other members of the sitting board. I strongly urge you to do the same."

* * *

"You got that right," Alex muttered into the car phone, his hand methodically rubbing the back of his neck. "Not only did it hit the fan, it splattered all over Deshler's face."

Casey heard Evan's raucous laughter come through the receiver, and she closed her eyes, picturing Con's shocked expression. Almost all of his supporters came from out of state, while the majority of hers were local. There was a good possibility most of his people wouldn't be able to attend on such short notice. And since it was the weekend, they wouldn't be able to send in their proxies in time.

The moment Alex had stepped down from the stage, the Grange Hall had exploded with sound. It had taken her nearly fifteen minutes to work her way to the door where Alex was waiting.

The parking lot had been clogged with departing cars, and Alex had used the delay to call Evan at the inn. Suddenly exhausted, Casey listened idly, grateful that he had taken charge. At the moment she doubted that she could make a rational decision of any kind, let alone one of vital importance.

"...and one more thing, Evan. Arrange for a team of independent auditors to be here by Sunday morning. If nothing else, we're going to have an honest count."

The limousine bounced over the curb and into the street. Alex winced at the sudden movement, and Casey hurt for him. He needed sleep.

After a few more words, he hung up and leaned back. "One thing you gotta say about Con," he said slowly, only his eyes turning toward her. "He gives a hell of a party."

Casey burst out laughing. "I have a feeling he didn't enjoy this one very much."

His grin was stiff with pain and fatigue. "I think you're right." He pressed a button near the phone console, and soft music surrounded them.

He hesitated, then lifted her hand from the seat between them and placed it on his leg, just above his knee. Casey snuggled against his side and rested her head on his shoulder and closed her eyes.

Tears pressed her throat, but she swallowed them away. They'd ridden home countless times just like this. But in those days, when the trip had ended, Alex had taken her upstairs and made love to her.

"Mr. Torres." The chauffeur's voice carried an urgent note of warning, and Casey sat up quickly, her eyes wide.

They'd just made the turn onto her street, and her house was two doors down. The streetlight was shining brightly, and a man was sprawled facedown on her front steps.

"Is it Mr. Newton?" she whispered, her nails digging into Alex's leg.

"No, the other one. Buddy."

Miklos pulled the long black car to a smooth halt behind the rusted-out pickup truck belonging to the young security guard. He set the brake, then reached into the glove compartment to draw out a snub-nosed revolver.

"Alex?" She stared at the gun.

"It's okay," he said in a grim tone. "He has a license to carry it." The two men exchanged glances in the rearview mirror. Alex nodded slightly, and the chauffeur climbed out.

Alex opened the door. "Get on that phone and call an ambulance. And the marshal."

Grabbing his hand, she tried to gulp down her fright. "Be careful."

Alex left the car without answering.

Her stomach leaping nervously, Casey picked up the phone and called the operator.

By the time she'd completed her calls and scrambled from the cavernous back seat, the guard was sitting up and talking. His voice was slurred, but strong. He seemed alert.

"Like I said, I was walking around the house, checkin' things out, ya know, and I heard this little scufflin' noise behind me. I started to turn around, but the guy musta hit me with somethin', 'cause the next thing I know, I'm wakin' up over there by that bush. I was goin' inside for the phone and got dizzy."

"Did you see the man's face?" Alex asked in a low voice, his gaze searching the porch and the blank windows facing the street for signs of life.

"No, sir. I didn't see nothin'."

"The ambulance is on the way," Casey said quietly, standing between Alex and the chauffeur. "The dispatcher said not to move him." She smiled reassuringly at the young guard.

"I don't believe I will move just yet. My head hurts like a sonofa...sorry, ma'am. Like the very devil."

Buddy blinked drowsily, trying to smile. He was a handsome young man, in a rawboned sort of way. Like Francis, she realized, but without the serious cast to his features.

"Casey, give me your key," Alex ordered, his eyes on the front door.

"Don't you think you should wait for the marshal?"

"No." Alex plucked the bag from her hand, then bent down to empty the contents onto the steps. Her key ring hit the cement with a metallic ping. He dropped the bag and grabbed the keys.

"Stay here," he ordered, taking the steps two at a time. He tried the door. It was locked.

Silently he used the key, then inched the heavy door open. It squeaked, and Casey, creeping up the steps only a few feet behind him, jumped. But she managed to swallow her gasp of surprise.

Alex pushed the door open another foot, then paused to listen. No sound. No signs of life inside. He stepped inside and flipped the switch by the door.

Casey heard only the sound of her own breathing. Walking on the balls of her feet so that her heels wouldn't clatter on the floor, she entered the foyer. Alex was standing in the open door to the parlor, his back stiffly straight, his face frozen.

"What is it?" she whispered, but he didn't seem to hear her.

Casey followed the direction of his unmoving stare. "Oh my God," she whispered in a choked voice. "It's... it's like someone went crazy in here."

Tears shimmered in her eyes. Her hand shaking, she pressed her fist to her mouth. The room was a shambles. Stuffing had been ripped from the madam's couch and the antique chairs. Oil paintings had been slashed, tables smashed to splinters. The cradle was a pile of kindling. All her carefully chosen things had been destroyed.

"The bastard," Alex said in a dangerous voice.

Casey took a closer look. This time the vandal had written "Chandler" over and over. And another single word even more frequently.

"Killer," she read in growing horror. She felt as though she were going to be sick. Pressing her hand against her stomach, she turned slowly to find Alex watching her, a look of terrible sadness on his face.

"Someone knows," she whispered.

Alex's voice was deathly quiet. "Yes, someone knows."

Chapter 13

The church was small, hardly more than a chapel. It was nestled in a stand of oaks on a little rise outside of Camden, Summerville's nearest neighbor, and reminded Alex of the little church in the barrio where he and Casey had been married.

It was cool inside, and quiet. The sunlight streaming through the stained-glass windows dappled the interior with colors, and the long, narrow sanctuary smelled of candle wax and incense.

The Sunday morning masses were over. No one was there but him.

Slowly, his footsteps sounding unnaturally loud in his ears, Alex crossed the small foyer and walked down the center aisle, a feeling of déjà vu shaking him. He saw again his younger brothers and sisters clambering over the backs of the pews in spite of his efforts to keep them contained. He remembered his mother in the old-fashioned black dress that grew shabbier every year. And he remembered Casey on their wedding day.

Something stirred inside, something that felt like a terrible sadness. She'd been so lovely, his bride. Radiant, everyone had said. To him she'd simply been his dearest love. The woman he'd needed all his life.

At the altar rail he genuflected as he'd been taught, crossing himself, his fingers lightly touching his forehead, his chest, his shoulders, saying the ritual words in his mind. He glanced up at the altar, his gaze brushing the figure of the man on the cross. The stirring inside him turned to a wrenching pain as he slipped into the second pew.

He bowed his head and closed his eyes. Sometimes the silence helped. Sometimes he could blank his mind and let the serenity flow over him. Sometimes he stopped remembering. Sometimes.

A sudden tension tightened his muscles, and he shifted uneasily against the hard seat. His words came back to him, haunting him. "Hard as a church pew," he'd said, referring to Casey's prized sofa.

That had been the same night he'd told her about Bart Chandler. About Randy.

Slowly he ran his hand over the lifeless wood. The madam's love seat was now splintered beyond repair, destroyed by Deshler or one of his hired hands.

Because of him. The great Alex Torres. The guy who'd thought winning was the only important thing in life.

A bitter taste rose in his throat, nearly choking him. All his life he'd worked hard, trying to make things better for the people he cared about. But in his drive for the top, he'd made others suffer for his success. People who didn't deserve to suffer. Like Randy Chandler and his mother. Like Casey.

Slowly he raised his gaze to the face of the Madonna smiling down from the side of the altar. Her eyes were soft, her face radiating love and forgiveness.

Those were Casey's eyes.

Alex dragged his hands down his face, fighting for control. The pain inside him spread, making him sick. He'd been without her for so long. So damn long. And now he had to leave her again.

Suddenly he saw her small face streaked with tears, her eyes wide with horror at the mess that, a few hours before, had been her treasured mementoes. He'd tried so hard to keep the ugliness away from her. To protect her from the stain of his guilt. But he'd failed.

Oh yeah, you're one hell of a man, Torres, he taunted himself silently. A real great guy. You can do it all, can't you? Work two jobs and go to school at night. Build a company from nothing. Force the bastards to smile when you walk into one of their private clubs.

But your money can't protect your woman from pain. And that so-called brilliant mind of yours can't save her company. And as for making love, forget it.

Alex broke out in a cold sweat, his heart beginning to slam against his ribs. In his dreams he was the perfect lover. In his dreams he filled Casey with his love, the way a man does when his woman is aroused and eager and waiting for him. In his dreams he was a whole man. But only in his dreams.

For a few seconds Alex couldn't breathe. He knew, and now Casey knew, that he wasn't a whole man. He never would be again. No matter how much he wanted to use his body to show her the things in his heart, that part of him would always fail.

He was inadequate, a failure at the one thing a man prizes most—his ability to satisfy his woman.

Alex stared at the carved crucifix over the altar. At the lines of suffering and sorrow worked into the wood. At the bloody wound.

A slow, agonizing death, crucifixion. In catechism the priests had talked about it a lot. It had always embarrassed Alex, all the talk of suffering and sacrifice. "If that had been me," he remembered proclaiming. "I would have fought the *cabrones*."

"But Christ would have been betraying the people he loved," the priest had told him with a sad smile. "And that would have hurt even more."

"You were right, padre," Alex muttered. "It hurts like hell." He dragged his gaze from the cross, staring blindly at the snowy altar cloth.

Casey was waiting for him at the foundry. Waiting for him to keep his promise to save her company.

But there were no more tricks, no more clever moves, no more surprises to pull out of a hat at the last minute. For the first time since he'd begun his climb to the top, the great Alex Torres was about to crash and burn.

He opened his eyes and stared down at the ring on his finger, the ring he'd never removed since Casey had put it there. No matter how the vote went, he'd already lost. He'd lost the one thing most precious to him. His wife.

Alex took a weary breath, his gaze lighting on a missal lying on the seat. He'd said the ancient prayers all his life. Prayers asking for forgiveness and compassion, muttered quickly, by rote. Had he ever truly felt them in his heart?

To him, forgiveness came from the part of God that every man carried inside himself. And that God refused to grant him absolution.

Tell me what to do, damn it! he cried in his mind, slamming his fist against the seat. I'll do it. *Anything.* Only take this hell from me!

Slowly, his teeth bared, Alex slipped to his knees, gripping the back of the pew in front of him so tightly that the veins in his hands stood out. Bowing his head, he pressed his forehead against his knuckles and closed his eyes.

"Dios, por favor," he prayed aloud, lapsing instinctively into the comforting language of his childhood. "Give me strength. Help me..."

His voice broke, and he stopped, his hands tightening until the muscles burned. No matter what he promised that cold, stern God, no matter how desperately he'd tried to remake the man he hated, it wasn't enough. How could he make up for the death of an innocent child? How could he wash the blood from his hands, so that he could touch Casey without feeling dirty and unworthy?

A pain like none he'd ever felt before came over him, making him feel as though he'd been suddenly gutted by a sharp knife and left for dead. Crying out, he shook the pew so violently that the hymnals fell from the racks and crashed to the floor.

But it didn't help. Nothing helped. Nothing ever would. Life didn't give second chances, not to people like him. Casey would never be his again.

In silence, Alex got slowly to his feet and left the church. It was time.

"For heaven's sake, Evan, you have to know where he is. Casey paced her office, stopping to look out the window every few seconds, searching for the black limousine.

Evan had been at her side since seven, teasing her, bolstering her, ordering her to eat when her breakfast stuck in her throat. Francis Newton was stationed by the elevator, and Sam Rickert had posted a deputy in the cafeteria, where the meeting was to be held. Still, she felt vulnerable and alone—because Alex wasn't with her.

Seated behind her desk, Evan looked up from the papers he'd been scanning, his face drawn. "He and the car and the driver were gone when I got up at six. That's *all* I know." He bowed his head, but not before Casey saw the flash of guilt in his green eyes.

"Evan, look at me."

Slowly he complied. The guilt was gone, but not the frown between his rusty brows. "Alex will be here, Casey. I'd stake my life on it." Methodically he arranged the papers in front of him, one on top of the other.

"There's something you're not telling me. What is it?"

His frown didn't ease. "I think Alex had better tell you himself."

Something in his tone alerted her. "He's leaving right after the meeting, isn't he?" It was a guess, but Evan's sudden flush told her that it had been accurate.

"That's the plan, yes. The Jetstar is waiting at the airport in Covington."

Casey turned away, her motions wooden. But that was exactly how she felt, she realized. Like a puppet, dangling from the strings of her emotions.

Yesterday she and Alex been together nearly every minute, phoning investors. He'd called those with the most shares, the ones already pledged to her and the ones who were still undecided, while she'd phoned all her supporters within driving distance, urging them to attend the meeting.

It had been a tense time for both of them. Neither had mentioned the problem that lay like an unexploded bomb between them. They'd talked only of business, as though they'd made an unspoken pact to avoid anything personal. But Casey had thought about it constantly.

Alex was too vital, too masculine, to live out his life like one of the *penitentes* she'd once read about, condemned to flay himself forever for one mistake. There had to be some way of reaching him. Of convincing him that he'd paid long and hard enough. But how?

Last night she'd thought about the problem until her head ached and exhaustion made the room spin. She'd finally cried herself to sleep, something she hadn't done since her father had left her. Tonight . . .

Her mind shut down, refusing to venture along that dangerous path. Alex hadn't left yet—at least, Evan didn't think so.

As long as he was still here, with her, there was hope. She'd solved harder problems than this. She would find a way to convince him to try one more time to work things out.

The sound of the elevator doors opening interrupted her thoughts. She inhaled sharply. Alex was here.

But it was Rachel Eiler who appeared in the doorway. From the top of her feathered hat to the tips of her sensible Oxfords, she was dressed in black.

For a funeral? Casey wondered cynically, forcing a smile.

"Cassandra, pay attention. I've come to tell you my decision." Her tone was imperious, but Casey thought she heard a note of regret, too.

"Come in, please, Mrs. Eiler," she said, the warmth in her voice genuinely felt. No matter what happened, she couldn't help liking the feisty little woman. "I believe you already know Evan Michaels."

Like a queen greeting a subject Mrs. Eiler regally inclined her head, her alert gaze sweeping the room. A strange look crossed her face as though she were disappointed. Could she be looking for Alex? Casey wondered, crossing the room to press the hand Mrs. Eiler extended impatiently.

Evan rose politely, but remained standing behind the desk. "Mrs. Eiler," he said with a reserved smile. Mrs. Eiler had been puzzled when Evan had canceled his appointment with her, and then incensed when first Alex and then Casey refused to elaborate on the reason.

"You need to get out in the sun, young man." Rachel's tone carried a stinging rebuke. "You're too pale."

"Yes, ma'am."

The old lady's gaze skipped to Casey, her thin white brows arching above the rims of her glasses. "As for you, I'm here to tell you how disappointed I am. You had me fooled, Cassandra. I thought I saw myself in you, but you let me down. I don't know if the rumors I've heard are true or not, if you've cheated the way Jeff claims or plotted with Alejandro like the papers are saying, but too many strange things have happened for me to take a chance."

For an instant she looked terribly tired, and the plumes on her hat seemed to droop in sympathy. "I am truly sorry, Cassandra, but I intend to vote my shares with that man Deshler." She paused, her bird-bright eyes snapping with something that looked like hope. "Unless you have...something to tell me that might change my mind?"

Casey clasped her hands tightly in front of her. Outside, cars were arriving steadily, filled with the shareholders who would decide if she was to stay or go. Whether she was to win or lose.

Evan had just told her that Con had gotten a significant number of his supporters here in time. In chartered planes, by hired cars, any way he could. Without Rachel the odds were about even.

One word now, she realized, and she would win. But that would mean breaking her word to Emily Plunkett, and that was something she couldn't do.

Casey took a steadying breath. She felt Evan's eyes on her, but she didn't dare look at him. She was afraid she would burst into tears.

"No, nothing, Mrs. Eiler. Except this: I've never lied to you. Nor will I. I can only say that every decision I've ever made has been in the best interests of our employees and the town."

Casey saw the sadness come into the old lady's eyes. And the resolve. "So be it," the other woman pronounced sadly. She turned, retracing her steps slowly until she disappeared from sight.

Casey felt a pang of compassion. This mess had taken a toll on Rachel, too.

Silence filled the pine-paneled office. Evan busied himself with his papers. Casey stared at the floor. At the wall. At the open doorway.

In a few hours it would all be over. She would be vindicated or not. Either way, she would never be the same again.

Evan cleared his throat. "Casey, however this goes, I want you to know that you did one terrific job with this company. Anyone with any knowledge of business can see that just by looking at the record."

Casey managed a genuine smile. "Thanks, Evan. I...needed that."

He gave her a brief smile. "About Alex..."

"I love him," she said simply, her voice wobbling.

"I know. So does he. That's what's eating at him. He doesn't want to hurt you again."

Casey studied his somber face. What was he trying to tell her? "You...know? About Chandler?"

"I know. Alex set up a trust fund for Bart Chandler's wife, and I did the work." He fiddled with the handle of his brief-case. "Alex went through hell before he could finally make himself leave you, Casey. He was afraid the press would find out. That you would be dragged through the mud with him. I've always been astounded that a man could go through that kind of torment without cracking wide open, but he did. He just took the pain inside himself so it wouldn't touch you. I have a feeling it's still there."

She nodded sadly. "I know that now. At the time I thought he'd found someone else."

Evan's brows furrowed. "Not from the moment he met you." He moved around the desk and took her hand. "You two belong together."

Casey curled her hand around his. "You know that, and I know that. But how can we convince Alex?"

"Convince me of what?"

Evan's hand tightened, and Casey clung to him, her com-posure shaky. Alex was standing in the doorway, looking so handsome in a perfectly cut gray suit she wanted to cry.

"To stay for the...victory celebration Becky has planned for tonight," she answered.

Alex's eyes narrowed, and his demanding gaze shifted to Evan.

"I didn't tell her," the attorney said quietly. "She guessed."

Evan pressed her hand, then released her. Quickly repack-ing his case, he gave Alex a brief grin. "See you two down-stairs." He glanced at his watch. "In five minutes." He gave Casey a thumbs-up and left.

Casey felt the air in the room change. It was warmer some-how, now that Alex was with her. And the knotty pine walls took on a cozy closeness.

But that was illusion. She and Alex had never been further apart. Not even in those sad last days in Manhattan. Then, at least, she'd had her anger to sustain her. Now she felt exposed, stripped bare by her own helplessness.

"I was afraid you'd left," she said softly, walking to the window. The lot below was nearly full, and one of Dutch Shrader's men was directing the overflow traffic to the grassy lot beyond the plant.

"I told you I'd stay until the end."

She turned to look at him. He seemed different somehow. Not physically. Physically, he was every woman's dream. Tall, dark, more than handsome. But something had changed inside, something vital, as though a door had closed on a part of him.

She ran her hand over her hip, trying to ease the need to smooth the lines of suffering from his face. "No matter what happens downstairs, I want you to...to know that I'll never forget what you tried to do for us...for me. I know now how much courage it took." She twisted her hands together and fought the tears that threatened to overwhelm her.

Alex's throat worked, as though he was having trouble swallowing. "I wanted to win one more time. For you." His smile was fleeting. "If we'd had more to work with..." He shrugged. *"Quien sabe?"*

"Yes, who knows?"

She glanced at the scene below. Most of the people had arrived by now. There was no reason to delay. A thick lock of curling hair fell across her cheek, and she brushed it away with an impatient hand. A month ago she would have worried about how she looked. Now she only cared about how she felt inside. And right now, she'd never felt worse.

Alex watched her fidget with her sun-tipped hair, her silky white blouse, the large silver pin on the lapel of her suit. He'd never seen Casey look so nervous or, damn it, so desirable. A part of him died a little more.

One hour, two, he would get through the days a few minutes at a time, until it stopped hurting so much. And then he would be able to breathe again.

"Ready?" Alex fingered the coins in his pocket, his gaze tracing the gentle curve of her cheek. Her skin had a delicate bloom, like the tawny color of a cactus flower at dawn.

"Ready as I'll ever be, I guess." She tried for a smile but failed. "I wish I had my lucky blouse."

"Your what?"

"The cinnamon silk that goes with this suit. I wore it on the day I interviewed for my first job as a management consultant. And I...I was wearing it the day you walked into my office in Pittsburgh."

A faint smile deepened the hollows below his chiseled cheekbones. "What happened to it?"

"It was ruined in the rain that day I came to see you at the school. Remember?"

His eyes clouded, and his smile stiffened at the corners. "Yes, I remember. I thought you were a mirage. A living vision out of my dreams come to torment me." An aura of pain, worse than anything caused by his migraines, surrounded him.

"Oh, Alex," she whispered achingly, "I don't want to torment you. I want to love you."

He longed to kiss the shadows from her eyes, but he knew that would only prolong the agony. A clean break was better for both of them. "And I...want to love you, *querida*. I'll always wish that I'd been a better man so that I could."

He straightened his already rigid shoulders and held out his hand. Tears clogged her throat as she took it. Side by side they walked to the elevator, where the guard was waiting.

Casey's pulse began to race. This was it. "Ready or not," she muttered, giving her linen skirt one more tug. "Here we come."

The cafeteria was filled to capacity. The fire chief stood at the door, keeping latecomers in the hall. Next to him stood the imposing bulk of Marshal Rickert, his attentive brown eyes continuously scanning the rows of attendees.

In spite of the air conditioning, which had been cranked up to high, the large room was uncomfortably warm, and many of the people in the audience were using the annual report they'd found on their seat as a fan.

Casey shifted her weight against the uncomfortable backrest of the molded plastic chair and uncrossed her ankles. The meeting had been in session for nearly two hours, and her back was beginning to ache.

She and the other members of the board were seated at a table to the right of the speaker's podium. The rest of the cafeteria tables had been removed, and chairs had been lined up in narrow rows to the back wall.

Ben, again wearing his new suit, this time with a white shirt, sat in the middle of the second row, bracketed by Becky and the rest of Casey's staff. Alex and Evan sat in the front row on one side of the center aisle. Mrs. Eiler and Jeff Plunkett were seated directly opposite. Next to the somber-faced old lady was an empty chair where Con Deshler had been seated.

At the moment the suave raider was at the podium, speaking, and the crowd was with him. Casey had never seen such a performance. Alternately charming and forceful, he'd praised her accomplishments in glowing terms while at the same time insinuating that she'd taken the foundry as far as it could go.

"It's time for a change," he'd said several times in several different ways. And each time he'd said it, it had sounded more convincing. The crowd was loving it—along with his glowing predictions of escalating dividends.

Stifling a sigh, Casey contemplated the sea of faces in front of her. Alex's dark hair and skin stood out starkly, a man out of place in this world of peaches-and-cream complexions, German names and Georgian architecture. And yet he was clearly the most impressive presence in the room.

Their eyes met, and he smiled his encouragement. Lines that had come more from suffering than laughter fanned out from the corners of his eyes, reminding her of the burden he'd borne alone and without complaint for so long.

A heavy weight of grief settled into a sheltered corner deep inside her. Without him here, buoying her, smiling encouragingly at her, she never would have made it this far.

She had spoken first, her nerves making her voice thin. But she'd poured her heart into her words, holding nothing back. By the time she'd finished everyone knew exactly how she felt about her employees and the town. The applause had been deafening. But a proxy fight came down to numbers, and those were still against her.

Strangely, though, the idea that she might lose didn't hurt as much as it once had. A few blocks away was a room filled with ruined furniture and shattered mementoes. Things that had withstood the dangers of a sea voyage and the ravages of age were now gone forever. Like her dream of a life with Alex.

"...and so, my fellow shareholders, if you want to see those dividend checks grow fatter and fatter every quarter, if you want to see Summerville Foundry more profitable than ever before, I ask you to vote your proxies for me and the directors I support." Deshler's all-American grin flashed, and he held up his hands in a victory salute. "Thank you."

Applause rose from the audience in a wave, pounding against Casey's eardrums in a mocking crescendo. Con milked it skillfully, picking out influential supporters in the audience for a special smile, a wave, a knowing look.

The man should be running for office, she thought wearily. But maybe that was in the plan someday. He would make a perfect politician, television handsome and exuding charisma from every pore.

"It's all yours, honey," he muttered, giving her a look that said the opposite. He'd won, and they both knew it.

Casey rose and returned to the podium. Her knees were shaking, but she managed to keep a calm smile on her face. "Thank you, Mr. Deshler. And now I'd like to throw the floor open for questions or remarks from any of you who own shares."

She waited, scanning the audience for hands. There was only one. "Mr. Torres," she said, her throat dry. Alex hadn't been scheduled to speak. She had no idea what he intended to say.

Unless he planned to tell the truth about Jeffrey Plunkett. Her heart skipped, then accelerated.

No, she thought, relinquishing the podium with a nervous smile. He wouldn't betray her. Not the man she'd come to know these past few weeks.

"Hang in there, *gatita*," Alex said in a voice too low to be heard by anyone but her.

She managed a nod before she turned away.

By the time she sat down she was shaking so hard she was grateful for the punishing vinyl seat that keep her rigidly erect. Alex turned his head to catch her eye, and for an instant she saw pain. And a plea. As though he were asking for her support.

Her throat closed. Alex had never once needed her help, but for some reason, he did now. She gave it willingly, letting him see the absolute trust she'd promised in her eyes. A look of stark gratitude glinted in his black pupils for a heartbeat before he turned away to face the crowd.

His hands gripped the sides of the podium, and he stood tall, a man who never had to bow his head to anyone again. The man she loved.

He cleared his throat, then smiled. "Good afternoon," he began in a deep, resonant voice. The amplification emphasized his slight accent, giving his words an intensity that Con's rounded tones had lacked.

"For those of you who don't know me, my name is Alex Torres. I am, or was before I retired, a corporate raider like…Mr. Deshler here. In fourteen years I took over thirty-two companies. Some were much bigger than yours, some smaller, but all had something I wanted."

Alex paused. The room was hushed, and there was a charged feel to the air. He tightened his grip on the podium and made himself look toward the half dozen or more reporters seated in a special section to his left. They were busy scribbling in their notebooks, their expressions greedy. By tonight his words would be plastered all over the country.

He took a deep breath. This was Casey's only hope, and even then, it was the longest of long shots.

"I tell you this because I want you to know how a raider like me thinks. A raider's bottom line is profit. Money in his pocket." He speared Deshler with a hard look. "In this case, that means patents and customers, both of which will benefit his own high-tech foundry in California. And I mean California."

A sound like a ragged gasp rose from the spectators, followed by a low undertone of urgent conversation that spread like a wave before Alex stopped it by glancing around the room, one brow cocked.

Deshler's face didn't change, but Alex saw the fury in the cold blue eyes. "What he *doesn't* want are these old buildings and the workers inside them. It might take a few months, it might take a year, but eventually, no matter what he tells you now, this operation will be shut down, the buildings locked up tight or sold off, the assets stripped, the workers laid off. Terminated."

This time the noise swelled louder, and angry words of protest and disbelief were heard over the din.

Alex waited for the buzz of comment to die. "I know this because that's exactly what I did six years ago with a company called Chandler Aerospace."

No! Casey shouted silently, her spine growing rigid.

He paused, as though he'd heard her silent plea. Casey held her breath, watching him fight for control. She knew—and he knew—what he was facing if he told the truth about Chandler: the headlines, the public scorn, the humiliation.

Don't, she pleaded with her eyes, her stomach lurching violently. Don't humble yourself for me, my darling. Please don't.

Alex straightened his shoulders and continued in a strong, clear voice. "Chandler was about this size, and I wanted it just about as much as Mr. Deshler seems to want Summerville Foundry. And I worked as hard as he's worked to get it.''

As he talked, Alex felt Casey's spirit reaching out to him, loving him. It gave him the strength to tell it all—his ruthlessness, his disregard for Bart's impassioned pleas, his determination to wipe out all traces of previous management.

He made himself accept the looks of horror that flashed over the faces he could see and the whispered words of censure. He made himself ignore the cunning look of triumph on Deshler's bland face. He'd given the bastard a sword. As sure as there was a hell, he would pay for what he was doing. But if Casey won, it would be worth it.

Alex was sweating when he was finished with the hard part, and he was sick inside. But he was strangely relieved to have the secret he'd carried so long exposed. Maybe now, in some small way, he could find a measure of peace.

"On the day that Bart Chandler and his son were buried, I swore that I'd never go after another company. I never have. I never will.''

The microphone picked up the throb of grief in his deep voice, and Casey wanted to weep. But she made herself sit perfectly still. She was afraid that any movement, however slight, might break the spell that Alex's blunt confession had cast over the listeners.

He paused, glancing pointedly toward the press. "In spite of the stories you've read and the rumors you've heard, I came here for one reason only, to help Casey O'Neill maintain control of the company she almost single-handedly resurrected from the dead.''

His eyes grew warm, and his voice rang with praise as he said slowly and distinctly, "I don't know of anyone, not even me on my best day, who could have done what she did. This place was history when she took over. I wouldn't have put a dime into it, but because she believed in people instead of statistics, she turned it around. And that's why it will continue to grow and prosper—because your CEO knows what's really important.''

Unerringly his gaze found hers. His eyes warmed, grew loving. Casey felt the contact in every part of her. This was personal. She knew it. Everyone who heard the tenderness in Alex's voice knew it, but she didn't care. Having his respect was more important to her than any company.

She let her love for him shine on her face for everyone to see. Maybe these people didn't know what he was doing for her, but she did. Alex was making himself completely vulnerable—because he cared. A silent sob shook her. He was the bravest man she'd ever known.

"People make a company, ladies and gentlemen," Alex said in conclusion. He stopped, fighting the feeling of shame that always tortured him when he thought about what he'd done. "I was dead wrong in what I did, and I'll live with regret every day of my life because of it." His voice vibrated with emotion. "Don't you make the same mistake. A vote for Deshler and his people might not cause the loss of a life, but it *will* cause the death of a dream."

He bowed his head, waiting for the swell of comment to die, but there was no sound, no hum of derision.

Alex took a deep breath and raised his head. No matter what happened, he'd given Casey everything he had to give. He hoped that it was enough. "Thank you for listening to me," he said into the hush.

Suddenly the room exploded, the spectators all seeming to talk at once. The reporters sat on the edges of their chairs, waiting for the results. Deshler whispered furiously into Mrs. Eiler's ear, but she was staring fixedly at Alex, her wrinkled face flushed.

Alex left the podium and returned to his seat, exhausted. He looked up to see tears streaming down Casey's cheeks. For him.

Inside, a powerful emotion swelled to life, shaking him hard. He loved her. He'd never stopped. He'd only tried to convince himself that he had in order to survive.

Please, he prayed to the spirit of Cadiz, the seed of his ancestor that John said was in his blood. Please don't let me hurt her again. His big hand clenched into an impotent fist, and he bowed his head.

Fighting for composure, Casey called for the vote. When it was over, she'd won. By a landslide.

Chapter 14

The victory celebration was held in Casey's backyard. It was nearly six-thirty, and the party had been going on for an hour. Half the foundry's employees were there, and many of the shareholders. Even Francis Newton, off duty now that the battle was over, had joined in the fun.

Most of the guests were crowded around the table of hors d'oeuvres set up in the large gazebo at the edge of the patio. Evan was acting as one of the bartenders at a makeshift bar.

With one hand he gripped a sweating bottle of champagne, tugging at the cork with the other. The cork popped free with a loud crack, and the bubbly wine fountained over his hand.

Casey held out her glass for a refill. She was slightly tipsy.

Squinting into the setting sun, she tried to remember how many glasses she'd had. Three, four, something like that. But it wasn't enough. Not nearly enough.

Alex stood apart from the others, his champagne untouched except for the sip he'd taken to toast Casey's triumph. He shouldn't have come. It was only going to make it harder on both of them when the time came to leave. But she had wanted him to share the victory, and he hadn't been able to turn her down.

"Here's to Mrs. Eiler," Becky cried, raising her glass. "She sure came through for us, the old dear."

"To Mrs. Eiler," the others echoed, downing their drinks.

Casey grimaced. Everyone sounded so happy. And they were smiling. She should be smiling, too. But she wasn't. She wasn't sure she would ever smile again.

Sighing, she stepped backward until she was standing at Alex's side. He'd shed his suit coat and tie, and rolled his sleeves to the middle of his forearms.

"Having fun?" she asked in a conspiratorial tone, not quite meeting his gaze. How was she going to get through the night? Tomorrow? The next day?

"Not as much as you are," he said dryly, swirling the bubbly liquid in his glass.

"Great. Terrific." She forced a laugh. "I want you to have a good time. You . . . we won. I won. Hurray for me."

Silently Alex emptied his glass onto the grass, then took hers from her hand and did the same. "Getting drunk isn't going to help," he told her gently.

Pain welled up inside her, but she fought it down. "Then what is, Alex? Tell me. I'd like to know."

She turned away, wanting to kiss him so much that she ached with it and knowing that she didn't dare. Because if she kissed him or touched him or felt his arms around her, she would never be able to let him go.

And he was going. Already he'd withdrawn from her, becoming more and more like the man in the stone house.

"Come inside, Casey," Alex urged in a low voice, his narrowed gaze indicating the dozens of curious eyes all around. "You'll make yourself sick if you stay out here."

"Maybe I want to be sick, so sick I won't remember any...any of this." She stared at the thick grass under her feet. Had there been grass in New Mexico? she wondered, scowling. Surely there had been grass.

A memory stabbed her. There had been grass by the creek. She hadn't understood then why he hadn't made love to her, but she did now. And it hurt so much.

Another cork popped, and a cheer went up. She blinked at the cheery laughter and loud hoots. Her people were celebrating the greatest victory of her career while she was slowly dying inside.

"Did you see Deshler's face during the voting when the old lady marched up to the microphone and ordered everyone to vote for Casey?" Becky chortled, holding out her glass. "I thought the man was going to pop a vein."

Evan grinned and pulled another bottle from the icy water. "He deserved it."

"You got that right, buddy," shouted one of the lab technicians, who was feeling no pain. "He all but threatened my boss with castration if he didn't switch sides. Ol' Ben told him to bug off."

Casey felt as though a pail of icy water had hit her squarely in the face. Next to her, Alex stiffened. Her gaze flew to her face. He was white.

"It's just a word," she whispered, gripping his arm with both hands. His muscles were rigid under her palms.

Without a word he pulled away from her and went into the house. Casey caught up with him in the kitchen.

"Alex, don't go! Not . . . not yet. Please."

He stopped, but he didn't turn around. "It's not going to get any easier, Casey."

She was close enough to feel the tension radiating from him, warning her to keep her distance. "Kiss me before you go."

He shook his head. "No." Slowly he turned to face her, his face ravaged with the same pain she felt inside. "That won't do either of us any good."

His stubborn mouth was only a few inches away, so close she could almost feel his breath on her face. A hazy smile grew in her mind, and she thought about tracing the hard curve of his bottom lip with her tongue, then remembered what that would do to him. His body would respond, only to torment him minutes later with another failure. But surely it didn't have to be that way.

"Don't go. Please don't go. We can work it out. I know we can." She waved her hand toward the noise coming from the backyard. "We beat the odds once, Alex. Together . . . together we can do anything."

She reached up to touch his face. His skin was damp and slightly rough from five o'clock shadow. Her palm flattened against his cheek, and for an instant, only an instant, he leaned into her touch.

And then his hand was dragging hers from his face. "Don't," he whispered. "I can't want what you're offering, Casey. It will only make it harder for me. I . . . can't stay with you. It would be the worst kind of torture to watch you become more and more frustrated. And it would kill me if . . . that frustration drove you to another man."

Casey's eyes filled with tears. For the first time she realized the enormity of the pain he must feel every day of his life. "I'd never do that, Alex. I want you. Just the way you are. I don't care about the sex—"

"But I do!" His voice shook with the kind of emotion she'd only guessed was inside him. "It's the way a man shows his woman what she means to him."

"But I know how much you care," she cried, her voice breaking. "You . . . you humbled yourself in front of a terrible man like Con and all those people to save me, Alex. It was an act of love."

He swallowed hard, but his voice was carefully controlled, as though that were the only way he could master his feelings. "All the love in the world won't change the fact that I can't make love to you. It's like an excruciating pain, Casey, that never goes away. At least when I'm alone, I can manage to live with it, but when I'm with you, it's . . . it's damn near unbearable."

Casey closed her eyes against the agony that was filling her. Tears welled, then escaped the dam of her lashes. With a heavy sigh, Alex pulled her into his arms. Her head rested against his chest, her hair brushing his chin. His hands encircled her shoulders, holding her loosely.

His breathing was erratic, tortured, but no more so than hers. His body was straight, his muscles sculpted with power and magnificently male. She would never think him less a man because of his affliction. To her it was the same as a physical handicap, unfortunate, but surmountable.

But to Alex the ability to satisfy his woman was a part of him, the same elemental core that had made him a success at thirty.

Living with her, not being able to love her, would cripple him. In spite of her own pain, she knew that she could never do that to him.

"I'll never forget you," she whispered, hugging him close. *"Mi amor."*

His arms tightened once, then dropped away. Without looking at her, he pulled the ring from his left hand. He hesitated, his face tortured, then carefully placed it on the counter. It meant that he was truly leaving her, even in his heart.

"Goodbye, Casey."

She nodded, her mouth tightly compressed against the sobs that threatened to escape.

Alex turned to go, then froze.

"Very touching," said a snarling voice. "Too bad I was the only one who heard." Ben Jameson appeared in the doorway, a gun with a long barrel pointed directly at Alex's midsection.

Alex went cold inside. He stared into the man's eyes, seeing the madness there. And the hatred. Suddenly he knew who'd nearly killed Casey. Who'd ruined her things. It was this kid with the vicious eyes.

Alex calculated the distance to the gun and bent his knees, ready to spring. A killing rage swept through him, but he made himself wait. The distance was too far. He might not be able to get his body between the gun and Casey before the kid fired.

Casey stared at the gun, then raised her gaze slowly to Ben's twisted face. "Oh my God," she whispered, hugging herself. "It was you. *You* ruined my things."

"It was easy. You really should have better locks on this old place." The disheveled scientist's wild-eyed gaze shifted to her momentarily, then returned to Alex's face. "Don't even think about running out that door, Casey, or I'll kill Torres where he stands."

Her heart began racing until she couldn't distinguish the separate beats. Her palms grew clammy. "Ben, why...why are you doing this?" She was suddenly cold sober.

Ben took another step, his sneakers silent on the linoleum. The gun never wavered. "I *told* you not to go to New Mexico. And I told you this man was no good. I even broke into your house, thinking it would shock you into changing your mind. But you *wouldn't listen* to me!"

Frantically Casey tried to think, to come up with the words that would take the madness from Ben's eyes. "What about the toolbox?" she asked calmly. "Was that you, too?"

"Yes, it was me. You were too happy to see him. I could see it in your eyes. I didn't want you to be excited about him, Casey. I told you he wasn't good enough for you." He took a quick breath. "You should have listened to me. I wanted to protect you, the way I couldn't protect my sister."

Casey swallowed the stinging taste of fear. "Ben, I appreciate that, but . . . but I've never done anything to you personally. Why do you want to kill me?"

His face grew ugly. "Because you were married to the man who destroyed my sister's life." His voice rose shrilly. "Bart Chandler was Deirdre's husband."

Alex flinched. He felt the blood leave his jaw. Suddenly he was face-to-face with the same pain he'd seen in this man's sister, and he felt as though his skin was being stripped from him inch by inch.

"I'm sorry," he told Ben, his voice low. "Truly sorry. I never wanted to hurt your sister or . . . her son."

A ragged flush streaked Ben's pale skin. "That's where we differ. I want to hurt *you*. Very badly, in fact."

Alex took a step to one side, putting his body between the gun and Casey. "Me, yes, but not Casey. She had nothing to do with what I did. Let her go, Jameson."

Ben's smile was a malignant parody of the grin Casey had always liked. "I couldn't figure out why she was so hot on bringing you back here to fight Deshler, so I did some checking. It hurt, finding out the woman I idolized had been married to a bastard like you. I would have forgiven her if she'd listened to me, but she didn't, and that makes her a part of this now, part of your punishment." His voice rose in pitch until it was almost a falsetto. "It'll hurt you worse to see her die, won't it? Much worse."

Casey clamped her lip between her teeth and tried to think. Somehow she had to get outside. Newton and the marshal were out there, and both were armed. Fervently praying that her voice sounded natural, she said casually, "You're right, Ben. I should have listened to you, just the way I've always done. Why don't you put down the gun, and we'll talk about it? I'll get you some champagne, and—"

"Don't take another step, Casey, or so help me, I'll blow you both away. I've got nothing to lose."

She stopped her backward movement and made herself smile. "Okay, whatever you say."

Ben was sweating profusely, glistening drops beading along his forehead and his upper lip. His hair stood up in dirty blond spikes, as though he'd repeatedly dragged his hands through the unkempt strands.

"I'm sorry I have to kill you, Casey," he said in a ragged voice. "But I...I promise you won't suffer. Not like my sister. Not like Dierdre."

Casey inhaled sharply. "Ben," she said softly, "you can't get away with this. Someone will hear the shots, and—"

"Oh no, they won't." A cunning look crossed his face. "I made a silencer." His fingers lightly caressed the black pipe-like device on the end of the barrel. "I told you I could do anything."

Alex felt his sweat plastering his shirt to his shoulder blades, but his mouth was dry. The man had eyes like a rabid dog, the kind they shot on sight in the pueblo. He would kill this man with his bare hands if he had to. To protect Casey.

"Look, Jameson," he said in what he hoped sounded like a reasonable tone. "This isn't going to do you or your sister any good."

"My sister's dead, you bastard," the young man cried, his voice rising hysterically. "She just...gave up. Because you took everything from her." The gun in his hand dipped and rose erratically, as though he were having trouble controlling his movements.

Alex took a step forward, his hand outstretched. If he could only distract the kid long enough, Casey would be able to run out the door.

"Think what Casey's done for you, Ben. She believed in you. She gave you a chance when no one else would. Let her go, and I'll go with you. Anyplace you say."

Ben jerked backward, the gun pointing directly at Alex's heart. "Beg for her life," he ordered, a malicious glint in his strange yellow eyes. "Get down on your knees, Torres, and beg, the way Bart begged for his company. If you do a good job, I'll let her go." Hatred boiled in his voice.

Alex heard Casey gasp, but he knew that he had no choice. He couldn't let her die for his sin. A rage like nothing he'd ever felt before swept through him, but he managed to control the wild need to lash out in fury.

Sweat ran down his brow, stinging his eyes and blurring his vision. Gritting his teeth against the scalding humiliation, he swayed, then dropped to one knee. His breath came in furious gasps, and his muscles knotted in protest.

"No!" Casey shouted, taking a step forward. "Ben, *please* don't do this."

Ben swung the gun a fraction to the right until it was lined up on her belly, and his finger tightened. "Sorry, Cas—"

Alex propelled himself toward the gun, knocking Ben's hand upward, but Ben managed to spin away. Alex leaped forward, and Ben fired. The shot sounded like a soft ping.

Alex felt the bullet rip into his side. He staggered but managed to stay on his feet. "Casey, run," he shouted, throwing himself at the gun that was again pointing toward her.

He caught Ben's arm, and the two crashed to the floor. They rolled together, fighting for the pistol. Casey ran forward, trying to help Alex, but the men's thrashing bodies smashed into her shins, and she fell backward.

She looked up in time to see Alex's fist catch Ben squarely in the face. There was a loud crack, and blood began pouring from Ben's nose before he crumpled into unconsciousness.

Alex grabbed the gun and flung it across the kitchen. It crashed into the baseboard and spun wildly beneath the table. The room began spinning just as wildly, pain searing the right side of his body. He fought for breath, every movement of his chest an agony. He swayed, then slumped to his knees. Everything was getting gray. There was a terrible roaring in his ears. He crumpled forward and lay still.

"Oh my God," Casey cried, scrambling over the floor to reach him. Gently she rolled him over. Blood seeped from a jagged black hole in his side, spreading quickly over his belly, saturating his shirt.

She crouched over him, her fingers caressing his face. "Alex darling, darling," she whispered frantically. "Don't leave me. Please don't leave me."

"Get Evan," he whispered, his hand pressing the wound. His eyes were open, but his face was gray, and his lips were white.

Fighting the weakness that threatened to overwhelm her, Casey hastily retrieved the gun from under the table, then ran to the screen door and pushed it open.

"Evan," she screamed over the din. "Help! Alex has been shot." Cries of disbelief answered her, and she saw Evan running toward her, his mouth open in shock.

He caught her arm. "What happened?" he cried, before his frightened gaze spotted the blood pooling by Alex's side. He cursed succinctly. "I'll call an ambulance. You get something to stop the bleeding."

He hurried to the phone on the wall and snatched up the receiver, his gaze never leaving Alex's bloody chest. Casey could hear his voice, but not his words. The buzzing in her ears was too loud.

Without knowing that she was doing it, she grabbed a clean towel from the drawer. Sinking to her knees, she quickly folded it and pressed it tightly against the wound, her hands trembling violently.

Alex groaned, tossing his head from side to side as though trying to escape. His breathing was sounding more and more labored, and his ashen face was drenched in sweat. "Lie still, Alex," she pleaded. "Evan's calling for help."

There was blood everywhere. Too much blood. His blood. *God, she hated blood.* She fought down the nausea that stung her throat and strove for calm. Alex needed her. She couldn't faint now. Not now.

The screen door banged, and Sam Rickert burst into the kitchen, his gun drawn. He was followed closely by the security guard.

"Damn it to hell," the marshal exclaimed, seeing Ben's slack face and wild appearance.

He was trying to sit up, his eyes vacantly staring at the blood all over his hands. On his shirt. On Alex's shirt.

"I'm sorry," he said over and over, the words sounding like a sigh.

Haltingly, her gaze never leaving Alex's face, Casey recounted what had happened. Francis Newton replaced his gun in his holster, then closed the door to the patio and locked it, keeping the others out.

The marshal sighed; then he, too, holstered his gun and reached for his handcuffs. "You're in a pile of trouble, boy," he muttered, pulling Ben to his feet, cuffing him.

"Promised Dierdre to make him pay," Ben muttered, his eyes vacant. " . . . pay his debts."

The marshal gave Casey an apologetic look, then led Ben toward the front door.

Evan and Francis bent down, matching looks of masculine helplessness reflected on their pale faces. "Looks like shock," the guard muttered. "I'll get a blanket." He stood and ran out of the room.

"The ambulance will be here in fifteen minutes," Evan told her in a low voice, handing her another folded towel. Silently, her hands still shaking, she replaced the one that was now sticky with Alex's blood.

Trapped in a gray icy fog that was clogging his mouth and throat, Alex thrashed violently, trying to escape the hot poker stabbing him in the side. It was cold. So damn cold.

But a part of him was warm. He turned toward the warmth, but his body was heavy. Too heavy.

Useless, he thought in an icy haze. That's what he was.

"Casey," he whispered. He wanted to tell her what she'd meant to him. But he couldn't. He was leaving her. He had to leave her. Leave her.

"Lie still, darling," Casey pleaded, caressing his white face with her free hand. His skin felt clammy against her palm.

His face contorted in pain, and he groaned. His eyes closed, then opened slowly, as though he were forcing himself to stay awake. His hand lifted, each slow inch costing him terrible pain, until the back of his hand brushed her cheek.

"Alex, please don't move. You're bleeding. Lie still. Please lie still." She clutched his hand against her cheek. His palm was terribly cold.

Alex fought to see her. One more time. His woman of light.

"...love you." His voice was less than a whisper, but Casey heard him. Terror filled her. He couldn't leave her now. Not now. Dear God, she prayed. Not now.

"I love you, too. Oh, Alex, I love you, I love you."

"Sorry...so...sorry."

His eyes closed, and his hand fell.

"No!" she screamed. "Don't die. Please don't let him die."

Chapter 15

It's been two days, Evan. Why doesn't he wake up?'' Casey paced the small lounge outside the ICU, her red-rimmed eyes pleading.

"The doctor said he's fighting, Casey, but he's lost a lot of blood, and the surgery to remove his splintered rib took a lot out of him."

The doctor had also said that Alex was lucky to be alive. Another inch to the right and the bullet would have hit his liver.

Casey shivered and dropped her head to her chest. "He can't die, Evan. He just can't."

"He won't, Casey. Alex is as tough as those prickly desert plants outside his window. Remember those?"

A tired smile curved her lips. "I hated the desert when I first saw it. Now I'd give anything to see it again—with Alex."

Evan started to say something, but the pneumatic doors behind them suddenly slid open. Alex's nurse appeared, beckoning to her. Every hour, one person only was allowed to spend ten minutes at his bedside.

Casey greedily clutched at those minutes like a woman facing the last few hours of her life.

"How is he?" she asked at once, her voice husky with the anxiety that never left her.

"Still unconscious, but his vitals are stronger." The nurse smiled, and her plain, middle-aged face seemed almost angelic.

Casey drew a steadying breath. She hadn't left the hospital since she'd arrived, only minutes behind the ambulance, and the little sleep she'd had had come in snatches. Her clothes were rumpled, her face scrubbed free of makeup, her hair hanging in her eyes.

"I'll wait for you in the cafeteria," Evan said, giving her a bracing hug. "You need to eat."

"I will, when Alex is out of danger." Casey followed the nurse to the first cubicle to the left. The bars of the bed were raised, and beyond them, amid a network of tubes and beeping electronic paraphernalia, Alex lay flat on his back, his eyes closed, his features slack. His face was ashen, and his thick brows and long lashes stood out starkly against his unnaturally pale skin.

His chest was bare, revealing small gray cups where the monitoring equipment was attached, and the sheet only partially hid the thick bandage covering the incision in his chest.

Casey gently lowered the side rail and pressed against the hard mattress, getting as close to him as she could. Alex groaned, but he didn't wake.

Her hand found his, and she lifted it to her lips. His skin was reassuringly warm, but not hot from fever the way it had been yesterday. Slowly, her hand shaking, she reached out to press her fingertips against his cheek.

"Don't you dare die," she whispered fiercely, feeling her love flow through her in a warm rush. "Don't you dare leave me, Alejandro. Not now. Not ever." Her voice broke, and she closed her eyes, praying the same simple prayer over and over.

Please save him. Please save my love.

"Casey." His voice was a whisper, so soft she was sure she'd imagined it.

But his eyes were open, and he was trying to smile. She bent closer, tears streaming down her cheeks, to kiss his forehead. His hand tightened against hers, and she held on to him. "You saved my life," she whispered urgently, afraid he wouldn't hear her. "You can't leave me now. I won't let you."

His brows slowly drew together. "Afraid...to...try," he said, his words labored, his eyes dull with pain. "...fail...you again."

Casey smiled through her tears. "It's over, Alex. No more penance. Don't you understand? You're free." She caressed his face as she spoke, her fingers tracing the harsh lines that his guilt had etched in his face, trying to absorb his pain.

He sighed heavily, then winced at the pain it cost him. "I want...to believe...you," he said through careful breaths. "So much."

"You have to believe me. I can't live without you, Alex. Not emotionally. So in a sense, if you leave me again, you'll be killing me." A sob shook her. "You have to fight."

Alex stared at her, a raw, tortured look on his face. And then, slowly, the strain eased, and a soft sigh escaped him. "I'll... try... to fight for you."

Casey felt a burst of joy. He wanted to believe her. It might take some time, but she would convince him. That was what she did best—convince people to believe in themselves.

"I love you," she whispered.

"*Te amo.* I love you."

Casey traced the sensuous outline of his lower lip, then leaned over to kiss him. Her hair tumbled over his face, and she pushed it back.

"Beautiful." His hand slowly rose to touch the soft, thick strands.

Casey's smile was shaky. "Promise me you won't leave me. You keep your promises, Alex. Promise me."

This time his smile reached his eyes. "I promise."

Casey sat with her back to the rock and stared at the slow-moving creek. The land was caught in a sweltering August drought, and the water level was low enough for the setting sun to bounce off the round stones lining the creek bed.

"I can't believe I'm really here at last." She turned her head and smiled into the piercing dark eyes watching her instead of the sunset. "I thought I'd never find someone to replace me, but I think Taffy Mannheim will do a terrific job."

Alex shook his head, and a lock of shaggy hair fell over his forehead. There was more gray mixed with the black now, and Casey thought it made him even more attractive. He'd earned those traces of silver.

"Taffy," he muttered in what sounded like wry amusement "I can't believe your board actually approved a CEO with a name like that."

Casey giggled. "Me, either, but once they heard her and saw her résumé, they were bowled over. She knows almost as much about metallurgy as Ben, and once he's out of treatment, they'll be a good team. Two brilliant, weird people. They'll understand each other perfectly."

"I don't know, Case. Maybe Ben's ready to face the world, like his doctor claims, but I'm not sure he's ready for a Taffy in the president's chair."

Alex's hand came up to brush back the hair that was feathering her cheek, and she smiled in pleasure. It had been almost a month since she'd seen Alex, and she was as eager for his touch as a new bride. Which she would be in just five days.

"Maybe he's not ready, but I am. It wasn't so bad when you were in the hospital and I could be with you for a few hours a day, but when you left, I kept feeling lost, like a big part of me was missing."

"Hurts like hell, doesn't it?"

"Yes, like hell."

She twisted until she could bury her face against his chest. She loved being in Alex's arms again, listening to his breathing, strong and steady. She'd come so close to losing him.

His recovery had been difficult. On the fourth day another infection had raised his temperature dangerously, and he'd tossed for hours in a delirium until the fever broke.

It was then that she had heard how terribly he'd suffered in his self-imposed exile. How desperately he'd missed her. Sitting by his bedside, holding his hand to calm his restless tossing, she'd vowed that nothing would keep them apart again.

"It's such a pretty night. Relaxing," she murmured, listening to his heart pound beneath her. Alex might appear calm on the surface, even impassive, but she could feel the tension in his muscles and hear the agitated pace of his heartbeat. "A great way to start my new life as a consultant."

"Helping me come up with a plan to thwart Deshler's bid for Towers Industries isn't exactly my idea of relaxing."

Languidly she ran her fingers over the solid forearm resting on her thigh. Because of the heat, she was wearing shorts and the skimpiest halter top she owned. Alex was wearing only shorts.

"Ah, but it is, my dear husband-to-be," she said, playing with the whorls of hair above his nipples. "After all the terrible things Con said about you in the newspapers and on television, it will be a pleasure whipping him again."

Deshler hadn't even waited until Alex was out of danger before declaring his intention to absorb Towers Industries into Deshler Enterprises.

"We could lose," Alex warned. "I've had a lot of bad press."

She ran her hand over his wrist to entwine her fingers with his. His grip tightened. His other hand ran up and down her arm, sending messages of pleasure through her body.

"You've also had a lot of praise for your courage in making a public admission of guilt. Especially from your employees. It must have cost them a fortune to buy a full page in the *Wall Street Journal* in order to print that vote of confidence. They want you back."

She ran her bare foot over his shin, feeling the downy hair against her instep. It felt wonderful being here with him like this. With no more secrets between them, and all the barriers down. Except one.

Alex sighed and looked out over the land that had saved him.

"Even if I do decide to go back, I can't stay away from here for too long a stretch."

"I know. And I understand. Besides, now that I've sold my house, we'll need a base." Casey idly traced the curving line of his thigh muscle. He'd regained the weight that he'd lost, and the sun had taken the pallor from his skin.

He sat up straighter, and the limestone behind him rubbed his spine. The sun was a golden ball on the horizon, and the air was still.

In the distance a coyote howled, and somewhere in the branches overhead, an owl hooted. He was used to these cries in the night. Once they'd made him feel less alone.

As if anything could do that.

But he wasn't alone tonight. And that was what scared him. He pulled up one knee and tried to ignore the tension snaking through him. In just a few hours it would be time for bed. Casey would expect him to sleep with her. To make love.

His mind slid away from the thought, just as it had for the past six weeks. He'd promised to try, and he would. But he was still terrified that his body would betray him again.

Slowly he turned to look at her. She was lovely in the amber light. Breathtaking. After all the weeks of waiting, he still couldn't believe that she was here.

Casey raised her face to his and smiled. He touched her cheek, and she turned to kiss his wrist. "I missed you so much."

Alex loved the husky note in her voice. "Not as much as I missed you. Butch nearly drove me nuts. He kept wandering all over the house, looking for you."

Casey giggled. "Maybe he's not so crazy, after all."

"I was the one going crazy. I wanted you here." He kissed her, then pulled her closer. His cheek rested against her temple. "In the hospital, when I woke up and saw you bending over me, I knew I couldn't make it without you. I was just kidding myself, thinking I could." He breathed a kiss into her hair.

Casey's gaze fell to the spot above the band of his shorts where a pink crescent scar curved from back to front. She shuddered, touching the puckered flesh with her finger. "And I can't make it without you."

"Are you sure, Casey? If I can't—"

Swiftly she moved out of his arms and pressed her hand to his mouth. "I have a present for you," she murmured, tracing the hard line of his jaw with her finger.

His eyes widened in confusion. "A present? What kind of a present?"

She reached behind her for the small satchel she'd brought out with her. Inside was the small package she'd retrieved from John Olvera on her way here. The leather wrapping was warm against her fingers.

"It's a reward for being such a good boy in the hospital."

Alex frowned, a wary look on his face. "You said I was bad tempered and impossible and threatened not to come to see me anymore if I didn't listen to the doctors."

She wiped a trickle of sweat from his temple with her finger. "That's true. You were a terrible patient, but I love you, anyway." She kissed him, feeling his instant response, then took his hand and placed the present gently into his palm. "Go ahead and open it before it's too dark to see."

Slowly he unfolded the soft square. In the center was a heavy silver chain, intricately wrought, with the look of antiquity woven into the metal. Resting on the coiled chain, attached to it by a heavy silver ring, was a single fang taken from a mountain cat, yellow with age.

"John told me that you gave it to the council when you first came here. He...kept it safe for you, because he knew that one day you would earn it."

Casey watched the play of emotions over Alex's face. She couldn't tell if he was pleased, but she could see that he'd been shaken by her gift.

"Casey, I...can't wear this." His voice was raw. His hand closed over the totem as though it hurt to hold it.

"Yes, you can. You *deserve* to wear it." She scrambled to her knees and faced him, her palms pressed against his shoulders. Somehow she knew she had to reach him now, or she might never get through.

"According to the legend, a man is worthy when he faces his flaw and overcomes it. You've done that, Alex. You did that when you humbled yourself in front of the whole world."

He stared at her, his expression unreadable. She could feel the tension radiating from her. She felt that same tension inside.

"Just as Cadiz went to prison to save his people, you went into a prison of your own making to...to save me from the shame that you knew I would suffer if the story ever got out."

Alex swallowed hard, and his eyes glinted. "It's still not easy to forgive myself. I try, but..." He sighed.

"Open your hand, darling." Her fingers shaking, she lifted the chain and slowly slipped it over his head. The ancient totem settled around his neck, glinting in the glow from the setting sun.

"I love you," she murmured, bending to kiss his chest just above the place where the cougar's fang nestled in the black hair.

The tremor started deep inside him and shook him so hard that Casey cried out. She wrapped her arms around his waist and tried to gentle the shudders that were shaking him.

"I need you," he muttered, his words sounding like a groan. "*Dios, te quiero mucho.* So much." His voice choked, and another tremor shook him.

"I'm here, my love. I'll always be here."

His hands ran up and down her spine, and she began to come alive. She felt the urgency in him, and her soul sang.

"It's been so long. So damn long." His mouth found the spot behind her ear that had always made her crazy with longing when he'd kissed her there.

She gasped and arched her neck, feeling the desire begin to build. "Too long for me, too."

His breathing grew harsher, as did hers.

She moved closer, curling around him until there was nothing but the soft material of her halter top separating skin from skin. His breath hissed past her ear, warm and moist. A faint scent of cigar smoke mingled with the musky odor of sweat dampening his skin. Masculine scents. Powerful. Arousing.

Warm air brushed the skin of her back, but his hands were even warmer as they stroked her waist. "I love your hands," she whispered.

"I love your body." He kissed the swell of her breast. "Your stubborn little jaw." His mouth moved upward to kiss the spot just below her jaw. "Your smile." His mouth hesitated over hers until her lips began to curve. His tongue lightly traced her lower lip, making her shiver.

"I'll never get enough of you, *querida*. Not in a dozen lifetimes."

Casey rubbed her cheek against his. "You feel so good. So warm. Strong."

He kissed her again. She responded, feeling his body quicken beneath hers. He froze, then wrapped his arms around her.

The coarse grass, sweet smelling and still warm from the sun, cradled them like a nubby blanket. They lay side by side, embracing, kissing tenderly. Sighing in pleasure, Casey let her legs relax. Alex stroked her cheek, her mouth, the saucy tilt of her nose.

Her hands combed through his hair, and the thick strands felt wonderfully soft against her palms. His thighs entwined with hers, their weight heavy and warm. Pressed so tightly together, she knew the moment his body began to harden against her. She held her breath, waiting. Alex muttered something in Spanish. A plea? A curse?

"We'll go slowly," she whispered into his hair. "As slowly as you want."

Alex groaned and buried his face in her neck, his arms crushing her.

"Kiss me," she whispered. "You have a big deficit to cover."

He raised his head and looked down at her. Some of the tension left his face. "I do?"

"Mmm. Six years' worth." She touched the sexy curve of his mouth with her fingertip. "Think you can handle that, Torres?"

"Is that a challenge, O'Neill?"

"Yes."

His smile slowly spread. "I accept." Alex lowered his head until his lips lightly touched hers. His kiss was gentle, making no demands. Adoring. Tender. Even reverent.

Her hands stroked the tension from his jaw, then moved lower to lightly caress his shoulders. He leaned on one forearm and played with the hair curling around her ear.

"You're so tiny."

"And you're so big."

She allowed herself to look at him, reveling in the supreme masculinity of his big scarred body. He was magnificent, his chest a forged expanse of muscle and bone that made her long to press her lips to each hard, powerful line.

Her fingertips eagerly stroked the midnight hair that grew in a furry line to a point somewhere below the material of his shorts. His skin was hot, the silky hair soft against her skin. She pressed her hand flat against his belly, her fingers lightly tracing the puckered skin of his incision, and the granite muscles jerked uncontrollably at her exploring touch.

Her fingertips brushed the hard edge of his waistband, and a thrill shot through her, accelerating the tempo of her heartbeat. He was breathing hard, his arousal pushing against his cotton shorts.

"Casey," he whispered, his voice strident and harsh. "God help me, I love you so much." He lifted his head, his face lined and twisted with a savage need, and his mouth opened over hers, hard and hungry.

His hand loosened the ties behind her neck, then worked at the knot under her breasts until the halter top fell away, exposing her breasts. He kissed one, then the other, and her nipples puckered instantly under his tongue. Shivers of arousal roughened her skin. His tongue lapped at her, exciting her more with each stroke.

Alex heard the little sounds in her throat. He felt her soft body beneath him, trembling with desire. She was ready for him. For her man.

He ran his hands down her body to her shorts. "Help me," he murmured, kissing her belly.

She sighed and raised her hips. Swiftly he removed her shorts and panties, flinging them aside. An amber glow lay over the land, turning her skin to gold. "My woman of light." He wanted her so desperately he was shaking inside.

"My husband. My love."

Alex looked into her eyes. At the promises she was making without asking anything in return. His hand touched the totem she'd put around his neck. The sign of a winner.

It was really hers, but he would wear it. Because she wanted him to. Because she believed in him. And because she believed in him, he believed in himself. Because she forgave him, he would learn to forgive himself.

Slowly, his gaze never leaving hers, he shed his shorts, then lay next to her again. They were so close, but not touching. In his dreams this was the moment when he filled her with his love. When he made them one.

But this time, if he failed . . .

"Love me, Alex," Casey whispered, her gaze never leaving his face.

Alex could barely speak. He loved her more than life, but he would never be able to find words strong enough to tell her. He kissed her, pouring all the love he felt into his kiss. Into his touch.

He felt the little shivers take over her body. His hands absorbed the heat from her skin. His mouth caught her urgent whimpers. Slowly he moved until he was lying between her thighs. Her hands caught his arms, urging him closer. He felt her open for him, welcoming him with the love that would heal him. His body surged into hers, strong, potent.

"Alex, oh, *Alex*." Casey felt him inside her, powerfully male. Hers.

She was filled with him. With his love.

He was gentle at first, moving slowly, letting himself feel all of her. Letting himself believe.

But the hunger that had driven him without relief for so long soon took over, and he began to move, his eyes never leaving her face. She was radiant, her face filled with love. He was filled with the wonder of her.

He pulled her closer, thrusting harder, out of control.

Casey was consumed with the joy of being Alex's woman. Over and over she cried his name, a pledge, an affirmation that she was his.

His breath rasped against her skin, and she clung to his sweat-drenched shoulders, letting the pleasure overtake her.

Lifting his head, Alex watched her respond, watched the pleasure illuminate her face. It was hard to breathe, hard to hold back, but he waited, waited for her.

"Yes," she whispered on a moan. "Oh, yes, *Alex*."

The beauty of her release took him over the edge. His body tightened, then surrendered, his release coming in a hot wave that shook them both.

Gradually their movements slowed to a mutual contentment. They remained together, wrapped in each other's arms, watching the land settle into night.

Casey had never felt such peace. "Don't leave me," she whispered, pressing a drowsy kiss against his shoulder.

Alex smiled, his hand stroking her damp back. "Never."

He lay on his side, still buried deeply inside her. His woman. Lightly, he touched her lips with his finger.

"I love you," she whispered. "So much."

Alex buried his face in her hair. Every day he lived he would show her how much he needed that love. How much he loved her in return. A feeling of deep peace settled over him. Slowly he raised his head and looked into the eyes of his woman.

Casey.

"Thank you, *mi amor*," he whispered. "For giving me back my life."

* * * * *

SILHOUETTE

Desire™

**Just when you thought all the good men
had gotten away along comes...**

MAN OF THE MONTH 1990

From January to December, you will once again have the chance to go wild with Desire *and* with each *Man of the Month*—twelve heart-stopping new heroes created by twelve of your favorite authors.

Man of the Month 1990 kicks off with FIRE AND RAIN by Elizabeth Lowell. And as the year continues, look for winning love stories by Diana Palmer, Annette Broadrick, Ann Major and many more.

You can be sure each and every *Man of the Month* is just as dynamic, masterful, intriguing, irritating and sexy as before. These truly are men you'll want to get to know... and *love*.

So don't let these perfect heroes out of your sight. Get out there and find your man!

Silhouette Intimate Moments®

It's time ... for Nora Roberts

There's no time like the present to have an experience that's out of this world. When Caleb Hornblower "drops in" on Liberty Stone there's nothing casual about the results!

This month, look for Silhouette Intimate Moments #313

TIME WAS

And there's something in the future for you, too! Coming next month, Jacob Hornblower is determined to stop his brother from making the mistake of his life—but his timing's off, and he encounters Sunny Stone instead. Can this mismatched couple learn to share their tomorrows? You won't want to miss Silhouette Intimate Moments #317

TIMES CHANGE

Hurry and get your copy ... while there's still time!

Indulge a Little
Give a Lot

An irresistible opportunity to pamper yourself with free gifts (plus proofs-of-purchase and postage and handling) and help raise up to $100,000.00 for **Big Brothers/Big Sisters Programs and Services** in Canada and the United States.

Each specially marked "Indulge A Little" Harlequin or Silhouette book purchased during October, November and December contains a proof-of-purchase that will enable you to qualify for luxurious gifts. And, for every specially marked book purchased during this limited time, Harlequin/Silhouette will donate 5¢ toward **Big Brothers/Big Sisters Programs and Services**, for a maximum contribution of $100,000.00.

For details on how you can indulge yourself, look for information at your favorite retail store or send a self-addressed stamped envelope to:

INDULGE A LITTLE
P.O. Box 618
Fort Erie, Ontario
L2A 5I3

ONE PROOF OF PURCHASE

To collect your free gift you must include the necessary number of proofs-of- purchase, plus postage and handling, along with the offer certificate available in retail stores or from the above address.

CSIM-3

Harlequin®/Silhouette®